Dedication

Thank you to all the men and woman serving in The United States Coast Guard for keeping our country safe and protecting our shores. A special shout out to Jacob Mamire Petty Officer BM2/E-5 Boatswain's mate. Your kindness was greatly appreciated.

THE LETTER:

Dear Michael

UNRAVELED: THE NEXT GENERATION BOOK 1

THERESA SEDERHOLT

The Letter: Dear Michael
Unraveled: The Next Generation Book One
Copyright© 2016 by Theresa Sederholt

The author acknowledges the copyrighted or trademarked status and trademark owners of the following wordmarks mentions in this work of fiction: The United States Coast Guard. Skype. The Four Seasons in Santa Barbara. La' Pâtisserie des Rêves. Doctor Who. American Express. Bouchon. Sterns Wharf. Guns N' Roses. In-N-Out. Jell-O. Arnold Palmer. Richie Sambora. Aston Martin. Tiffany. Beverly Hills Hotel. Lamborghini. Ferrari. Rolls Royce. Inspiration Point. Butch Harmon School of Golf. Cypress Point Country Club. Advil. Epsom Salt. Ray-Bans. Rincon Beach. Jeep. Range Rover. Bath and Body Works. A Thousand Wishes. Dr. Seuss. Pepto-Bismol. Calistoga Mineral Hot Springs. Eight Coast Guard District. Titanic. Leo Christopher. Wonder Woman. Humpty Dumpty. NORACAL Boxer Rescue.

This is a work of fiction. Names, characters, businesses, places, events, and incidents are either the products of the author's imagination or used in a fictitious manner. Any resemblance to actual persons, living or dead, or actual events is purely coincidental.

This book contains strong language, graphic sexual situations, and violence. It is not intended for anyone under the age of 18.

ISBN: 978-0-9976692-0-6

Publisher: Theresa Sederholt ©
Cover designer: Robin Harper, Wicked By Design.
Editor: Jacquelyn Ayres.
Formatter: Stacey Blake, Champagne Formats.
Photographer: CJC Photography
Model: Michael Federico

Thank you, Debbie Cooper naming Cooper and Bennett Holiday and for your donation to A Christmas Prayer For Patty. A Cancer fundraiser and awareness for Patty Erickson.

The Letter: Dear Michael

A life of privilege isn't always what it seems. Kidnapped at the age of seven and diagnosed with Leukemia at nine; Michael is all grown up now, with what he thought was the perfect life. He was ready to take the next step: get married and eventually start a family. Then, a "Dear John" letter and the unearthing of a deeply buried secret turned his dream into a nightmare.

Now, Michael's hope of a life without limitations seems too far out of reach to ever be truly realized. The pressure of family, safety, and secrets is overwhelming. Everyone turns to him, but who can he turn to?

Chapter One

Michael

ONE WEEK AND MY WORLD WILL CHANGE COMPLETELY. Only one more week and I'll be marrying the girl of my dreams. Today, however, is all about me. My bachelor party weekend begins now. Well, actually—it began last night. My best friend Bo is already passed out on the couch in the living room. If that's any indication on how this weekend is going to be—Lord, have mercy. There is a constant banging on my front door and for fuck's sake, its reeking havoc on my hangover. When I finally open it, I find both my uncles standing outside with a grim look on their faces. At least Uncle Jax had the decency to knock. That's probably because Uncle Max was in control, for a change. That, however, doesn't last long as they both come barreling in.

"What's the problem? Is everyone okay?"

Uncle Jax is pulling his hair, which, after all of these years, can only mean two things: stress and mayhem. Uncle Max attempts to clear his throat as if he's about to speak. "Junior, sometimes, in life, things don't always go as we plan. We make plans and life takes us in a different direction," he pauses. Uncle Jax takes this opportunity to yell at him to shut the fuck up. This has to be bad if it has them at each other's throats.

"Junior, I received a letter last night from Heather. It's addressed to you and your Aunt Raven said I can't open it," Uncle Jax informs me then thrusts a letter in my hand.

"Why would she send you a letter?" I'm not really asking him; I'm more or less just talking out loud.

"Well, whatever happens, Max and I are here for you."

Uncle Max begins to pace while Uncle Jax stands there, his arms crossed with a scowl on his face, not so patiently, waiting for me to open the letter. Heather has seemed a little off recently but I figured she was stressed about her thesis and everything leading up to the wedding. A part of me wants some privacy but my gut is telling me I might need my family right now. I quickly rip open the letter.

Dear Michael,

I'm sorry, I never meant for this to happen. I thought we would be together forever. I really believed that you were my soul mate. Recently, I've felt a change in our relationship. It's an unexplainable shift, but something is missing. What that something is, I don't know. It's not your fault; it's mine. I've decided to go back to Switzerland and explore different possibilities. I will always love you, Michael, but I finally realized I'm not in love with you. I know how close you are to Jax, so I sent this to him so you would have your family around you for support. I hope one day, you will find someone who can love you the way you should be loved, I just know that person is not me.

Forgive me,
Heather

What the fuck? She can't be serious. "I need to call her, this has to be some kind of sick, cruel joke." I'm searching around my flat for my phone and when Uncle Max calls it, Bo's arse starts ringing, finally getting a moan out of him. He lifts the pillow slightly off of his face.

"Mike, turn down the television and shut the fucking phone off; my head hurts."

"Not as much as it's going to hurt when I'm done with you. Wake the fuck up and get the phone out from under your arse or I'll do it for you—*now!*"

Bo immediately opens his eyes and sees Uncle Max squatting down, only inches from his face. He quickly reaches under his arse and pulls out my phone. "I'm sorry, sir, I didn't know anyone else was here. I thought it was the television."

I quickly grab my phone. "This has got to be some sort of sick joke. One phone call and I can get this all cleared up." I drop the letter and call Heather but it goes directly to her voice mail. I try her dad and it also goes to his voice mail. This can't be happening. "Why? Why would she just walk away without any explanation?"

"Junior, I promise; Jax and I will get to the bottom of this." That usually means my uncles will do what ever it takes to make things right and God help anyone who gets in their way.

"No, both of you have to stop. I need to handle this on my own, and you need to respect that I'm capable of doing it."

"Junior, please, Max and I are here to help you; let us."

I'm not giving in on this one. "*Don't* make me call Aunt Raven." She is the only person who can rein him in. I'm not opposed to using that to my advantage.

"You wouldn't."

I hold up my phone and wave it at him. Uncle Max stops pacing and looks at the two of us. "Jax, let's give him some privacy; he knows we are here for him."

He throws his hands up. "Fine, have it your way. I swear you are more like your mother everyday." The two of them head out but not before issuing me a warning not to do anything stupid and, of course, issuing the same warning to Bo.

"So, Mike, is it what I think it is?" he asks. I slump into the couch and stare into space. I don't know how much time has passed, but he hands me a beer. "It's five o'clock somewhere. I read the letter; it's cold, Mike, even for her."

I take a long pull on my beer. "What the fuck does that mean, *even for her*?"

"Look, when it comes to Heather, you have blinders on. You always see past her flaws. Hell, you do that with everyone, even me. She hates me, and she slowly pulled you away from all your friends. Take a look around; who do you see? I'm the only one who won't back down from her, which is why she hates me."

"If that's the case, then why did you stick around for so long?"

"Someone has to keep you on your toes. Besides, I'm your greatest source of amusement. So, what's the plan?" He slams back the rest of his beer and quietly waits for me to take the lead.

"If I learned anything from my family, it's to never except anything without all the facts. I'm not going to sit around here and take this letter at face value. She wants out, then she needs to have the balls to tell me to my face. Get ready, we're going to Switzerland."

He's not moving, still picking at the label on the empty beer bottle. "What if she doesn't want to see you? I mean, really, she already took the coward's way out. Are you prepared for that? What if the answers are not what you want to hear?"

I'm already out of the chair and headed towards my room. "Before this night is over, I'll have my answers. You've got thirty minutes to get your shit together or I'll leave without you."

Chapter Two

THE FLIGHT FROM HEATHROW IS ONLY AN HOUR AND thirty minutes. Sometimes it's a lot quicker to hop on a commercial airline than call up one of my uncles and tell them I need the jet. Although, doing this throws the airline and my detail into a tailspin. Not that they don't already know my every move. People that didn't grow up in a mega-rich lifestyle always think 'if only I had his money;' they have no fucking clue what it's like to grow up isolated. The only person who really truly understands the loneliness is my Aunt Jackie. She's never let it define who she is and I've tried to follow her example.

It wasn't until a month into my masters program that I met Bogart Turner, a California expat, and we became friends. His laid back attitude towards life drives my family nuts, especially Uncle Jax. Bo's family is wealthy but not off the charts. Unfortunately because of me, he now has a permanent bodyguard.

The letter is practically burning a hole in my pocket. Why? What the fuck does she mean she loves me but she's not in love with me? "What kind of bullshit nonsense is that?"

Bo nudges me, hard. "Mike, what kind of bullshit nonsense is what?"

"Nothing; I didn't realize I said that out loud. How much longer before we get there?"

"We are getting ready to land now. Don't worry; we will get to the bottom of this, but you better be prepared, dude, she might not want to see you," he warns. I know he's probably trying to prepare me for the worst, but really how much worse can it get?

"Oh, trust me, she *will* see me."

We land and since we have no luggage, our guards quickly usher us to our waiting car. I knew my uncles would make sure I had everything I would need.

The drive is quiet; Bo is busy checking stuff on his phone and I'm trying to prepare myself for what I'm going to say. If she wants out, I would never force her to stay, but don't fucking drop a note to my Uncle Jax, of all people, and expect me to be okay with it. I'm not a confrontational person, I've been through too much in my life to be bothered with that shit, but I'm also no one's doormat.

Heather's father has a huge estate in the country. We head down the long drive and I feel my heart race as Bo squeezes my arm. "Before we get up to that door, tell me, Mike, how do you want to handle this? I mean, I'll hang in the background and make sure you keep it together, but what if she doesn't want to see you or what if the father won't let you see her, then what?"

The car barely comes to a stop and I'm out the door. "Balls to the wall, Bo."

I don't even reach the front door and her father is already standing there . . . waiting. "Michael, she said everything that needs to be said. You need to accept it, son, and move on. It's best that you leave."

Accept it? Move on? Leave? He can't possibly be serious. "With all due respect, sir, would you? I need to hear it from her and not some lame arse letter. I think I deserve the same respect I've always given her." I take a step forward, indicating to him I'm not leaving.

"Come in, I'll let her know you're here."

Bo squeezes my arm and pulls me aside. "Before she comes down here, you better rein it in. You're wound so tight, you're ready to explode." I take a few deep breaths and try to calm my racing heart. "I know. Don't worry; I'll be fine." Just then, she enters the room, and she looks so sad; this can't possibly be what she wants. "Heather, babe, tell me this is some sick joke."

Her eyes dart to Bo and then back to me. "Bo, can you give us a few minutes, please," her voice is soft and she seems to barely get the words out.

"Mike, I'll be right outside the door." He doesn't wait for me to answer.

"You want to explain to me why my uncles showed up this morning with a letter from you, dumping me? If you had a problem with me, why wait till a week before the wedding? You didn't even have the decency to tell me to my face?!"

"Michael, please, I need you to respect my decision. I can't live in your world. I'm not in love with you."

"You're not in love with me—since when? You can't live in *my* world? What the fuck does that even mean? If you're not in love with me, then why the hell are you crying?" I know I'm yelling, but fuck it all to hell I'm pissed off.

"I can't live with all the baggage that comes with you and your family! I'm. Not. In. Love. With. You!" Her words are cold and they sting. I reach for her but she backs away. What the fuck is going on?

"What baggage? For Christ sake, none of this makes any fucking sense."

"Everything, Michael; the constant need for guards, and the never ending secrets."

"Secrets? What secrets? What the hell are you talking about?! I've always been an open book with you."

Before she can answer, her dad steps back into the room. "Michael, this is a conversation that you should be having with your family, not Heather."

"My family? What the hell do they have to do with any of this? This is my life, not theirs."

"Look, I never liked the fact that there were always so many guards around you. I know having money means people will do anything to take it away, but I felt that maybe it was something more. I ran a more extensive background check on your entire family's history—everyone—Michael. I wasn't going to tell my daughter what I was doing but after everything I found out, I felt she had a right to know. I know you're a good and honorable man, however, with you, comes your family's baggage. I will not have my daughter put in constant danger." He walks up to his desk, pulls out an envelope and hands it to me. "I'm not sure how much you actually know, but these are the results. I suggest you go home and talk to your parents about them. I told Heather if she really wanted to marry you, I would find a way to make it work, but she doesn't. I think you should leave now."

Just like that, it's over. No logical explanation, just she doesn't love me and my family is too much for her. Secrets? There are no secrets in my family. Hell, they even live in the same damn bloody house! Who the hell can keep any thing secret with them around?

"Mark my words, Heather, someday you'll look back on all of this and regret your decision. You'll miss me and by then, it will be too late." I turn and walk away, leaving a world of pain behind me. When I open the door, Bo is standing there waiting for me. I don't bother to explain. I can't explain something I don't understand myself. I head directly into the waiting car with Bo racing to keep up with me.

"Where are we going?"

"To see the one person who has all the answers."

When we get into the car, the guards inform me that the jet is on standby, ready to take me wherever I want to go. That didn't take them long.

"Thank you. Let the pilot know we'll be heading home to Scotland."

I want to rip open that envelope but I also want privacy when I do. "Bo, you don't have to go with me. I've dragged you through enough."

He holds his hand up stopping me from saying anymore. "Hey, even though your uncles—especially Max—scare the living shit out of me, you're my best friend and I wouldn't be anywhere else. Besides, I'm finally going the see the '*compound*' and meeting your cousins."

The thought of Bo around my cousins snaps me back to reality. "Listen I'm warning you now, so we have no problems, stay clear of the girls, especially Antonia. You will never see the light of day ever again if you mess with her." The only thing that gets me is a wave of his hand, and a 'whatever.' Bo's a player and that's the last thing I need to worry about.

We get to the airport and the jet waiting for us is a new one, smaller than the usual. The pilot informs me it's Uncle Max's new toy. He is detailing all the specs and the advantages of having a smaller private plane. Personally, I don't give a fuck. I just want to get home. Bo, on the other hand, loves to fly. He has his license and even toyed with the idea of doing it for a living, until his parents stepped in. His duel degree in Oceanography and Environmental Engineering will open a lot of doors for him when he goes back home to California. A lot more than a pilot's license.

Finally, we're airborne. I grab a bottle of scotch and two glasses, another one of my uncle's companies. My gut is telling me I'm going to need it. I pour us each a glass and open the envelope. I pull out the huge report, and Heather's engagement ring tumbles out, yet another fucking smack in my face. I sit back and begin to read. The investigator has a summary page on each family member followed up with all the details. It's all old bullshit, detailing Aunt Raven's family history. These people are all dead or, for the most part, locked away; why would any of this matter to Heather? Finally, the report gets to the information on me. Everything is pretty much as I

9

remember it. I was sick at the time, so some of the details that were told to me are a little hazy. Who cares, that my grandfather is a bigamist, he still managed to save my life. It doesn't change anything. Then, I get to my mother's page and my stomach flips as the word *raped* jumps out at me. I turn to the details and there's a copy of a police report. It's saying that she was drugged, beaten, raped and became pregnant. That can't be; I know for a fact that I'm the only baby she was able to have. It states that she gave birth to a healthy boy . . . *me. What the fuck?!* I flip through the report to the part with all of my information and all of my medical history is here. How is that even possible? The notes from the clinic detailing all of my blood work and there it is—my dad is not my dad. I look at the date on the report and it's dated over a month ago, yet, she chose this time and in this way to give this to me? I've got such a tight grip on my glass that it shatters in my hand, cutting into my palm. The scotch instantly burns and then numbs it. Bo grabs the papers and the flight attendant is trying to clean it up. The buzzing in my ears sounds like some bad static.

"Mike, what the hell is it?" He begins to flip through the report and I grab it from him.

"I was just startled by something. I need to talk to my mum. We should be landing soon." Conversation is over. I take my seat and tune everything out. Everything, that is, except that one word that keeps swirling around in my head—*raped.*

We arrive home and Bo is apparently blown away since his mouth is hanging open and his head is like something in a tennis match. "How big is this place?"

"A couple of thousand acres . . . give or take." When we pass the garage, he literally grabs the seat, and the look on his face makes me laugh . . . the first laugh I've had since this nightmare started.

"Yeah, Uncle Max has a thing for toys. Once a week, they are all brought out, washed and waxed. Today's your lucky day."

"My God, this is not what I was expecting. I know you said it was big but this is insane. Did you see all those cars? That's not a garage; it's a fucking warehouse!"

"Yeah, and we haven't even gotten to the castle, yet."

When the castle finally comes into view I look at Bo and he's suddenly very quiet. "Hey, what's wrong?"

"I think I finally realize how lonely this must have been for you. I thought my childhood was sheltered but this is off the fucking charts."

"Well, at least you had some friends. All I had growing up was my family. There were some foster kids that came through here but no one I was ever really close to. When we first moved here, I would explore all the tunnels with Rose. But, when she died, I was on my own."

"Who was Rose?"

"Aunt Raven's mum. That's a story for another day."

"I can't believe all this time and you've never brought me here."

"Life gets in the way of living, you know that. We were always studying or partying. Remember what I told you?"

"Don't worry, just take care of your business."

The closer I get to home the faster my heart beats. Why the hell did I have to find out this way? The ride seems to take forever. Finally, we pull up to the castle and my uncles are standing out front waiting. I expected nothing less.

Uncle Jax grips my arm, pulling it towards him, glaring at my bandaged hand. "Junior, what happened to your hand? What happened with Heather?"

I shrug it off, hand Uncle Max the folder, and walk past both of them. "Where is my mum?"

"She's upstairs in her office going over some stuff for the winery with your dad. Junior, you're upset. What happened with Heather?"

"Uncle Jax, I need to talk to my mum first. Everything is in that envelope." I run up the steps, leaving Bo behind. I knock on the door but don't wait for an answer. "Mum, Dad, we need to talk."

"Michael, what happened to your hand? Why are you here? I thought it was your bachelor party weekend?" That seems like a lifetime ago.

"Didn't Uncle Jax tell you? Heather sent him a letter calling off the wedding."

"No. We just got back from Italy. Why would she call off the wedding and why send a letter to Jax?"

"I went to see her to find all of that out. She spewed some bull-shit story that she loved me but wasn't in love with me. She said our family had too much baggage and too many secrets. Her father then gave me a detailed report of our entire family history. Most of the stuff was all old bullshit that I already knew, but imagine my sur-prise when I got to the part about my parents. Why the hell didn't you ever tell me? Dad, do you know? Did you know all along?"

My mum begins to shake and my dad pulls her into his arms. "Bella, I've got you; it will be okay. Michael, calm down and let's talk about this like adults."

"Adults, Dad, really? Maybe you both should have thought about talking to me long before now. If I didn't find out, would you have ever told me?" I'm yelling and my mum is crying, but I can't back down, not now.

"I have loved you as my own from before you were born—DNA never changed that and never will."

"I know you love me, but I still had a right to know. I should not have found out the way I did. This is so fucked up."

My mum takes my hand and squeezes it. "Michael, I think you need to hear the entire story and you need to hear it from me."

My dad wipes away mum's tears and kisses her forehead. "I'll give you both some privacy, my love." I watch him reluctantly head out the door.

"Please, Michael, have a seat."

"I'd rather not."

"Have it your way, but please put aside your anger and listen. I was very young and naïve. I was going to a trade show in Las Vegas. It was my first business trip and I didn't have my big brother watching my every move. I thought—finally—I would be able to have some fun with no one constantly looking over my shoulder. There was an after party and some of the girls I went to the event with were going, so I decided to go." She closes her eyes and takes a deep breath. I know it must be hard to relive but I need to—no—I have a right to know. "All I know is one minute, I was in a club, having a good time, and the next, I woke up in the hospital. The doctor told me I was drugged, beaten, and raped. Your uncle Jax and Grams came and took me home. It was right after that Jax brought Max on board to head up security. Your dad and I were friends before I went to the event and when I came home, he saw something was different. I pushed everyone away, including him. But, he was so persistent. Finally, he wore me down and I let him in. When I found out I was pregnant, I tried to end it with him, but he didn't care. No matter how hard I tried, he wouldn't leave."

I hold my hand up, stopping her. "Why did you decide to continue the pregnancy?"

"That's a personal choice that every woman must decide for herself. I decided to continue the pregnancy. I felt nothing that happened was your fault, so why should you pay the price? I was all set to be a single parent but your dad insisted we get married before you were born. Before the wedding, he went to his parents and told them everything. His excitement quickly disappeared when his parents disowned him for his decision to marry me." She closes her eyes and her voice is barely above a whisper.

"We thought we would have a big family, but I had so many complications and then a priest was brought in to administer my last rites. I fought hard and, after surviving multiple surgeries, I was told I couldn't have any more children. Your dad didn't care that he would never have a child of his own; he told me you will always be his son, and he's never let me down. Then, when you became ill and needed a bone marrow transplant, my past came crashing into my future. My entire world was spinning out of control." She stops and tries to pour herself some water but she spills it. I pour it for her and wait for her to continue.

"Everyone was tested to see if anyone was a match. I was close but not close enough. That's when your grandfather came into the picture. Jax went to see him and he was a perfect match."

"I know he was a match and he ultimately saved my life, but what does that have to do with any of this?"

She takes a deep breath, and takes my hand. I'm not sure if it's for her support or mine, but this part seems to be the hardest for her to tell me. "Your grandfather's cousin set me up to be raped as a payback for some stuff that went on between the two of them."

Her words are hanging in the air.

"What kind of sick bastard does something like that?"

"The same man who was responsible for the cold-blooded murder of Uncle Max's first wife and son."

I skimmed over the stuff in the report about my grandfather. Maybe this is what freaked Heather out. It still doesn't justify why she dumped me. I'm still the same man I've been all along. "How much of this did Grams know?"

"Oh, Michael, none of it. She was a victim along with the rest of us."

"None of this explains why you never told me about my father."

"You were a happy boy who adored his father. With every passing day, that bond grew. I didn't want to take that away from either of you. I thought maybe, when you were older, I would tell you but it became easier as time went by not to."

"Easier? The only one it was easier for was you. Didn't you think I would eventually find out?"

"No, I always thought that if and when the time came, I would be the one to tell you. I never thought you would find out this way. Is that why Heather called off the wedding?"

"That coupled with the fact that she has decided she is no longer in love with me."

"What kind of person walks away because of a past that you had no control over? After all this time, doesn't she know the type of man you are?"

"Yes, well, one would think so, but it doesn't change the fact that all this crap comes along with me. The bottom line is I had the right to know. It should have come from you and not from some report. Look, I applaud you, that you had the strength to continue the pregnancy. I have even more respect for my dad than ever before, but secrets never really stay hidden." I finally sit down and let it all sink in, staring out into nothingness.

"Michael, I know you're hurting, but I only wanted to do what I thought was best for you."

"How is hiding all of this from me in my best interest?"

"I didn't want you branded by anyone else's actions. I know nothing about the man that raped me. You tell me how knowing all of this helps you?"

"That's not the point, Mum; I had a right to know. I should be the one to share it if I wanted to. You can't begin to imagine how I felt reading about all of this in a fucking bloody report!"

Her hands are trembling and part of me feels so bad that I've made her feel this way, but I can't help feeling hurt. "Michael, I'm so sorry." With her trembling fingers she wipes away a lone tear trailing down her cheek, and now I feel even worse.

"I need to talk to my dad—*alone.*"

She gets up and squeezes my shoulder. "I'll get him. I'm sure he's right outside that door." Sure enough, she opens the door, and he comes racing in.

"Bella Mia." He takes her in his arms. He's always showing her how much he loves her, not just saying it.

"I'm going to leave the two of you alone to talk. I'll be down-stairs if you need me." My mum leaves and he sits next to me. I don't even know where to begin.

"I have questions."

"I figured you would, but first, I have something I'd like to say." He gets up and pours himself a dram of scotch, which is rare for him. "I have loved you and considered you mine from before you were even born. I've watched you grow into a fine young man, one that I would like to think I played a part in creating. I honestly be-lieve with all my heart that it doesn't matter whose DNA you have, it's whose love you have that really matters. You're my son and you will always have my love and respect. Please understand your moth-er loves you and she really thought it was in your best interest to keep this secret."

Something my mum said about Dad's family jumps out at me. "Dad, why did your family disown you?"

"Are you really sure you want to hear all of this?"

"Yes, don't you think the time for secrets is long gone?"

He puts his glass down and takes a seat next to me. "I asked your mother to marry me at least a dozen times and every time she said no; stubborn woman. Finally, in a moment of weakness, or to shut me up, she finally said yes. I was so excited and wanted to share that with my family. I went to see them and told them everything. My dad said if I married your mom I would be disowned from the family. I was in shock; they both said such terrible things. Things I would never repeat. I knew my life would never be complete with-out her. I left that day with the intention of never going back there again. I set out to prove to them I didn't need any of them. I had my Bella and that's all I would ever need. After that, I thought your mom and I would get married and have lots of children. You know what they say about plans . . . anyway, once your mom was home and recovered, I focused on raising you and creating my own winery to pass on to you or your children one day. Then, you got sick, I did the one thing I vowed I would never do again—speak to my family. I went back with my hat in my hand and begged them to be tested. As you know, they weren't a match and, even though they said they wanted to be a part of your world, they never really have."

"So you walked away from your family because of me?"

"No, son, I walked away from ignorant people. I will always choose love over everything else. Your mom loves me and I love her. One day you'll find that type of love, a love so intense that it threatens to take the wind out of your sails and rocks you to your core. I know you thought Heather was that great love, but if she could walk away from you, then it wasn't true love. I will go to my grave and beyond loving your mom with all that I've got. It's a once in a lifetime kind of love." He takes a deep breath and he gets a far away look on his face. I know he loves her—hell—he shows it in so many ways, but when he talks about her, it's so intense.

"Dad, I love you. I know I don't say it all the time but I do. I'm proud to call you my father. I only hope that one day I can live up to the standards you've set for me."

"Thank you; you already have. I love you, too, but I sense there's something else bothering you; what is it?"

"I'm pissed off at Uncle Jax," I admit. He begins to laugh and I'm floored. "What's so funny?"

"We all get pissed off at him; so what else is new? What the hell did he do now?"

"We had a deal. We've never ever kept secrets from each other, yet, he kept this from me." The more I think about this the more it pisses me off.

"Well, before you get all crazy mad at him, why don't you sit him down and hear what he has to say. You might be surprised."

"Why would I be surprised?"

"Your mom asked him to keep the secret, and you know Jax; he's not easily swayed. Maybe if you talk to him calmly, you can find out why he agreed to go along with her plan."

In a matter of twenty-four hours, my entire world has turned upside down. I don't think I can handle any more surprises.

"I will as soon as I find him. Do you know where he is?"

"Well, the last I saw him, he was threatening to castrate Bo if he got within five feet of Antonia. I hope to God you warned Bo before you brought him here."

"Um, yeah, but, Bo does whatever he wants to do. We better go rescue him, and I want to talk to Uncle Jax." We head out the door and my mum is standing there. I give her a hug and search out my uncle. He has some explaining to do.

Chapter Three

JAX

MAX AND I ARE SITTING IN MY OFFICE GOING OVER THE file that Junior brought home. I sense her and I know I'm probably in trouble. Max doesn't even bother to turn around.

"Jax, you can't be threatening to castrate anyone who gets within an inch of Antonia."

I glance over to Max before I turn to face the music. He's smirking, clearly trying not to laugh. I turn around and see my beautiful wife is standing with her hand on her hip ready to lay into me.

"Sweetheart, in my defense, it's all your fault." The key to winning this argument is putting the blame on her. Although, her face is now flushed, and I wish I could rethink that strategy.

"Me? Why the hell is any of it my fault? He's a perfectly nice guy, Jax. He's a friend of Michael's and it's his first time here. He very rarely brings anyone home and all she did was offer to show him around. Maybe you should stop reading into everything. And Max, don't even think you're off the hook. I don't know what you did to Bo, but he won't even come within five feet of you. Every time your name is mentioned, the poor guy breaks out into a cold sweat. Both of you need to rein it in. Now, where is Michael?"

"Right behind you, Aunt Raven. Is Bo okay?"

"Yeah, Antonia took him on a tour of the property. I'm sorry about everything that happened. You did nothing wrong, and I'm always here for you. Never let the insecure actions of one person make you bitter." She gives him a big hug.

Michael

"Thank you. I need to talk to Uncle Jax alone for a bit. Can you make sure Bo is okay, please?"

Everyone leaves and now it's just us. I don't even know where to begin. The two of us are standing here toe to toe, neither one saying a word.

"You have questions for me," he ends the awkward silence.

"Really just one: why?"

"Why, what?"

"Why did you promise to always tell me the truth when you knew it was a promise you couldn't keep? I get that it wasn't up to you to tell me, but our relationship has always been based on truth. When I was so sick, you told me the truth. When Rose died, you came to me as soon as you could and told me. I've always trusted you to tell me everything, no matter what. I've never second-guessed you ever, but now, I'm not so sure." His face pales at my words. I don't want to hurt him, but I need to understand it all.

"Never second-guess me, please. It was not my secret to tell. I had to abide by your parents wishes and do what they thought was best for you, even if I thought they were wrong. Are you sure you really want to hear this?"

Deep down I know I don't have a choice. "Yes, I need the truth—all of it—not just what Mum and Dad told me," I demand. His jaw is tight and he seems apprehensive, but I'm not backing down.

"First, I love you. I don't regret a single second of having you in my life. But, honestly, I felt responsible for your mum's rape. To see my sister, so broken, nearly destroyed me. He didn't just rape her, Junior; he beat her to within an inch of her life. That day, I walked into the hospital and didn't even recognize my own sister, and the way your Grams looked at me nearly destroyed me. I realized that I was making a name for myself, and that name was attracting a lot of attention. I should have thought to put security in place sooner. I live with that guilt every day. It was only after talking to James that I found out the rape was planned all along, but it still doesn't change how guilty I feel. That guilt has fueled everything I have done since. This is why I'm always so over the top when it comes to keeping everyone safe." There's a crack in his voice and for a moment he turns away from me. He clears his throat, turns towards me and takes a deep breath before he continues. "When we got Bella back home, she was extremely withdrawn. The outside wounds eventually healed but on the inside, she was broken. The light in her was gone. She was no longer that happy girl and it was all my fault. What was even worse was, for the first time in my life, I couldn't fix it. When she found out she was pregnant, at first I feared she would terminate the pregnancy. I didn't think she would be strong enough to go through with it. I thank God, that, for her, that wasn't an option. She found her strength and little by little the pregnancy seemed to bring her back to us. You put a light back in her eyes that I thought was lost to us forever. I vowed I would protect you and provide for you no matter what happened. Your dad was in the picture before the rape and quite frankly I was surprised that he stayed around afterwards. Most of her friends slowly shied away from her, especially when Max put tight security on all of us. Then one day, Michael came to me and asked my permission to marry your mum. I did what I thought was best and tried to buy him off, and trust me, I threw everything but the kitchen sink at him, but he wouldn't go away. I think deep down inside, I feared they might move to Italy and then I wouldn't get to watch you grow up. In the end, he offered to sign away all of his rights to you and any of her money just to marry her. He had only one request, that the wedding take place before you were born. I asked why he agreed to the terms and he said 'Someday you'll understand what it's like to love beyond all reason.' When Bella had you, there were so many complications and, at one point, we almost lost her. He stood by her, his love and faith never waivered. He's such a good man, Junior. I admire his strength and his ability to love unconditionally. Then one day, your parents came to me and said they didn't want to ever talk about the rape. As far as they were concerned, Michael was your dad. I fought them on their decision to hold back, but, in the end, I had to abide by their wishes. You know me better than just about anyone. You've got to know how hard that was for me, but I had to respect their decision. I couldn't let my guilt get in the way of how they chose to raise you. When you got sick, I saw the past slam into the future. Again, I asked them to tell you the truth, but they refused. Instead, Michael went to his parents and begged them for help. I had ads and commercials made up that offered millions for a perfect match, but I knew in the end it would be James."

"Were you hoping on a off chance that my real father would somehow be one of the donors?"

"Junior, I was a desperate man, throwing everything I could at the wall and seeing what would stick."

"Do you know who he is?"

"No, I don't. Would you want to know? Would it make a difference in the man you are today? Would you do anything differently?"

"No, I don't think so."

We are still standing only inches apart, his jaw is ticking and I know there has to be more.

"Is that it, cause if there is anything more, now would be a good time for you to come clean. I don't think I could tolerate another secret, least of all, from you."

He walks over to his desk and pulls out a bottle of scotch and two glasses, which I'm sure is reserved for him and Uncle Max. He passes me a glass and swirls the amber liquid around in his before taking a sip. "Yeah, there is one more thing I have kept from you but with good reason. There are only a few select people who know this and I would like to keep it that way. The day you were born, I put a percentage of Raiders Inc. in your name. I never thought I would have children of my own, so I made you my whole life. I never told your mum because I didn't want her to ever wonder if the person she was with was just in it for the money. As time went on, Michael was more than able to provide for you both. When Max and I sold the company, that money was put into a trust, which I continue to manage. What I'm trying to tell you is, you're a very wealthy man."

My grasp on the glass gets tighter and I down my scotch. That familiar burn is almost welcoming. "Are you fucking kidding me? Why the bloody hell would you do that? Exactly how rich are we talking here and who actually knows?"

He pours me another drink. "Maybe you should sit down." By the look of angst on his face, I figure I better take his advice.

"Aside from my attorneys, Max and Raven are the only ones who know. For safety purposes, I want to keep it that way. As far as how rich, well, if I wanted to turn all of your holdings into liquid cash within the next forty-eight hours, I would say about 6.5 billion, give or take a few."

"Like billion with a B?" That loud buzzing in my head is back again.

"Yeah, like billion with a B. When I first did it, I knew that the trust would be able to provide you with a comfortable income, but I never expected it to grow that much. Junior, you understand why no one can know. I already have two full time guards on you, if this got out, you would lose whatever freedom you have. I'm sorry; I never meant it to be like this." He sits next to me and both of us are quiet, staring into our now empty glasses. I look at him and for the first time I see such sadness.

"How exactly did you mean it to be?" my voice is barely above a whisper.

"I never wanted your Grams to have to work three jobs again. I never wanted to hear Bella crying because she was hungry. I wanted to make my mum proud and before I found out what my father was really all about, I wanted to make him proud too, just in case he ever came back. I know the intensity of which I do things can be a bit much, but every one of those things have forced me to find my focus in life," his voice trails off.

"What if I don't want any of it? Did you ever think of that?"

He turns and stares at me, a stoic expression on his face. "If you decide that you don't want it, I will put it in a trust for your future children. You need to understand all of this is because of you. The winery your parents own. The distillery Uncle Max built, all the subsidiaries and all the toys are here to stay. A percentage of everything we have is split up between different charities. I would hope that once you find your footing in life, you would do the same. There are safe guards in place so you can never give it all away but you can use some of it for something good."

"What do you mean because of me?"

He gets really quiet, puts his glass down and closes his eyes for a moment. Like someone organizing their thoughts. "You remember Erica."

"God, I haven't heard that name in years. How could I forget her; she was responsible for my kidnapping. What does she have to do with anything?"

"We were in a long term relationship. She was also involved in some aspects of Raiders. She did some things that could have ended my career and sent me to jail. One day, I left her to watch you while I showered. She gave you my phone to keep you busy while she was on a call that I was not supposed to hear. You inadvertently recorded it. When I saw it, Max and I put together everything she did and we were able to stop it all before I ended up in jail. She was blackballed from the industry and from her family. It's what fueled her rage and made her want revenge. If you didn't do what you did, no telling how different life would be today. So you see, in so many ways, we all got a second chance in life. You need to focus on that; go out into the real world and find out what your something special is and run with it. Make a difference, Junior."

"So I'm just supposed to go on with life as if I don't know about this ridiculous amount of money. How do you suggest I do that?"

"Exactly as you have been all along. Go out and make a life . . . find your way. Put aside everything I told you today. It's nothing that you have to deal with. It will all be waiting for you when you're ready. The best advice I can give you is never let material things define who you are. If all this stuff went away tomorrow, it wouldn't matter. What matters most in life is love, respect, and your family. Those things can't be replaced. You need to be able to take a long hard look in the mirror and respect the person looking back at you. I read somewhere that 'a man will be judged by the family he leaves behind.' I look at our family and I think we're doing okay. No matter what shit is thrown at us, we are a great family."

"Where the hell do you read that?"

"A fortune cookie."

I look at him and he burst out laughing. "Are you serious?"

"Hey there is something to be said for fortune cookies."

"What about Heather?"

"What about her? After what she's done, her lack of compassion and respect makes me sick. Do you really want to be with someone that was so quick to toss you aside like yesterday's leftovers?"

"No, you of all people know better; I will never go back. I think I'm more shocked that she was so selfish, and I blame myself for having blinders on. Why didn't I see her for who she really is?"

"You're tender-hearted and always see the best in people, even when they don't deserve it. Don't let her make you jaded."

"How can I not? I thought she was my end all. How could I have been so wrong?"

"Listen, you might not believe this now, but someday you will find that one person who really does make you whole. She will make you see the world in a different way, make you a better person, you'll know it and you'll have no doubts."

"Is that the way it was with you and Aunt Raven?"

"She gave me purpose. For the first time in my life, everything I did or said mattered to me. That's how you'll know."

"Maybe it's not realistic to think that everyone finds that type of love."

"You've got to believe, Junior. You can't let this make you a jaded man."

"I don't know what to believe anymore."

"Give yourself time." He passes me a business card. "If you need someone to talk to that's not in the family, she is a good listener."

I never thought he would talk to anyone outside this family.

"Do you know how her father was able to get his hands on my medical records?"

"Max is already working on figuring it out, but you know—where there's a will there's a way. Money is power and her father has plenty of it. Have you given any thought as to what you want to do next? Last time we talked, you were in the process of narrowing down which job you were going to take, have you decided? I mean, I know that everything just happened and if you want to hang out here for a while, you should. This is your home, it will always be."

"Why do I hear a *but* coming?"

"Because you know me too well. Do you really want to deal with your Grams? She's in Paris this weekend with Mick but she will be back on Monday."

The thought of Grams giving me the third degree right now makes me want to hightail it out of here.

"Actually, I was offered a position in the States. I was on the fence about it, but I think I'm going to take it. Maybe the change will do me some good," I inform him. He becomes very quiet, and knowing him the way I do, he probably doesn't want me that far away.

"Where is it and with which company?"

"California, off the coast of Santa Barbara. It's a pilot program with the federal government. My PhD in Civil Engineering, Geo-technical Engineering, and Geology coupled with my two years of post doctorate research put me at the top of the list for the job. I will be working on and off of the existing offshore oil fields; I won't bore you with the details. I will have the opportunity to go to different sites from Santa Barbara to the Gulf Coast. After all my years of schooling, it will be great to finally apply everything I learned to real life. Bo is moving back home, so the timing is great. I'll at least have my best friend to keep me busy."

"I know he's your best friend, but are you sure going back to California with him is the best thing right now? He does seem to be a little bit of a loose cannon."

"Look, I know he can be a little wild at times but he always has and always will go balls to the wall for me. I'll be okay, but I'm going to hightail it out of here before Grams comes back; you need to smooth things over for me with her. You know she will be calling me all hours of the day and night, interrogating me. Besides, you owe me."

He laughs. "You are more like me than you realize. I've got your back and I always will. I know you're hurting but don't do anything stupid. Take all the time you need and don't jump right into another relationship."

"Trust me, my focus right now is going to be work and only work." We get up and he pulls me into a bear hug.

"Okay, I'm going to trust you on this one. I'll smooth things over with your Grams. In the meantime, let's go find your friend before Max kills him."

We head out in search of Bo.

Chapter Four

SPENDING THE WEEKEND WITH MY FAMILY WAS GREAT, BUT now it's time to get on with my life. It's been said looking good is the best revenge well, my success will be my revenge. I sent a confirmation email accepting the position in California. I decided not to go back to my flat in London. I closed that door and I don't want to return—too many memories. I spoke to Aunt Raven about it and she made arrangements for everything to be packed up. She's even made arrangements for Bo's stuff to get packed up, too. He actually made it through the weekend without having either one of my uncles castrate him. Which was surprising considering Antonia couldn't take her eyes off of him. If there is anyone who will put Uncle Jax in an early grave it's Antonia. For the long flight to LA, we have one of the larger jets. This bad boy has all the bells and whistles, and Bo is ecstatic to mess around with everything.

"Do you think you can tear yourself away from everything long enough so we can make some plans?"

"Are you ready to tell me what was in the envelope?"

"The past, which is where it needs to stay. Now I booked a suite at The Four Seasons in Santa Barbara. The first order of business when we land is to get a car and then go clothes shopping. Do your parent's know you're coming home?"

"No, I didn't tell them. Besides, my dad is probably busy directing his latest project. I haven't spoken to my mom or my sister yet.

Let's get settled in first and then we can deal with all of that. I don't understand why did you decided to take the job. You originally said you were going to talk to your uncle about opening your own firm. Besides everything with Heather, what changed and why Cali?"

How the hell do I explain it to him? God, this is why I hate secrets and lies.

"California is as far away from London as I can get. I want to get my feet wet and work for someone before I branch out and possibly open my own business. I want to enjoy life without anyone knowing much about me." Even to myself, I don't sound to convincing.

"Right, Mike, like that's even possible. You're moving to Cali with two bodyguards in tow and you think no one will notice? Get your head out of your ass. I think if that's what you really want then don't stay at the best hotel in town. Maybe we could go back to my parent's house and use their place as our home base before you have to start work. Granted it's a long drive from Santa Barbara, but my sister does real estate and she can either secure a long-term rental or you can buy something with some sort of privacy relatively quickly. Oh and why are we going clothes shopping?"

"Since the only thing I have right now are the jeans covering my arse, I think it would be a good idea to get some clothes. Call your sister and tell her to start working on finding something I can buy that will give us the privacy I need," I instruct. He gets very quiet and begins picking the label off of his beer bottle, a nervous habit of his.

"What's the problem? Just tell me whatever it is and I will deal with it. No secrets, Bo."

"On second thought, I'm thinking maybe going back to my parent's house is not the best idea. We've video chatted with them, but I never told anyone about the bodyguards and shit. I wouldn't even know how to. I mean, what am I supposed to say? 'Say hello to Mike and these are his guards so he doesn't get kidnapped again. Oh and by the way I have a full time guard, too.' They will fucking freak out. Maybe we need to avoid my family for now."

Sometimes having it all is like having nothing. The problems might be different yet, at some point in life, we all have our hands tied behind our backs.

"If you need to back away from me, I totally understand. I don't want to be a problem. Besides, once I start work, I will be gone for extended periods of time."

"Don't be an ass; we will figure it out. We will stay at the hotel. The Four Seasons is top notch and it does have plenty of privacy. If you want, we can put the reservation in my name along with the Limo. I know you like to drive yourself when ever possible but you have no clue what it's like to drive in the States, let alone California, so for now, you have a car and a driver at all times. Believe me, if you do that you'll blend right in. Think of Santa Barbara like the American Riviera and you'll do just fine. When are you supposed to start work?"

"I have about two weeks off before I have to start. That should be more than enough of time for us to get settled in. Did you decide which job you're going to take?"

"Yeah, I had no clue that you were coming back with me so it's ironic that I already accepted that position I told you about at the special research lab in Santa Barbara. I'll be in the Marine Ecology and Conservation division. Maybe down the road, when you're ready to open your company, we can work together. For now, I'll have my sister try and find us a place to live."

I get up and get us each another beer, even though there's enough staff on board to take care of a small army; that's not my thing.

"Mike, what's wrong? Don't tell me *nothing* cause I know you better than anyone. Is it something in those papers?"

If only it was just that. "Listen, it might be in your best interest to distance yourself from me."

He holds his hand up stopping me from continuing on. "What

has you so worried? Was there some sort of threat?"

"No, but now that we will be in the States, I'm worried about being more out in the open. I'm probably just over reacting, but I want to talk to Uncle Max about it, maybe bounce some options off him."

"We'll figure it out, in the meantime get some rest; it's a long ass flight and I want to explore this bad boy."

Just like that, the conversation is over. Bo never talks about his sister much or any of his family. If he's worried, he's not letting on. Not only do I have to be more conscious of Bo's safety and mine but now I have to worry about his family, too. Up until a couple of days ago, I thought I'd be married and living in London, boy was I mistaken. Fucking Heather has me second-guessing myself at every turn. I think I would feel better going over everything again with Uncle Max. Bo is already in the flight deck with the crew, no doubt in all his glory. I head into the office for some privacy, and I'm not surprised when he picks up on the first ring.

"Junior, is everything okay?"

I don't want to come off sounding paranoid but I'd rather be safe than sorry. "Yeah, everything is okay. Since there has been a change in plans, I need to go over them with you and get some advice." He's very quiet as I give him the low down on everything, including Bo's family.

"So, let me get this straight, you and Bo are going to stay at the hotel until his sister finds you a home to buy or lease, instead of just staying at the hotel indefinitely. What hasn't changed is when you are not staying at your place, you will be staying on the offshore oil fields. You are worried about Bo's family's safety, is that everything?" He makes it sound so simple.

"Yeah, after everything Uncle Jax told me, I'm worried about the safety of everyone around me. I feel like I'm becoming paranoid and a part of me wishes he never told me." I close my eyes and rub my temples, trying to ward off the migraine I feel coming on.

"This is nothing to stress about, Junior; I've had security on Bo's family for about a year now. I've kept them at a distance, not as close as your guards. Now that you have decided to settle in California, as a precaution, I will up security on all of you. If you try to explain the situation to his parents, they might not be as receptive to it. I think it would be best if I talk to them. I've done this before and I know how to handle it. I will fly out tomorrow. In the meantime, get checked into the hotel and stay there until I get in."

"You've had security on them all this time? Why didn't I know this?"

"This is why I'm good at what I do. There hasn't been any increased threats. However, I will never leave anything to chance ever again. If that means putting extra guards on everyone, so be it. Let me do my job and don't worry." Easy for him to say!

"Maybe you could tell me what I should tell them and I can do it myself. You don't need to fly all the way out here for a conversation." Now I feel stupid that I even called him.

"It's not just a conversation; I need to make sure all security is properly in place. Would you rather I send Jax?"

I leap out of my chair and nearly knock the phone off the conference table. "Dear God, Uncle Max, don't you dare do that to me."

He's hysterical laughing! "Relax, Junior, I wouldn't do that to you. Keep your guards close and I'll see you soon." He hangs up and, whether I'm ready for it or not, California, here I come.

Chapter Five

BO WASN'T KIDDING ABOUT IT BEING A LONG ARSE FLIGHT. I'm glad I'll have at least two weeks before I have to start work. It will probably take me that long to get my bearings. All of my interviews were done via Skype, so it will be nice to finally meet everyone. When we get into the car, Bo tells the driver where he wants to stop before we check into the hotel. Two hours and about thirty shopping bags later, we are finally checking into our hotel.

This place is beautiful, very serene, and fucking sunny as hell. Thank God I listened to Bo and picked up a half dozen pairs of sunglasses. After a very long, hot shower, Bo and I order a ridiculous amount of food. There's something to be said for sitting on the balcony watching the waves roll in while sipping on a beer.

"I can understand your need to be back home; this place is tranquil." I take a deep, satisfying breath and continue to watch the waves.

"Mike, what's wrong? You seem off, did something happen?"

"I spoke to Uncle Max. He said he's had security on your family from day one. He's kept them at a distance since we were in a different country but now that we are here, he is going to increase coverage," I inform him.

He lifts his shades and glares at me. The look on his face is not good. "My parents are going to fucking freak out. Is this really necessary? What the hell am I supposed to tell them?"

He's really going to lose it over what I have to tell him next. I take a deep breath and continue. "You don't have to tell them anything. Uncle Max will be here soon to talk to them and get everything into place."

"He's coming here?! Oh for the love of Pete and all that's holy, please shoot me the fuck now."

"Be thankful; he threatened to send Uncle Jax. Why the hell are you so afraid of him anyway?"

"Oh I don't know, maybe because he's actually killed people for a living . . . that might have something to do with it. My sister is going to freak out."

Now I feel even worse. "Did you try calling her yet?"

"No, she will know right away something is off; twins have a way of knowing that shit. I'll shoot her a text and tell her to drive up. Max can explain it to my parents and you can explain it to Dagen when she gets here."

I watch him send the text and my stomach instantly knots. How the hell am I going to explain to a girl I've never met that because of me, she has to have a permanent bodyguard? It's not like I'm the fucking King of England, for Christ's sake. I'm a nobody, just some unknown, filthy-arse rich guy who never earned a dime of it. The kicker is, I can't even give that shit away. Billion with a B—fuck me.

"Tell me about Dagen. What do I need to know before I meet her? I mean, if I have to try and explain all this shit to her, I need to know what approach to take." I grab us each another beer and watch the sun begin to set.

"As you know, we are twins, but she is older. She is bossy and doesn't take any shit from anyone. She has my dad wrapped around her finger. I was named after Humphrey Bogart and she was named after Ronald Reagan. Yeah, her real name is Reagan but when I started talking, it came out as Dagen. She got her degree from Stanford University. She studied abroad and went on to open her own boutique real estate office. She caters to the kids of the rich and

34

famous. She loves Boxers and helps run a rescue for them. What are you so worried about?" He's not going to let this go until I give him some sort of answer that makes sense.

"Of course I'm worried. I have to tell some girl I never met that she has to have a bodyguard close by . . . forever. Oh, and you've had one for a long time now, you just didn't know it. It's a fucking total invasion of privacy. I'm a nobody to her and yet I'm about to fuck with her world. Bloody hell, Bo, I'm sitting here thinking about how I'm going to explain it to her when half the time it doesn't even make sense to me. You know me, this is all shit I never wanted. There are a lot of sick people in the world and they will do anything for money. Sometimes I think it's better to be alone, that way, I don't have to have the responsibility of anyone but me." The sun is almost gone and it's like watching a fireball drop into the sea.

"I got it just tell her 'Hi, I'm Mike and I'm going to fuck with your world' that should work." He's laughing, no doubt trying to lighten the mood.

"Some days, Bo, you are such an arse." The front desk rings us to let us know she's here; it's game on.

"I'll go down and bring her up here while you scramble to figure out what you're going to tell her."

I head back out to the balcony and call Uncle Max. Maybe he can give me a clue as to what to tell her.

He picks up right away. "Junior, is everything okay?"

"I need some advice. Bo's sister Dagen is here. I told you I was going to have her help me find a place, but I also have to tell her about the additional security she will have. Exactly how am I supposed to do that?"

"Don't tell her anything yet. I was able to tie up my other business sooner than I thought. I just landed, so I should be there soon. Let me discuss it with her and her parents. Focus on finding a secure place to live. She has a guard that is maintaining her distance right now. You have two guards and Bo has one. Don't worry; everyone is safe. Stop reading so much into everything."

"I've always hated this part but after what Uncle Jax told me I hate it even more. I didn't ask for any of this shit. All this money did is seal me to a lonely existence and now everyone around me has to deal with the same shit."

"Hey, don't talk like that. We'll get it all figured out and you'll be able to have a life—I promise. I'll see you soon."

I hang up and head back inside. I was not prepared for what came walking through the door. Bo is blond, tall with well-defined muscles. Throughout college he was on the swim team. Dagen has thick brown hair, and her eyes are a very dark brown. They are extremely intense and her curves have no end to them. How the fuck are these two twins? I snap out of it and realize Bo is laughing.

"Don't worry, Mike, we get that reaction all the time. This is Dagen."

I extend my hand out to introduce myself and she pulls me into a hug! "The whole Brit thing is cute and all but this is Cali, we hug . . . or, at least, I do."

"Okay, well first off I was born in America, but raised in Scotland. Can I offer you a beer or is that too Un-American of me?"

She cocks her head to the side and smiles. Those eyes are like nothing I've ever seen before. "I'd rather have a Chardonnay, please," she asks. I scrape together my wits, get her a drink and we head out to the balcony. "So, Michael, I understand that you and Bo want to share a place. Tell me what you're looking for."

If I could get my head out of my arse, I might be able to.

"I have a large family, which I'm sure will visit me, so lots of rooms. Something very secluded, maybe with some land. Something with a view would be nice." As I go through my list, she takes out her iPad and enters my information.

"What's your budget?" I take a long slow pull off of my beer, trying to figure out what the hell to tell her.

"Sis, money is not a problem but time is. Mike will be working a lot so we need to get this wrapped up quickly. Hotel living is not our style." Bo interjects, helping me out.

She doesn't even bat an eye at the absurdity of all of this. She turns her attention back towards me. "So if we find something, how quick would you like to close?"

"Within two weeks—sooner, if that's possible."

"If I find something but it needs some work, would you be willing to move in and have the work done while you're living there?"

"I'll be going to the offshore oil fields to work where I'm sure I will be staying for an extended period of time, so if Bo can handle it, then I'm fine with it."

My phone rings and I excuse myself, step back inside to answer it. It's Uncle Max letting me know he's on his way up. When I open the door, he's standing there. "So I didn't have to come down to get you because?"

"Because I'm your uncle but, more importantly, I'm in charge of your security. Your guards already put me on the approved list. Now, where is she?" He looks over my shoulder. I roll my eyes and head back outside grabbing some beers along the way. I pass Bo a beer and he instantly pales at the sight of my uncle.

"Uncle Max, meet Dagen Turner, Bo's sister," I do the introductions. If he's surprised, he doesn't let on.

"Pleasure to meet you, Miss Dagen. Do you have a list of homes that are available?" Uncle Max is in his take no prisoners mode, God help her.

"You can call me Dagen, sir, and yes, I've narrowed it down to three that I think might work, depending upon how secluded the guys would like to be." She passes him her iPad, showing him the options. Would be nice if I was a part of all of this.

"Junior, have you looked at these yet?"

"I was just about to when you came in."

"Miss Dagen, Bo, would you mind giving us a moment?" He waits for them to go inside and then calmly passes me the iPad. "I don't want to demand or dictate what you should do. You're not a child anymore. I'm only here to make sure you make the safest choice for everyone involved. I realize that I've always protected you and, quite frankly, I always will, however, I need to teach you what to look for. That being said, look at the three properties and tell me what you see?"

I finally look at the iPad and begin to compare the three properties.

"One of them is right on the water, although it is beautiful, I don't think that would be a good choice. It's not gated and not very secure. That leaves the one that is ridiculously too big. I mean, *really*, fifty rooms? Also, there's the smaller five bedroom home on nineteen acres. I like that one; it's gated and has two separate buildings for staff and a guest house." I shrug and look back up at him. He's smiling for the first time since he got here.

"You have a good eye, so stop doubting yourself. You looked at it logically and made a good decision. Now tell me what you know about Dagen."

"I only met her five minutes before you did! You probably know more about her than I do." I look at him incredulously. His face never gives anything away, but his avoidance tells it all.

"Okay, why don't we go look at the place and then I'll talk to her about security. You take the lead and I'll follow."

He can't be serious. He's holding the door open for me and I realize—he *is* serious. I can do this. *Yeah, keep telling yourself that, Michael, maybe you might even believe it.* I wish Bo wasn't so scared of Uncle Max; maybe it would be a little easier if he would help me.

"Dagen, I'd like to see the home on nineteen acres as soon as possible, please. If I pay cash, how quick can I expect to close?" I hand her back her iPad, and the mention of paying twenty-nine million in cash doesn't seem to rattle her at all.

"It's not occupied, so with a good nudge, we can do a title search and have it closed in seven to ten days. In California, a home inspection is not required, and the inspector doesn't need to be licensed, however, I would be more comfortable if you had one. I can refer you to one or you can bring in one of your own. Let me make a quick call to the listing agent to set up a showing. Would you like to wait and see it in the daylight?"

"First thing in the morning will be fine, thank you."

She excuses herself to make a call and Uncle Max goes and sits down right next to Bo. Now it's his turn to be in the hot seat.

"Bo, tell me about your sister." Honestly I don't know why he's so scared; it's actually quite funny.

"Sir, what do you need to know?"

Uncle Max gets a sly smirk and I'm holding in my laughter. He probably knows more about her than her own brother. I realize he's just having a little fun at poor Bo's expense.

"You need to relax, I'm not going to hurt you. Well, not unless you do something so bloody stupid that I can't control myself."

That's it I lose it. I'm laughing so hard I can hardly see through the tears. "Uncle Max, lighten up on him. I know you're having a lot of fun but time is of the essence."

Bo puts his beer down and focuses on Uncle Max. "Dagen is stubborn as a mule. She doesn't take no for an answer. She doesn't stop until the job is done. She is opinionated and strong-willed. I don't know what else I can tell you, that you probably don't already know."

She comes back in the room and smiles before taking a seat directly across from Uncle Max. "Michael, we have an appointment for ten a.m. Will all the guards be joining us or just yours?" She's smiling and her eyes are piercing. She turns her attention towards Uncle Max. "Sir, my business caters to the children of Hollywood's superstars. I know all about stalkers and security detail."

"Miss Dagen, what do you mean by all the guards?"

"Didn't you think I would look into who my brother's best friend is? Not everyone who lives in California is laid back with a 'no big deal' type of attitude."

"Well then, Miss Dagen, if you researched correctly, you know that the guards are permanent and the one that is on you and your parents will no longer be kept at a distance."

"What if I don't want the guard, have you thought about that? And, again, can you please just call me Dagen?"

"I'm a gentleman with old school manners, so please forgive me, but that's not an option, *Miss* Dagen," he enunciates slowly. "As far as the guards are concerned, you don't have a choice. I'm sure you wouldn't want anything to happen to your parents, and your brother wouldn't want anything to happen to you. I would think you would be happy that I've put the safety of your family before anything else." Watching them go back and forth is like watching a line judge in a tennis match. Neither one of them is backing down.

"Sir, I will table this for now. I need to make some phone calls if this is going to close quickly." She turns her attention back towards me. "Michael, I'm going to my suite to make some calls. I will meet you in the lobby at nine a.m. for coffee before we head out."

Bo quickly gets up, no doubt to escape Uncle Max. "I'm going to hang out with Dagen tonight. I'll see you in the morning."

Just like that, everyone is gone.

Chapter Six

I'M ON THE BALCONY STILL NURSING MY BEER WHEN UNCLE Max comes out with a bottle of scotch and two glasses. "If you're offering me scotch then it must be bad."

He pours a glass and passes it to me. "It's nothing bad, but I want to know how sure you are that you want to live with Bo? I understand he's your best friend but that doesn't mean you have to live with him. Hell, even Jax and I were never able to live under the same roof."

"Why don't you like him?" I'm not backing down on this one. I've lost so much in the past few days; I'm not losing my best friend, too.

"It's not that I don't like him. On the contrary, I like him and his family. I'm concerned about putting them in harms way. Before you flip out, there are no threats. However, moving to California puts you in the open more. You're a good-looking guy and you will attract attention. I want to make sure you're prepared for anything," he states. I slam back my scotch and I'm about to flip out on him when he holds up his hand to stop me. "I know I can protect them; that's not the problem. They might not want the protection. You saw Dagen get all unhinged tonight. If she doesn't follow the rules, she could unwittingly put herself in danger. If anything happened to her or any of them, would you be able to live with yourself?"

Damn it, just another reason why billionaire with a B is going to fuck me up the arse.

"What do you suggest I do? I feel like the walls are closing in around me. How the fuck am I supposed to have a normal life? Please make me understand it. At this point, I don't even know what normal is."

"The first thing you need to do is never act out of fear and panic. If the home tomorrow is anything like the pictures, we can have extra guards without too much disruption. I believe I can get Bo and his family in line with the changes, but the only one that will give us a problem is Dagen."

"You just met her for a whole five minutes, how could you know that?" He's got a Cheshire cat grin on his face.

"Junior, five minutes with her is all it takes to see she is strong and not about to back away from her beliefs. She was not afraid to go toe-to-toe with me, yet her brother pales every time I look at him. Like I said, I know I can protect everyone, that's not even an issue. You've grown up always having security around to the point that they blend into the back ground for you. Bo followed your lead and usually ignores them. Dagen will be a problem and I need for you to be prepared to deal with that when I leave."

He can't be serious; deal with all this? I'm still trying to deal with being tossed to the bloody curb because of something I had no control over. "Exactly how the hell am I supposed to deal with this on top of everything else that's been thrown at me?"

He squeezes my shoulder as if that will offer me some sort of comfort. "I get that you're gutted by everything that has happened. Heather walking away the way she did was fucking low. I'm sorry that you found out about your parents in a report, but we had to abide by their wishes. As far as the money, your mum doesn't even know about it. Really, Junior, it was for the best to keep it quiet, and personally, I think it should stay that way. If it gets out, you will have a slew of new shit to deal with. Go on with your daily routine as if nothing has changed, because in reality, it hasn't. Jax dropping that bombshell on you was huge but he trusts you and for Jax, that says a lot. As far as Dagen is concerned, you have two choices: keep her close or walk away from all of them. If you keep her close, she can see that security is a non-issue for you. In time, she will follow your lead." He pours another scotch and swirls the amber liquid around in his glass. I know he's right I just wish everything wasn't thrown at me all at once.

"Did you find out how Heather's father got his hands on my medical records?"

"Yeah, everyone has a price. Also, he owns one of the oldest and largest pharmaceutical companies in Switzerland; it really wasn't that hard. Unfortunately, there was no way to stop it."

"What's to prevent anyone from finding out about the money?"

"That information is buried so deep, no one will ever be able to unravel it. Can I ask you why you decided to take this job? Not that there is anything wrong with it, but there are plenty of other places closer to home. Are you running?"

"I need the distance right now. I don't want anyone to hover over me. I want time and space. I'm feeling overwhelmed—almost trapped—by things that are out of my control. I'm not running, just taking some time away from my family and all it encompasses," I lay it out. He takes another sip of his drink, no doubt to ease the sting of my words.

"You know you can have all the time you need, but we will always have your back no matter what. We are a tight family. We might get knocked about a bit, but that will never change the core of who we are."

"What did Grams say when she found out?"

"I'm no idiot; I threw all that in Jax's lap and hightailed it the hell out of there before she got back. I would suggest you ring her up soon or you risk her showing up on your doorstep." He gestures with his glass before taking another swig. I love my Grams but the thought of her showing up here is not what I need right now.

"Why is Bo so afraid of you?" I inquire. He has a huge grin and

I know he loves it.

"Have you asked him?"

"Of course I have. The only thing he will tell me is that you killed people for a living. Did you do something?"

His eyes grow wide and he's trying not to laugh. "I might have had a chat with the boy, letting him know what I did during my time with MI6. I might have let it slip in great detail how I did it. I might have also let him know that I have no problem hurting anyone who fucked with you." The two of us begin to laugh and it feels good. "I'll try to go easier on him, but he makes it so fucking fun for me. Let's get some rest, tomorrow is going to be another busy day."

We say goodnight and he heads into his room. I hang back and enjoy the sound of the waves. There is an eight-hour time difference between here and Scotland. If I call my Grams now, I can catch her having her morning tea. I grab my iPad and Facetime her, I know she'll want to see that I'm okay. She might not be the best with the electronics, but she can muddle her way through. She answers right away.

"Hi, Grams, how was Paris?"

"Michael, I know everything. I have a good mind to ring her up and give her a piece of my mind, not to mention that father of hers. He had no right to do what he did and he hasn't seen the last of me." *Oh, dear Lord.*

"Grams, I need you to do something for me."

"Of course, do you want me to come to California? I can have Jax get the plane ready right now. Why did you leave before I got home? You better not be running away."

"Grams, calm down, I'm not running away. I just want some time to figure out what I want to do next. I took the job in California that I told you about. I think it will be a good opportunity for me to learn everything from the bottom up." At least she's listening for a change.

"So what do you need me to do?"

"Don't contact Heather or her father. Just please, for me, let it go. I agree with you; what she did was wrong but my parents should have told me. It doesn't change who I am; it never will. DNA didn't make me into the man I am today—good, bad, or otherwise—my family did that all on their own. I need some time and I'm asking you to give me that. Uncle Max is here and he is setting up security so there really is nothing for you to worry about."

She leans in closer, as if she is trying to see clear into my soul. She is the strongest woman I know, but her family makes her very vulnerable. Finally, she smiles. "Okay, I won't contact Heather or her father. It always comes back around, Michael. Mark my words, it always comes back around. I'm giving you three months from today and then I will be paying you a visit. No one and nothing is going to stop me."

Well, at least I bought myself some time. "Now tell me about your trip? I'm surprised you got Mick to leave Scotland. How did he handle all the crowds?"

"Paris was fun. It was Mick's first time there so we did the tourist stuff. He was not too happy about the crowds at the Eiffel Tower but he handled it. You know his sweet tooth was in heaven at all those pastry shops. I took him to La Pâtisserie des Rêves and he made friends with the owner. Before long, they had him in the kitchen working. Don't be surprised if you get a care package from him. Michael, are you really okay?" It always comes back to me and I love her for it.

"I will be. I have Bo with me, and his sister Dagen. She's a real estate agent and helping me find a place to buy."

"Okay, well tell Maxwell I'll check in with him and don't let him scare your friend too much." She laughs and, in a strange way, it's comforting.

"I won't. I love you, Grams."

She waves goodbye, "I love you, too. Three months, Michael." When I hang up, I feel better. She has a way of bringing calm to a situation, at least for a little while. I decide to call it a night; tomorrow is going to be another long day.

Dagen

What the fuck has my brother gotten us into? I don't know if I want to punch him or grab him and run. All I know is, I need answers before I do anything more for his friend. He is quietly following me back to my room. He knows. He always knows that when I'm this pissed—just shut up. Give me my space and I might just calm down. We get inside the room and I head directly for the fridge to pull out a couple of beers.

"Bo, I'm going to ask you some questions and please be honest. Let's start with the basics: what the hell is your friend in to? I tried researching him, but there really isn't that much out there other than the usual stuff. I get they have money, I get that he was kidnapped as a child and now he has constant guards. Why have the guards on all of us?"

Bo has a nervous habit of cracking his knuckles. Tonight the popping is out of control. He sinks into the couch next to me. "Okay, sis, here is what I know. Mike was supposed to be getting married next week but she dumped him in a 'Dear John' letter. We went to see Heather, the ex, and I don't know what happened; he wouldn't say. What I do know is we left her house in Switzerland with an envelope and went directly to his family compound in Scotland. What ever was in that envelope really upset him. When I asked him about it all he would say is that it was about the past." He shrugs. "Scotland was insane!" he throws in quickly. "I knew he grew up rich and isolated, but until I saw his place, I really had no idea. They have an *extreme* amount of money. We were only there a couple of days and, before I knew it, we were on our way here. He was offered a lot of jobs and I thought he was leaning toward opening his own company, but then he decided to move to Cali. He's moving on and I know that it seems quick, but with Mike, when he's done, he's done. He never goes back, he's very direct, honest, extremely logical and humble. Family and loyalty is everything to him. I know that his Uncle Max, who, by the way, scares the shit out of me, is in charge of security. He is over the top when it comes to safety, but I don't know why. I only just found out when you did that he's had eyes on Mom, Dad, and you for a while now," he finally finishes and I half wonder if it's the beer or his fear that is making him throw everything he knows about them at me all at once

I'm trying to process this all but something is off. "Do you think he is going to have the guards closer to us because Michael is living with you now?"

He gets up and tosses his empty beer bottle in the trash while grabbing a bottle of water. "I think so. I just wish I knew why. I still think it has something to do with what was in that envelope."

"Maybe there is some sort of danger that you are not aware of. Did you ask him?"

"I asked when he first put a guard on me, and all he would say is 'people are crazy, Bo, and my family will never take any chances again.' I figured it had to do with the kidnapping."

"What's Max's story?" His jaw gets tight and he sinks back into the sofa next to me.

"That guy is scary; you need to stay away from him. He's killed people, Sis—bad people, but still—dead is dead." He waves his hand as if it will emphasize his point. I get there is no coming back from dead. Then, it hits me, he's really scared of this man. I've never seen him like this.

"If you're so afraid of Max, why have you remained friends with Michael?"

"I don't know how to explain it. Mike is my best friend. He

would go to hell and back for me if I asked him. I trust him; he's never let me down. He doesn't judge me but he'd be the first person to call me out if I did something wrong. That type of friendship is hard to find and I'm not prepared to walk away from it—*ever.*"

"How the hell are you going to explain to Mom and Dad why we have guards?"

He is picking at the label on his water bottle, no doubt totally clueless on what he's going to do. "I don't know. How did you know you had a guard on you and why didn't you ever tell me?"

"I didn't; it was a bluff. I figured if there were guards on you and Michael, chances are there's one on me."

"Maybe you could talk to Max about the guards on Mom and Dad; you seem to have a way with him."

"You want me to talk to him?"

He doesn't answer, only gifts me with his huge smile. I shake my head, knowing he just charmed me better than any snake charmer ever could. "Fine, I'll talk to him in the morning and find out what his plan is. He seems like the type of person that always has a plan. For now, get some sleep. I think the next few weeks are going to be crazy for all of us." I give him a hug before I get up and head into my room. I still have some work to do but he's got to be exhausted after his long flight. There's a lot more to this family then meets the eye and I aim to find out exactly what that is.

Michael

Morning comes but I got very little sleep, if any. Every time I closed my eyes I thought about what she did and I would get really upset. I think more with myself than with Heather. I really thought I knew her so well, when in reality, I didn't know her at all. I always thought that she would be my rock, strong like all the women in my family are. The only thing she was strong about was walking away. It will be a long time before I ever trust myself to believe in someone again.

I need to figure out what I want to do about Bo. Maybe it's selfish, but I really need my friend right now. He has always stood by me through the good and the bad, expecting nothing. He's dealt with having a full-time guard and having to live a life with limitations all because of me. I just wish to hell Dagen would cooperate but after yesterday, I don't think she will. She didn't back down from Uncle Max and he can put the fear of God in just about anybody. Sometimes I wish I really was a time lord, just like Doctor Who. I would go back and never ask Uncle Jax if there were any more secrets. Never in my wildest of dreams did I expect him to say yes there was more I didn't know. I always knew we were wealthy, but it was never flaunted in anyone's face. We went about our business, working hard and giving back to the community. I was never handed anything. Well, maybe my Lamborghini golf cart, but I think that was more for Uncle Max than for me. I hate secrets and the fact that I have to keep this one is killing me. I don't think I should be expected to keep this from my family. The more I think about this, the more pissed off I'm getting. I grab my phone and call him.

"Hey, Junior, is everything okay?"

"Uncle Jax, I'm pissed off at you for telling me this secret—*your* secret. Now how the hell am I supposed to just forget about it? Don't you think my parents and Grams need to know? By the way, I spoke to Grams yesterday and she's going to give me some space. But you know her, that might last a week, and if she comes here, it's game over."

"Calm down, Junior. After you left, I thought about everything and I decided to tell Bella, Michael, and Mum about the money. I didn't go into great lengths only that you owned a large portion of Raiders, and after we sold it, I put it in a trust for you. I kept it very simple. Now you need to go about your business like you've always done and forget about it. As far as you're concerned, you only have the money you are earning. What's the bigger issue here?"

He always knows. Damn it, how the hell does he always know? I tell him about Dagen. "What if she refuses tighter security? I know Uncle Max said he will deal with it, but I'm trying to start a life here. I was hoping for some anonymity. I thought I would get that here. Now, I'm not so sure."

"I spoke to Max, and he as brought me up to speed. If anonymity is what you want then don't draw attention to yourself. Once you have a place and get into a routine, things will go smoothly. I know how important Bo is to you. Having that one friend that you can trust no matter what is important. Don't stress about it; between Max and me we will help you. But remember, nothing has changed. The money was there before you and will be there long after you're gone."

"You make me laugh; live on the money I earn? I'm buying a house for twenty-nine million in cash! Normal people don't do that. Normal people have a mortgage and take months to close on a house, not two frigging weeks!" I know I'm yelling, but I can't help it and I hate that it's him I'm yelling at.

"Sometimes, like in life, Junior, you have no choice. This is one of those times. Once Max has you set up in a house and security in place, you can go about your business. Please, just give me the two weeks to get it all together. If Max can't deal with Dagen, then I will."

"That, Uncle Jax, does not in any way make me feel better. I'll give you the two weeks. What did the family say when you told them?"

"Well, your mum yelled a lot and Grams laughed until I told her that you knew. I venture to say you will be lucky if she gives you a week before you find her on your doorstep."

That's the last thing I need or want right now. I love my Grams but her intensity can be a bit overwhelming. "I'm trusting you to keep them in line while I get settled."

I look at my watch and realize if I don't leave now, I'll be late. "I have to go meet everyone now; we have an appointment to look at a house. I'm sure Uncle Max will keep you updated."

"Hang in there, Junior. I promise it will work out."

At this point I really don't have a choice. "Yeah, give my love to everyone."

I hang up, finish getting ready, and head out to the balcony, thinking I would have a few minutes to myself to organize my thoughts, but Uncle Max is already having coffee and yelling at someone on the phone. It doesn't take me long to realize it's Uncle Jax on the line. I swear they are up each other's arse all the time. I grab my coffee and sit back, hoping I could watch the waves pound into the shore, but June Gloom is in effect right now so there is a beautiful fog hanging in the air.

He finishes his call and pulls up a chair next to me. "Hey, are you okay? I spoke to Jax and he told me you're worried."

"That's putting it mildly. I'm going to just act like I never found any of this out. I'm going to trust that you will have tight guards on everyone. I'm going to leave Dagen and her parents for you to deal with, because I honestly don't think I can handle another thing."

"You don't have to deal with any of this; that's what family is for. You didn't bring any of this on yourself. Can I ask why you are so freaked out about all of this? You've always known that we had money."

"Yeah, I know, but it was always your money and Uncle Jax's money, not mine. Even my parent's vineyard was never mine. It was my father's dream, not mine. For years my heads been buried in books and research. I never paid attention to any of this. You know I don't like the unknown. I like to have a plan and I like to stick to the plan. I thought I would marry Heather and we would start out like every other normal person does, maybe even struggle a little."

He gives me his usual "you can't fucking be serious?" look and hearing it out loud, I have to agree, what the fuck was I thinking? He begins to laugh and tears are rolling down his cheeks.

"What the fuck is so funny that you can barely catch your breath?"

"Most people dream of winning the lottery and sailing off into the sunset. My crazy arse nephew dreams of being poor and struggling through life. Clearly you can see how ironic that is." His words ring true and I begin to laugh. "Ultimately, Junior, you need to be happy with whatever choices you make. Your duel citizenship makes it easy for you to stay here, but just remember—you can't run from who you are."

"Do you think that's what I'm doing?"

"I don't know; only you can answer that. Are you? Lately, every time we are alone, you act as if there's something you want to talk to me about but then you back down. Almost like something is nagging you. What is it?"

"Do you know who raped my mum?" I'm barely able to get the words out.

"Why are you asking me this?"

"What if. . ."

"STOP! Are you afraid you could be like him?"

"Yeah. No, I don't know. I can't help but wonder if I have siblings? I mean, look at you and Uncle Jax. You have the same father but different mums. You didn't grow up together, yet you're so much alike."

"Did you talk to Jax about this?"

I can't form the words. I can't even look him in the eye.

"Look at me, Junior."

When I finally do, I see such sadness etched all over his face. He's a man who silently carries everyone's secrets, and bears everyone's hell. "Did you ask him?"

"Yes, when he told me about all that he did to find a donor. He said no and I believed him. I knew if I asked him—good, bad, or otherwise—he would tell me. Part of me wants to know and part of me is afraid of what I will find."

"So if Jax already told you, then why are you asking me?"

"Some stuff you play pretty close to the vest and I think that would be one of them."

"Look at Jax and me; we have the same evil blood from our father, your grandfather, running through our veins. We weren't even raised by the same mums, yet we are nothing like him. It goes back to *nature vs. nurture*. There is nothing to wonder about. You don't have a bad bone in your body. Let's focus on the future and stop dipping into the past. It can't be changed, so why go back?"

So, that's his way of telling me, even if he did know, he would take it to his grave.

"What should I do if I decide to get into another relationship? Should I tell her about my past? Will she find it repulsive? Do I dare open myself up to all of this ever again? How do I deal with all of it? How did you tell Aunt Jackie? How did she react when you told her?"

"Wow. Okay, first, Jackie was with me when I found out everything my father was responsible for. When you decide to get serious with someone again, you will have the courage to share the past with her. If she really loves you, she won't judge you by the mistakes of others. Your family is an example of the loving and positive home that you come from. That should speak for itself."

"Okay, one day at a time."

"Exactly. Now, on a positive note; I called Tony and he will be here tomorrow. If you decide to go with the house we are seeing today, he will need time to design a security system that will fit your needs."

"Wow, it will be good to catch up with him. I thought he never leaves the island."

"When I told him it was you, he jumped at the chance. We better head downstairs and meet everyone."

"One more thing before we go. I know everyone is worried about me, but honestly, I need some time for me. I promise I'm not running away."

He gets up and begins to pace. It's how he processes information and finds comfort. "I will give you some time, but if I don't like what I see, then all bets are off." He offers me his hand and we shake before he pulls me into a bear hug. Everyone in my family is so strong and so powerful; I hope I can live up to their expectations. We head out to meet Bo and Dagen, and I thank God this is almost over. Now I just need to find a house, start a new job and a get a new life . . . all within two weeks time. Piece a cake.

Chapter Seven

Dagen

I SPENT A GOOD PORTION OF THE NIGHT SEARCHING THE Internet, trying to find out anything that I might have missed the first time about Michael and his family—nothing. Once they left the States, it's like they never existed. I hate to go into any situation without knowing all the facts, but at this point, I have no choice. I look up from my tablet and see them approaching. I quickly close everything. Michael hits me with his million-watt smile.

"Good morning, Dagen. Where is Bo?"

"He had some stuff to tend to for his new job. He said he would check in with you later. Look, before we take this any further, I have some questions that I need answered from both of you about the possible danger surrounding you."

Max smiles, "Well, Miss Dagen, perhaps we should take this someplace a little bit more private."

Michael quickly holds his hand up to stop him and takes a seat next to me. "Actually, Uncle Max, I'd like to take care of this." I didn't notice last night how deep his voice is. He leans closer to me and the closeness is unnerving. "Dagen, there is nothing sinister about my family. I'm sure you know that when I was younger I was kidnapped. After that, my family has become very security conscious. The extra guards are necessary; I would rather air on the side of caution. I'm sure you wouldn't want anything to happen to anyone. I can't stress enough how important it is that my business remains private." His answer doesn't sound rehearsed but then again, I hardly know this guy. I glance at Max and he's smiling like a Cheshire cat, again. He makes me want to wipe it right off of his face.

"Michael, your personal information will always remain private. I'm not someone that you need to be worried about. I'm concerned about the safety of my family. Surely you must understand that."

"I do understand, but you need to let the guards do their job and go about your life as if they aren't even there." His eyes sweep across the guards stationed at every entranceway.

"Exactly how do you suggest I do that?" I'm trying not to be sarcastic but it isn't always easy.

"One day at a time. Do what you usually do on a daily basis. Everything else will fall into place. Now, why don't we go see the house you found for me." He quickly signs the check for my coffee and when he gets up, he offers me his hand. I'm usually so good at figuring people out right away but I can't with him. He's either a really nice guy with impeccable manners or a very cunning bastard. Why would someone dump him in such a cruel manner? I look down at his outstretched hand and I don't reach for it. I won't be charmed and I sure as hell will never be someone's rebound. I gather up my stuff and when I get up, he places his hand on the small of my back. The gesture is so simple yet so powerful. I need to remind myself to keep my head out of the clouds. He is a distraction, one I don't want or need right now. When we get outside, the waiting cars and guards snap me back to reality.

"Michael, I lined up another property for you to see today. It just came on the market and I thought you might be interested in it. Plus, you will have something to compare. It's bigger with a lot more acreage, which offers you even more privacy. It's listed at forty-five million."

He doesn't flinch at the price, not that I thought he would. We head over to the first property and while Michael is looking around the house, Max is walking around the outside perimeter. I usually wait outside for my clients so they don't feel like I'm a pushy sales lady but, with Max outside, I follow Michael around.

"So, Michael, you're awful quiet, what do you think? Do you have any questions?"

"I'm amazed how large the rooms are. Granted I grew up in a castle, but still these rooms are huge. There would be no problem closing very quickly?"

"As you can tell, the house is empty so a quick closing is not a problem." I wish I knew how to read him better, but the only thing I can figure out is right now, he has a deer in the headlights look in his eyes. Maybe he's overwhelmed by all of this?

"Once I show you the other property you will have a better gauge on what this price point will buy you. Is this your first home purchase?"

"Yes. Lately, it's a first time for a lot of things."

Maybe that's it, new home jitters. I wonder what the other firsts are. "You don't have to do this alone. You have your family and friends to catch you if you fall," I remind him. His eyes are intense, taking me in. I'm almost afraid to look away. Finally, he smiles and when he does, his eyes sparkle.

"Okay, Dagen, why don't you show me the rest of this ridiculously large arse house. I'm sure my uncle will catch up to us when he's done."

I give him the guided tour and then leave him to wander around while I make some calls. I'm sure he doesn't want me up his ass the whole time. When I step out back to give him his privacy, I notice a very animated Max, pacing and yelling. When he notices me, he quickly calms down and walks the other way, no doubt wanting me out of ear shot. I'm about to check in with my office when my phone chirps with a text from Bo:

Bo: Hey, how's it going?

Me: We are at the first place and he seems overwhelmed, but I'm not sure since I don't really know him. Are you coming here?

Bo: No, I'm stuck at work. Is Max with you?

Me: Of course, did you expect anything else? I feel sorry for Michael it must be hard having to live a life under everyone's watchful eyes.

Bo: We'll talk later. In the meantime, get Max to explain to Mom and Dad what is going on.

Me: Coward lol.

Bo: Love you. . .

Me: Ditto.

When I look up, Max is standing in front of me. I nearly leap out of my skin. "Miss Dagen, when you're done with your text, we are ready to head to the next place."

"You seemed upset earlier, is everything okay?"

His icy blue eyes are so intense even when he smiles. "Yes, it can be said that my brother brings out the best or possibly the worst in me. The jury is still out on that one. I will be heading to Beverly Hills this afternoon to speak with your mum. I understand that your father is filming in Spain; Jax is on his way to talk to him now."

"I think it's time for that discussion we tabled last night. Are we in danger?"

"Right to the point, Miss Dagen. There are no threats against anyone; it's merely a precaution."

I take a deep breath and attempt to choose my words wisely. "You make it seem like no big deal but for someone who has never had to live like this, it can be a bit unnerving, at best."

"Did you find it difficult to go about your business when your guard was first assigned to you, or should I say when you realized she was even there?"

"Honestly, I bluffed last night. I had no clue I had a guard. I'm okay with the constant protection, however I just need to know if it's precaution or if there is an immanent threat. That's what I have a problem with. I don't want to be kept in the dark. I can't make any decisions with only half the facts." I don't even think I took a breath during that ramble but he has a way of unnerving me.

"There is no threat, totally precautionary measures," he reiterates. It feels like I'm pulling teeth trying to get anything out of him!

I step closer; only a few inches separate us. "If you're holding back or lying to me, it won't be pretty." The only thing that gets me is a smirk that I want to smack off of his face.

"Miss Dagen, Junior is back, why don't we look at that other house so he can make his decision?" Just like that all conversation is over. I storm past him, mumbling under my breath, which only gets me a laugh from both of them.

Michael

After reviewing two properties, I decided to go with the first one. It offered up everything I needed. Plus, paying cash did the trick and I was able to close within a week of getting here. Tony showed up and in one day he was able to get all the high tech security installed without too much disruption. He even left me with a new high tech gadget that he wants me to test out with my acoustic guitar, which made Uncle Max very jealous. Uncle Max taught me how to play but when it comes to new tech stuff, Tony always sends them to me first. Uncle Max is getting ready to go home today and as much as I love him, it's time. I need to start the next chapter in my life and I can't do that with everyone hovering over me. I head out to the balcony for one last breakfast with him before he goes and I find him on the phone, pacing and yelling—the usual. Before I can step back inside, he hangs up.

"You didn't have to end your call on my account."

"I didn't. Jax and I were done with our disagreement. Eventually he will get that thick head out of his arse, but for now, I'll just let him stew. Let's sit down and enjoy breakfast. I'll stay if you want me to, but I don't think you need me to."

I laugh and he cocks his head to the side with a look of confusion. "Uncle Max, if you stay any longer I will make you watch *Doctor Who* with me." My laughter is contagious and it feels good to have these carefree moments again. Lately, they've been so far and few between.

"Bloody hell no! I'll be gone within the hour."

"So, what did Uncle Jax do to piss you off?"

"Honestly, he's having a hard time leaving you here on your own; he's barely keeping it together. When you wanted to go to school in London, that was bad enough, but with an ocean between us, he is teetering on the edge. . ." he trails off.

"And you? How do you feel about all of this?" Might as well get all this out now.

"How I feel really doesn't matter; it's what you want and need. That is all that matters to me."

"So, you're not good with all of this?"

"I know you're safe and I've put everything in place to protect you. But ultimately, you need to make a life for yourself. You can't do that with any more limitations placed on you. Just promise me you won't make any rash decisions."

We get up and he pulls me into a bear hug. "I promise I will be fine." He lets go and agrees with me before he heads out the door.

Now that I'm finally alone, I head out, determined to get some furniture for this huge house. After wandering around numerous shops, I realize this is a lot harder than I thought. Heather picked out everything in my flat, so I never gave it much thought. I'm really the opposite of the rich persona and I think that's helped to not draw attention to myself. Dagen has been helping Bo furnish his suite and his office. She seems to have a good eye for this stuff so maybe I will just ask her. Really, it's not like I will be here much anyway. I decide to shoot her a text to see if she is interested.

Me: Hey Dagen, I was wondering if you weren't too busy, would you want to help me furnish this huge arse place?

Dagen: Do I get free reign?

Me: Well, that depends; what's in it for me?

Dagen: Besides a kick ass place, what do you suggest?

Me: If I'm giving you free reign, then you should have dinner with me. After all, your brother has been working late every night and I only know the two of you.

Dagen: Deal. I'll be by in about an hour. ☺

That was a lot easier than I thought. If I'm going to make a life here, I need to start with making some friends.

Chapter Eight

TRUE TO HER WORD, EXACTLY ONE HOUR LATER THE GUARD at the gate makes me aware of her arrival. When I open the door, she is standing there with a dog that I presume is hers.

"Michael, say hello to Preston. He's one of my rescues and I'm trying to get him acclimated to different people."

I give Preston my hand to smell and he decides I'm a keeper. "When did you get him?"

"I've had him for three months. This is the final stage before I have to rehome him. Have you thought about getting a pet?"

"Actually, I had a wonderful dog growing up, Vito. When he passed, it left a huge void in my life. I didn't want that heartache again. Besides, I will be gone for weeks on end. What made you get involved with pet rescue?"

"That's a long story for another time. Why don't you show me what you're thinking of doing here?" Just like that, the conversation is over. She allowed me a small glimpse into her sweet side, and then the walls came back up.

"The one thing I can't stress enough is that I want a home. I want it to be comfortable and lived in. I don't want anything dark, lots of light. I grew up in a castle that was modernized but it was still a castle." As I say this she pulls a sketchpad out of her bag and begins drawing.

"You really grew up in a castle?" She cocks her head to the side and the sunlight makes her eyes seem more intense.

"Yes, I really grew up in a castle. There were a lot of good things about it, but growing up that isolated with a security detail shadowing your every move makes for a very lonely existence. That's enough about my childhood. Let's focus on the here and now. I don't dwell on the past. I fought too hard to live and enjoy my future. What else do you need from me?"

She laughs, "Money, oh and that dinner you promised; I'm starving."

"I will have an Amex card for you in the morning. What about Preston? Will he be okay here?"

"He will be fine. We can leave him with the guards at the gate. I'm sure he will keep them amused."

"I found a place that sounded very interesting called Bouchon. I took the liberty of making a reservation. I hope you don't mind."

"Not at all, I've been wanting to try it."

We head out and I have to remind myself this is not a date, just two friends having a meal. When I place my hand at the small of her back, I swear I could feel a very subtle shudder. She cocks her head to the side and smiles up at me; her eyes sparkle like nothing I've ever seen before.

"Rather than leaving Preston with the guards, I have a better idea. Let's take him with us." I scratch his neck and his little stump of a tail is going crazy.

"We can't take him into a restaurant!"

"I know that, but, Dagen, look at that face and those eyes. How could you leave him home? We can grab something to go and take him to the beach." Preston picks that moment to roll around on the grass on his back. *Show off.* "Besides, you will be here a lot, decorating this place, so we can go to Bouchon another night." I just ensured myself a second go round with her. *Thank you, Preston.*

"There is a historic pier near here called Sterns Wharf. We can grab something to eat and stroll the water's edge. I can drive us or we can let your entourage take us." She bites her bottom lip, trying to suppress her laugh.

"We can take your car but you have to put the top down and you have to let me drive."

She slowly releases her lip, tilts her head back and laughs. "You want me to let you drive my car? Do you even have a license?" Her laughter is like sunshine piercing the heavy fog.

"I'll have you know, I went this week and I now have an official California driver's license." I pull out my wallet and show her my card.

"Just because you passed the test doesn't mean you can drive. Besides, we drive on the opposite side of the road."

"I'm an excellent driver. I learned at very early age how to drive a Lamborghini; Uncle Max taught me." I won't tell her it was a golf cart; no need to worry her. She presses a button on her remote and the top automatically begins to go down. She tosses me the keys while she gets Preston situated in the back seat. Once his harness is attached we are good to go. Of course the *entourage* follows us. The car handles like a dream but she still has a white-knuckle grip on the dash. When I finally find a parking spot, I kill the engine, reach over and pry her fingers off the dash. "Really, Dagen, my driving is bang on . . . smooth like a fine wine."

"You do realize, Michael, that the speed limit is not a suggestion." She takes in a deep breath. I'm laughing so hard I can hardly catch my breath. "Do you mind sharing what's so funny?"

"Preston's jowls were flapping in the wind and he was wiggling his rump, I couldn't help but speed up for his enjoyment." I quickly get out and open the door for her. She graces me with another beautiful smile. I mentally remind myself I will not get sucked in anytime soon. She grabs a blanket from the boot of the car as I grab the sweatshirts and try to keep Preston under some sort of control. We stroll down the pier and get something to eat from one of the local restaurants and then walk along the waters edge. She finally declares she's found the perfect spot, spreads out the blanket, and we begin to enjoy dinner.

"So, Michael, are you enjoying Cali? It's got to be a huge change from what you're used to."

I don't know what she knows about me or what I'm used to. "It's different, always sunny and the people are relaxed and very friendly."

"Do you feel it's something you can get used to?"

"Sure, why not? People are people no matter where we live. It's simply a matter of showing someone the same respect they show you."

"Have you always been so black and white?"

I mull over her question for a bit while I give Preston another piece of my sandwich. "In all aspects of my life, I give my all and expect the same in return, otherwise, why bother? Black and white? Not sure about that . . . maybe

"Tell me more about you. The only thing your brother told me is general stuff I could find on a resume. What makes you tick?" I ask after a few moments of silence from us as we're serenaded by the pounding surf. She remains quiet and I hope I haven't scared her away already. I really want her to be comfortable and not shy away from me. "How about I ask you something that I wouldn't find on your resume? I'll start off simple; why did you get involved in Boxer rescue?"

She's twirling her hair around one of her fingers. "Wow, okay. Well, that's actually not a simple one. When I was sixteen I was dating a guy who was two years older than me. I was young and he was my first real boyfriend. I quickly realized that he was obsessive and controlling. I broke up with him, but he had different ideas. One day he came to my high school, barged into my math class, picked me up and left. No one did a damn thing to help me, not even my teacher. He took me to a small abandoned beach shack. It took my family and the police two days to find me. After that, I vowed I would never be a victim ever again. I learned how to defend myself, and I also got a dog. His name was Sidney; he was very special. I told myself that I was adopting him to save him, but in reality, it was Sidney who saved me. After he passed, I didn't feel like I was ready for another companion, so I got involved with rescuing Boxers. I foster them and then place them in the correct homes."

Preston has since rolled over on his back and both of us are mindlessly scratching his belly. "Well, you're right; that's not simple. What happened to the guy?"

"He accepted a plea bargain and agreed to counseling. I have a permanent restraining order in place. I've never heard from him again. Now tell me something about you that's not on the Internet or your resume."

"I don't know what Bo has shared with you. Maybe you should tell me what you already know."

"I know as a child you were kidnapped. You recently split from your fiancée. You grew up in a castle, which has to be really cool. He also said you're very direct, honest, and when you're done—you're done—no going back."

"Yes, well it seems Bo has nailed it. My ex sent me a letter a week before the wedding, calling it off. That was a total mind fuck. Growing up in a castle was fun but it was also lonely. The castle has secret caves and tunnels that I spent many hours exploring."

"Wait, she sent you a letter? When Bo mentioned it I thought he was exaggerating. God, how awful and cruel."

"Yes, well apparently, you can love someone and not be in love with them. It was quite a revelation, if I must say so." The evening air is cool and I pass her a sweatshirt. "What made you decide to go into real estate?" I want to quickly steer the topic off of Heather.

"I love architecture and design. I wanted to take it to a different level. I don't want to just sell someone a house; I want to make it a home for them. I keep my business small for a reason. I don't want to lose that personal touch. I help find the perfect home and then take it through the renovation process. By the time that is done, I know all of my clients wants and needs. It's at that point they usually ask me to help them decorate it and tailor it to their style."

"So my request and bribe with dinner was not new for you?"

Her laugh is infectious and I laugh too. "No, Michael, it's not, but I really wanted to have dinner and get to know you better. It has nothing to do with work. My brother has so many friends but no one as close as you. I wanted to know why. What makes you so different?"

"Did you ask him?"

"Of course I did. He said it was too hard to explain but he trusts you like no other. I trust my brother so I'm giving you the benefit of the doubt. Now tell me about your family."

"Well you've already met my Uncle Max. He's married to Aunt Jackie and they have triplets: Jeffery, Samuel, and Grace. My parents own a winery in Italy, they split their time between there and Scotland. My Uncle Jax, well, he's hard to explain. He's married to Aunt Raven and they have two girls: Antonia and Gabriella. My Grams is married to Mick, he's a great guy and takes everything in stride."

"The thought of Max with triplets is off the charts crazy. Why is your uncle hard to explain? They all live in Scotland?" She's peppering me with questions and I'm trying to keep up with them.

"Yes, the castle is huge and sits on thousands of acres. There are different businesses and other smaller homes that surround it. My Aunt Jackie runs a riding school for children with special needs. Aunt Raven reshaped the Foster Care program. There is a distillery, another of my uncle's adventures. As far as Uncle Jax is concerned, you'll just have to meet him yourself to understand."

"Why did you pick California to settle down in?"

"I wanted to go someplace where no one knows me or my family. I want to make it on my own and not rely upon what others have achieved. I've always wanted to make a difference in the world.

Anyone can make a living but not everyone can make a life. I want to make a life for myself. I want to be the one to define who I am. Ultimately leave something good behind. It might sound old school, but I learned at a very young age that there is so much more to life than just stuff. Stuff can come and go, but what we leave behind is what matters most."

"You're right, that is a very old school way of thinking. You said you learned it at a very young age, how?"

"When I was nine, I was diagnosed with Leukemia." I let the words sink in for her before I continue. "I'm fine now, but it scared me. It changed me in ways I never expected, made me appreciate life more."

"I saw a picture of you on the Internet receiving an award from a hospital for your work with children dealing with Leukemia. I just thought you did the standard volunteer work that everyone does to pad their resume." She seems sad and that's the last thing I want or need.

"Don't be sad; I love spending time with children who are sick. I've been through it and I understand their fears and needs. Their parents see me as a beacon of hope. I'm happy knowing that I can help them."

"Tell me about your new job. What exactly will you be doing?" Finally, something I feel comfortable talking about.

"I will be out on the offshore oil and gas rigs, determining if they are safe for the workers and the environment. I would love to see the world use more alternative energy sources. I'm really look-ing forward to getting started. I will stay out there for a few weeks at a time. Later on, I might have to travel to other sites."

"If the world used more alternative energy wouldn't that put you out of work?"

"No, there will always be a need for natural resources. Technol-ogy changes and people become complacent. We will always have to find a way to safely extract the oil and gas, while doing the least amount of damage to the environment. We need to find ways to use the resources here before we tap into other countries. In the United States, thirteen hundred oilrigs shut down in one year. If the economy gets better and the oil companies decide to bring those rigs on line, they will need safety updates," I finish and realize that she actually seems interested in my job, which is a first for me. Heather was never interested in any of this.

"Well, you picked a great place to work. California has some of the strictest environmental laws in the country. Will you stay here or will you go to different countries and try to do what you are doing here?"

"I'm not sure. Bo and I have a few ideas we are kicking around. Right now, we are both applying what we learned to real life situations. I don't want to work for someone forever; I want to be that someone. Enough about me, please tell me more about you."

"How about you find out more over time. What would make your house a home for you?"

"Smooth move taking the spotlight off of you. Comfort is number one for me. I don't want a show place. I guess you can call me kind of a minimalist."

"So you don't like a lot of stuff around, everything has a place. Is there anything that is a must have? Like Bo had to have an area in his office for all his surfing trophies."

"Yeah, I would like some quotes from my favorite television show put up in my office."

"What show and how many?"

"*Doctor Who*, probably about six or so. Have you watched it?"

"No, but my brother loves it," she states without looking up. I shake my head in disbelief.

"Are you opposed to watching *Doctor Who*? This could be a game changer here." She laughs and I could swear she even snorted!

"You would end a friendship over a television show?"

"No, I would have to work extra hard to show you the error

of your ways, and my time is limited, so I think we need to start tonight," I surmise. She smiles and it warms me in ways I never thought possible.

"Oh, Michael, I can see we are going to be good friends. Do you have any hobbies?"

"I've played Rugby all throughout college and I have an obscene love of Golf. What about you?"

"I play sand volleyball. I will let you know when the next game is and maybe you can come. It's a good way for you to meet different people. I've never golfed; maybe you can take me. Is it hard? Is there a player that you absolutely love?"

"I can only dream of golfing as well as Arnold Palmer. It can be hard, it's not just physical but mental too. I think that's why I enjoy the game so much. You are competing against yourself."

With the setting sun and the distinct chill in the air, we decided to pack up and head back to the boardwalk. There are so many little shops and when we stumble upon an artist doing caricatures, I quickly commission him to draw the three of us. His completed picture makes me smile and I hand it to Dagen.

"This is my first art purchase for my new home. I want you to decorate my bedroom around this picture, please."

"You can't be serious?"

"Oh, but I am very serious. Art is very subjective. I don't want some stuffy crap hanging in my home. I want the place to be real and feel real. This picture represents all of that."

She stares at the picture for a long time and then finally smiles. "Well, believe it or not, I get it. There is a lot I can do to decorate around this picture, but for now, it will have to wait. I have a long drive home and I want to get an early start tomorrow on your home."

"I have an idea, why not stay at my place this week and work from there? I know the guest rooms are sparsely finished, but I think Preston would really love running the grounds here."

She is very quiet and I hope I'm not scaring her off. Finally, she looks up at me, but I still can't get a read on what she is really thinking.

"Michael. . ."

I hold my hand up, stopping her mid thought. "I don't want you to feel uncomfortable in any way. I know I just got out of a relationship. I also know all about the ills of rebound relationships. I assure you, right now, what I really want is to build a friendship that will last over all the good and the bad in life."

"I didn't think you would want any type of relationship other than friendship with me. What I was going to say is that I can't stay the whole week but I can at least stay a few days."

"Hold up, what do you mean by any type of relationship with you? Aside from the fact that I just got blindsided by someone who I thought was in love with me, why wouldn't I?" Why the hell is she's looking down at Preston, avoiding eye contact?

"I'm not your type." She waves her hand up and down her body for emphasis. I reach out and lift her chin so she can look into my eyes.

"What the fuck, Dagen, is that supposed to mean? You don't even know me well enough to know what type of women I'm attracted to!" my voice, a lot louder than I intended. She steps back and looks at me. When she does, I swear I can see tears in her eyes.

"You're right, I don't know you well enough, but most guys are looking for the skinny, sexy girls, not girls like me."

I take a step forward, my face only inches from hers. "Listen to me, cause I'll only tell you this once. The day you walked into the room, I was blown away. You have curves that dreams are made of, eyes that light up and dance with delight. You're a breathtakingly beautiful woman. I would jump on the chance to get to know you better but I'm not in a good place right now and it wouldn't be fair to you. You deserve the best and not a rebound. Give me time, please."

She finally smiles and whispers "Okay, my friend. Let's get home; we have an early day tomorrow."

We walk back to the car with my treasured picture. I take her hand and I realize, with time, I'm going to be okay.

Chapter Nine

LAST NIGHT WAS COMFORTABLE; PRESTON FELL ASLEEP between the two of us as I introduced her to *Doctor Who*. Apparently, the jury is still out on that one for her. We stopped at a local store on the way home, where she picked up some toiletries along with odds and ends she thought she might need. I didn't really know what to give her in the way of clothing, so I left her one of my rugby jerseys.

I grab a mug and pour my coffee, thinking I would take it and go sit outside when I see her. Her thick long chocolate hair is everywhere. Her lips have a morning puffiness to them and my jersey—holy fuck—it's pulling in all the right places. "T-Shirt" by Thomas Rhett pops into my head. Hell yeah, "Your hair messed up like a Guns and Roses Video." I look down and realize I'm still pouring my coffee and it's everywhere. Fuck, I need to get my head out of my arse.

"Morning, Michael, are you okay?" That's a loaded question.

"Yeah, I was just startled. Can I pour you a cup?"

She grabs some paper towels and quickly helps me clean up the mess, and then she lets Preston out while I attempt to keep the coffee in the cups.

"Why don't we take it out back? I've come to enjoy watching the June Gloom in the morning."

"Most people don't like it, they feel like it takes away from the coastal beauty. Why do you enjoy it so much?"

"Minus the coast, it reminds me of home. The morning fog rolling over the fields was always comforting."

She curls into the sofa and attempts to pull her shirt to cover her assets. I'm trying not to stare but damn my Rugby shirt never looked so good. "So what part of your home in Scotland would you like me to incorporate into this home? Are there colors that you must have or absolutely hate?"

I'm trying to concentrate on what she's asking me, but my cock on the other hand has a different idea. "Last night I gave some thought as to what I want to see when I come home from work. I decided I have to have one room that is totally dedicated to *Doctor Who*." Her eyes grow wide and I'm not sure if she is going to laugh or give up on me.

"You said you wanted some quotes, now it's an entire room?!"

"Before you form an opinion, let me tell you a story. From when I was a very young boy, my uncle Jax got me hooked on *Doctor Who*. It was our thing that we shared that no one else in the family quite understood. When I was kidnapped along with my Aunt Raven. She's made me focus on the Doctor and what he would do if he were in that situation. Later on, when I was diagnosed with cancer, I was so scared that I ran away. It wasn't one of my best thought-out plans, and my Aunt Raven finally found me hiding in one of the tunnels under the castle. Instead of getting mad at me, Uncle Jax showed me how to be strong like the Doctor. My initial treatments were at a hospital in the States. When I got to the hospital, my entire room was transformed into a TARDIS. I know all this must sound absolutely crazy to you, but through-out my entire life, I have found that whether I was happy or scared I could find some sort of comfort from that show. I know it's not reality and it's only a television show but to a lonely little boy it meant there was a huge world to explore. It meant I would be safe and I could survive anything that was thrown at me. It gave me hope."

She takes my hand and gives it a small squeeze. The jolt is unnerving. "Wow, just wow. I'm blown away and I'm also sad for that little lonely boy."

"Please don't be sad; those experiences made me who I am today. I know I can survive anything and I think that's why I'm, as you call it, a very black and white person. Whatever is thrown at me, I push forward through it."

Bo chooses this time to finally grace us with an appearance.

"Hey, sis, what are you doing here?"

"I'm decorating this place and transforming it into a real home. How's work going?"

"It's going, but very busy. Just a heads up, Dad is back in town and he is coming here tonight with Mom. They want to see where I'm living and Dad said he wants to have a face to face chat with you, Mike."

"Well, now that's interesting. Should I be worried?" All I can think of is Uncle Jax went to talk to him, and that can't be good.

"Honestly, I didn't think he would have any problems with all of this, but he did meet your Uncle Jax and then flew right home."

"I think I would like to meet this man that everyone seems so intimidated by, I mean, really, he's just one man. I don't understand what the big deal is."

Bo begins to choke on his coffee and I can't help but laugh, if she only knew.

"Someday you will have that opportunity but in the meantime, we need to get this place done. I have to get that Amex card set up for you and make some phone calls. I'll have everything set up within the hour." I get up and give them some privacy. I head into my room and shoot a quick text to Aunt Raven:

Me: Hey are you available to FaceTime now?

Raven: Of course, for you I'm always available. Give me a few minutes to get someplace private and I'll ring

you.

Me: OK.

While I'm waiting, I sit back and stare at my guitar. I haven't picked it up since everything went down with Heather. I pick it up and start to tune it when the phone rings. "Hey, Michael, is everything okay?"

"I'm not sure and I need you to get to the bottom of it. You know Uncle Jax went to see Bo's father and filled him in on the security detail. I thought it was all over and done but now his parents are coming here tonight to talk to me. I need you to find out exactly what Uncle Jax said. You know the way he can be and I don't want any surprises."

"Oh for the love of Pete, what the hell did that man do now? Okay, I will figure it out. How is everything else going? Max said you have a couple of weeks to get acclimated until you start work."

"Yeah, I'm doing good. I've got an official California driver's license. Dagen, Bo's sister, is decorating my house so I'm hoping it will feel more like a home real soon. I'm looking forward to going out to one of the drill sites and begin work. I'm getting on with my life. How is everything over there?"

"Oh my God, Michael, how the hell did you pass the test for the license?"

"After everything I told you and that's what you're worried about?! Just because Uncle Max taught me to drive doesn't mean I'm a bad driver."

"Well at least it wasn't your mother that taught you. So tell me about Dagen. Max mentioned her and of course how much fun he had at poor Bo's expense."

"She is kind and beautiful. She is a friend that I would like to keep for a very long time. And before you say anything right now, I'm only interested in friendship. How is everyone else?"

"Antonia has decided she doesn't want to go to a college in Scotland. She has been applying to colleges in the States without any of us knowing. When Jax found out, it sent him over the edge. To make matters worse, Grace is graduating early and has decided that she is going wherever Antonia goes. I don't see this ending well for any of us. Other than that everything is fine. I'll get with Jax and then get back to you on what I find out."

"Okay, thanks." She hangs up and no doubt I'll hear it from Uncle Jax for throwing him under the bus, but I need to know what to expect. I wonder what schools Antonia is applying to. She loves photography and has such a good eye for capturing the unexpected. I'm about to pick up the phone to call her but before I do, Uncle Jax is already calling me. Nothing is ever easy.

"Hey, that was quick. What do I need to know before they get here? What exactly did you tell Mr. Turner?"

"I swear, Junior, I didn't do anything crazy. He probably wants to see for himself that his son is okay. I wish you would give me a little more credit. I do know how to play nice with others." Crap, now I feel bad.

"I'm sorry, it's just that I've seen you in action and lately everything that's been thrown at me has me a little bit on edge."

"I understand, but next time please come to me first. How is everything else going?"

"Everything is good. I start work soon. Dagen and Bo have been showing me around. I asked Dagen to help decorate the house, so that should help it come together faster. What's going on with Antonia?" Before I can even finish I hear his typical growl.

"We have, as your Aunt Raven says 'butt heads like two year olds'. In her mind she is an adult and can do whatever the bloody hell she wants. We all know how this is going to end. She is applying to colleges in the States, for Christ's sake why would she want to leave here? She could have everything the world has to offer right here in her own backyard."

I don't think he'll ever understand the need to go out into the real world.

"Go easy on her. Growing up isolated from a lot of the outside world is not easy. How will she discover who she is if you don't let her spread her wings?"

"Have you been eating fortune cookies?"

I can't help but laugh. "No, but you know it's the truth. You can't let your fear take over our lives."

"Yeah, I hear you. Keep me posted on what happens with the Turners and if you need me to smooth things over with them, just let me know."

I hang up with the promise that I will try and get through to Antonia. Before I attempt to tackle my email, I call American Express and get Dagen her own card. They give me a temporary number and will have a courier deliver the card today. It was much easier than I thought. The first thing I see when I fire up my computer is an email from Heather. I hover over the delete key but curiosity gets the best of me and I open it.

Michael,

By now you've read the report. I'm sorry, so very sorry for the way I handled it all. I picked up the phone a million times to call you, but I didn't know what to say. Every time I held the phone, my anger got the better of me. What I read in that report scared me. Did you know about your dad? Did you purposely hide it from me? All of the stuff about your grandfather! Not to mention your Aunt Raven's evil violent family. We spoke about your family all the time and yet you never told me any of the stuff that was in that report.

It made me wonder what else you've hidden from me. I understand why you wouldn't broadcast the details about your mother's rape, but why didn't you trust me enough to tell me? I'm hurt and I feel betrayed. Can you deal with the unknown? What if you're more like him than you realize? Maybe he's why you got so sick as a child. Maybe it's his genes that are bad? These are all questions we should workout together, then maybe we can get past all this. Please call me and let me know where you are and how you are doing.
Heather

I've read it three times now and I'm still in shock. She is all over the place, blaming me for keeping a secret I never even knew and then in the next breath she wants to talk to me to get past all of this? The time for talking is long gone. I've always been an open book with her and her thinking I knew about my mother's rape and kept it from her is a real smack in the face. My family's history is private and their business, not hers. Again, I hover over that delete button, but my rage gets the better of me. Before I even knew what was going on she closed the book on me. Now she wants to talk, well now I want my say.

Heather,
   I was just as surprised by the rape as you were, but if you really knew me then you would know, unlike you, I would never have kept that from you. I'm very proud of my family and I always will be. My mother has endured a horrific experience. She was beaten,

drugged, and raped. Maybe someone else would have terminated the pregnancy, but she's a strong woman with a very supportive family and decided not to have an abortion. Giving birth to me almost killed her, yet she never regretted her decision. My dad has loved me as his own from before I was born, and always will. I've known nothing but love, honesty, and respect. My family has taught me how to be a better man. What has your father taught you?

I hope someday you will get past worrying about what others think. Maybe then you can turn your attention on how to be a better person. Perhaps then you could learn to love someone more than you love yourself. Maybe, just maybe, you can learn to be less judgmental. No family tree is without some sort of skeletons, it's how we choose to deal with it that matters. You shouldn't have judged me by my DNA, but by the man I am. The same man I was from the day I met you. How could you even suggest that maybe I'm like him or that I have bad genes? That is so cruel, yet somehow I'm not surprised you even suggested it.

Please don't bother calling me or writing to me again. If you've learned anything about me over the past few years, you would know that when I'm done, I'm done. Michael

After I send it I mark her email as spam and if she contacts me again I will have all communication with her blocked. I've had a lot of time to think about everything. Hindsight is always 20/20 and I realize Bo is right; she was slowly pulling me away from my friends and, if I let her, my family, too. I will never let anyone have that type of power over me ever again. I need to get out of here and blow off some steam. I love to run and escape the world, so I let my detail know that we will be leaving within the hour. Before I head out, I make sure to leave the American Express information for Dagen along with a note that I took Preston for a long run.

The weather is perfect for a run on the beach, not too hot and a slight breeze. I start out slow, not really sure what Preston can do, but when I pick up my pace he is right beside me the entire time. My thoughts stray to Dagen. I promised myself I wouldn't get involved with anyone for at least one year. Why the hell did she have to come crashing into my world? Why now? Maybe work will be a great distraction. Preston veers off and heads into the surf. He is a big baby, barking at the waves, but one whistle and he's back at my side. We head down the beach for about another mile and finally start to slow down. Rico, one of my guards who has been with me for eight years, hands me two bottles of water, one for me and one for Preston. I would love to keep him but I know it wouldn't be fair to him. He's amusing himself with the empty water bottle, and I could watch him for hours. "Hey, Preston, why did she have to come into my life now?" I need to wrap my mind around all the changes and then move forward. Do I really want to suck her into my world? Would that be fair to her? She is just so different. A beautiful girl, hiding in the shadows of her own insecurity. If only she could see herself through my eyes, maybe then she would realize how beautiful she really is. "Come on, boy, we better get back." We head back but take our time strolling along the beach. I'm not sure where my relationship with her is going, I only know I have a comfort with her that I've never had with anyone and I'm not about to jeopardize it.

Michael and Preston went for a run, which left me with lots of time on my hands for research. I take the picture from last night with me and step into the master bedroom. I look at the picture of us, trying to figure out where I would hang it. I can't help but smile at its quirkiness. You would never know that we barely know each other. All my instincts are telling me this, whatever this is, is not going to end well for me. It's too soon to jump from one relationship to another, hell he said so himself. How do I shut off what my heart is feeling? Whenever he put his hand on the small of my back I felt a shiver run up my spine. He sees past my obvious insecurities. My weight doesn't match my height. Maybe if I was six feet tall it would. Short and wide is not exactly all the rage right now. My whole life I've always felt like the outcast, not part of the *in* crowd. When Shaun abducted me from school all that got me was the standard fifteen minutes of fame, followed by the whispers. "Why would he want her?" That was not a boost to my sixteen-year-old ego. Ugh, I finally meet someone interesting and he comes with baggage, bodyguards, and Lord knows what other crap.

Why would Heather end her engagement to him in such a cruel way? I mean, geez, a letter? That's so fucked up. Unless she was afraid he would be violent, but he doesn't seem that way. However, looks can be deceiving. I learned that the hard way. Why would my dad want to talk to Michael? What could his uncle possibly have said to make him fly home from Spain so quickly? I'll admit the whole guard thing can be very unnerving. When they were watching from a distance it was different especially since I had no clue.

My heart broke when Michael was talking about his childhood. It must have been so lonely. Would getting involved with him mean the same thing for me? I take another look around this empty room and realize I've got my work cut out for me. Even though he says his

childhood was lonely, when he talks about his home—Scotland—
his face lights up like a little boy on some great adventure. I want to
see that look when he talks about this place. That's it, decision made.
I need to see where he grew up. It's the only way I will get a true
sense of who he is and what is going to make him happy. One last
look at our quirky picture and I head out to look for him.

I find him out back, attempting to give Preston a bath. I don't
think the two of them rolling around in the grass with the hose is
going to work. I want to go help but Michael's laughter is infectious
and I don't want to interrupt it. So carefree without the weight of
the world upon his shoulders. I wish everyday could be like that for
him. When he finally sees me, he motions me outside. He cocks his
head to the side and smiles. Fuck me; I'm so screwed.

"You could have joined us. I'm sure Preston would have loved
it."

"You were having so much fun I didn't want it to end. How was
your run?" I take control of Preston while Michael finishes hosing
him down, but not before he finishes with a good doggie shake and
now I'm wet too.

"It was good. Running helps clear my mind of the clutter. Did
you find the Amex info I left for you?"

"Yes, but there's something I wanted to talk to you about. Since
you don't have to start work till next week, I thought it would be a
good idea for you to take me to Scotland," I say. His eyes are intense
and I fight the urge to look away.

"Why? I mean if you want to go I will take you, but what purpose would it serve?"

"I hardly know anything about you. I would see for myself what
you like and what you don't. This way I would get a better feel for
what I need to make this place your home."

"And me telling you is not enough?"

"No, I want to see where you grew up through your eyes. It
would be very easy for me to furnish this place, make it comfort-

able. What I'm trying to do is make it a home. A place that when you walk in the door you get what you can't get outside these walls. That same adventurous look you get when you talk about Scotland. The only way I can do that is seeing it for myself."

He's very quiet. Maybe he is unsure about bringing me around his family. I'm sure he doesn't want to give them the wrong idea. "Dagen, the look on your face says a lot. Never play poker, babe. Stop thinking I don't want you around them. Please get past any self-doubts. If you want to see it, then we leave in the morning. However, you need to be prepared for the entire experience . . . my family is not for the faint of heart." He leads me to the patio and motions me to sit next to him. "My Uncle Max is just the tip of the iceberg. When everyone is together, it can get a little crazy. Do you think you are up for it?"

"Are you issuing me a challenge? If so then bring it on, Bucky."

He gets a huge smile on his face, picks up Preston's ball and tosses it for him. "Okay, you got it. We can leave right after your parents leave or first thing in the morning, the choice is yours."

"Right after my parents leave. It's a long flight and since we don't have a lot of time, I'd rather fly through the night. I need to go home and pack. What about Preston?"

"He comes, too. I've been thinking about adopting him. I figured when I have to be away, I could hire someone to be his companion. Why are you laughing?"

"I knew that you would be adopting him from the first time you met him. You just needed time to see the light." We get up and head back inside, his hand on the small of my back and that feeling is instantly back. Why does my skin prickle every time he touches me?

"Okay, I'll make all the arrangements while you head home to pack. Make sure you have all of Preston's paperwork." I watch him walk away with Preston on his heels. Yup—definitely screwed.

Michael

She wants to see my home. Lord help me, I hope she's ready. If they don't scare her away then maybe there's hope. I head into my office and call Uncle Jax. He answers on the first ring.

"Junior, what happened with Mr. Turner?"

"I haven't met him yet, I need the jet available tonight please. I'm coming home for a few days. Before you get excited, it's just a quick trip. I asked Dagen to decorate my home and she would like to see where I grew up. Oh and I'm bringing Preston, he's a dog I've adopted."

"Wait you got a dog? Why? What kind? Are you sure about this?"

"Well, if you let me get a word in edgewise. Preston is a rescue Boxer. Dagen has been working with him and he kind of adopted me. You know how I feel about dogs and I think we need each other. I figure while I'm not home I will have someone come in and take care of him."

"Okay, you sound pretty sure about this. I'll make sure I have him documented as a service animal, that way he avoids quarantine coming into the country. I'll have everything set up for you within the hour," his voice trails off and he becomes very quiet, too quiet for my liking.

"Uncle Jax, what's the problem?"

"Are you getting involved with this girl?" Always direct and to the point.

"We're friends. I won't lie to you; I am attracted to her but I'm not ready to go there. It wouldn't be fair to her or to me. I'm just going to take one day at a time. I do need you to do me a favor and give Grams a heads up. Tell her she is not to interrogate Dagen."

He's laughing! "I can try but I won't make any promises. You need to do me a favor. I need you to talk to Antonia in person about college. Maybe you can get a better read on her."

"I'll try and get her alone for a little bit. I gather you're not having much luck convincing her to stay put."

"No, and I'm trying to stay calm, but she's not making it easy."

"Have you tried listening to her with an open mind? I know you; you can get tunnel vision." There's that familiar growl and I can't help but laugh.

"The plane will be ready. I'll see you when you get in." He doesn't even wait for me to answer. He hangs up. No doubt, I hit a nerve.

I really don't need much. I throw a few things in a bag along with my passport. While I'm there, I need to go over security with Uncle Max. I'm not sure how it will work with me being out on the different rigs for weeks at a time. I want to make sure these arrangements are in place before I start work. Maybe I should have told her not to worry about packing too much, but really it's only for a few days. I'm sure she won't have that much stuff. With her parents coming here tonight, I better get something to put out. I don't think my standard coffee, water, beer, and scotch is going to cut it. I really need to hire a live-in housekeeper who loves dogs. At least that will guarantee that we both get fed. The timing of this trip isn't the best but I didn't want her to think that I didn't want her to meet my family. Especially after seeing the look on her face. I don't understand why she doubts herself. A quick shower and I'll be ready to head into town.

I love the downtown area the best, it's busy yet there are so many specialty shops. I can walk around unnoticed for hours, which is so different for me. I've never had to grocery shop; everything was done by someone else. When I think about it, it's a lot of work trying to live a simple life. I stumble upon a really nice gourmet food store and after walking around, lost and confused, a very nice lady took pity upon me. First she tried to match me up with her granddaughter, and then she helped me figure out the food for tonight. I finally left armed with enough food and wine for a small army. I decide to shoot Bo a text before I head home, just incase I should pick up something else.

Me: Hey, I got some stuff to put out tonight but not sure if there's something special you think I should have.

Bo: Did you get your man card revoked?

Me: No, arsehole! I figured I disrupted everyone's life enough, so this is me smoothing things over.

Bo: Don't worry; they probably just want to make sure you're not some deranged serial killer. Lol.

Me: Dagen and I are leaving for Scotland tonight, how do you think they are going to take that?

Bo: Really? Why? Oh shit, don't tell me you're with my sister? Damn, Mike, you didn't waste any time. Do we have to have a talk?

Me: No, and no she wants to see where I grew up before she tackles the decorating job. Oh and I adopted Preston. I'm also looking for a live-in housekeeper for us. Before you say anything, she needs to be a real housekeeper. Would it be so bad?

Bo: Now who's being the asshole? So now we have a dog . . . great. Would what be so bad?

Me: If I wanted to get to know Dagen better? Do you think they will freak out?

Bo: Not sure about them freaking out, but I did talk to my mom today and I believe she's lost her mind. I was trying to find out why they were coming and she kept going on and on about how sweet your uncle Max is! You and Dagen are adults but I think you should give yourself time. I'm getting paged, I'll see you later.

And just like that, he's gone. Uncle Max and sweet in the same sentence makes me laugh. God only knows what he told her. I was going to look for a new car but if I wait, it will be another non-date I can ask Dagen to go on. Instead, I better get home and figure out the housekeeper situation.

Chapter Ten

Dagen

WHAT THE HELL WAS I THINKING? LIFE ALWAYS SEEMS to sound so much better on paper until you have to actually follow through with it. I don't think I really thought this through. Sometimes my mouth operates before my mind can catch up. I mean what in the world possessed me to suggest going to Scotland?! I know why, because I don't do things half-assed. If I'm going to make his house a home, then I need to give it my all. Maybe then he'll want to stay. And there it is: the truth. "Oh Hell no, Dagen, don't even go down that road." Great, now I'm talking to myself. I throw open my closet in hopes of something jumping out and saying "I promise to make you look tall and lean." Yeah, like that would happen. What am I thinking? Bo has been there. Trying to find my phone in my bag is nothing short of solving world peace! I'm always hunting for the damn thing. Finally, I find it at the bottom of the infamous black whole.

> **Me:** I'm taking a quick trip to Scotland with Michael, what should I pack?

> **Bo:** Really, that's why you're texting me? How about explaining what the fuck you're thinking?

Me: If I'm going to make his place into a home, I need to see where he grew up. What makes him comfortable and happy.

Bo: You might be able to feed that bullshit to Mike, but not me. You like him, so just face it and we can all move along here.

Me: Is that a bad thing?

Bo: I don't want to see either of you get hurt. Time heals and maybe you need to give him that; don't rush it.

Me: What if time changes him? What if it makes him bitter?

Bo: Never gonna happen, his crazy family would never let it. Speaking of which, I spoke to Mom today. She has lost her marbles. She thinks Max is very sweet!

Me: I'm sure he has a side to him that we didn't see. He probably shows it when he wants something. Did she say why they are coming over tonight?

Bo: No, I thought you might know. All she would say is, after Dad met Jax, he felt he wanted to meet Mike and flew home right away.

Me: You're worried, why?

Bo: I know we are adults and can do whatever we want, but you know I don't want them upset. The whole bodyguard thing never freaked me out cause it was like that from the day I met Mike, but it can be unnerving.

Me: You don't have to tell me. When Ms. Salvano first introduced herself, I thought it was odd, but when she followed me into the ladies room. I damn near died from embarrassment! Do you have any idea how hard it is to pee with someone standing outside the door waiting for you? Anyway, what should I be prepared for on this trip? Hell, I don't even know what to pack?

Bo: Jeans, they have horses among other things. Everyone is very nice, just remember to have patience with Jax and you'll be fine.

Me: What is his story?

Bo: Intense. He has a plaque hanging over his desk, 'Can't means won't' I'll just leave it at that. I gotta run. I'll see you tonight.

Well, the only thing I learned from him is to pack jeans . . . great. I throw some jeans in an overnight bag, along with a long sundress, head out and hope for the best.

Ms. Salvano and I have come to an agreement. She can come into the ladies room with me. She can follow me wherever the hell she wants, but under no circumstance will she ever drive me around—Miss Daisy I'm not. It's a long drive up the coast and once I get to the scenic part of the trip, I put on the music and Lady Antebellum's "Ready to Love Again" comes blaring to life. Am I really ready to love again? I've been closed down for so long, afraid to take that first step. The words "building walls around my heart to save me" are making my heart pound. That's what I've been doing for so long. Can I really let myself feel again? What if I give him my heart and he crushes it? What if I'm a stepping-stone? I quickly wipe away a lone tear, not wanting Ms. Salvano to notice. Too late, she squeezes my shoulder.

"I know you don't want me to drive you like Miss Daisy, but maybe it would be best if I did."

"Thank you, but I'm fine and don't worry, you will be too. Can I ask you how you got into your line of work?" I need a distraction and maybe getting to know her better will help.

She reaches over and lowers the music. "I was in the Italian Navy and when I was injured I needed to find something else to do. My father is a friend of Mr. Fleming and he introduced us. He offered me employment, and then put me through a very extensive training program. Nothing like the Navy."

"How long have you been working for Mr. Fleming?"

"Two years." I'm waiting for her to elaborate but boy she's a woman of few words.

"Before you were watching over me, what did you do for Mr. Fleming?" We pull up to the guard gate and they let us through.

"I believe your parents just pulled up behind us; would you like me to bring your suitcase into the house for you?"

"I gather you are not going to tell me anything more," I surmise. She barely manages a smile. "Okay, have it your way, but eventually, I will find out your story. You can leave my suitcase, I'll get it later. Thank you." No sense pushing her for anymore answers I know I'll never get.

Michael

I need a housekeeper and, unlike the average person, I can't just pick up the phone and call an agency. Hell, I've never had to think about any of this shit, everything was just always in place. The simple things in life are usually the things that are so quickly taken for granted. I hate that I have to keep asking for help but, until I have all my ducks in a row, I have no choice. With the eight-hour time difference, I'll text Uncle Max first to make sure he's up.

Me: Hey are you able to facetime now?

Uncle Max: Of course, give me five.

I don't have to wait very long before the screen comes to life.

"Hey, Junior, is everything okay? Shouldn't you be heading out soon?"

"Not yet, there are a few things I need to go over with you first. I need to hire a live-in housekeeper. I know I can't just call an agency and I'm not sure how you want to go about doing that? It's not like my small flat in London that I was able to maintain myself. This place is massive and I don't have the time to maintain it all. Also, how are we going to work security when I'm out on a rig?"

He looks tired, more so than usual. When he's troubled, he tends to not sleep much. "I realized when I was there that with the size of that place you were going to need some live-in help. I've already been making the arrangements. Your new housekeeper, Mrs. Cooper Holiday, and her husband, Bennett, will be going back with you. They are in their late fifties. Mr. Holiday is a master gardener and is really looking forward to taking care of the grounds. Mrs. Holiday has impeccable credentials and I think they would be a good fit. If you don't like them, I can find someone else."

He's mindlessly rubbing the scar on his temple, it's almost as if something else is bothering him and I don't think it's just my crap that he has to deal with. "Relax, I'm sure they will be fine. What's the problem?"

"Antonia and Grace, they are driving me crazy. Even Sam and Jeff can't take it, add to that your Uncle Jax, do I have to say any more?"

"No, I get it. I'll try talking to the girls when I get there. What did Uncle Jax do?"

"This whole Antonia thing is making him nuts, well more than his usual crazy. You know the two of them are butting heads. Well, let's just say the stress level around here is off the charts."

"I can only imagine. I'll try talking to him again when I'm there. What about security while I'm on a rig?"

"I'm working on that now. I know you want to feel like everyone else. I'm trying to figure out how this is going to play out. I will have that all worked out when you get here. Oh and Jax told me you got a rescue dog. You know the way I feel about rescue animals—very proud of you." He finally smiles.

"Thanks. He's a Boxer; his name is Preston. He's very entertaining. One more thing, what did you say to Bo's mum? She told him that you're very sweet."

He begins to laugh. "I have my shining moments, but I wish I could have seen the look on Bo's face."

"Well, I don't know what Uncle Jax told Mr. Turner, but they are on their way here now. He swears he behaved and we all know what that means. Anyway, thanks for helping me with all of this stuff. I'll see you soon."

"Safe travels and if you need me to smooth things over with Mr. Turner, let me know."

I hang up and head out just as everyone pulls up. Game on.

Preston is racing around apparently very excited to see everyone or just plain excited, can't tell yet which. Dagen looks a lot like her mum, whereas Bo looks like his dad. Bo pulls up right behind his dad and Preston nearly tackles him.

"Hey, everyone, sorry I'm late. I got stuck at work."

"Hello, Mr. Turner, Mrs. Turner, glad to finally meet everyone in person. Please, come in." I'm not usually nervous around anyone but for some reason tonight I am. Mr. Turner extends his hand, his grip is firm. I'm not sure if it's meant to intimidate me. Like that would ever happen.

"Michael, no reason to be so formal. Please, Hector and Lana will do just fine. So, how about a tour of this place before the sun sets?"

"Of course, there's not much here, yet; I put that ball in Dagen's court."

It's a pretty big home but with not much in it, the tour doesn't take too long. He is, however, very impressed with the extensive security system. Since it's another beautiful evening, we all converge on the patio. Bo sets up the fire pit, which I've come to learn is his favorite part of the yard.

"So, Hector, I understand you met with my Uncle Jax."

His smile quickly fades and I feel like I've been hit in the gut.

"Yes, he is a very interesting man. After my meeting with him, I have a better understanding as to why we all must have guards. I really just wanted to see for myself where my son is living and where my daughter is spending so much time. He impressed upon me that my children are safer than they've ever been. After seeing everything for myself, I venture to say he is correct." He nods in agreement with himself. I shouldn't have doubted my uncle, but I've also seen how persuasive he can be.

"My understanding is it's your Uncle Max who is responsible for all of the security. I'm sorry I was not back from Spain in time to meet him, but Lana said he is thorough and very sweet," he mentions. I look over at Bo who almost chokes on his beer and I'm trying very hard not to laugh. I swear I'm getting as bad as Uncle Max.

"Well, I'm glad you and Lana got to meet my uncles. They are a very important part of my life. Family is everything to me."

"I get that, Michael, but I have to tell you, I'm still apprehensive about all of this." He waves his hand around for emphasis, his eyes focused on the security guards in the distance.

"Hector, you of all people should understand what happens when someone has any kind of wealth or fame. Granted I'm not the King of England, but in today's world, we must be careful. You work with the rich and famous, you know it doesn't take much to bring the crazies out. Security around all of us is extremely tight but that's what is needed to keep everyone safe. I would rather be a little bit over cautious than complacent about security. What can I say to assure you no one is in any danger?"

He gets up and pours himself another glass of wine, no doubt processing all of this. "Nothing, my children are adults and no matter how much I complain or threaten them, they will do whatever they decide is best for them. Even if it goes against my better judgment."

So—bottom line—no matter what I say, he doesn't want his family around me and, frankly, I understand better than he thinks.

"Hector, I don't know what I can say that would ease your mind."

Bo gets up, grabs a beer and takes a seat next to his dad. "Dad, Mike is my best friend. I have no problem with this, trust me," he says before taking a swig. Hector lets out a heavy sigh; Bo's speech seems to have calmed him down a bit.

"So, when do you start your new job, and what exactly will you be doing?" Hector asks.

My new job is easy to talk about. I only hope Dagen told them we are leaving for Scotland. "I start next week. I made sure to allow myself some time to get settled in. I'll be working on offshore oil and gas rigs. I'll be analyzing safety procedures to make sure they are being followed properly. I'll also be developing and implementing new ones to improve drilling while keeping the workers and the environment safe. The world will always need oil, gas, coal and alternative energy sources, it's just a matter of retrieving them safely and efficiently," I go through the specifics. He seems genuinely interested in what I will be doing, either that or, unlike his daughter, he has a great poker face.

"Do you have any other plans before you start work?"

Well, here goes nothing. "I was going to buy a car this week and explore California but, instead, I will be heading back to Scotland this evening."

"Is everything okay?"

"Yes, apparently my interior designer needs to see where I grew up so she can get a feel for how to decorate this place."

"Dagen, you never said you were leaving. How long will you be gone?" He totally cuts me right out of the conversation. His voice is raised and I think I just landed on his shit list, or possibly hers.

"It was a spontaneous decision, Dad. You've seen the size of this place. I have to come up with a lot of creative ideas to bring some warmth into it. If I'm going to do that, I need to see where Michael grew up and meet his family."

Bo, wasn't kidding when he said Dagen has her father wrapped around her finger, almost as bad as Antonia has Uncle Jax.

"Dad, did you finish up the film you were working on?" Bo, probably picking up on the angst in his sister's voice, quickly steers the conversation away from the trip.

"There is still a lot of editing that needs to be done. How is your new job going?"

"It's going great, but there is a lot that needs to get done." Preston is back and throwing his ball in Bo's lap. "Mike, what are you going to do with Preston while you're gone?"

"He's coming with us. I'm sure he will have a blast running around with the horses."

"It's a long flight are you sure he will be okay?"

"I didn't even think about that. Dagen, has he flown before?"

"Yes, I have some stuff the vet gave me to keep him calm. He should be fine. What time are we leaving?"

I don't want it to seem that I'm pushing them out the door, but the sooner they leave the sooner we can get out of here. "No rush, whenever you're ready."

"Michael, how long will you be allowed to stay in this country?" Hector asks. I'm taken back by his question. I would have thought Bo would have, at least, given them the basics about me, but then again, it's Bo we are talking about here.

"I was born in New York City but raised in Scotland so I have maintained a duel citizenship. I'm looking at this as a permanent move. Eventually, I would like to open my own company, but first, I need to learn from actually doing it. Learning in school and doing it in real life are two totally different things." Preston drops his ball at my feet and nudges me to toss it for him. He is a welcome distraction from what feels like an interrogation.

"Well, it sounds like you have everything planned out, but keep in mind, life has a way of turning on a dime. Plans we make and real life tend to collide at the worst possible times."

Dagen tries to stifle a yawn but her mum doesn't miss it. "Hector, I think you've interrogated poor Michael enough. We have a long drive back and they have a flight to catch." Right now, I could give Lana a huge hug.

They get up to leave and when he hugs Dagen I hear him tell her to be safe. We get to the door he pulls me aside. "Keep my daughter safe, no matter what."

He kisses Dagen goodbye and they head out. I'm left standing there, staring at the closed door.

Bo nudges me, "Mike, you okay?"

"What the hell was that all about? Your dad acts as though there are crazy arse gunmen around every corner. Everything that has been set up is just a precaution. If either one of you feel the way your parents do, then just go. No one is holding you hostage. I've survived all these years on my own; I'll be just fine."

He grabs my arm holding me back. "Mike, they are just worried. They never had to deal with the intense security that you deal with on a daily basis. They'll get use to it, give them some time. Go home and have some fun before you have to start work."

"Okay, I'm sorry. I know you're right, but he threw me off with all his questions. Dagen, if you still want to go, I'll get Preston and we can head out." She's been quiet and I hope it doesn't mean she's changed her mind.

"Of course I still want to go. I'm not easily influenced by anyone, including my father. I'll get my stuff and meet you at the car."

I've never met anyone like her, so self-assured and determined, yet, so insecure. I watch her walk away, her beautiful hips swaying like the waves in the ocean. I'm quickly snapped out of my daydream by a crash in the kitchen. I don't have to go far to find Preston, playing with a box of crackers and an empty cheese platter on the floor. Bo wrestles the box away from him and I begin the clean up.

"Mike, I hope you find a housekeeper soon and you better make sure she can handle this monster. I still don't know why you decided to adopt him."

"I think he adopted me. Uncle Max has the housekeeper and gardener all set up. They will fly back with me. Providing Preston likes them," I add. He rolls his eyes at me and I can't help but laugh.

"Go, Dagen is probably waiting for you. I'll finish cleaning this up."

I head out and sure enough she is waiting by the car with a suitcase that could fit a dead body. "Hey, you realize it's only for a couple of days, right?"

"I had no idea what to pack, so I opted for a few different things." I know when to shut up and now being one of those times. Finally, we are headed to the airport.

Bella

Michael is coming home for a few days. Jax said he's bringing Bo's sister. I want to be there for my son, but right now I need to do this, not just for him, but for me, too. The guard at the gate lets me pass and I head up the long drive to the house. I barely wait for my driver to bring the car to a stop before I step out. She's waiting in the doorway for me. I need to show self-control. As a compassionate woman, I want to understand why she did what she did. As a mother, I want to snap her fucking neck. She's smiling and I ball my fist, prepared to wipe it right off her face.

"Hello, Bella, is Michael okay?" Like she really cares.

"Can I come in?"

"Of course, please." As she steps aside, I expect to see her father, but there's no sign of him.

"How's Michael? I tried to email and call him, but he won't answer me."

"Why did you do it? Why would you hurt him like that when you profess you love him so much? If you were concerned about your safety, you could have come to me. All you had to do was ask."

The smile is instantly gone from her face. "Bella, I was shocked when I read that report. It was apparent that your family keeps secrets, so why would I trust you to tell me the truth? How could I trust any of you?"

I take a few breaths to try and steady my nerves when all I want to do is bitch slap some sense into her. "You lived your whole life in a glass bubble. You have no idea of the pain and humiliation I went through. It was up to me to tell Michael when I felt I could, when I thought it was best for him to know the truth—not you. All you did was read about it on a piece of paper. I lived it. All the pain and uncertainty—I dealt with it everyday. It was my personal business—

not yours. You should have trusted the man that you say you loved. Apparently, Heather, the only one you really love is yourself."

"I know I made a mistake. I realize that I should have talked to him about it first, but I was in shock. After he left, I tried to contact him, but he wants nothing to do with me."

She's got some pair if she thinks she can say "I made a mistake" and that would make it all better. "Of course he wants nothing more to do with you, not only did you hurt him, but you also hurt his father and me. You had no regard for anyone's feelings but your own. If you really knew him then you would know when it comes to family and the people he holds close to his heart, he would never let anyone hurt us." I thought she would at least show some remorse, maybe even shed some crocodile tears, instead, she has a stern icy stare.

"I thought you believed in forgiveness and second chances, who's the hypocrite now, Bella?" her words and tone, pure evil.

"You're right, Heather. I do believe in forgiveness and second chances when the person is truly sorry for what they've done. But, you're not sorry, and I will never forget what you put my son through. I don't need to hang on to my hatred of you and what you've done because that would only make me pathetic just like you. My family has worked through all of this, but you will never be rid of what you've done and I hope that it will haunt you for the rest of your life. I know that you have tried to contact my nieces and my sisters-in-law. Don't ever try to contact any of us again, or this will not end well for you."

She throws her head back and laughs. It's so sinister that the hair on the back of my neck stands up. "Are you threatening me? What would your precious Michael think of the almighty Bella if I told him?"

I get up and head towards the door with her quickly on my heels. When I turn around, her face is just inches from mine. "It's not a threat . . . I only make promises I can easily keep. My son loves and trusts me unconditionally, something you know nothing about. Stay away from my family or all bets are off." I leave her there with her mouth hanging open. I shove my hands in my pockets to stop the trembling and once inside the safety of the car, I let out the breath I was holding and the tears begin to fall.

Chapter Eleven

Michael

THE RIDE TO THE AIRPORT WAS LONG, BOTH OF US LOST IN our own thoughts. I don't know her well enough to know why she's so quiet. Once on board and all settled in, she seems to finally relax a little.

"Are you okay, you seem very quiet?"

"Do you always fly like this?"

I'm quickly reminded that what seems normal to me can be a bit much for other people. "If you mean on a private plane, no, not always. It depends upon my circumstance. Sometimes it is for the benefit of others that I fly on a private jet, less disruption for everyone around me." The flight crew informs us that we're ready for takeoff. When we are safely at cruising altitude I reach over and unbuckle her seatbelt. When I take her hand in mine, I feel her tremble. "Let me give you a quick tour before dinner."

We go from room to room, the entire time she doesn't say much. When we get to one of the bedrooms, she freezes. "Are you okay?"

"Yes, it's just a little overwhelming. I've never been on a plane that has all these rooms." We head back into the dining area, my hand on the small of her back. I like to feel the constant connection.

"Dagen, you need to understand, none of this defines who I am."

"Maybe not, but you still take advantage of everything that is available to you. It's very easy to say none of this matters when you are still using the private jets and buying a twenty-nine million dollar mansion for cash." Her eyes quickly dart around our surroundings.

"Dinner is ready, let's eat." We head into the dining area and I let the flight attendant know I've got this.

"So if you don't like the conversation you just cut it off?"

"On the contrary, this trip is to help you understand me more. I'm not going to discount your opinion. What I will do is show you the real me. Not what you perceive me to be." I pour her some Chardonnay. "After this trip, if you still have questions, I will answer them all. The only thing I ask is that you keep an open mind and don't judge me by my family's wealth. Other than being born a Vizzano, I did nothing to earn it."

She lifts her glass and offers up a toast. "Here's to getting to know the real Michael Vizzano." She takes a sip. "So, how many of these planes do you have?" her words sting, maybe it's just my distaste for the extremes in my life.

"I'm not really sure. Uncle Max takes care of all of this stuff." I shrug. She wrinkles her nose and I'm not sure if it's the mention of Uncle Max or everything as a whole. "Does it bother you?"

"It just seems so over the top, especially if you're trying not to draw attention to yourself. Why not fly commercial?"

"That would draw even more attention. Think about it, I can't just walk on a plane. I have guards who are armed with me twenty-four seven. The few times I have jumped on a short commuter flight, I've nearly given Uncle Max heart failure. If possible, I would much rather not disrupt everyone's life. How about we eat before our dinner gets cold?" I sit back and wait for her to lift the lid on the silver dome covering her plate. She slowly lifts it, her eyes grow wide and she begins to giggle. When she giggles, it's like a ray of sunshine on a foggy morning.

"Really?"

"Yes, really. In-N-Out double-double, no onion burger with fries is my new favorite. You see, I really am just a regular guy who was born into all of this, but it doesn't define who I am. I really want you to understand me so that you can make my home the place I always want to go back to."

She lifts her glass and clinks it to mine. "Deal, now tell me a little bit about your life growing up. Favorite memories, things that made you laugh or even cry." She takes my hand and gives it a good squeeze. "Relax, Michael, you secrets are safe with me."

"I told you about the riding academy, do you ride?"

"No, I've never been on a horse. Is that something we need to do?!" Her eyes are wide and she practically squeaks.

"There is nothing to be afraid of. I would never let anything happen to you. If you don't feel comfortable, you don't have to. There is also a working farm on the property. A person can get lost for a long time if they wanted to." My words trail off along with my mind.

"Hello, Michael, I seem to have lost you for a little bit, where did your mind wander off to?"

"I'm sorry, sometimes looking back on the past, I'm reminded of so much that was lost." I briefly close my eyes and remember Rose. The adventures and the laughter we shared.

"You've told me what your family does, but what about you? What did you like to do?"

"There are caves and tunnels all throughout the estate. I spent a lot of my time exploring them. As I got older, I would campout in them. I would pretend I was an archeologist on an exciting dig, kind of like Indiana Jones."

"How were you able to do that with the guards constantly up your ass? I would think that would seem to defeat the purpose."

"As long as I was on the property and carried a two-way radio, I was given some freedom to wander around. I think when you see the place you will have a better understanding."

"Is that when you fell in love with the earth? I mean you must love it if you're doing everything you can to preserve it?"

"I never really thought of it like that, but I guess so. For a while, I thought I would go in to archeology, but I soon realized I wanted to preserve what we have for future generations and not look back on what was."

"Will you show me some of the tunnels that were your favorite?"

My cousins have been in some of them with me but the very best ones were the ones I found with Rose. That was our special time and I've never shared it with anyone else, not even Heather. "If we have time, but this is a short trip and I'm sure my cousins will keep you entertained."

"Will they all be there?"

"Yes, they will all be there. While we are there, I need to speak to Antonia and Grace about their choices for college."

"Is there a problem?"

"Antonia was doing classes online but now she started applying to colleges in the States. Where she goes, Grace goes. They are thick as thieves. My uncles asked me to try and reason with them."

"So Max is the typical overprotective dad that doesn't want his daughter to go away to college, is that why he is so over the top with security?"

"No, that started before any of us were even born. He experienced a horrific loss that changed his life forever."

"I'm sorry to hear that. Do they all live in the same house?"

"Everyone but Uncle Max's family lives in the main house. Uncle Max's house is between the stables and the main house. We are a very close family, sometimes *too* close."

She pushes away her plate and leans in closer. "What do you mean *too* close?"

"Picture yourself being stranded on a deserted island with the same dozen people for twenty years, how would you feel? Its not like reality TV where someone gets booted off the island. No one ever leaves."

Her smile quickly fades. "I can see where it would get old real quick."

"Don't get me wrong; I love them all, but it was lonely at times."

"Would your children have to grow up the same way?" She touches upon a fear I've never shared with anyone, not even Heather.

"I hope not. I love kids and would like to have a lot of them, but not if they have to be isolated. Look, it's getting late, let's turn in." I get up not giving her a chance to protest.

"I'll show you to your room." I offer her my hand and she keeps a tight hold as we head towards one of the bedrooms.

She gives it a squeeze, quickly reaches up and brushes her lips on my cheek. "Good night, Michael."

Before I can react, it's over and she is closing the door behind her. I brush my fingers where her lips just were. "Preston, what the hell am I doing?" Oh bloody hell if you answer, I'll commit myself. "Come on, buddy, we need to try and get some sleep."

We head into the cabin next to hers, but I know the only one getting sleep tonight is Preston.

All the reasons I shouldn't get involved are swirling around inside my head, yet the only thing I can focus on are her soft lips brushing my cheek. Maybe seeing my home and all my life entails will push her away.

Dagen

What the hell was I thinking? I told him I was not a rebound girl yet I made the first move. "What a schmuck, Dagen!" Jesus, now

I'm talking to myself again. What the hell is this man doing to me? I can't sleep. I can't concentrate on anything and it shows in my business. The only thing I can think about is him . . . *Mr. tall, dark, and handsome.* There are so many facets to him. He's a loner but not by choice. Could I fit into his world or am I setting myself up for guaranteed heartache? Why the hell did Heather dump him? He seems so sincere, even when he said he liked my curves, but is he telling me what he thinks I want to hear? I know I'm not the California dreaming kind of girl. I'm an average girl with above average curves. It took me a long time to come to the realization that it's okay to be different. Who am I kidding?—I'm still fighting for that realization.

I think spending time with him in his environment, surrounded by the people that love him, will tell me a lot. His guard will be down and maybe that will give me a good feel for the truth, whatever it may be. I could have furnished his house without this trip, but my interest in him has been piqued. My brother always had lots of friends but not one best friend until Michael. From the day he met him, they have been inseparable, why? Whenever I question him all he would say is 'he always has my back.' Why is he so close to his uncles? Is it because of the way he grew up? Ugh, the questions keep swirling around in my head. I can only hope the answers are not too far out of my reach. Somewhere over the Atlantic, I finally drift off to sleep.

Michael

Sleep never came plus Preston's constant snoring didn't help me at all. The captain buzzes me to let me know we are an hour outside of landing. I head out to the galley and get coffee for both of us. I'm about to knock on her door, but before I can, she opens it. Her beauty leaves me standing there speechless.

"I hope one of those coffees are for me."

"Oh, yeah, sorry, I fogged out for a sec. We will be landing within the hour and I thought you might like a cup."

"Thank you, you're a lifesaver." She takes a sip and I could swear she moaned.

"I hope you were comfortable. Did you get some sleep?"

"Not really, you know strange surroundings and all. How did Preston sleep?"

"He slept like a rock and I must say we need to do something about his snoring." Her laughter stirs something in me, just not sure what that something is.

"I was wondering how he would do on such a long plane ride." Preston rolls onto his back and is doing an arse wiggle with a groan.

"Well, looking at him, anyone would think I brought him up from a pup."

"Yes, he did take to you right away. He's a good dog but was lacking attention. Have you figured out what you are going to do with him when you're at work?"

"Yes, I have a live-in housekeeper and gardener coming back with us. They will maintain the property and help me with Preston. I better let you get ready. I'll meet you in the lounge." Even though I don't want to leave, I give her some privacy.

Dagen

The coffee is wonderful but I can't sit around daydreaming, I need to get ready. My room has an en suite and one look in the mirror makes me want to scream. I fell asleep with my makeup on so now I have raccoon eyes. My hair is a wild mess, no wonder he was staring at me! He will probably be scarred for life. I quickly jump in the shower and try to make some sort of normal with my hair. I'm not sure what I'm walking into with his family so I opt for a simple sundress with a matching sweater. When I walk into the lounge area he looks up and smiles. Okay, maybe I chose well.

"I wasn't sure about the weather, I hope this will be okay?"

"You look beautiful. Have you ever been to Scotland?"

"No, I've been to Spain, Israel, and New Zealand."

He cocks his head and seems surprised. "Wow, that's different."

"Yes, I went to Spain with my dad on a shoot. When Bo and I graduated from high school, we went to New Zealand for an extended vacation. I did an exchange program in Israel."

"Why Israel?"

"My mother is Jewish and my father is Catholic. My parents let us choose which religion we wanted to follow. I chose Judaism and Bo chose Catholicism, probably just to have something to debate with me. I had an opportunity to study for one year abroad that eventually turned into three years. When I graduated, I wanted to stay, however, my father had other ideas. With the constant threats of violence he put his foot down and dragged me home."

"So what did you study?"

"I majored in architectural history with a minor in music. Unfortunately, there weren't a lot of jobs for a girl with that type of degree, so when I got back home, I went to school for design and from there went into real estate. I figured I would do it for a while to pay the bills, but then I found that I could incorporate the two. I usually stick to small boutique jobs. Yours is the largest one I've ever taken on. That's part of the reason I needed to see where you grew up, the real Michael."

"What's the other part?" He laughs and his smile prickles my skin. "You had to know I would ask."

"Busted. I wanted to learn more about you and what better way than from your family."

He leans in and brushes the back of his hand up my cheek. "Careful what you wish for, sunshine. Buckle up, we're getting ready to land." I'm a flustered mess but somehow get myself buckled in.

Michael

When we exit the plane, I let Preston do his business and head towards the car. I'm about to open the door for Dagen when it flies open and my Grams steps out.

"Michael, why do I have to find out from Antonia that you're coming home?"

"Hi to you too, Grams. This is Bo's sister, Dagen." Maybe I should have warned her about my Grams? Nah, she'll figure it out all on her own.

"Hello, Dagen, I don't know what you did to get my grandson to come home so soon, but whatever it was, thank you." She gives Dagen a hug, which is not like her. Who knows, maybe she's getting soft in her old age. "Is that drooling monster yours?"

"His name is Preston and he is a new addition to the family, so be nice. Where is Mick?"

"Tinkering on his new tractor. He believes he is a farmer." She waves her hand and mumbles something about nothing he plants grows; poor Mick.

"They are usually always together. I'm a little surprised he's not here," I quietly mention to Dagen.

We get in the car and Preston sits up front with Marshall, Grams' driver. I hope she doesn't start her interrogation; I had enough from Mr. Turner; I don't need any more.

"So, Dagen, is this the first time you've been to Scotland?"

"Yes, and my first impression is it's very green. How far is your home from here?"

"Michael will give you a complete tour tomorrow, but this is the furthest point on the property. This is where Maxwell keeps all the planes and helicopters."

"Oh, so we are here?!"

Grams reaches over and squeezes Dagen's knee. "Don't be overwhelmed by all of this nonsense, dear. We are just like everyone else."

I begin to laugh and I'm sure they think I'm nuts, but I can't stop. That is until Grams gives me the look.

"Did your brother tell you about the castle? I know my granddaughter gave him the complete tour much to her father's dismay."

"He just said it was big and I needed to see it for myself."

"Okay, so look to your left. You see the clearing? that's where Mick has decided to become the great farmer."

"Well, it looks like something is growing."

"My dear, those are weeds, but let's keep that to ourselves. You know every now and again, you have to stroke their egos." Grams begins filling Dagen in on her trip to Paris. Next thing I know, she is asking if she can take her to Paris shopping. Dagen's eyes grow wide and I'm sure she's looking to me for help.

"We are only here for a short time. If she wants to come back another time to shop I'm sure we can work something out. For now, let's not overwhelm her . . . please."

"Well, while you're here, you need to talk to your cousin about her decision to go to school in the States. We have all tried and she won't listen."

"I don't know why everyone thinks she will listen to me?"

"She idolizes you, that's why. Just try, please because right now there is no living with Jaxson or Maxwell. You know if Antonia goes, Grace will follow. I swear those two will be the death of all of us."

We pull up to the house and Mick is standing out front. He doesn't like when she is out of his sight for too long. We get out and he quickly takes her hand.

"Mick, this is Dagen."

"Pleasure to meet you. Everyone is out back waiting for you."

I take her hand and lead her inside. She freezes in the entrance-way. Her eyes are looking every which way. She doesn't seem to know where to look first. "I know at first it's intimidating, but really, just relax. Come on." I pull her towards the back of the house and out on the patio where I know everyone will be having coffee. Uncle Max is the first person to notice us.

"Hello, Miss Dagen." He has a grin probably because he knows how much it irks her when he calls her Miss.

"Hello, *Mister* Maxwell Fleming."

"Touché, Dagen. I will try, I promise. Let me introduce you to everyone while Michael goes upstairs to get Jax."

That's my cue that Uncle Jax wants to talk to me in private. I pull Aunt Jackie into a hug and whisper "Make sure he behaves, please." I excuse myself and head upstairs.

"Hey, why aren't you downstairs with everyone else?"

He's running his hands through his hair, one of his habits when he's stressed.

"I wanted to talk to you alone. It's Heather, Junior, she contact-ed Antonia about you. She also tried to contact Raven but that fell on deaf ears."

I feel my chest tighten. I put all this behind me and I wish ev-eryone else would too. "What did she want? I told her never to con-tact me again."

"Antonia wouldn't tell me what she said only that she wants you back. I know I said I would leave it all up to you but when she contacted Antonia, I couldn't take it and I went to see her. I asked her to be an adult about all of this."

I roll my eyes cause I know better. "What exactly did you tell her? And, I mean everything."

"I explained to her that she chose to end it with you. She should have judged you by the man you are today and not the gene pool of others. Too bad, so sad, life goes on and so should she."

His direct approach might be good in business but when it comes to dealing with people, it leaves something to be desired. "Dare I ask what she said?"

"She turned on those crocodile tears. I told her they won't work on me and she needs to move on. She started this ball rolling and we don't go back. I left, but you need to be aware, I don't think she is done with you. Has she tried contacting you?"

"Yeah, I told her basically the same thing. I marked her emails as spam and she hasn't tried to call me. If she contacts Antonia or anyone else, let me know and I'll handle it. You don't need to be dealing with my crap." I know all of this stuff makes him want to shelter me even more but it's life and I'm moving on. I can't live in a bubble and that's the part he has the most trouble dealing with. That's why he's having such a hard time with Antonia.

"I know you can handle whatever is thrown at you, but we are family and I'll always have your back. Now, about Dagen. . ."

"Before you go any further, we are friends. Let's just leave it alone for now."

"I get it but. . ."

"No but's about it; just drop it. I need to get back downstairs and you need to meet her."

"You're right. By the way, how did things work out with Mr. Turner?"

"He was everything I expected him to be. I gave him an extensive tour of everything but the panic room. Tony really went all out with the security system, Hector seemed impressed."

"Who knows about the panic room?"

"I haven't told anyone but, eventually, I will have to tell Bo and Dagen."

"Okay, remember—less is more. We better get downstairs before we are missed."

Dagen

Oh my God, this place is off the charts huge. I hope Michael doesn't want his home to look like this. It will not fit into the California lifestyle. While he is upstairs, Max introduces me to Michael's parents and aunts before getting into a heated debate with Mick and Michael Sr. about some smokehouse. Thankfully, Jackie comes to my rescue with the offer of coffee.

"I thought Michael's cousins were going to be here?"

"The girls are still asleep and the boys went for a ride. Don't worry, you'll get your fill of them. Max said you are helping Michael decorate his new home. Has he talked you into watching that show for *research* purposes?"

Raven begins to laugh so hard she's practically in tears. "Don't feel bad, Dagen, we've all been suckered one way or another into watching *Doctor Who*. You'll find it will be easier if you just go with the flow. Every time Jackie lost a bet, she would have to watch it."

"I asked Michael to take me here so I could see where he grew up and meet his family. I don't know him very well but I figured this would be a good place to start. I want his home to be a reflection of who he is and not a show place. He might not be there all the time but, when he is, I want it to feel like a home. I think knowing more about his childhood will help." Maybe my explanation will help them relax and open up to me about Michael as a boy.

Raven, Jackie and even Grams are telling me funny childhood stories. Everyone is happy to share. Everyone except Michael's mom, Bella. She is very quiet, watching me very closely. I'm trying not to read anything into it but I'm becoming very uncomfortable. Maybe she is just being protective. After all, he did just get a DJ letter. Finally she puts her coffee down and slowly joins in the conversation.

"I'm sure my son will want to show you all the tunnels and the stables. Hopefully you will come back when you have more time and we can go to the vineyard. We are usually there all summer but when I heard my son was coming home, I came home too." Well, at least she wants me to come back again, that's something.

"He told me about the vineyard and I would love to see it. I've tasted your Chardonnay and it is wonderful. Unfortunately, we are limited on time since he has to be back for work in a couple of days. Maybe before the summer is out we can come back." She doesn't say anything more and I pray my answer satisfied her.

"Did you help Michael find Preston?"

"No, Raven, it was more like Preston found him. I do rescues and I was at the final stage, which is placing him in his forever home. He took a liking to Michael and that was it."

Raven smiles and then suddenly gets a faraway look. "I can understand that. Michael has a way with all animals. I first met him when he was in my second grade class. He had a dog, Vito, or as Jax always called him, The Beast. He was a German Shepherd, trained for protection but very gentle. You should teach Preston hand signals. I had a service dog for years. All I had to do was give him a sign and would do whatever I needed. Don't tell your brother; his name was Bo."

I don't ask her why she needed a service animal; that is very personal. However, I find it very interesting that she had him trained for sign language. "Did you train him?"

"No, Max trained him."

Why am I not surprised? "He seems to be a Jack of all trades."

Jackie laughs, "My husband and his crazy brother don't believe in the word *can't,* but those are stories for another day."

I'm beginning to wonder where Michael is when three girls

come strolling outside. One is more beautiful than the other, but it is easy to see who their parents are. Grace has Maxwell's piercing light blue eyes but she is tall and very lean like Jackie. Antonia and Gabriella have Raven's deep violet eyes. Both girls have long, thick, dark, wavy hair. God, everyone in this house is so beautiful and it's very intimidating. When Antonia finds out who I am, she hits me with a million questions about Bo. Yikes, I think she's got it bad. Needless to say, she was disappointed to find out he didn't come with us.

"So, I understand you are thinking of going to school in the States."

"Yeah, I'm looking at UCLA or Cal Tech."

"Both are good schools. What are you thinking of majoring in?" She glances around the room and then shrugs her shoulders.

"I'm not sure, but I don't have to declare right away. I just need to make sure my current online classes I've been taking are transferable."

"True, but how do you know you are picking the right school. The key is to finish up as quickly as you can. Why not some of the local Universities here?" That only gets me a *what the fuck is wrong with you* look.

"Dagen, I was born in this house. Uncle Max actually delivered me. I need to experience life. I'm not going to be able to do that if I never leave here. Besides, Michael lives in California so at least I will have some family to fall back on. Plus, Grace will be with me. She's majoring in language arts," she rambles. More like my brother is there, but I don't know her well enough to call her out on it.

"Sounds like you have this all figured out."

"I'm working on it."

"What about you, Gabriella, what do you like?"

"The symphony is my life. When I'm not playing my violin, I'm studying music."

"Where would you like to continue your studies?"

"I'm not really sure. Where did you go to school?"

"California and Israel. I graduated with a degree in architectural History with a minor in music. I play the piano but my degree was not going to get me any type of employment. I decided to go back to school for design. From there I got my real estate license. Now I own my own business. But it took me some time to find my way." I can only hope that some of what I'm telling them sinks in.

Finally, Michael is back and with him is a man who would put Michael Angelo's David to shame. My legs won't move and my mind is mush. I can't get past his deep blue eyes and chiseled cheekbones.

"Hello, Dagen, it is a pleasure to finally meet you, I'm Jax." He takes my hand and I snap out of my trance, hopefully none the wiser. His voice is very deep and smooth, and when he smiles, he's got dimples.

"Thank you. I understand you met with my father in Spain."

"Yes, I'm glad I got to speak to him in person. I think I made him feel more comfortable about the added security. I hope you're okay with it too?"

"Yes, after today I think I have a better understanding." Now that I met the man, I can understand why Michael said I have to meet him to understand. There is an intensity about him that can't be explained.

"Well, I think everyone monopolized your time enough. Michael will show you around, and I'm looking forward to seeing his place when you're done with it."

Michael takes my hand and it doesn't go unnoticed by Jax. We head into the house and he leads me into a massive kitchen. This is a chef's dream kitchen with two Vulcan-Hart ranges and gadgets galore! I love to cook and while I'm basking in this beautiful, off the charts, kitchen I realize Michael is talking to me.

"I'm sorry I was mesmerized by this wonderful kitchen."

"Do you like to cook?"

We really know nothing about each other, which in a way is

kind of nice. "Yes, I love to cook and bake. Do you know how to cook?"

"Yes. I spend my summers with my parents at the vineyard. My father taught me to cook and how to make wine. My mum taught me how to make the best coffee and desserts. We can talk about all that later, I want to show you some stuff before sunset." He takes my hand and leads me to a blank wall in the kitchen. "Press the wall."

I press on the wall and it pops open, revealing a tunnel. He takes my hand and pulls me inside. The lighting is very dim but he leads me to a staircase. When we get to the top there is another panel. He opens it and we are in an upstairs hallway.

"Oh. My. God. That is so frigging cool!"

He laughs, "Yeah, the first time I took Aunt Raven in there it freaked her out."

He leads me to a door, opens it and I'm instantly transported back in time. It's a child's room. "You kept it the same all these years?"

"Yes and no. This room has a lot of good memories for me but also a lot of bad ones. This was my room when I was diagnosed with Leukemia. I went from here to stay in a hospital in the States and then eventually a Swiss Clinic. I did come back here but, in my mind, I was afraid if I stayed in here I would get sick again. As much as I loved this room, I still thought something bad would happen to me. I really didn't want to give it up, but I couldn't sleep in here. At night, I would pretend I was sleepwalking and I would head down the hall to another room or sleep on the floor. I figured everyone knows not to wake a sleep walker and my plan worked for a few nights."

"Really, what happened?"

"Uncle Jax happened; he knew what was going on. When I went back to the clinic for some follow up treatments, he had a contractor come in and renovate one of the other rooms for me. I would still come in here, but only once in awhile. Come, I'll show you the other room." We head down the long hallway to another room and when we enter it, I'm amazed. The room is huge and does not go along with the rest of the home's décor.

"Oh, wow. This is very modern and large. Did you choose everything in here?"

"Uncle Jax picked the bed and left the rest up to me. He wanted to make sure I had some place that I felt was totally mine."

I take my time looking at everything. I walk up to a wall that has numerous models on the shelves. "Did you make all of these yourself?"

"Yes. Some of them took me months. Most are bridges or famous buildings." He takes my hand, "Come, I want to show you something." He takes me to a very large picture; it's a set of framed blue prints.

"These prints are of the original castle before all the modifications were made. I used these to find some of the tunnels."

"These prints are amazing, would you want to put this in your office?"

"That's a great idea. Maybe I'll take some of my models, too."

"I can finally understand how lonely this must have been. This place is huge and easy to get lost in. At least there is history here. Did you research to see who this place was originally built for?"

"Yes, but the records get a little muddled up. Let's go, I want to show you some of the outlying area's before it gets dark."

"Am I dressed okay or should I put on jeans?"

"Tomorrow you can wear jeans when we go riding. Today, I'm liking the dress."

I feel my cheeks flush and quickly turn away. "What about Preston?"

"Uncle Max is putting him through his paces. He'll be fine and I'm sure he is loving all the attention he is getting."

We head outside and waiting for us is a charcoal Aston Martin. I instinctively head towards the passenger side only it's really the drivers side. I can't stop laughing.

"Mind sharing what's so amusing?"

"I was thinking how much Preston would love this car."

"Want to drive? You can really open it up."

"Maybe tomorrow; today I want to take in everything around me."

We quickly take off, he wasn't kidding when he said he could open it up. The scenery is breathtaking as it's whizzing by me. He finally comes to a stop, gets out, and quickly opens my door.

"There's a clearing at the top of the hill. I thought we could watch the sun set at the top over a bottle of Chardonnay." He pops the trunk and pulls out a basket and blanket before taking my hand. He's pulling me along but I'm trying not to stumble. The last thing I need is to perform a humpty dumpty moment. When we reach the top, I finally look up and I swear if I reached up I could touch the heavens. He leans in, his hot breathe on my neck.

"Beautiful, isn't it?"

"There are no words to describe it."

He let's go of my hand and I'm startled by how much I feel the emptiness left behind. He spreads out the blanket for us and pours the wine. We sit down to watch the sunset. There are a multitude of colors streaked across the sky. He taps his glass to mine.

"To many more spectacular moments frozen in time."

He's very quiet and I wonder if he took Heather here. If he made these grand jesters to her. Why wouldn't he? I mean she was his fiancée. Is this his shtick?

"Did you come to this spot a lot when you lived here?"

"When I wanted time alone to think, I would ride my horse up here."

"Well, this would have made quite an impression with the ladies." Oh that was subtle, Dagen.

"The only person I ever brought home was Heather."

"Why? I mean surely you had lots of dates."

"It was hard knowing if the person wanted to be with me or was she just after the money that comes with the name. Heather's family is very wealthy, so I thought she would be more understanding. Clearly I was wrong."

All I can think is how sad and lonely of a life this man has had. "Why did you bring me here?"

"Honestly, I don't know. Maybe I need you to really understand me. I mean, I like our friendship. I've never had a woman as a friend. Hell, I don't even know if you want me around. All I know is, I feel comfortable with you. You make me laugh over the simplest things. You don't want anything from me and you don't judge me. I can be me and you're not scared off by all of this." He tilts his glass up towards the setting sun.

"So, no one has ever been here, not even Heather?" He gets really quiet and picks at the grass. "Michael, it's okay if you don't want to talk about it."

"It's just hard dipping into the past, the pain of a loss never really goes away, does it?"

"No, we put it in a safe place, safe for us to deal with it."

He picks up his glass and swirls the liquid around. "Her name was Rose, and she saved me. In the end, she paid with her life."

I feel a knot in my throat. He gets really quiet again, picking at the blades of grass until the spot is bare. I want to know but yet, I don't. When he's ready, he'll tell me. I take his hand and gently squeeze it. "Someday, when you're ready to share, I'll always be here to listen."

"Oh, Dagen, where have you been all my life?" He gets up pulling me with him.

"Come, it's getting dark and there's a lot more house for you to see." It doesn't take long before we are speeding into the night and I'm hanging on for dear life.

Chapter Twelve

JAX

JUNIOR AND DAGEN LEFT AND THERE'S NO SIGN OF MAX.
"Jackie, where did Max go?"

"He's working with Michael's dog. I think they were headed towards the distillery. Did you talk to Michael about Heather?"

"Yeah, no worries; he already spoke to her. I don't think we will be hearing from her anymore."

She rolls her eyes and is giving me a look like I'm a clueless bloke. "Either way, Jax, I've instructed everyone that if she contacts them, they are not to talk to her and to let one of us know. I know you think we've seen the last of her, but I don't think so."

Jackie's usually spot-on, and now I'm worried.

"Thanks, I'll go look for Max."

I head out but I don't have to go far. I find him in the field near the stables. "So this is Junior's new found beast?"

"He's a sweet dog and very playful. I can see why Junior took to him so easily. Did you talk to him about Heather?"

"Yes, hopefully it's the end of it, although, Jackie doesn't think so."

"Yeah, she spoke to me about it, too. She's usually right, but don't tell her I said so."

"What do you know about Dagen?"

"You know everything I know."

"Cheeky bastard, what's your tingle sense telling you? Don't even try denying it." He's got a sixth sense that has saved our arses on many occasions.

"She's tough and I think Junior is attracted to her, but I think he's going to be gun shy, lack of self trust. When he finally let someone in, he got burned in the worst way. He's going to need time. Have you suggested therapy to him?"

"Yeah, I agree with you. I think he just needs time."

"Well, remember how long it took you after Erica. Let's hope he can bounce back quickly but not recklessly. I think having him in California is a good thing. He's able to find his footing in life and I'm still able to keep close tabs on him."

"Did he ask you about the man that raped Bella?"

"Yes, he did and I told him exactly what I told you when you first asked. He's not that man, Jax, and he never will be. Just like we are nothing like our father. . . Let it go."

I'm mindlessly scratching Preston's neck. "So does this beast have potential?"

"Yeah, he's a good dog and I'm glad they found each other."

"Did you introduce Junior to Mr. and Mrs. Holiday?"

"No, not yet. I will in the morning. Right now I want to show Junior my new smoke house."

"I swear you're like a little kid sometimes." We walk back to the house and find Junior and Dagen just getting back from their drive.

"Jax, have you figured out what we are going to do about the girls?" Just the mention of it makes his jaw begin to tick. Max will never be able to let the girls out of his sight.

"Short of moving us all to California . . . no."

"Junior, have you thought about what you could possibly tell Antonia to get her to go to a local university?"

"Oh, Michael, I forgot to tell you I spoke to Antonia about college. I think I figured out why she's so hot to go to Cali and it's not for the schools," Dagen jumps in. We are all staring at her like she has three heads.

"Please, Dagen, I'm at my wits end with my daughter; if you figured something out, share it with the rest of us."

"Well, when I talked to her about school, she didn't even know what she wanted to major in. She did, however, have a million questions for me about my brother. I think it's about a crush and she's using school as her excuse to get near him."

I don't know who is going to lose it first, Max or me.

"Are you fucking kidding me?! All of this for a bloody crush?!" Max begins to pace and I know I've just let out a growl that was more like a roar and probably scared Dagen.

"Um, you both need to calm down. Flipping out is not going to help your cause. I have an idea, so just hear me out. I can let her know subtly that my brother is not available. She also mentioned that she wanted to spread her wings and the best way for you to clip them is to go along with her plan on moving to California."

"I'm sorry but maybe you don't understand—that's not a good option." I know I could easily follow my daughter but at what price?

"Tell her if she insists on going to California then the whole family will be going too. I'm sure by now she knows, when it comes to your family, you would do anything to protect them."

"You're a very shrewd, young lady, but I won't lie to my daughter."

She takes a few steps closer with her hands on her hips. "I'm not telling you to. There are plenty of places in Cali that you can rent month to month. Let her get it out of her system. You can get Gabriella an internship with the California Symphony. There are also a lot of language arts colleges for Grace. Look, I'm just giving you options; think about it."

Impressive that she's not afraid to go toe to toe with me. "I'll give it some thought, while I consider other options. In the meantime, I hope you're enjoying yourself. There is so much to see and do. I hope you have enough time to really get a feel for this place. I'm looking forward to seeing what you do with Junior's place."

"It's beautiful here, but it's also very isolated. What made you decide to move here?"

"Max, found this place; it was a good place to retire after we sold Raiders." She cocks her head to the side and raises her eyebrows as if she is surprised. Maybe she is but she doesn't need to know all the details of our past. "You seem surprised."

"Well, if this is your idea of retirement, then you have a skewed way of looking at life."

I can't help but laugh at her assessment of me. "I admit I look at life a lot differently then the average person, but then again, why go through life being average. I'll leave you to your exploring; I have business to attend to." I leave and Max begins to show them the progress he's made with Preston while he takes them to see the smoke house. I head into my office to think about what Dagen said. It's all starting to make sense now. Antonia's fascination grew after Junior brought Bo home.

"Jax, are you okay?"

I leap out of my chair at the sound of her voice. "Raven, you nearly gave me heart failure."

"You usually know whenever I'm near. What's going through that beautiful mind of yours?"

"Dagen said that Antonia has a crush on Bo and she thinks that's what is fueling her desire to go to school in the States. How am I supposed to deal with a crush?" I ask. She crawls into my lap and snuggles into me. When I pull her closer, I whisper in her ear "No matter what happens in life, this will never get old."

"I know that you want to shelter her from all the bad in the world but she needs to experience life. We will always be here for her, and Michael lives in California, so she will have some family there."

"What do you think if we all spent the summer in California? It would be an extended vacation."

"How is that giving her some space? How do you expect her to grow and mature if you are always hovering over her?"

"Sweetheart, you of all people know I could never let her go live in another country. Hell, remember what happened when she went to her friend's house for a sleepover?" My arms around her tighten at the memory.

"How could I forget? You and Max parked outside the girl's house all night with your state of the art listening devices. Remember the aftermath, Jax? Do you want to deal with that again?"

"Hell no, she didn't talk to us for six months. What if we all head over to California and try living in the States for a bit?"

She's quiet, her fingers trailing hearts on my chest. I know it would be hardest on Raven, the past coming back to life. "You know I would do anything for my family, but going back there." Her voice trails off and I know what a struggle it would be for her. I mindlessly stroke her back as I hold her tightly in my arms.

"I'll try to figure something else out. Hopefully it won't come to that. What's your take on Dagen?"

"Right to the point, Jax. I don't know her well enough to form an opinion but hell, look how well we thought we knew Heather. Time is a healer and I think he needs it more than he will say. Don't forget, it's not just the breakup that he's dealing with. He has to come to terms about his father and about the money. I know you kept that from him for his protection but, in the end, like you, he bases everything on honesty."

"I understand what you're saying, but what if he loses his trust in me?"

"He knows the reason why you kept the secret and I know he gets it, but you have to give him some time and space. He's a lot like you, but you operate at 100 mph. Not everyone operates like that or can even remotely keep up with you." I mindlessly twirl her hair, lost in her words of reason.

"If we have to go to California, I promise I will keep you safe. I know it will be hard but you know I'll always have your back."

"I love you, Jax."

"More, sweetheart, always more."

Dagen

After Max shows off his smokehouse, we continue our endless tour around the castle and each room is more spectacular then the last. Never over done and each room has warmth that I never would have expected in a castle. The last room he takes me to is a music room with it's own recording studio.

"Wow, Michael, this is amazing. Do you play any of these?" He watches me as I trail my fingers across the baby grand piano.

"Yes, Uncle Max, taught me to play the guitar. We all enjoy this room whether it's playing an instrument or singing. What about you? I know you said you minored in music, do you play?"

I sit down at the piano and rest my fingers upon the keys. "I've played the piano since I was seven years old. There was a time it was all I ever wanted to do."

"Why didn't you?"

"I realized I loved to play for me. The thought of putting myself out there for the world to judge made me . . . made me want to crawl into a hole and hide. Fame is not for everyone and certainly not for me."

He reaches over and tucks my hair behind my ear, his thumb rubs across my cheek, causing my skin to prickle in response.

"Play something for me . . . please."

My fingers trail along the keys as if they have a mind of their own. "Honesty" by Billy Joel" pops into my head. Maybe it's what we need, real honesty. He picks up the guitar and plays along with me. When he starts to sing, I'm blown away; his voice is deep and so raw with emotion. Hearing him and knowing what he's been through makes my stomach twist into knots. I want to hug him and beat the daylights out of Heather all in one sweep. I quietly play and listen to him pour out his emotions through the song. When he's finished, I can't help myself; I turn, lean up, and brush my lips over his. "That was so beautiful," my voice, barely a whisper. I glance over toward the door and I notice Max standing in the doorway. I'm sure the kiss was not lost on him. Before I can acknowledge him, he's gone.

"When you play the piano, you close your eyes and part your beautiful lips." He skirts his thumb across my bottom one and I feel a shiver run up my spine.

"Dagen, why did you kiss me?"

"I was caught up in the emotions from the song." My version of a lame excuse, trying to hide my feelings. "Are you ever going to tell me about Heather?" I quickly change the subject to hide my embarrassment.

"What's there to tell? She decided she wanted to move on."

I squeeze his hand, "Didn't you ask why? I mean you seem like a nice guy, why would she end it in a DJ letter? That's just cruel."

"You think I'm nice?"

"Well, yeah, except that sometimes, getting any information out of you is like pulling teeth. Other than that, you're a nice guy. Did she make you question that?"

"Let's go for a walk."

"Are you going to take me into another one of those tunnels?"

He laughs and takes my hand. "No, my Grams planted a white garden on the side of the house. In the moonlight, it is absolutely stunning." We head out the French doors, he takes my hand and we begin to walk around the west side of the castle.

"There are different benches placed around the garden. Depending upon the position of the moon, each one will give you a different view. Tonight, it's a full moon so let's sit on the outside perimeter. I want you to close your eyes and let me lead you."

He puts an arm around my waist and lets go of my hand. It doesn't take long to get to the bench. "Okay, Dagen, open your eyes."

When I open my eyes, I'm blown away at the sight before me. The moon has cast a glow upon the flowers and they all look like the tips were dipped in purple glitter. The fireflies are dancing everywhere and the garden looks magical.

"Oh, Michael, this is so amazing!"

"I thought you would enjoy it."

When we sit down he instantly takes hold of my hand again.

"I'm enjoying the garden but you know you're not going to get out of answering my question." His grip tightens at my words.

"She sent the DJ letter to Uncle Jax, which that, in itself, was pretty low. I was not about to let her walk away without a face to face. I confronted her and she handed me a detailed report about my family. She accused me of keeping secrets when in reality, I never knew any of what she accused me of hiding. If she really trusted me she could have just asked me. It was very personal and not something my family was ready to share with anyone, including me. She has since regretted her decision and tried to contact me and other members of my family, but it's too late."

"So let me get this straight. She blames you for keeping secrets from her that you knew nothing about and they weren't your secrets to tell?"

"Exactly. In exposing all of this to me she hurt not only me, but my parents, too.

I believe in forgiveness and second chances but some things just can't be forgiven."

I don't ask him what was exposed, if he wants to tell me he will in his own way.

"Why did you pick that particular Billy Joel song to play?"

"I don't know, it's like my fingers had a mind of their own. You have a beautiful voice. Did you take lessons?"

"No, Aunt Jackie uses music as another form of therapy for the children that she works with. Sometimes Uncle Max and I would help her out. When a child is upset, singing can help calm them down. It's no big deal."

"Somehow I can't picture Max singing. You, on the other hand, have a beautiful voice. You should sing more."

"Are you going to tell me why you really kissed me? I mean, not that I didn't like it, on the contrary, I liked it a lot, but why?"

I attempt to pull my hand from his but his grip gets tighter. "I don't know, it just felt right."

"More than right, Dagen."

Chapter Thirteen

Michael

I FORGOT TO WARN DAGEN THAT THIS TIME OF YEAR SUNRISE comes very early coupled with seventeen and a half hours of some sort of daylight. I'm sure she will want to sleep in so she can get adjusted to the change. I love the early mornings, but by the way Preston is snoring, I don't think he will be getting up anytime soon. I get up and head downstairs, determined to get in a long run before everyone wakes up. When I step out back, Antonia is waiting for me. "Jesus, you damn near gave me a heart attack. Why are you lurking around back here?" I grab my chest.

"I'm not lurking; I wanted to catch you alone. I figured this was the best way to talk to you without everyone all up in my business."

"Well, if you want to talk, then you're going to have to run with me." I know she's not a fan of running but when her mind is made up, nothing will stop her. We head off towards the distillery, which is away from the houses. "So what's going on with you? Why are you so intent on going to a university in the States?"

"I'm being smothered and the older I'm getting, the worse it is. I want to experience life and not under my father's thumb."

"Next, you're going to tell me this has nothing to do with Bo." I glance over and her face gives nothing away. Maybe Dagen was wrong about the crush.

"I'm not going to lie to you; I'm attracted to him but it's more than that. I need to get a life. How were you able to get out from my father's tight grasp?"

"Oh. My. God, Antonia, look around you, does it look like I have freedom to do whatever the fuck I want? No, I don't, but I also know first hand what the real dangers are. You need to realize that you can have your freedom but it comes with conditions."

"Then how is that having freedom?"

"You have to learn to pick and choose your battles. Figure out what is really important to you and what you can actually let go. It really is a balancing act and something you learn as you go along. You need to earn his trust in your decision-making. Mainly, you can't expect that, after you turned eighteen, you can just flip a switch. It doesn't work like that. Let's sit by the pond for a bit." We head over and I know she is grateful for the break.

"He doesn't even give an inch. God forbid I do something to upset his applecart; all hell breaks loose. And Uncle Max—he's just as bad. I'm surprised they haven't microchipped us like they do the dogs!"

"You have a lot of valid points. But, what makes you think that they wouldn't follow you to the States?" The shocked look on her face tells me she never even considered it.

"My God, do you think he would go that far?"

"Think of the man, Antonia; of course he will. Do you want my opinion?"

"Of course but not a lecture, please."

"Enroll in the University of Saint Andrews. Tell him that even though you want to be in the general housing, you understand that's not an option. You will, however, agree to get an apartment with Grace. That shows him you are willing to negotiate with him. I know you've been doing online classes and those can transfer to Saint Andrews. Then, after a year, you reassess your situation. If you feel a university in the States will have what you need, then you at least have something to negotiate with. Right now, you're coming to the table with nothing. You don't even know what course of study you want. How do you expect him to take you seriously when you don't take yourself seriously?" She's very quiet, tossing pebbles into the pond.

"Why Saint Andrews?"

"Couple of reasons. First, it's the furthest away from here without leaving Scotland. So it would make sense for you to go there. Secondly, they have a joint program with William and Mary in the States. You do the first two years at the main campus here and then the last two years you finish up at the campus in the States. You'd be going in with credits, so it wouldn't take you two years. If you want to go toe to toe with him, then you're going to have to start thinking like he does. Now, as far as Uncle Max is concerned, you're on your own with that one. When it comes to security, you know nothing I have said or done has ever made him change his mind and probably never will. Do you have any idea what you want to go to school for?" She looks away from me and I know she's hiding something. "Hey, look at me." When she does, I see tears in her eyes and it breaks my heart. "You know you can talk to me about anything. Why are you holding back on me, of all people?"

"I don't want to put you in the middle."

"I'm already in the middle, everyone has asked me to talk to you, but right now, it's just us; spill the beans."

"I want to study photojournalism."

"So, what's wrong with that? I've always said you have a great eye when it comes to photography."

"I want to be where the action is and not behind some desk or in a studio. I want to be out in the field."

"What do you mean by 'out in the field?'"

"What I really want to do is travel with the British Army."

"Oh for fucks sake, Antonia! Why not just strap a grenade on your arse and call it a day?!"

"That's why I haven't said anything to anyone. You're the most easy going, understanding person in this family and look how you're reacting, can you imagine what he would say?"

"Why can't you photograph stuff closer to home?"

"What like puppies and babies? Do you hear what you sound like?"

"What about Grace? Don't tell me she wants to do something equally as off the wall."

"She wants to be a translator for MI6."

"Why am I not surprised? Do you want me to talk to both of them?"

"Oh, Michael, would you?!"

"I can't make any promises, but I'll try and figure something out."

"I know I can always count on you to help. Thank you."

"Now I have a question for you. What did Heather say when she contacted you?" I pray she didn't tell her about my mum's rape.

"She wanted to know how you were doing and she kept saying she was sorry. She wanted the family to know that she never meant to cause friction. She kept saying she was worried about you. She acted like you were going to off yourself."

"What did you tell her? Don't even try to tell me nothing. I know you better than anyone and I'm surprised you didn't try to go and kick her arse."

"Oh, I was tempted, that's for sure, but I didn't want her to think we were wasting any time on her or her feelings. I told her you were doing great. Making a new life for yourself in the States, and that maybe it was for the best that she walked away. She asked me why I felt that way and I believe my exact words were 'He brought so much to the table and what did you bring?' I also told her that if she tried to contact any of us again, I wouldn't be so nice. She hung up and I haven't heard from her again, none of us have."

"Thank you for defending me, but you didn't have to. If she tries to contact you again just ignore it and then let me know." I get up and offer her my hand to pull her up. "Come on, we better start heading back."

"So, what's the story with you and Dagen? I'm not an idiot, so don't tell me nothing."

"I never could hide anything from you. I like her . . . a lot. Right now, we are friends and I will see where that leads us. Time is not my enemy for a change, and I don't want to rush into anything. We may be destined to just be friends and that's okay, too. One day at a time."

"Sometimes friends turn into lovers. Just don't let what Heather did to you make you afraid to take a chance."

"Never. I fought too hard to live and I'm not about to close down now. I'm glad I came home and she got to meet everyone."

"Hey, if we didn't send her running for the hills, then she just might be a keeper. So, tell me about your new house."

"It's huge and I'm very excited to see what Dagen is going to do with it. Bo lives with me but he has a separate wing. When I'm all settled, you will have to come and visit."

"I plan on it and not because of your roommate."

"Very funny. Come on, I'll race you back to the house. Last one in makes the coffee." We take off and I figure I would go easy on her but at the home stretch, she slingshots past me! We race into the kitchen and Uncle Max is waiting for us.

"Well, you two were out bright and early."

"Yes and, since Michael lost the bet, he'll be making coffee."

"Oh, well I wouldn't want to get in the way of a bet. While you're at it, I'll take a cup too, then I want to introduce you to Mr. and Mrs. Holiday and go over the security for when you're on site."

"Well, if you guys are going to talk shop, I'll take my coffee to go."

I quickly get the coffee going. I don't want to waste my last day here going over business stuff. I pass Antonia her cup, "Here's your coffee and do me a favor, on your way upstairs, if Dagen is up, let her know I'm in the kitchen, please." She mumbles *friends* under her breath and I try not to laugh.

"So where are the Holidays?"

"They are at the stables with Preston. I wanted him to get used to them. Let's go over security first and then we can head down there. I have a new guy that has the qualifications and certifications to work on the rigs. I had to make sure for insurance purposes, that he was legit. His name is Neville Marcus and he is originally from Louisiana. He has previous experience working on the rigs that you will be working on."

He begins to pace which doesn't make me feel good at all.

"What's wrong?"

"I hate only having one guard, but that's all I could get the state to agree to. If it was a private company, I could have had more but they have so many bloody regulations. I thought about anchoring a boat nearby with more personnel but again—more regulations. The rig is two miles offshore; I might be able to anchor a boat one mile further out. That would put us in international waters. Mick has a good friend with the US Coast Guard; I'll get in touch with him and find out if it's possible. In the meantime, let's go with what we've got in place."

"You know. I can take care of myself. You taught me well and now you need to give me the chance to prove it. Besides, what could possibly happen? I'm two miles offshore and security is already tight." I pour some more coffee and top his off.

"Come on, I want to meet the Holidays and then rouse Dagen before the day slips away from us."

"Junior, can I ask. . ."

"Oh for the love of Pete, do I need a friggin neon sign? Friends, Uncle Max, just friends." I look at him and he's got a smirk on his face. "What?"

"That's not what I was asking."

"Oh, sorry, it's just that I feel like all eyes are on me. Don't worry, I'm not broken. What did you want to ask me?"

"Did you talk to Antonia?"

"Let's head down to the stables and we'll talk along the way." I'd rather be out of anyone's earshot. When we step outside, Uncle Jax is waiting. Why am I not surprised?

"Well good morning to you both. When are you heading out?"

"Not until tonight. I'm glad you're here; I can fill you both in at the same time. I didn't get a chance to talk to Grace yet, but as promised, I spoke with Antonia about college. I listened to her side of the story and she has some valid points. Before you flip out, I explained to her that she was going about it all wrong. I think she should start out in a University in Scotland and get a year or two under her belt. After that, she can decide the next step, but she doesn't have to do it on her own. You both need to listen to her and Grace when they are trying to talk to you about the future. Uncle Max, I know what you've been through and I know how difficult it is for you to give any us a little bit of breathing room, but you have to try. Instead of coming at both of them with guns blazing, stop and listen. No matter how much you hate this, they have to go out into the real world and experience life, otherwise, why bother? And as much as I hate to say it, you need to negotiate with them. Approach it like any other business deal and maybe you will be able to meet somewhere in the middle."

Both of them are very quiet. Maybe I got through to them on a different level but only time will tell. If I tell them about their future plans they will freak out, and who knows if that's what they really end up doing. Most people change their majors at least once.

"Uncle Jax, if you don't try, you will lose her. She is, after all, an adult and can walk out that door tomorrow. And, it's only a matter of time before Grace follows."

All I can do now is hope for the best, otherwise Antonia will hightail it out of here and there is nothing they can do about it. As we approach the stables, Preston notices me and takes off running.

Just as I'm prepared for him to pounce on me, Uncle Max holds his hand up and Preston instantly stops.

"Wow, I'm impressed. He learned your signs so quickly."

"He's a smart dog, Junior. I think he will do fine. I went over all the signs with Mr. and Mrs. Holiday. They can show you all of them when you get back home. Come, let me introduce you."

We head into the stables and after chatting with the Holidays, I finally feel like everything is coming together. They are very excited about the move and Preston has taken a liking to Mrs. Holiday. No doubt because she made him homemade treats—traitor. I excuse myself from the conversation and head up to the house to rouse Dagen.

Chapter Fourteen

WHEN I GET INTO THE KITCHEN, I FIND DAGEN ALREADY up, having coffee and, sweet Jesus, she's wearing my Rugby shirt again.

"Good morning, I was hoping to be here when you got up but I was going over some stuff with my uncles. Did you get enough of sleep?"

"Yes, even though I used the blackout drapes, my mind kept telling me it was still daylight outside. What have you been up to?"

"I put together a list of the stuff we talked about taking. Went for a run with Antonia; I'll tell you all about that later. Are you up for horseback riding today or would you rather do something else?"

"I'm willing to give it a try." Her uncertainty is practically written all over her face.

"I promise you will be fine. I would never put you in harm's way. I'm going to run upstairs and shower."

"Am I okay with jeans?"

She's got on Jeans, chucks, and of course, my Rugby shirt. I lean in and whisper in her ear. "More than okay, sunshine. My shirt never looked so good." I pop open the panel in the kitchen so I can take the short cut to my room. When I turn back her cheeks are flushed and she's smiling. Yeah.

Dagen

I'm enjoying my coffee in my Michael-induced trance when I realize someone is talking. I look up and there is an elderly lady that I've never met, asking me something but I can't understand what she's saying.

"I'm sorry I was lost in thought. I'm Dagen Turner, a friend of Michaels."

"I know who you are, my dear. I'm Mrs. Osla. I was spending a few days in town, but when I heard Michael was home, I came back. Have you been given a tour of the place, yet?"

Good Lord, I only got every other word. "Yes, Ma'am, it's very peaceful here."

"More like isolated, dear. Where is the lad?"

"He went to shower before we go horseback riding. He should be back any minute." *I hope.* She sits down across from me and I feel like any minute she's going to pull a light out of her bag, shine it in my face and start peppering me with questions. "Would you like me to make you a cup of coffee?" Anything to get out of her glare.

"If you don't mind, I would love a cup of tea. You know, it can be said that you can judge a person by the way they make their tea."

Oh great like I wasn't scared of this lady before, now I'm starting to sweat.

"I promise I will do my best." I get up and begin looking around the kitchen for the kettle. I mean, how hard can this be? I find the kettle and while I'm waiting for the whistle, I set out cream and sugar. I think I'm doing okay until I find the tea. There's loose tea, bag tea, flavored tea—what the fuck?! Why don't they just have normal Lipton frigging tea bags?! I'm staring at the tea cabinet and I'm about to cry when she comes over and puts her arm around me.

"Relax, dear, Anwan, that's Michael's Grams, says it's the act of making the tea that settles the nerves not the tea itself. I promise I won't bite you." The kettle whistles and she sets the tea up to steep. "I met your brother recently. I understand from Maxwell that you're twins."

"Yes, although, I was born New Year's Eve at 11:59 pm and he was born New Year's Day at 12:05 am, so I tease him that I'm a year older. Are you related to Michael?" I can't figure out how she fits in here and Michael never mentioned her before.

"I'm an old family friend. Are you enjoying your time here?"

"Yes. I wish we could stay longer. I'm sure there is so much to see and do."

"Well, you'll have to come back when you have more time."

Michael picks that time to come to my rescue. "Good Morning, Mrs. Osla. I see you met Dagen. I thought you were away for a few days?"

"I heard you were home and I don't get to see much of you anymore. Besides, I can visit with friends anytime."

"We're not leaving until tonight, so why don't we have a big family dinner? In the meantime, I'm going to take Dagen horseback riding."

She raises her eyebrows and clears her throat. "My dear, have you ever ridden?"

"No, should I be worried?"

"Oh you're in fine hands. Run along now. I'll let everyone know about dinner tonight."

He takes my hand and we head out the door under the watchful eye of Mrs. Osla.

We head down toward the stables. The closer we get, the more nervous I'm getting.

"Oh. My. God, Michael, they are huge!"

He hands me a bag of apple slices that they keep in a small fridge in the barn. "You can offer them the apples but place it in the palm of your hand so they don't get your fingers. Watch me." He puts the apple slice in the palm of his hand and one of the horses walks up and takes it. Okay, Dagen, you can do this. Don't be such a baby. Mentally trying to talk myself into doing something that has me scared to death is no easy feat.

"Dagen, you can't let fear rule your life, otherwise, life will pass you by. You never want to say 'what if.' Trust me."

I open my palm and with a shaky hand I offer the apple slice.

"Good Lord, Dagen, it would help if you opened your eyes."

"You caught that."

"Yeah, come on, try again. This is Tequila, he is very laid back."

"He seems to like me, either that or he wants more apples."

"Probably both; he has a thing for apples. You can ride him today. I will teach you how to saddle him up." He's explaining step-by-step what he's doing, but the only thing I can focus on is him. The way he fills out those tight jeans, add to that the boots he's wearing and I swear I'm about to lose my mind.

"I don't know where you went on me but you might want to pay attention now." His killer smile is making my heart race. I mentally chastise myself and try to pay attention.

"Now comes the part when you have to actually get on him."

It only takes me two tries, and his hand on my ass might be why I needed a second try. He quickly saddles up his horse and we head out. The countryside is magnificent. No matter where I look, there are fields of wild flowers. When I turn around to ask him where we are headed, he has his phone out and he's taking pictures of me.

"How the hell are you taking pictures, steering your horse, and not falling off?"

"I'm gifted. Let's go towards the left, there's something I want to show you."

"Everywhere I look I find something more beautiful than the last."

"I could say the same thing. We're here; hold on and I'll help you down." He quickly jumps off of his horse and helps me, this time his hands are around my waist.

"My legs feel like Jell-O. I can hardly stand."

"You need to walk a bit and you'll get your land legs back." He takes my hand and leads me to a clearing. It's filled with lavender. Everywhere I look, it's purple.

"Oh wow, Michael, it's beautiful. I don't think I will ever see anything like this anywhere else in the world!"

"Probably not. Uncle Jax planted the lavender when we first moved here. He said it reminded him of Aunt Raven's eyes. Every year, the plants multiply. Now the fields are filled with it. Let's walk the horses to the left side of the field. There's a stream where they can get a drink."

When we get there the horses go right up to drink.

"I'm glad I let you talk me into horseback riding, although tomorrow I might not think so. Tell me about Mrs. Osla. I have to confess I only got half of what she was saying."

"Most people don't even get that. She is Uncle Max's first wife's aunt. She worked at my uncles' company and when they sold it, she came to live with us. Remember when I told you that when I went into the hospital my entire room was transformed into a TARDIS, well it was Mrs. Osla who pulled it off. She has a heart of gold when she's not scaring the living daylights out of everyone."

"What happened to Max's first wife?"

"She was murdered along with his son."

"Oh my God, I'm so sorry. That is so terrible, but it explains why he is the way he is with security." I can't imagine what happened and I don't want to pry.

"Yeah, he knows he's over the top—we all do—but we also understand why, so we don't question it. Besides, most of the time, he has good reason to be."

I need to lighten the mood. "What happened with Antonia?"

"We had a good talk. I asked her about Bo and she said she is attracted to him but after talking to her I know it has more to do with finding her independence than anything else. I did what I could to help. In the end, everyone is going to have to come to an agreement. I suggested that they go to school in Scotland and then transfer to the States. That might give everyone some breathing room."

"Did you get everything settled with your new staff and security?"

"Yeah, you'll meet everyone when we fly out later. We better get going; there's a lot more that I want to show you." He helps me up and I get back on my horse, grateful that I didn't land flat on my ass.

"I think I'm beginning to like horseback riding. We will have to do this again."

He's laughing so hard and holding his sides. "Mind telling me what's so funny?"

"Oh, sunshine, I love your enthusiasm but trust me, tonight you won't be suggesting we ride any time soon."

Chapter Fifteen

Michael

DINNER WITH THE ENTIRE FAMILY WAS TYPICAL INSANITY. Dagen was able to hold her own with all of them and towards the end of the trip, she even understood Mrs. Osla. It was sad to say goodbye to everyone, but I'm really excited to start my new job. When we hit cruising altitude, we went into the media room and put on a movie. She lasted a whole five minutes before her head was on my shoulder and she was fast asleep. I shut off the movie but I don't want to disturb her. Oh, who am I kidding? I love how comfortable she is with me. I've never seen anyone sleep with a smile on their face. I twist myself around and wrap my legs around her before I cover us with a throw. How can someone be so beautiful, yet so insecure? There's no pretense, all her cards are on the table. I rub her head and she lets out a little moan that gets my cock's attention. Down, boy, there'll be none of that anytime soon. I want to take my time and, whatever this is, I don't want to mess it up. I wrap my legs a little bit tighter and somewhere over the Atlantic drift off to sleep.

My eyes fly open at the sound of the Pilots buzzer. He informs me that we will be landing in thirty minutes. She begins to stir and when she opens her eyes she looks up at me. I feel like all the air has left my lungs. Her hair is everywhere, her lips have that puffy look that I can't resist and her eyes, so soulful. Fuck me, I'm done.

"Good morning, sunshine."

"I'm sorry, I must have fallen asleep."

She tries to move but I lock my legs tighter. "Not yet." I lean in and brush my lips over hers ever so slightly. "Those lips are begging to be touched by mine." She parts them and her eyes grow wide. Before she can respond, I gently brush them again. "Beautiful." I unlock my legs and help her up. "We're landing in thirty minutes."

She presses her fingertips to her lips. "Why?"

"Well, we can't fly around forever."

"You know what I mean, why did you do that?"

"I could make up all kinds of excuses but, in the end, that's all they are, excuses. Like I said, they were begging."

She smiles and her cheeks flush. Every time I watch her walk away, it sets alarms bells ringing in my balls. After a cold shower, I check my emails. The first thing I notice is a message from my boss, asking me if I can possibly start sooner. I shoot him an email letting him know I'll be in later today. When I head out to the cabin, I find Dagen already out there having coffee with Mrs. Holiday while Preston is eyeing their toast.

"Good morning, everyone. Mrs. Holiday, I have to head to work sooner than I anticipated. I'll get you settled in as best I can before I leave."

"Don't worry about it. I'm sure I can make the best of it."

"Michael, you don't have to worry. I will be working on your place non-stop for the next two weeks, so I'll be around to help."

"I know I've monopolized your time. I don't want your business to suffer because of me."

"My assistant has everything under control, believe me, he's even more organized than I am."

I'm excited to start my job but not so excited to leave her. "Thank you."

After getting everyone settled in and my bag packed, I make my goodbyes and head out. I didn't think it would be so hard, but the look on Dagen's face made me realize just how much I'm going to miss her. While I wait for my launch, I begin to flip through the pictures I took of her. There is one that I instantly know I want framed for my office. She's on Tequila and I snapped it just as they both turn their heads towards me. I can't stop staring at it. This is crazy, I need to put her out of my head. I'll text Bo; he's always good for a laugh.

Me: We're back and I got called into work sooner. Dagen is staying at the house. Make sure you introduce yourself to Mr. and Mrs. Holiday. Anything new that I need to know?

BO: Nah, how was the trip?

Me: Short but good.

BO: I take it my sister survived.

Me: Yes, she is fine. I'll be gone for the next two weeks, so make yourself available.

BO: What are you worried about?

Me: That house is huge and I'm sure Dagen will get bored if she is left alone.

BO: She's a big girl Mike; she can take care of herself. Sounds like you got it bad.

Me: You're an arse.

BO: So the housekeeper is married, but is she hot?

Me: She's around your mum's age. Lol

BO: Way to spoil my fantasy, Mike.

Me: Anytime, my friend. My launch is here. TTYL.

I get to the platform without any problems and I find Neville waiting for me.

"Good morning, sir. In order to keep a close eye on you, I will be your assistant whenever you're here. Your regular detail will takeover when you get back on the launch."

"I get it, Neville. I assure you, I'm not new to any of this. I'm more than capable of taking care of myself, so this should be a walk in the park for you." He gives me a slight nod as if in agreement.

I spend the rest of the day familiarizing myself with the layout and getting to know who's who and who does what. My goal is to make sure everything is up to date and in proper working order. First things first, I set out to find my boss, Mr. Cassidy. When I ask one of the workers where I might find him, he points me to two men in, what appears to be, a very heated discussion. Rather than interrupt them, I decide to wait and see if things calm down. From what I can gather, the Mud Engineer is upset about my being there. He's shouting that it's second-guessing the crew's work. I don't need people hating me before I even get started.

"Excuse me, I'm Michael Vizzano. I can assure you that I'm not here to second-guess anyone's work. I'm here to help make improvements that will make your job easier and safer. I hope we can work together to make it happen." I reach out to shake his hand. He looks at me and back down to my hand. Finally he grips it, no doubt trying to intimidate me with an iron grip.

"I'm Brynjar, but everyone calls me Bryn."

"Nice to meet you, Bryn. I hope you don't mind but I need to steal Mr. Cassidy for a bit. How about we meet tonight and we can go over some of the things you might want me to address."

"That's fine; dinner tonight at eight."

"Mr. Cassidy, I hope my being here won't pose a problem for the crew?"

"Michael, let's head to my office and we can go over everything, and please call me Glen. We are very informal here."

On the way to his office he introduces me to many of the workers. Everyone seems pleasant enough but I'll never remember all their names. His office is small and cluttered.

"So, Michael, I'm sorry I had to push you to start sooner, but I got the updated reports for the Atlantic hurricane season. The prediction is that after August, we could see quite a bit of action. I don't usually buy into all of the hypothetical shit but I would rather be safe than sorry." He hands me a stack of reports.

"These are the most current reports, review them and let me know your thoughts."

"Okay, I'll get started on this right away."

"I'll show you your office and where you and Neville will bunk." I've never bunked with anyone in my life so this should be interesting.

I thought my office was small until I saw the sleeping quarters. I'm a simple man but this takes it to a whole new level. I snap a few pictures and decide to send them to Dagen. It's also a good excuse to see what she is up to.

Me: Hey Sunshine, check out my new sleeping quarters and my postage stamp office. Maybe I should hire you to do something with them.

Dagen: That should be a piece of cake after this place. I'm making a lot of progress. Oh and Preston is keeping

Mr. Holiday very busy digging craters in the garden. ☺

Me: I have some huge bones for him in the kitchen pantry. They should keep him busy for hours. I told Bo that I left and to make sure he makes himself available in case you need anything.

Dagen: Thank you, but I'm a big girl and I will be just fine. Have you ever bunked with anyone before?

Me: No, this should be very interesting. I know you can take care of yourself; just humor me.

Dagen: Okay. Maybe you should watch one of those Tiny House shows. You can get decorating ideas for your cubbyhole. Lol

Me: Very funny, I see you and Bo have the same sense of humor. I better get going. I'm supposed to meet a crewmember for dinner. I'll be knee deep in work, but I will try and text you during the week.

Dagen: Okay, have fun. Bye ☺

Me: Fun is being with you, sunshine.

She doesn't answer back, I hope I haven't scared her off. Staring at the screen I finally see the three little dots.

Dagen: I have fun with you, too. Let's plan something when you get back. Hugs.

Wow, she signed it *Hugs*.

"Come on, Neville, let's go meet with Bryn and see what all the yelling was about."

When we get to the dining hall, Bryn is there with about six men and a couple of women. I introduce Neville as my assistant, and after some quick introductions, they begin to layout all the problems on the rig. I have to remind them I'm not here as a liaison for human resources; I'm here to inspect the safety of the rig and to make recommendations that would be more environmentally friendly. The group begins to filter out and the only one left is Bryn.

"Michael, how long do you think it will take you to assess everything?"

"I won't know until I start digging in."

"Did Cassidy give you the latest weather predictions?"

"Yeah, it seems that this season might be a bad one. I'm hoping that everything here moves quickly and I can hop over to the Gulf before any of the storms hit."

"This is a tight-knit community, so If you need help with anything, let me know."

"Thanks. I just relocated here from Scotland, so I'm still getting used to everything. Any help is always welcome. Do you live in Santa Barbara?"

"I live in Montecito, just outside of Santa Barbara. Have you found a place to live yet?"

"Yes, I found a place in Santa Barbara." Thoughts of Dagen instantly come to mind and her beautiful smile makes me calm and happy.

"Did I lose you there, Michael?" He laughs.

"Sorry, still suffering from jetlag. I'm going to call it a night. I'll see you in the morning." I get up and head to the showers before hitting the hay.

Me: Hey Sunshine, you up?

Dagen: Yeah, I figured you'd be sleeping by now.

Me: Couldn't sleep. I was flipping through the pictures I took in Scotland.

Dagen: Ugh, how many goofy pictures of me were you able to snag?

Me: Tons of beautiful pictures.

I attach one of my favorites, she has her eyes closed, her bottom lip between her teeth and she's feeding Tequila an apple.

Me: That's one of my favourites.

Dagen: He's beautiful.

Me: You're beautiful, sunshine.

Dagen: You better get some sleep; I think you're suffering from jetlag.

Me: Why can't you see what I see?

She's not responding, maybe I pushed too hard to fast?

Me: Hello???

Dagen: Sorry, it's hard for me to have self confidence. I live in Beverly Hills where everyone is thin, blonde, with perfect perky breast. I'm nothing like that so it's always been hard for me to fit in.

Me: Your breast seem perky to me. I think I've even seen them salute me when you wear my Rugby shirt. ;)
Dagen: OMG are you serious?

Me: Yeah, and I know you just snort-laughed. Everytime I see you in my shirt I hear "T-Shirt" by Thomas Rhett over and over again in my head. Do you know that song?

Dagen: No, and I don't snort-laugh!

Me: Yeah, you do and it's great . . . the song and the snort. Why do you want to fit into someone else's box?

Dagen: I want to have friends.

Me: I hope you realize how insane that sounds. If you have to change to have friends then they aren't friends. Do you remember what I told you our first night on the beach? Breathtakingly beautiful, never forget that. If anything, let those fuckers follow you. Got it?

Dagen: You're going to make me cry. Can we talk about something else, please.

Me: For now, yes. How is Preston?

Dagen: He has been very busy with the dinosaur bones you got him. Mr. Holiday repaired all the holes he dug and Mrs. Holiday baked him snacks.

Me: He's a traitor.

Dagen: Don't worry, he won't forget you. In the meantime, it's getting late. You better get some sleep.

Michael: I know, goodnight, Sunshine.

Dagen: Night

Me: One last thing, in my bottom dresser drawer there are about a half dozen of my Rugby shirts. Wear them . . .*please.*

Dagen: lol goodnight. Hugs.

Chapter Sixteen

Dagen

He's been gone for ten days and it feels like ten months. I never thought I would get so attached to him. It hit me hard and fast. Maybe it's because I've been surrounded by everything Michael. Or his daily text messages that really pack a punch. He always starts his day with a "good morning, I miss you" text and ends it with a "good night, Sunshine ☺." I keep looking at those pictures he sent of his living conditions and it's worse than any summer camp. This place is going to feel like a palace to him. I can't believe how quickly I was able to pull so much together. As much as I never want it to end, I want to surprise him and have it done when he gets back. Only one more day and he'll be home. Part of me is excited and part of me is sad.

Music is my energy and I always have it playing while I work. I love the new Michael playlist I put together. Earbuds in, singing to one of my favorite groups, Lady Antebellum "Just A Kiss." While I'm putting the finishing touches on his office, I can't help but remember his lips brushing over mine. *'Are we gonna do this or what?'* When I turn around he's standing there. With his beautiful smile and golden tan, he takes my breath away. He reaches in and pulls one of my earbuds out, his hand stroking my cheek.

"I wasn't expecting you back until tomorrow."

"I see you took my advice and you're wearing my shirt." His voice is so deep and sensual.

"It made me feel like you were still here. Let me show you everything."

"Where is everyone?"

"Running errands but they should be back any minute." Before he can say anything, Preston comes barreling in and nearly knocks us both over. "I guess everyone is back. I told you he wouldn't forget you."

"How about you show me everything."

"Sure, well, as you can see I incorporated all of your models and the blueprints into your office." He's not saying anything, only staring at the plaque I had made for him.

"Success depends less on strength of body than upon strength of mind and character." —Arnold Palmer.

"I hope you like it. I know how much you love golf and, when I saw it, I knew you had to have it."

"I love it." He turns his attention to a long glass shelf that I filled with family pictures. "Where on earth did you get these?"

"Mrs. Osla. Once I learned to finally relax around her, it was easy. I still get tripped up every now and then on some of the things she says but, if nothing else, we have a good laugh about it. I'm not really sure who everyone is but Mrs. Osla said you would." He's not saying anything and now I'm really nervous. He picks up a picture of him at Jax and Raven's wedding. He's very young and absolutely adorable. He's in a tux and he's dancing with a beautiful lady. "I'm sorry; maybe I should have asked you first before I did this."

He finally looks up at me and the look of sadness on his face breaks my heart. "This was Rose. She was Aunt Raven's mum." He puts the picture back; apparently, he's not ready to talk about her. "How about I show you the rest of the house before Bo gets home?"

When we get to his *special* room, I step aside and let him open the door and go inside.

"Sweet Jesus, woman, it's un-fucking believable! How the hell did you get this together so fast? *Oh my God*, there's even a fully stocked TARDIS bar. This is the best man cave ever! Everywhere I look, I find another quote, some that I never gave you, how?"

I love his enthusiasm for everything. "I started by watching every Doctor Who episode I could get my hands on. You didn't tell me I would cry! Why didn't you warn me? Oh my God, the *Doomsday* episode shattered me."

"I didn't want to ruin it for you. The feels only come once. So now I have to ask you the question that every fan always asks: who is your favorite Doctor?"

"Even though every actor brought something to the role, it was David Tennant that owned it. Why the hell are there no women Doctors?"

"The world isn't ready for that, yet. Who is your favorite companion?"

"Rose, they were all good but she stole my heart."

"Come here." He pulls me into his arms, gently presses his lips against mine and whispers, "Thank you."

"We have one more room left, your bedroom." The shakiness in my voice at the mention of his bedroom is not lost on either of us. When we step into the room, I rapidly begin explaining the little bit I did in here. "I know you like a minimal amount of stuff so I kept it very simple with clean lines and a lot of white and gray tones."

"I love where you placed my first art purchase. Every night when I go to bed and in the morning when I wake up, it will be the first thing I see. I love it all."

I've convinced myself that as soon as the opportunity was right I'm going to take the plunge. Well, no time like the present. I take a breath to steady my nerves and step closer to him. My focus is on his lips. I want to feel them again, this time everywhere. I reach up and run my finger over them, just like he's done to mine. "Michael," I start. Preston takes this opportunity to drop his dinosaur bone on

Michael's bare foot. Michael jerks and our foreheads bang together. *Are you fucking kidding me?* We both laugh because honestly, that's all we can do at that point.

"I owe you a dinner at Bouchon, would you like to go tonight?"
Well, snap me back to reality; I'm an I.O.U.

"You just got home after ten days away, I'm sure there are a lot of things you need to catch up on. We can do it another time. I'm going to head home."

"Dagen, stop. What did I say that just shut the door in my face?"

"You don't owe me anything. I include a decorating service when my clients purchase a house from me, especially one of this magnitude."

"Time out. I thought we were past the business end of our relationship. I thought we were friends, what changed? Oh, for fucks sake." He pushes me up against the wall, his hands pressed onto the wall while his body is up against mine, so I'm trapped. The heat coming off of his body is insane. "I asked you to dinner because I'm trying to do anything and everything to spend time with you. You need to stop reading into things. I thought after Scotland you would understand that I say what I mean and mean what I say. I don't play games. Now, are you finally going to kiss me?"

"What happened to never a rebound and we need to stay friends?"

"I had ten long arse fucking days to think about all of this. We will always be friends, but for us that will never be enough; you're my more. All I'm asking for right now is one thing, so are you going to kiss me or not?"

I'm staring at him and I'm not sure what to do. *Should I take the chance or say no and regret it my whole life?*

"Get out of your head and listen to your heart."

Before he can say anything more I kiss him, hard. My tongue swirling around his like the *Dance of The Sugar Plum Fairy*, the slow steady movements of the ballerina building up to the big finish. I finally pull back and gently tug his bottom lip between my teeth. My legs are trembling and I don't know how much longer I can stand. He puts his arms around me, holding me tight. Holy hell, I can feel his cock pressing up against me, he is huge. If he continues to press into me, my damn panties will melt right off.

"I'm going to jump in the shower, be ready in thirty minutes. I want to have a picnic on the beach, just you and me." He pulls back, kisses the tip of my nose, and heads into the bathroom. The water is running and all I can think about is joining him. Not yet—too soon. I'm about to leave when I hear him singing. "You make me crazy and I kinda like it." It's Brett Eldredge's song "'Lose My Mind." I'm frozen in place, my legs not willing to move. Do I make him crazy? He sure as hell makes me crazy. The water shuts off and he steps out of the bathroom with only a towel wrapped around his waist. There is some sort of tat just below the V from his six-pack abs. I want to ask what it is but if he drops that towel any lower I might faint. My legs feel like Jell-O and now I really can't move.

"You might want to get ready unless you want me to put on a show for you."

My face is hotter than a five-alarm fire. "I love that song you were singing. I'll be going now and you can hang on to that towel." I turn and leave but not before he tosses his towel past me. I fight the urge to turn around, plus I know I'm a chicken shit when it comes to this stuff. He's laughing, and I close the door behind me.

Michael

The kiss. I've been thinking about those lips for ten long days and nights. They were worth the wait. Now I'm like a junkie who needs his fix. I've never had to wait for anyone, not even Heather. While she gets ready, I need to get everything together for a picnic on the beach. I find Mrs. Holiday busy in the kitchen.

"Hello, Mrs. Holiday, I hope some of those are for people."

"Oh, yes, Mr. Vizzano, but I can't help but spoil Preston."

"It's okay, but can you please call me Michael? I'm not a formal guy and I rather you save that for my dad."

"Well, if I'm going to call you Michael, then you need to be less formal with me."

"How about Mrs. H?"

"Perfect. Now what can I do for you?"

"Did my car get delivered and were you able to keep it hidden from Dagen?"

"Yes, my husband stashed it in the garage behind the guest house. It's beautiful. I think she will be surprised. Do you want me to have him pull it up front?"

"Yes, please. I want to put together a picnic basket to take to the beach; what do you have for me?"

"Give me a few minutes and I will pack everything for you."

"Thank you, I'll be in my office for a bit."

I head to the office and I notice so many little touches of Dagen everywhere. She really made this place my home. I would love to call Mrs. Osla, but the time difference makes it impossible. I pull up my email; there are six messages in my spam folder from Heather and that's where they'll stay. Why can't she just let it go? I don't want to deal with any of this. Besides, Dagen should be about ready to go. I get up to leave and my guitar catches my eye. I grab it and head out. Hopefully she's ready. I head towards the kitchen and I hear her talking to Bo.

"Hey, you're back. How was work?"

"It was intense but good. The days fly but the nights drag. We'll catch up tomorrow; Dagen and I are going to dinner." With my arm around her waist I'm practically pushing her towards the door, leaving him no chance to suggest that he come too.

"Before we go any further, I need you to close your eyes."

"Why?"

"Humor me, please."

When I know they are closed, I guide her along to the side of the house where my car is waiting. Damn, it's a beauty.

"Okay, you can open them now."

"Oh my God, it's beautiful! When did you find the time to get it ordered and delivered here? I've been here the whole time, how did I not see this?"

"I'm a Ninja when it comes to keeping a secret. I might even let you drive her."

"Oh, so how do you know it's a girl?"

"I know because the Aston Martin DB11 is beautiful, yet powerful. It takes a man to be able to handle her, and she has the power to bring a grown man to his knees. So, you see, she is a girl."

"Well, there is no arguing with that logic." She smiles. I open the door and she steps in.

"Perfect."

"I made a playlist for us, it's on my phone." I unlock my phone and hand it to her. She is staring at it with a funny look on her face. "What?"

"I'm your screensaver."

"Yeah, the apple picture is one of my favorites."

"I have a lot of the same songs." She hits play and "Ready Set Roll" by Chase Rice comes on and I can't help myself, I sing along, "You've gone and turned your sexy all the way up to ten."

"You have such a great voice, I can listen to you sing all day long."

"I love music, like good books, you can get lost in it for hours. I was thinking about having a small studio built, what do you think?"

"There's tons of room and it would be great for resale purposes."

"Dagen, I'm not selling my home; I'm here to stay. Can I hire you to oversea the project?"

"Are you coming up with things to keep me around or do you

really want a studio?"

I pull into a parking spot and cut the engine. "I really want a studio, but, more than that, I want you around. I don't need to come up with excuses to make you stay." I lean in and gently kiss her, over and over again. "Now, about that picnic. . ." I get out and grab everything from the boot. When I look for her, she's still sitting in the car, her fingers pressed on her lips. She's startled when I open the door for her.

"Sorry, I got a little lost there for a bit."

"Nothing to be sorry about. Let's go find a spot to catch the sunset."

We find a secluded area and have everything set up in no time. Mrs. H packs one hell of a picnic basket, even including candles.

"So, tell me how did you really like living in such tight quarters?"

"It was very different than anything I've ever done before. I tried to stay very busy until I was ready to drop, otherwise, I would have gone nuts. I'm not going to be on that rig much longer."

"Why?"

"Part of my contract states that I have to travel to other rigs within the United States and make sure all of them are operating at or above current safety standards. With the prediction of a bad hurricane season, I might go to the Gulf of Mexico and work my way back to the west coast."

"Are you not going to come back home?" She looks sad and I never want to see that on her beautiful face.

"I promise you, sunshine, I will always come home. I'm not done yet at the rig that I'm currently working on; I'll go back there in two weeks to finish up. So you're stuck with me for at least the next two weeks."

She hands me my guitar. "Will you play something for me?"

"Any requests?"

"Whatever you want."

I play a few cords, trying to figure out what to play and then it hits me and I go right into Sam Hunt's "Make You Miss Me." It seems like the perfect choice. "No more waiting, hesitating, it's guaranteed." She slides a little closer. "I'm gonna make you want to kiss me." All I can think of is those sweet lips. I put the guitar aside, and put my hands on her neck, pulling her close and kiss her. Gentle at first but then she slides her hands under my t-shirt and I lose all reason. Trying to gain some sort of control of the situation, I stop kissing her lips and work my way down her neck and nip at her shoulder.

"Your skin prickles at my touch, every time. I swear every inch is begging for a kiss."

She tilts her head giving me full access to that sexy neck. I trail my tongue slowly from her shoulder up her neck. I nip at her ear and she moans, parting her lips, the perfect invitation for me. With every swirl of her tongue my cock is fighting his restraints. I pull back and take a breath.

"If we don't slow this down, I won't be able to control myself."

"Is that a bad thing?"

"When I have you and, sunshine, I will have you, it will not be a quick shag on the beach with our detail in the shadows."

"Sometimes I forget they are there."

"I haven't. Besides, I want to devour every inch of your beautiful body, nice and slow. I want to make you scream over and over again."

"A little cocky, don't you think?"

"No, I'm being honest. I want to take my time, enjoy you. It's not a race to the finish line, it's the journey along the way that makes it all worth while." I pour some more wine.

She holds up her glass, "Here's to a fantastic journey."

I pull her close to me and capture those lips again. I can't seem to get enough of them. They're full, warm, and sweet. My hand brushes across her breast and her nipples are hard. I trail kisses up and down her neck. I pull away before I can't stop.

"Can you stay with me for the next two weeks?"

"I have to go home tomorrow. I have stuff pending at work that I need to handle. You could come down to my place for dinner tomorrow."

"Okay, I can get stuff done around here and I will drive down to you. We better start packing up; there's a storm that's going to hit pretty quickly."

"How can you tell?"

"Count from when you see the lightening and then hear the thunder. The closer the gap the closer the storm." I watch her counting and I can't help but laugh.

"What's so funny?"

"I haven't heard 'One Mississippi, Two Mississippi' since I was a kid."

We race to the car, but the heavens open up before we get there. When we get in the car, I turn towards her and I'm blown away. The dim light of the car casts a glow, her hair is wild and wet, her lips are parted and, dear God, if I don't look away, I won't be able to control myself. She reaches out and takes my hand. My jaw is tight and I'm fighting for control. I tell myself to breath but then I glance over and her wet shirt is fighting a losing battle to keep her nipples restrained. When the next thunder claps and the lightening strike lights up the sky, she grabs my thigh. "Oh bloody hell, woman."

I hit the button for her seat and it glides back giving me more access to her. I pull her into a kiss and then work my way down her neck. She lets out another fucking moan. "If you moan like that again, my cock will explode." I kiss her nipples through her shirt and I swear they are the perkiest damn things I've ever seen. When I nip at them she loses all control, and tries to pull me into her seat with her.

"Michael, I thought you wanted—." Before she can finish, I kiss her long and hard, over and over again. When I finally pull back

I look at her and her lips are puffy and her hair is wild. I rest my forehead on hers.

"You're going to be the death of me, sunshine." I adjust myself as I sit back up, start the car, and head towards home, knowing this night is far from over for both of us.

Chapter Seventeen

THE RIDE HOME SEEMED TO TAKE FOREVER WHEN, IN reality, it only took fifteen minutes. I wanted to wait, build up to this. I wanted to show her that I'm all in here, no fucking about. When it comes to this woman, I have lost my frigging mind; all reasoning is shot to hell. When I pull up in front of the house, I cut the engine. I want to talk to her. I need to put all my cards on the table, but before I can say anything, she pulls me towards her and kisses me, hard. Fuck me; I'm done.

"I want you, Michael," she whispers when she pulls back.

My eyes search hers and she doesn't look away. "Are you sure?"

She kisses me again, "Yes."

I'm out of the car in a flash. I open her door, reach in and lift her into my arms. I'm kissing her with no intention of stopping for anyone or anything. I race in the door and head directly to my bedroom kicking the door closed behind me.

"Michael, can you dim the lights."

I look at her and I know why and I'll have no part of it. "No, when are you going to realize that your are beautiful? Please don't hide from me, not now, not ever." I put her on the edge of the bed and kneel down in front of her. I want to make this all about her. I need to make her feel beautiful and not with just my words. I reach for her again and I freeze. When I close my eyes that fucking report is all I can see. The words swirling around like water going down the drain—*rape*.

"Michael, are you okay?"

Why do I have to always be so righteous? "We need to talk."

Before I can say anything, she pushes me, I land on my arse and she's trying to race out the door. "Dagen, stop, please let me talk."

"If you don't want me, be man enough and just say so."

I get up and run to stop her. "Will you please sit down and let me talk. After that, if you want to walk away, I won't stop you." She takes a seat on the bed, quickly wiping away her tears. It guts me to think I put them there. "I told you only part of why Heather left. I wasn't sure I would ever share any of this with anyone, but I realized tonight that if I want more with you, then you have the right to know. I won't go into great detail, but you need to know that my family has been hurt a lot. You've seen first hand how overprotective they are." I take a breath and steady my nerves. "It all started with my grandfather; he's a bigamist. Uncle Max has a different mum than Uncle Jax and my mum. This next part is really sick, but I feel you have the right to know everything. My grandfather was responsible for the murder of Uncle Max's first wife and son. Apparently, his cousin set my mum up to be raped as a warning to him. I'm the product of that rape. To top it all off, he's also the one who donated the plasma that saved my life."

She's not saying anything. I don't know what I expected when I dropped this bombshell but silence wasn't it. "My mum was at a convention, she was drugged, beaten, and raped. She has no idea who my real father is. My dad married her right before I was born and raised me as his own."

"Why are you telling me this now?"

"I wasn't going to ever tell anyone, but I realized that's wrong. You know I base everything on honesty. What kind of man would that make me if I didn't tell you? My silence would go against everything I believe in."

"So, this is why Heather left you?"

"Yes, her dad had a report waiting for me with all of my family's history. I never knew about the rape. I only learned about it when I read the report. She thought I knew and kept it from her."

"When you finally read the report did you confront her?"

"I wasn't going to but then she emailed me, and if that's not bad enough she made it sound like she would be doing me a favor if we tried to get back together." Her cheeks instantly flush and her grip on my arm just got a hell of a lot tighter.

"Oh my God, are you serious? What the fuck is wrong with her? It's not like you had any say in any of this. Did she even know you? I mean I think I know you better in this short time then she ever did."

Her defending me is beautiful. "I'm an open book and I thought she knew that. If she had questions, all she had to do is ask. As far as I'm concerned, she took the coward's way out."

"Does my brother know any of this?"

"No."

"You know what, Michael, it's no one's business but yours and your parents. Were you worried that I would look at you different-ly?"

"Yes, maybe. I don't know. All I know is I don't like secrets, which is why I'm usually an open book." I'm looking down, afraid to look at her, afraid of what I might see.

"Michael, look at me, please." I look into her eyes, expecting to see pity or disgust and instead I see compassion, something I didn't see when Heather gave me that report. "It doesn't change anything for me. You're a reflection of the parents who raised you, not some random guy's DNA. If we're being honest here, then I've got to tell you I went to Scotland with you, not just to decorate this place but to find out who the real Michael is. Seeing all the love and respect everyone in your family shows each other was beautiful."

I want to laugh, maybe she's reading the same fortune cookies as Uncle Jax. "Thank you."

"Heather's an asshole. I'm sorry, but I just had to put that out there."

"Yes she is, but I'm glad cause if she wasn't, I never would have met you." I kiss her, soft gentle kisses.

She pulls back and rests her fingers on my lips. "Michael, I thought tonight would end a lot differently, but when I have you, I want all of you. No distractions, no baggage, only us."

I can't help but smile. "Oh, when you have me? Is that the way this is going to go?"

Her cheeks flush and I can't help but laugh. "You know what I mean. Anyway, it's late. I'm wet, cold, and I have an early day tomorrow. Apparently, I have to impress a certain someone with my culinary skills for dinner tomorrow night."

"I'm looking forward to it."

"Goodnight, Michael."

I kiss her goodnight and walk her to the guest room. Knowing that she's on the other side of that wall is going to be a real test of my willpower.

After a long hot shower I'm still not able to sleep, so I might as well get some work done. I head into my office and take a longer look around at everything. She did such an amazing job. I sit at my desk and just take in the entire room. There's only one thing missing. I open my computer and pull up the pictures from our trip to Scotland. One is more beautiful than the next. I find the perfect one to display on my desk. Dagen is a few feet in front of me, sitting on Tequila. We are in the lavender field, her head is turned towards me and the sun is shining. She looks like she doesn't have a care in the world. I hit print and tomorrow I will find the perfect frame for it.

Next on my to-do list is to send an email to Antonia. I hope she finally came to a decision on school. When I open my email, I notice I now have nine messages from Heather. What the fuck is her problem? I glance through them, all the same drivel. She's either in love with me or feels sorry for me. She almost sounds like she's having a mental breakdown. When I get to the last one, I feel my blood pressure rising. Now she's saying that my mum is threatening her. If I ask Mum, she'll get upset and that's the last thing I want. Uncle Jax might know what's going on and if not, he'll get to the bottom of it.

Me: Hey, you busy?

Jax: Never too busy for you, what's up?

Me: I got a bunch of emails from Heather. She is claiming that Mum threatened her and she wants to get a non-harassment order. Did Mum do something?

Jax: Knowing your mum, probably. Do you want my opinion?

Me: Is it going to piss me off?

Jax: Wise arse. I would do nothing. If you acknowledge her emails, that keeps the line of communication open. She's grasping at straws.

Me: That was my plan, but I don't want Mum getting upset over this. It's my problem, not hers.

Jax: She's your mum and when someone hurts you, they hurt her. The lioness will always protect her cubs.

Me: Don't tell me more fortune cookies.

Jax: lol yep, gotta love those things. How's everything else?

Me: Work is very busy; sleeping in a bunk is an odd

experience. Not something on my bucket list. I'm only going to be on my current rig for maybe two more weeks and then I'm going to the Gulf of Mexico. The weather service is predicting a busy hurricane season. I need to make sure everything is running properly.

He's not answering me. I know he wants me in a bubble but that's not going to happen.

Me: Hello, are you there????

Jax: Yeah, why can't you do something safe? I was just getting somewhat used to you being out there and now you want to put yourself in the middle of hurricanes. Between you and Antonia, it's a wonder I have any hair left.

Me: lol I will be fine. What's going on with Antonia?

Jax: I don't know what you said to her but she has agreed to do her prerequisites at a University in Scotland as long as Grace goes along with it. So you bought me some time.

Me: Glad I was able to help. I made a decision; I told Dagen why Heather ended it. I can't live a lie, even if it is a lie of omission. I wouldn't want it done to me so how could I do it to someone else?

Jax: So you decided you want a relationship with her. What happened when you told her?

Me: It was hard for me cause I still feel like it's Mum's

business but it involves me. I don't know what I was expecting, but she said it doesn't change anything for her. She also said I'm the reflection of the parents who raised me and not some guys random DNA. I swear she must be reading the same fortune cookies as you.

Jax: I'm glad you haven't shut yourself off. I was worried you would shy away from having a relationship again. Just remember, you're not in a race.

Me: Thanks. She finished my house and it's wonderful. I really feel like it's my home. Wait till you see my man cave. There is a fully stocked TARDIS bar!

Jax: Wait! You have a TARDIS bar? You need to send me the pictures right away.

Me: Of course I will. I also decided I want to build a music studio and Dagen agreed to help me with it.

Jax: I know how much you love music. I think it will be a good outlet for you when you're not dealing with a hurricane.

Me: Funny, very funny. Good night.

Jax: lol Good night.

Chapter Eighteen

I DON'T KNOW WHAT TIME I FINALLY FELL ASLEEP LAST NIGHT; I only know the feeling of sleeping in my own bed and not a little bunk is surreal. When I finally get my sorry arse out of bed, the only one I see is Bo, out back, having coffee. I grab some and head out to join him.

"Where is everyone?"

"If you mean Dagen, she left early this morning. The Holidays went to town to pick up supplies. How the hell are you?"

"Good; work is very busy. Have you been following the weather forecast for this year's hurricane season?"

"Yeah, they are predicting a bad one. Will that change your schedule?"

"I will have to switch some things around but it shouldn't be that big of a deal. The worse part of my job is the fucking bunk I have to sleep in."

"It could always be worse. So, you and Dagen?"

"What about us?"

"So, it's an 'us'?"

"We talked about this already, is there a problem?"

"You're my best friend and she's my sister; just don't hurt her. I don't know how much she told you and honestly it's her business, but she doesn't trust very easily."

"She told me about the guy that took her from school. I have no intention of ever hurting her." I get up and pour us each more coffee.

"I trust you, Mike, it's just me wanting to protect her."

"Look, I'm going to her house for dinner tonight. I was planning on spending the day exploring outside of Santa Barbara. Why don't you come with me and I might even let you drive my new car." That should make him happy.

"Wait, you got a new car? What kind? When did this happen?"

"Well, if you slow down and let me get a word in edgewise I will tell you. It's an Aston Martin DB11. I was going to go car shopping but Uncle Max surprised me and had it on preorder for quite some time. I originally wanted the DB10 but they only made five of them specifically for the Bond movie. She's a beauty."

"You'll really let me drive her?"

I can't help but laugh at him. "Sure, come on let's see what she can do."

When we head towards the garage, my girl is waiting for us, nice and clean after last night's storm. "Now remember, she's got a lot of power, so take it easy."

He presses the ignition and she comes to life. "Jesus Christ, Mike, that alone is enough to make a grown man cry."

"Yep, there's nothing in the world quite like that sound."

"Where to?"

"Pacific Coast Highway, for starters. I want to pick something up for Dagen. So, what do you suggest?"

"Not for nothing but, for a guy, lately you do an awful lot of shopping. Are you sure you didn't lose your man card?"

"Keep laughing, arsehole, and I will take over the driving," I threaten. He changes his tune real quickly. "So, any suggestions? She worked hard on the house and even though she said it's a service that she provides with the purchase of a home from her, I want to give her something."

"Get her something that is important to you. She loves music, art, and animals. She's not a showy person. I don't know what else to tell you."

"So, a car is out of the question."

"Now who's the asshole?"

I pull out my phone and with a few clicks I've got it. The perfect gift that she'll have beyond this lifetime along with something from Tiffany's that I have to pick up.

"So, where do you want to go?"

"I want to do some tourist stuff: Rodeo Drive, Hollywood, and, if we have time, Venice Beach."

"You got it. Now put some damn music on."

I turn on the sound system and after messing around with it, I find some station playing an hour of driving music. I'm about to sync my phone and access my playlist when I hear Richie Sambora's opening to the classic Bon Jovi hit "It's My Life." The ultimate driving song and in the DB11 it's like sitting in the front row of the best damn concert ever. I swear this song could have been written about me. "I just want to live while I'm alive." Hell, yeah. Not sure who's singing louder, Bo or me. When it's over, they go back to some elevator nonsense, total mood killer.

"I asked Dagen if she would head up a project for me. I want to have a music studio built. She said she would. When we were in Scotland, she played the piano for me. She's fantastic."

"I always thought she would play professionally."

"What happened? I mean she's really very talented, so why do you think she didn't pursue it?"

"Even though she is a very strong person, she's also a very shy person. Most people don't realize that. Her self-esteem is not the greatest."

"That's the part I don't get. She's the whole package: sweet, kind, strong, and beautiful, yet she doesn't see it. Was she always like this or was she different when she was finally rescued from that guy?"

He changes lanes and slows to a somewhat normal speed. "Yeah, well, after we got her back, she was never the same. She was always positive, bright, and optimistic. After him, she became with-drawn and full of self-doubt. Let me ask you something, Mike. After you were kidnapped, how did you deal with life? I mean, I know you were younger than she was, but still, it had to be hard."

"When something like that happens, it's very easy to lose trust in people. I was a kid and the people around me fought to help me. The way she explained it, he took her right out of her class and no one helped. I had some counseling but then soon after, I got sick. I was constantly in survivor mode. It sounds like she retreated within herself."

"Maybe now that she has a guard on her all the time she might feel safe."

"If only it was that easy. She has to learn to trust herself again. Don't forget he was someone that she trusted and cared about. No one helped her, not even her teacher."

"Now that I'm home, I want to be around her more. Maybe that will help her. I hate that she lives so far away from me."

"Do you think she would ever move?" If only I could find a way to keep her around more.

"No, she has her friends and her business in Beverly Hills, plus our parents are only five minutes from her. Eventually, you will run out of things for her to do and you are gone for two weeks at a time."

I'm starting to understand why Uncle Jax likes everyone under one roof.

He pulls off the freeway and when we get to Rodeo Drive I'm taken back. It's a rich man's paradise. "This is amazing, it's like an outdoor who's who of the shopping world."

"Man card, Mike." He valets the car so we can take in the sites on foot.

"I've walked all over Paris, London, Switzerland, and Scotland, but I never had so many people stare at me before. What the fuck is their problem?"

He's laughing but I don't find this amusing at all, it's actually uncomfortable.

"We are two relatively good looking guys who just got out of a very expensive car. We are walking with four men in suits, following close behind. They either think we are rich, famous or both. Don't be surprised if women and men start slipping us their numbers."

"I thought you said we would fit in here?"

"Mike, look around; we do." I look around and he's right. My Aston fits right in with the Lamborghini, Ferrari, and the Rolls that lines the valet lot.

"I need to stop in Tiffany's and then let's have lunch at The Beverly Hills Hotel."

"Tiffany's, really? I told you to keep it simple."

I wave my hand and keep walking. "Yeah, yeah, I heard you. I know what I want and don't worry, it's simple." That finally shuts him up.

Tiffany's has my package ready for me and we are in and out in minutes. Now, for the tourist stuff. When we get to the Beverly Hills Hotel, it's like old time Hollywood.

"Mike, I can't believe how much you're enjoying this."

"Bo, remember where I grew up." That shuts him up right away.

"You better text Dagen and let her know I came with you. Unless, of course, you want to be alone. I can always drive home."

"Wipe that smirk off your face. You drove enough; I get to drive home. I'll text her."

Me: Hey, sunshine, guess where I am.

Dagen: Well, if I had that car, I would be driving up and down PCH.

Me: Close, I'm at the Beverly Hills Hotel, having lunch and movie star watching.

Dagen: OMG you're such a dork. Lol

Me: Not feeling the love here, babe. Bo is with me.

Dagen: Sorry. So it will be the three of us tonight?

Me: Guess you can't have your way with me tonight.

Dagen: Pretty confident that tonight was your night.

Me: Leaving it up to the stars, sunshine.

Dagen: What time are you coming over?

Me: I'm doing the tourist stuff today. My next stop: Hollywood Walk of Fame, Sunset Strip, and, if we have time, Venice Beach.

Dagen: OMG you crack me up. Dinner is at 8. Enjoy the experience. Hugs.

"Okay, she said dinner is at eight so we better get going, lots to see."

"I can't believe you're making me do all the tourist shit."

"Hello, David Tennant, has a star on the Hollywood Walk of Fame, did you really think I wouldn't have you take me there."

"Come on, Mike, we've got a lot to get done in a short time." When we get to the car I let him drive so I can take pictures. "So . . . what did you get at Tiffany's?"

"Don't worry; it's just a little trinket to go with something else I got her. I'm going to give it to her when the timing is right".

"Don't worry; I won't blow it for you. Seriously, man, if you want me to make myself scarce tonight, I can."

Part of me wants to say yes but I want everything to be perfect. "We're good, Bo; stick to the plan."

We get to Hollywood and it's everything I thought it would be. I got my picture taken with David Tennant's star.

"Mike, what are you doing?"

"I'm texting this picture to Uncle Jax." He's laughing and I almost get knocked over by a group of people that just got off a tour bus.

"If you want to get to the beach, we need to leave now. This is the only day I'm playing tour guide."

"I'll get Dagen to take me to San Francisco." I stand back up just as he rolls his eyes and I can't help but laugh at him. "Hey, life is short and I never want to say 'What if?' You never know what's waiting around the bend in the road."

"Oh, I know what's waiting: my ass, handed to me on a silver platter if we're late."

We head to Venice Beach and it is amazing. It reminds me, in some ways, of Camden Market in London. Our detail is not too happy with all the open areas and the massive crowds. We find a tattoo shop with some incredible designs and a line out the door. "Bo, do you know anything about this guy's work?"

"Yeah, he's pretty well known around here. He did the wave on my back. You thinking of getting another one?"

"No, mate, one's enough." I vividly remember the pain and that's not something I want to visit anytime soon.

"We better get going before we're late. Am I still driving?"

"Yeah, I'll drive home tonight."

After a bit of a commute, we pull up to Dagen's house and it's fantastic. It's very small, and it is tucked in between two very large homes. Massive trees and different level stone gardens surround the entire house. "This is amazing. I've never seen anything like this."

"Wait till you see the inside. She renovated the home herself. Come on, I'll let her tell you all about her baby, as she calls it." We step inside and she yells from the kitchen for Bo to show me around. It's a two bedroom, one bath Spanish style cottage home, probably built in the early 1920's. The living room has a huge fireplace, but it's the ceiling that is amazing. It's a pitched, wooden ceiling with beams that run the full length of the house. In one corner, overlooking the room, is a baby grand piano. When we get to the kitchen, it smells amazing.

"I figured we could eat out back. Michael, can you light the torches, please. Bo, start bringing the food out back," she barks out the orders. I'm watching the dishes go by me and each one looks better than the last. I cook to survive but she cooks with passion. "Michael, snap out of it. The sooner we get everything set up the sooner you can eat."

"Every thing looks and smells fantastic."

We head out back and dig into the most amazing Chinese food ever.

"You really made all this yourself from scratch?"

"Yes, I told you I love to cook. I just wish I had a bigger kitchen."

"This house is beautiful and the living room ceiling is unreal."

"I used all reclaimed wood. I picked this house up at an auction. It was slated to be demolished, but I knew it had good bones. I brought it down to the studs and worked my way up. It took me almost a year to get it all done."

"That's dedication."

"I read that when you're doing something you love, it's not work."

I hold up my fortune cookie. "Don't tell me you read it in a fortune cookie."

"As a matter of fact, yes," she replies. I can't stop laughing. "Mind sharing what's so funny?"

"Uncle Jax quotes them all the time. I swear I thought he just made that shit up."

"Never dis the fortune cookie."

"Oh, I have to show you my picture; hold on." I pull out my phone to show her and there's a text message from Heather. I quickly left swipe it to delete it hoping she didn't see it. I pull up the picture and she's smiling.

"I see you had fun today."

"Yes I did, and I still have some things I want to do."

"Dagen, you're taking him on the next adventure."

"I'd be happy to, just let me know when and where."

"I want to see San Francisco. Do you want to go tomorrow?"

"It's better if we do it during the week while everyone is at work, maybe it won't be so crowded. Besides, I have to work tomorrow."

"Okay, whatever day you decide, I'm in. Bo, you sure you don't want to come with us?"

"Positive. Come on, let's read our fortunes. Remember you have to add 'in bed' at the end of them."

"Okay, Michael, you go first."

I take a cookie out of the bowl and pop it open. "Are you sure I have to add 'in bed' at the end of it?"

"Yes, come on, what does it say?"

"Change can hurt, but it leads a path to something better, in bed. Well, that's interesting"

"Okay, Dagen, you're up next." Bo waves a finger at her.

"Don't be afraid to smile, you never know who's falling in love with you, in bed."

"I couldn't agree more." I wink at her before bringing my attention to her brother. "Come on, Bo, stop laughing and read yours."

"Never give up. Always find a reason to keep trying, in bed."

Dagen turns beet red and I can't stop laughing. "Oh my God, that's too fucking funny."

"I'm glad you're amused. Since you're driving, I'm getting another beer." He heads inside and before he's even out the door, my lips are on hers.

"Mmm, you taste so good."

"Don't." She pulls away from me.

"Hey, what's wrong?"

"Are you still in touch with Heather?"

She saw the text on my phone. I pull it out and hand it to her. "Go ahead and look at the text messages, you'll see I've never answered them." She pushes the phone back towards me.

"I don't want to look. I asked you and I would rather *you* tell me."

"She has been emailing me, and I don't answer her. She contacted Antonia and after talking to my cousin about it, I'm sure she was sorry she did. I answered her first email and told her not to contact me again. I told you you would never be a rebound. I would like to think that you trust me and believe me."

"I'm sorry, I just kind of freaked when I saw her name."

"She is the past and that's where she's going to stay. Come on, I'll help you clean up, then we've got to get going. Since you're working, I want to drag Bo's arse out of bed and hike Inspiration Point in the morning. Are you sure you can't come?"

"No. You guys have fun. Even though it's Sunday, I have a client coming in tomorrow. Michael, are we okay?"

I get up and pull her towards me and kiss her. When we finally pull apart my heart is racing. "Sunshine, we are fine. We're finding our way and there will be a few bumps, nothing that we can't get past."

"Okay. Will you please text me and let me know you got home safe?"

"We will be fine, no need to worry."

"Well, you have that new powerhouse car and you're just getting use to driving in the States, so yeah, I'm worried." She starts lifting the plates off the table. I help her carry everything in the house and find Bo falling asleep on the couch.

"Get your sorry arse up, we've got to get going."

After he chugs down the rest of his beer, we head out the door but not before I get another sweet kiss goodnight. When we get into the car, I pull out my phone and check Heather's message. It's another plea for me to call her.

"Mike, I thought we were going, what's going on?"

"Blocking Heather. She's been emailing me and I've been ignoring them but now she is texting."

"Knowing you, I'm surprised you waited this long to block her."

"She contacted Antonia and—"

"Wait why the hell did she contact Antonia?"

I'm look at him and alarm bells are ringing in my head. "You and Antonia aren't . . . you know?"

"No, Mike, I just know what a bitch Heather can be."

"Yeah, well, Antonia tore her a new arsehole. Which is what I expected. I didn't block her because it would be like poking a hungry bear. She hasn't tried to contact you has she?"

"Hell no, she hates me! But, if she gets desperate, she might. I'll let you know if she does. So, Antonia ripped into her, good?" He's smiling and the hair on the back of my neck is standing on end.

"Bo, I swear, you better stay away from her. She's young, very inexperienced and, if you value your life, you will stay away."

"Relax, Mike, I know better. Come on, let's get going, we have an early hike tomorrow." We head out but I don't think this is over, not by a long shot.

Chapter Nineteen

Dagen

I CAN'T BELIEVE I LET A STUPID TEXT MESSAGE FREAK ME OUT. I thought after all she did he would have blocked her. I can only imagine what Antonia said to her. The little bit I was around her, I was quick to figure out she wouldn't take anyone's bullshit.

Michael: Home safe and sound. What are you up to?

Me: I just got into bed with a book.

Michael: I would much rather be there with you instead of your book.

Me: It's a good book.

Michael: I'm better ☺

Me: I see Mr. Cocky has come out to play. Lol

Michael: What book?

Me: Why do you want to know?

Michael: I want to know everything about you.

Me: Oh, I thought you wanted some pointers.

Michael: Now, sunshine, I think I've got that department covered.

Me: We will see.

Michael: Careful what you wish for, babe.

Me: You better get some sleep; you have an early hike tomorrow.

Michael: After the hike, we are going to the beach. Bo is going to teach me how to surf. This should be interesting.

Me: Are you trying to fit everything you possibly can into each and every day?

Michael: Life is short and there's no luggage rack on the hearse.

Me: Fortune cookie?

Michael: No that's not from a fortune cookie; Aunt Raven always says that.

Me: Check in when you can; I won't be working late.

Michael: Sweet dreams, sunshine

Me: Night, hugs.

For the last two weeks I've been working on a surprise for him. As much as I really wanted to spend the day with him, tomorrow I will be in Nevada at the Butch Harmon School of Golf for my last private lesson. I can't wait to show him what I've learned. Thanks to my dad's connections, I was even able to snag a reservation for golf on Tuesday at Cypress Point Club in Pebble Beach.

I give up on reading my book and call it a night. Hopefully after all these lessons, I won't need as many Advil's and Epsom salt baths.

Michael

When we get home, I find Preston sprawled out on the sofa between Mr. and Mrs. H., watching a movie. I swear he's a traitor; he didn't even lift his head up to greet me.

Rather than disturb them, I head into my office to deal with this Heather bullshit. I start by checking her text message. It's nasty and vile. How the hell was I ever involved with this woman, let alone getting ready to marry her? After she sent the email about my mum I thought it was best to ignore her but, after reading this last one, I don't think she's going away.

Heather,

It was your choice to end our relationship, now you're having second thoughts? Don't. It was the best thing you've ever done for me. Do not contact me or anyone in my family, for that matter. I can't help it that you have regrets. You chose this path, now deal with it. Please be an adult about all of this and move on or it *will be you I get a non-harassment order on! Michael*

I hit send and then block her from everything. Preston comes strolling in and curls up under my desk. "What's the matter, traitor, movie over and no more popcorn?"

He moans and rests his head on my foot. I'm replaying my conversation with Bo in my head and I know he's not telling me everything. I know it's early there but I need to talk to her now.

Me: Facetime me now.

Antonia: I'm half asleep. Are you okay?

Me: Now!

Antonia: Grrrr

"Michael, what the hell is wrong with you, do you know what time it is?"

"I know, but I need to see your face when I ask you this. Are you getting involved with Bo?" Antonia can't lie to me to save her life. She can bullshit everyone and anyone but me. She's staring into the phone and she's not answering me.

"It's not what you think," she finally says.

"Oh, and you know what I'm thinking? If you did, you would be afraid for his life right now."

"Michael, all we do is talk sometimes. He listens to me. I swear there is nothing going on."

"If that's the case then why keep it from me?"

"Because you're as bat-shit-crazy as my dad!"

"Only with you; you're the only one who is able to push all my buttons!"

"Really? And all these years I thought I was just a tag along brat."

"You used to be able to talk to me about anything and everything, what changed?"

"Sometimes, Michael, I just need someone outside of this family to talk to. I still talk to you about stuff. You're the only one who knows what Grace and I really want to do. How's that make you feel?"

"Laughing and teasing me is not helping your case."

"He's your best friend, I would think you would trust him."

"I trust him with my life, but you're a lot younger than him and he's very experienced."

"Oh my God, when did you become my father?"

"Just promise me you won't do anything more then chat."

"Yes, I promise. Now, what happened? Don't try to deny it; the road for us goes both ways."

"Heather—that's what happened. She's sent numerous emails and now text messages. I was at Dagen's house for dinner and she saw a text come in from her."

"Oh, well you're just friends so it shouldn't be a big deal, right?"

"Wipe that smirk off your face. After being away from her for two weeks, I know I want more. She's honest, compassionate, funny, and beautiful. She's the real deal, Antonia. There—I said it, are you happy now?"

"I knew that when you brought her home. I'm amazed how dense men can be sometimes. Anyway, what happened when she saw it?"

"Of course she got upset. I assured her that Heather is in the past."

"What did you do about Heather?"

"I told her to stop all contact and blocked her on everything."

"I thought you did that already?"

"I emailed her before and told her there's no chance to get back together but I didn't block her."

"Why? That's not like you. What were you so worried about?"

"You and my mum. Apparently, my mum went to see Heather. I got an email that she wanted to take out a non-harassment order against her."

"Way to go, Aunt Bella! Wish I could have gone with her; I would have kicked her arse and enjoyed it. Oh I know we could have brought Grams along—now *that* would have been fun."

"You see what I mean? You don't need to encourage my mum or anyone else, for that matter."

"Look, Michael, you can block her all you want, but if she wants to get in touch with you, she'll find a way."

"Did you ever like her?"

"I did in the beginning but you know, it's like my mum always says, the first six months the cleaning lady is on her best behavior—after that—it's a crap shoot."

I can't help but laugh at her analogy. "Well, thanks for clearing that up for me. So what do you think will happen with Dagen in six months?"

"Well, what happened with Bo after six months? After all, they are twins."

"They're nothing alike. Bo goes with the flow. Dagen is just different; I can't explain it. I guess time will tell all. By the way, I'm going hiking tomorrow morning with Bo and then he is going to teach me how to surf."

"I want pictures of you trying to surf. When you get more into a routine maybe I can come for a visit. There are a lot of things to see and do in California."

More like Bo is here and she wants to see him. "We will figure something out. You should see my man cave."

"I already heard about it from my dad. He told my mum about it and she just waved him off. I swear the only one who will listen to him when he talks about that show is Mrs. Osla. In saying that, I think he took your move the hardest."

I feel a knot in my gut. "I know it's hard to explain, but he's always been more than just my uncle. I know Heather never got it."

"Maybe she was jealous of the relationship. If that's the case, it usually ends up a disaster."

"Why?"

"Why was she jealous or why is it a disaster?"

"Both."

"If she is jealous, she would try and pull you away from him and the rest of the family. Not that we would ever let that happen, but it would make for a lot of tension. If you become more involved with Dagen, you need to let her see from the start that you and my dad are not just family, He's your rock and you keep him humble."

"You amaze me."

"Don't get to excited; I read and pay attention. I mean, what the hell else is there to do around here?"

"It's getting late; I've got to try and get some sleep. We will talk soon."

"Don't forget my pictures of you surfing." She's laughing no doubt anticipating some blackmail material.

"Goodnight."

She hangs up but I'm still staring at the blank screen. I'm not tired at all, so I grab my guitar, a beer and head out back with Preston trailing behind me. No doubt annoyed that I keep waking him up. Losing myself in music helps to clear my head and tonight, I really need that. The breeze coming off the Pacific is just enough, and it doesn't take Preston long to fall back asleep. My thoughts tonight are all over the place. So much has happened in such a short time. Why did things with Heather go south? I think about what Bo said, how Heather was pulling me away from everyone. Why would she do that? Why didn't I see that for myself? Maybe Antonia is right, maybe she was jealous of my relationship with my family. After all, it's only her and her father. Her emails and text messages are showing a side of her I never knew. After all these years, how could that be? I understand how Uncle Jax would be worried that after everything that went down, it would be hard for me to trust anyone again, but everyone deserves to love and be loved. I was brought up to see the good, but it doesn't mean I have to be anyone's doormat. I keep playing around with my guitar and I realize the song I'm playing over and over again is Tim McGraw's "Humble and Kind." It reminds me of what I was taught at a very young age. Work hard and give back to society. But most of all, never take anything for granted.

The air is getting cold and I'm finally tired enough to call it a night. I wake Preston up and we head inside to get some sleep before our morning hike.

I feel like I just fell asleep and my alarm is already blaring. This hike will be interesting, especially after my conversation with Antonia. Bo and I grab some water and head out.

"Mike, you're very quiet this morning, everything okay?"

"Yeah, I'm tired. I was up late talking to Antonia."

He pushes his Ray-Bans up a little bit further. "Really? Everything okay?"

"Cut the crap; I know you've been talking to her. I'm the one person she can never lie to, so keep that in mind."

"I swear, Mike, we're friends. I know she's younger than me but she's like an old soul or something. I can't explain it; she's just so easy to talk to about anything." He's protesting too much; this is worse than I thought.

"Do you know what would happen to you if you so much as put a finger on her?"

"Trust me, I'm sure my body parts would be scattered all over the world."

"That's putting it mildly."

We make the rest of the trip in silence, both of us are lost in our thoughts. We start the hike at Tunnel Trail; it's not a long strenuous hike. The trail starts out flat and then it's an uphill climb. When we get to the summit, the view takes my breath away. Everywhere I look, I can see something different: the city, the ocean, and the Channel Islands. All of it—spectacular. The area is speckled with an unusual looking flower. "Bo, what kind of flower is that?"

He pulls out his phone and snaps a picture. "Not sure, but we can check it later. The area we are in now is a popular place for couples at sunset." He sits on one of the boulders overlooking the expansive view. "Why would you object to me going out with Antonia? I mean, it's not *that big of* an age difference."

"You're right it's not. It's not the number that matters; it's the emotional gap. You're light years ahead of her. Maybe if she went to a traditional school and did all the social events that went along with that, then it would be different. Unfortunately, we were homeschooled. I only realized the differences when I went away to college."

"You know eventually she is going to want to leave the nest and experience life. What happens then?"

"There will be a lot of craziness and, eventually, they will come together and let her go. But, it won't be pretty."

"Mike, why? I mean, I get that they have money and the guards are for our protection, but you have to admit, they are over the top."

"I know you're afraid of Uncle Max, but maybe this will help you understand him a little bit better. He was married before. At that time he was a policeman in England. His wife and baby son were in the park when a gunman shot them both. They died instantly and Uncle Max was first on the scene. It nearly destroyed him.

"Oh my God, that's awful."

"That's only the tip of the iceberg. My family has experienced a lot of loss. Keeping everyone safe is what drives them. Do you really want to be in the middle of that? Do you think you can survive it?"

"I have no idea. All I know is that right now she needs a friend and I intend on being that friend." He gets up, no doubt my words weighing heavy on him. "We better get going; I can't wait to get you on a board."

We head down the trail and now it's my turn to throw out some questions. "Let me ask you something, do you think Heather was jealous of my relationship with my family?"

"What makes you think that?"

"Antonia said that maybe Heather was jealous of my relationship with Uncle Jax. You said she slowly pushed all my friends away. How did I not see any of this?"

"Well, I could say you were thinking with your dick but I don't think that's the case. It was very subtle. She never said 'Mike, you can't go out with your friends,' she just made sure you guys always had other plans that didn't include any of your friends. After you got engaged, how many times did you bring Heather home?"

"In the beginning it was more frequent, but I was so wrapped up in school and then my post-graduate research that time slipped away."

"That's the point, it was gradual. Now you know what the signs are and you'll never let that happen again."

"So what beach are we going to?"

"You are getting your first surfing lesson at a world famous beach, it was even mentioned the Beach Boys song 'Surfin' Safari.' We are heading to Rincon Beach, which you probably know nothing about. Every January there is a championship held there. It is ranked number thirty-four on the list for the top one hundred spots to surf in the world."

"Pretty impressive as long as I don't kill myself."

"Trust me, you'll be fine. This time of the year it's not so intense." His Jeep is equipped with a sound system that he put together himself. Which helps take the sting out of the bumpy ride. He puts on a Thomas Rhett play list and we head on out. At least the music is great.

Chapter Twenty

EVERY OUNCE OF MY BODY HURTS. PARTS I DIDN'T EVEN know existed are screaming out in pain. Getting up on the board was hard, but staying up is a skill I don't have. I venture to say I drank a good portion of the Pacific Ocean today and, by the time we left, my detail probably needed a stiff drink. Now I have a better understanding of Bo's daily workouts and weekly Yoga classes. It's all about balance, strength, and endurance. I will say that I have flipping off the board, face first, down to a science. After a long hot shower and a very long nap, I'm almost back to normal. As promised, I sent Antonia a blackmail picture and I even send it to Dagen.

Dagen: Wow, that's some picture, lol. Did you enjoy your day?

Me: I had a lot of fun. The hike was spectacular and, well, we know how surfing was. How was your day? Did you get all your work done?

Dagen: I got a lot done. I have to work tomorrow but I wanted to take you on an adventure Tuesday. Are you available?

Me: For you? Of course I am! I can spend tomorrow

nursing my aches, pains, and ego. Where are we going?

Dagen: It's a surprise and don't try to get it out of me.

Me: I could come over and work on getting it out of you.

Dagen: Good night, Michael.

Me: What, no hugs?

Dagen: Sorry, Hugs.

Me: Night, sunshine.

I have a ton of paperwork to get done, but Mrs. H. must be cooking cause the smell coming from the kitchen is making my stomach rumble. I head out to get some food and find her baking Preston's treats.

"You realize you're spoiling him?"

"He does better with homemade treats. I made mac and cheese, if you're interested."

"I'm starved. I can get it."

She shoos me away. She reminds me of Grams, always wanting to take care of me. "Nonsense. Bo showed me the pictures from today. I'm surprised you can still walk. I thought for sure you would sleep through the night." Leave it to Bo to show everyone.

"It wasn't as bad as it looked. I thought it would be a lot easier. While I'm home, if you and Mr. H. want to take a little trip and see some sights, feel free. I can hold down the fort."

"Thank you. There is so much to see and do here, but one thing a day is more than enough for us."

I can't help but laugh at her subtlety. "Point taken. Dagen has something planned for Tuesday but I will be here all day tomorrow."

She dishes up dinner and it's wonderful. Sometimes there is nothing better than comfort food.

"Is Bo home?"

"Yes, he's in the man cave room." Hearing her call it the man cave room is hysterical.

"Michael, if you don't need us tonight, would it be okay if we left early? One of the local theaters in town is playing *Citizen Kane*. It's one of Bennett's favorite movies."

"Of course, go and enjoy yourselves. We will be fine."

Preston and I head into the cave and Bo is watching *House of Cards*.

"I didn't expect you to be able to move. I'll stick to golf from now on. Let me know when you can fit in a round."

"I'm working all week but I can fit something in this weekend."

"Okay, I'll get something set up. I've got some paperwork to get started on, I'll see you in the morning." I grab my beer and head into my office with Preston dragging his arse behind me. "You need to get some exercise and not be such a traitor. Tomorrow morning we are going for a run." Like he's really going to answer me.

I love being in my office, but I can be easily distracted from my work. I have to comb through a mountain of reports that Glen gave me before I left. If everyone would just adhere to the strict laws that California follows, my job would be a lot easier. I don't just look at the rig itself but the flowlines, blowout preventer, glider field—everything that could be a potential problem. I should be able to wrap up my current project within a few days and then head to the Gulf. After the Deep Water Horizon spill in 2010, I would like to think that every precaution has been taken to never have anything like that happen again, but I would never leave anything to chance.

I finally start to tackle the stack of junk mail that has accumulated over the last two weeks. After flipping through it all, I find the rest of Dagen's gift that I ordered. I already decided where to give it to her. Now I have to find the perfect time. I'm curious and excited about Tuesday, but I don't know if I can wait till then to see her.

I haven't spoken to my parents in a couple of weeks, which is odd, they usually check in every week with some sort of crazy story or adventure. The nine-hour time difference is a pain in the arse but my dad should be up. He picks up right away.

"Hey, Junior, everything okay?"

"Yeah, I haven't heard from you and Mum for a few weeks. Is everything good?"

"We were giving you some time to get settled in, plus we've been really busy. How's work?"

"It's good. I have to sleep in a bunk. Other than that, I'm enjoying it. I went surfing today."

"Oh dear God, don't tell your mother or I will never hear the end of it." I can't help but laugh. My mum will be encouraging and helpful and then she'll freak out on my dad.

"Too late; Antonia has a picture that she can use to blackmail me with. How is Mum doing?"

"If you're wondering, I know she went to see Heather. I told her that I didn't think it was good idea. I told her to close the book and move on, but you know she could never do that. She wouldn't even let me go, stubborn woman. Hold on and I'll let you talk to her."

"Hi, Michael, how are you?"

"I'm good. I got an email from Heather. She told me about your visit and threatened to get a non-harassment order against you. Are you okay?"

"I had to have my say, Michael. I couldn't let her get away with what she did. She invaded my privacy and tore your life apart. She's lucky I didn't snap her neck."

"Well, now that you got that off your chest, can you please stay away from her. I have blocked her from all contact. I'm moving on and hope she is too."

"Okay, are you dating someone?" I knew she would catch that right away.

"Yes. Dagen."

"I know I didn't get to spend much time with her, when she was here, but she seems very nice. Take your time, Michael, explore and enjoy life. Most of your adult life you were with *her*. Learn what it's like to be on your own, relying on no one. If she's a keeper, she will stick with you. So, is your house done?"

"Yes, and I love it."

"I heard all about the man cave from Jax. I think he's jealous, don't be surprised if he calls Dagen out to make one for him. What have you been up to?"

I might as well get this over with. "I went surfing today. Hold on, I'll text a picture."

"Are you out of your fucking mind?! Where the hell was your detail during all of this? You tell Bo when I see him, he's in big trouble."

"Calm down, it's not as bad as it looks. My detail was trying to keep up with me. I'm surprised they didn't rat me out to Uncle Max. I can honestly say I did it but I don't think I would do it ever again."

"Are you trying to fulfill some sort of bucket list?"

"I never thought of it like that, but you know, there's a whole big world out there and I kind of feel like I've been set free for the first time in years. Somehow, I feel like I'm playing catch up."

"I won't lecture you; all I ask is can you please keep a level head and keep the danger at a minimum? You're not playing catch up. I'm too old for this. Hold on, your dad wants to talk."

"Hey, I'm looking at this picture and I have one question, did you ever stay on the board or were you always upside down flying through the air?" He's laughing and I pull up the photo. He's got a point.

"Funny, Dad, very funny. When are you guys coming out to visit?"

"Before the harvest; probably soon. I'll give you a heads up."

"Okay, it's getting late. Love you both, and we'll talk soon."

I'm headed into bed, Preston dragging his arse behind me when I get a text from an unknown number. I open it up and realize it's from Heather.

Heather: Why did you block me? Can't we be adults and talk about this?

Me: Why are you stalking me? There is nothing left to say. You made your choice, now live with it. I've moved on and you need to do the same.

Heather: We were together for so long, how could you just walk away without a fight? I said I was sorry and confused by everything. Where is your compassion? Are you so perfect that you never made a mistake?

Me: I've never claimed to be perfect, far from it. Why would you want to go back? After I read that report and I replayed what you said in my head, the only thing I kept seeing is you pulling away when I reached for you. Were you afraid of me? Are you afraid what kind of children we would have? Will there always be doubt? So much has been said, and some things can't be changed. Please move on and stay away from my family. I don't want to change my number but, if you keep this up, I will.

Heather: You're showing what a bastard you really are. Maybe you're really like your father after all. Maybe your kids will end up the same as him. Label him what he is: a rapist. The apple doesn't really fall far from the tree.

And there it is—the truth—how she really feels. She couldn't deny her fear and, honestly, when I first found out, I had fears of my own. But after talking to my uncles, I finally understand. They experienced a similar fear with their own father. He's a bigamist, and evil to the core, yet, he saved my life. I've never asked him why he did it; I only thanked him and never looked back. I couldn't at the time; I was in a fight to survive. I will always believe that if we surround ourselves with good, try to teach others to be humble and kind, then the evil can't affect us. When I look back at what Aunt Raven accomplished with the foster kids, so many of them were on a dead end road. She helped guide them, nature vs nurture.

I block her latest number; I will not let her make me have doubts. Now I'm too wound up to sleep. Bo already went to bed. I'll text Uncle Jax and see what he's up to.

Me: Hey you available to Facetime?

My phone is ringing. He doesn't even hesitate. *He never does.*

"Hey, Junior, everything okay?"

"Yeah, I can't sleep, thought I would see what you were up to."

"You can't bullshit me; do you want to vent?"

He's right; I don't even know why I try. "It's Heather, I blocked her from everything. She still messaged me from a different number. She just said things that royally pissed me off."

"This is the best advice I can give you. Until you get to the point when you have nothing more to say to her, you will continue to let her twist your nuts. Add to that, if Dagen thinks you are still in some way connected to Heather, you will lose her and I don't think that's what you want."

"I don't want to mess things up with Dagen. I shared very personal stuff with her. I don't take that lightly."

"I know you don't, your opening up to her about everything was huge. Obviously, you're very comfortable with her. Someone like that doesn't come around often, don't jeopardize it. What will you do if Heather pulls this shit again?"

"I guess I'll keep blocking her. Eventually, she will have to go away."

"If it was me, I wouldn't take a back seat to all of this. Leave nothing to chance. Why don't you give Tony a call? Maybe he has some tech type of suggestion. You know he is always inventing new things. Maybe you can even take Dagen to the island for a little vacation."

"You're not going to get me out of going to the Gulf, so stop trying."

He tries not to laugh but no such luck.

"Busted my arse on that one. Antonia showed me the picture of your attempt at surfing. You can't imagine how many phone calls I got from Max. Apparently, your detail called him in a panic."

"Is he okay? Should I call him?"

"He's fine. He blamed it all on me. He always blames me for everything. Max and I are so much alike, yet, so different. I wouldn't call him just yet; give him a few days to calm down. Is there anything else you're planning that might give me heart failure?"

"I might go skydiving soon."

"Junior, for the love of God, just kill me now and get it over with!"

"Relax, just kidding. So did you start work on your man cave?"

"I have to talk Raven into it, but Mrs. Osla is on board."

"Of course she is; she's the coolest little old lady ever, but don't tell her I said that. When are you coming out to see my place?" I ask. He's running his hands through his hair and hesitating. "Hey, what's the problem?"

"A lot of bad things happened in the States. Aunt Raven might not ever be able to go back there. You know I would never go without her. I promise I will try and talk to her about it."

"I understand. Antonia said she wants to come soon, maybe

that will help Aunt Raven. It's getting late; I'll talk to you soon."

"Stay safe and call Tony."

"I will." we hang up and I head into bed, hoping my mind will finally shut off.

I tossed and turned all night. Maybe Uncle Jax is right. Maybe I need to take the bull by his balls. First things first, I get up and send Tony an email. There's no doubt in my mind that I want Heather out of my life for good. No one and nothing is going to stand in the way of my discovering all things Dagen.

A nice long morning run will do me a world of good and then it's time to work on my surprise for Dagen.

"Preston, you are getting very lazy. Get your sorry arse up; we're going for a run."

We head out with him dragging his arse behind me. "Maybe if you cut back on the treats from Mrs. H., you wouldn't feel like such a slug."

I love to run on the beach, and watching Preston fight with the waves is always very entertaining. I have to admit, the playlist I made for running is off the charts fantastic. I timed it for exactly one hour. It starts out easy and right when I hit that wall, it kicks me into high gear with Bruce Springsteen's "Born to Run." My cool down is to Pink singing "Fucking Perfect." I will make Dagen believe that she is perfect just the way she is. I will never have her second-guessing herself. Trying to fit into someone else's box is nothing but bullshit. Why would anyone want something the same as everyone else has? Uncle Jax always told me "Lead the Pack, don't follow." He probably got that from another one of his fortune cookies.

I head towards home and when I get there Mr. H. is waiting with everything I need to surprise Dagen. "Michael, from the picture you showed me, I labeled where each plant has to go. Are you sure you don't want me to go with you to do this?"

"Thank you, but it means so much more if I do it. If I run into problems, I'll call you."

"Okay, well, I loaded everything into the Rover. Remember, follow the diagram I made you." I can't help but laugh he's just as excited as I am. I made sure to pack my presents for her and my guitar.

It's a long ride to her house and there's no rhyme or reason to the traffic or the highways in this state. With the help of my detail, we get everything unloaded. Now comes the fun part. Following the design that Mr. H. made, I plant the vegetables on the wall that gets full sun, making sure I put the Basil plants in-between the tomato plants. Apparently it reduces bugs. Now for the flowers—an entire wall, all different levels, filled with white, pink, and blue Forget Me Not plants. My house is close to the water, so it's a lot cooler. It's hotter than hell here, so I take off my shirt and douse myself with the hose. When I turn around, I see Dagen standing there.

"Oh, you're home early. I wanted to surprise you."

"Well, consider it done. It's not everyday a girl comes home from work and finds a half-naked, wet guy in her yard."

"Well, when I was here the other day, I noticed that the ledges on these walls were empty. I thought I would fill one side with vegetables and the other side with flowers."

"They look wonderful. Now let's hope I don't kill them."

"You won't. I installed an irrigation system and it's on a timer."

"Wow, you think of everything. The flowers are beautiful. What kind are they?"

"The flowers are called Forget Me Not. Legend says that a knight and his girl were walking along the rivers edge when he picked so many flowers, the weight of them, with his armor, caused him to fall in the river. As he was drowning, he shouted out to her, 'Forget Me Not.'"

"Oh my God, Michael, that's horrible!"

"There are other meanings; it just depends where you look.

Women wore them as a sign of faithfulness and enduring love, so they wouldn't be forgotten by their lovers."

"Well, that sounds a hell of a lot better than drowning. Thank you. This is all so beautiful and thoughtful. Come inside, dry off and I'll make some coffee."

"I'm dirty, can I jump in your shower?"

"Of course, come on."

She takes me inside and is showing me where everything is, when I notice she's got a claw foot tub. I lean in and gently kiss her. "Next time, sunshine, we are doing the tub together." Her cheeks turn beet red and I can't help but laugh. I shoo her out and head into the shower. Her bathroom is very girly and everything in the shower is from someplace called Bath and Body Works. She must really like this one called A Thousand Wishes, there's soap, lotions, and some spray stuff. Now I know why she always smells so beautiful. I wrap a towel around myself, gather up my clothes and head out to find her. She's standing in her bedroom with a pair of sweats in her hands. She's got on cutoffs and my rugby shirt.

"I thought you could use a pair of Bo's sweats while I wash your clothes."

"Thanks, I'll take the sweats but you don't have to wash my clothes. You might want to turn around, unless you want a show." I can't take my eyes off of her wearing my shirt and she's not moving or saying a word.

"You have a tat, what is it?"

I look down and my towel slid down low, real low, exposing the top of my tat just below the start of my V. "Yes, it's a TARDIS with the quote from Doctor Who 'We're all stories, in the end. Just make it a good one, eh?' going around it. Would you like to see it?" I don't wait for her to answer, I step forward and lower my towel a little more, knowing I'm stepping into dangerous territory. Her finger trembles as she traces the words. I lift her chin up and kiss her as my towel falls to the floor. She pulls me up against her body holding my arse tightly as if she will never let me go. I finally let go of her lips with a slight tug between my teeth. "Dagen, I want you." I lift her and carry her to the bed. Slowly working my way down her neck, one tiny nip at a time, then back up. When I rest my forehead on hers, I run my fingers over her nipples. "I don't care what you say; those damn girls are so perky I swear they're saluting me." When I gently push her back, I slide my hands slowly up her sides, taking the shirt with them. I run my tongue around the jewel in her bellybutton, giving it a little flick. Her skin keeps prickling every time I kiss her from hip to hip. "Your skin is begging me to keep kissing you everywhere."

I need this to last. After all, I only have one shot at a first that she will remember for the rest of her life. I make quick work of her cutoffs and leave the pink lacey thong with a little bow on top for later. I look down at my cock and send him a mental note to take a back seat until later. I never break my connection with her. I kiss every inch of her. I swirl my tongue around the inside of her ankle, slowly working my way up to my beautifully pink lace gift-wrapped package. Avoiding it at all cost right now, or it's game over. Down the inside of her other leg and back up again. Across her hips and up to those beautiful, perky girls, swirling my tongue around her nipple and then I tug, gently at first, but when she moans, I nip it a little harder.

"Michael, Oh my God, please, more."

She pulls at her other nipple but I push her hand away. "Mine, sunshine, all mine." Now I'm working both nipples and driving her to the edge of total ecstasy. She's got her hands in my hair and she's pulling.

"Harder, Michael. I need more."

I slow it down.

"Noooooooooooo."

I'm trailing my tongue down to my pink lace present. I tug at the bow with my teeth, finally pulling her thong off. I'm back at her ankle and working my way up, always around never getting any-where near my prize, at least, not yet. Down her other leg and back up again. I slide lower and kiss her nub, which causes her to gasp. Slowly flicking my tongue over and over again. I reach up and take her hand and pull her into more of a sitting position.

"I want you to watch me when I take you over and over again."

When I push a finger deep inside, her teeth dig into her bottom lip. Now two fingers and I'm tugging on her nub. She's almost there; I can feel her legs begin to shake. When I push in three fingers and curve them up, I hit her g-spot. Her hips are going wild, she grabs my hair and pushes me harder in into her. Her whole body flushes and she's saying my name over and over again. I slowly work her down before I start again. This time with soft gentle kisses. I don't want to break the connection, but I need a condom.

"I need to get a condom."

Still placing gentle kisses up and down her little landing strip. Before I can move she reaches over and yanks open a drawer on her night table. After some fumbling around I get hit in the head with a whole box of condoms.

"A little enthusiastic, are we now?"

"Don't worry, I'll give you a break now and then."

I toss her one of the condoms. "Here you go, sunshine, put it on me."

I pull myself up on my knees and my cock is giving her the royal salute.

"Um, that's awfully big, I don't think this is going to fit."

I get up and grab my jeans and pull a couple of condoms out of my wallet and pass them to her. "You know I was a Scotland Scout for a whole day; try one of these."

"Why only one day?"

"Do you think now is the time to discuss that? At this moment I don't think you want my cock to deflate."

"Point taken."

While she's trying to get the package open, I'm between her legs mindlessly playing with her nipples. I forget all about the condom and work on my perky girls.

"I think you're ready for me now."

She finally gets the packet open and slowly rolls the condom on my cock. It takes a lot of willpower not to come when she touches me. With her feet resting on my shoulders I slowly enter her. I need to give her a chance to get used to me.

"Are we good, Dagen?"

She lets out a deep breath, "Yes."

I begin to move, and being like this with her is surreal. She slides her feet down and digs her heals into my arse. I give her what she needs and I push harder. I don't want this over in a flash, so I slow down. I put her legs over my shoulders and go even deeper. I pull out just to the point of breaking the connection and then push my way back in, each time a little bit harder, waiting a little bit longer. I begin rolling her perky nipples between my fingers and every time my cock slams into her, I tweak them a little harder.

"Oh my God, that's it, hell yeah!"

I'm trying to hold back and give her more but when she yells like that, I'm fucked. I come with such a force I feel like my balls are going to get sucked into the condom along with my cock. I'm kissing her long and slow until my heart finally comes back to somewhat normal. I quickly remove the condom, tie it up and toss it in the trash next to the bed. I pull her close and let her snuggle into me while I trail my fingers up and down her back.

"You're quite the tiger in bed." She looks up at me and she's blushing. "I like it, keeps things lively." She's flicking my nipples like I did to hers and slowly working her way down to my cock but not before she kisses my tat. When she finally takes a hold of my cock, she swirls her tongue around the head. Her hands and mouth are everywhere and I'm about ready to lose my mind. I try to pull back but she locks her arms around my legs and goes so deep, I hit the back of her throat. I can hold out for a long time, but the one thing that drives me wild is the throat bump, fuck me—I'm done. When I finally open my eyes, she's sitting between my legs smiling at me.

"So, why were you a Scotland Scout for just one day?"

I can't help but laugh. "After everything tonight, that's what you want to know?"

"Yep. Fess up, what happened?"

"Uncle Max happened. He found out there would be camping in the woods. No parents and no guards, and so no Michael."

"Well, that sucks. If you want to go camping, I will take you. I love camping."

"Where the hell have you been my whole life?"

"Here, Michael, waiting for you. You sure took your sweet ass time getting here."

We both laugh and it's comforting to know she's not just my lover but also my friend. "I'm starving, are you ever going to feed me?"

"Do you want me to cook, order in, or go out?"

"I can help you cook, it will be fun."

"Okay, let's get dress and then we can whip something up."

We get up, throw on our clothes and head out to the kitchen. In no time, we've put together pancakes, eggs, toast, bacon and coffee. Between my run this morning and my workout in bed, I'm really starving. She has a huge outdoor, round patio bed with lots of pillows. We take our food outside and I grab my guitar and her present.

"After dinner, are you going to serenade me?"

"I enjoy playing for you." We finish eating and I begin messing around with my guitar. I start singing "Yours" by Russell Dickerson. She knows this song and sings it with me. "I came to life when I first kissed you." I lean in and kiss her. "We should record something together when you get the music studio done. We harmonize great."

"I love that song, but I don't think I do it any justice."

I put my guitar aside and pull her close. "Hey, what did I tell you? You don't need to fit into anyone's box."

"Why fit in when we were born to stand out?"

"Fortune cookie?"

"No, Dr. Seuss." It's nice to know she can laugh at my quirkiness.

"The architect will have the plans for the studio ready for us tomorrow morning. We can stop there before your surprise and review the plans. Don't bother asking, you have to wait until tomorrow."

"You are one tough cookie, Dagen. Now I have a little something for you. It's a two part gift." I hand her the Tiffany box.

"Michael, none of this is necessary."

"I know that. It's something that I wanted to do." She opens the box and pulls out the bellybutton ring with a dangling Tiffany blue diamond shaped like a star.

"Oh my God, it's beautiful."

"Now this goes with it." I hand her an envelope. When she opens it up she begins to cry. "Now there will be none of that."

"You had a star named after me!"

"When I'm on the rig and far from home, you can look up and find your star. If it's cloudy, or daytime and you can't see it, you just have to look at your bellybutton and know that no matter where I am, a part of me will always be with you . . . promise."

"Thank you. Show me which one is the Dagen star."

We lie back and look at the directions and when we find it, I see a tear slide down her cheek. "Hey, are you okay?"

"More than okay, I'm happy for the first time in a long time." She snuggles into me, and trailing her finger over my heart, almost like she's writing something.

"What are you doing?"

"Writing my name on your heart."

"It's permanently stamped there, sunshine." I kiss her, pull the throw blanket over us and we fall asleep.

Chapter Twenty-One

Dagen

I CAN FEEL THE HEAT OF THE MORNING SUN ON MY FACE, AND when I open my eyes, I see Michael nestled between my boobs. How can a man be fast asleep with a smile on his face? I hate to disturb him but I need to do my morning business and we need to get started. I gently stroke his hair and he begins to moan. I don't think he realizes how sexy he is, either that, or he doesn't really care.

"Michael, you need to start waking up. Don't you want your surprise?"

"Hmm, I had the best dream ever. I was warm and snuggled in a cloud."

"No, Michael, you were snuggled in my boobs all night."

His eyes open and when he looks around him, he laughs. "I'm drawn to them like the beacon at the top of the lighthouse, guiding me home. Maybe that's why they always salute me." He's kissing my nipples, right and then left.

"We have no more condoms."

"I know. I just needed to give my girls their proper attention. They need to start the day off right. So, what is our plan today?"

"I'll show you after my shower."

"I'll help you shower."

"If you help me, we won't get done." Now he's behind me with my hair in his fist, nipping at my shoulders.

"What if I promise to behave?" He pulls my hair a little tighter.

"What if I can't behave?"

"If you have dessert all the time, then it doesn't mean as much, but if you have to wait for it, then you can appreciate it more." He leaps out of the patio bed, takes my hand and pulls up. "Let's go, sunshine, I have a surprise to collect."

We head into the shower and get all soaped up. It takes all of me not to take him right there especially when he shampoo's my hair.

"I need to bring my own shampoo and stuff here, so I don't smell girly."

I smile knowing that he's coming back and plans on staying around, at least, for a while. "Bo has some stuff in the linen closet I forgot to tell you about. There are also a dozen or so new toothbrushes."

"Why so many toothbrushes?"

"I have an electric toothbrush, but every time I get my teeth cleaned, I take the samples. You see, now they came in handy. I know Bo has some shorts here; I'll get you a pair." I give him some privacy while I look for something for him to throw on. I'm finally feeling a little bit more comfortable in my own skin when I'm with him. When he pulled me up and made me watch him, it was like seeing someone else, not me. I keep replaying the scene over in my head and he made it all about me. Pleasing me came first. When I wanted more, he gave it. I'm falling for him hard. I have to have faith that he won't shatter my heart into a million pieces. I don't think I could take it if he did. I snap out of my daydream and realize he's standing in the doorway totally in the buff.

"Dagen, want to tell me where that beautiful mind of yours wandered off too?"

"I was thinking about last night," I admit. He walks up to me, laces his fingers behind my neck, his thumbs stroking my cheeks. He brushes his lips over mine and then tugs at my bottom lip.

"I know it was more than that. I'm not going anywhere and when you're ready, you can share it with me. Now since we are out of condoms, you need to get me some clothes."

"Okay, first have a seat; I have to show you something. I'm going into my closet; don't follow me." I made sure when I remodeled my home I put in a huge walk-in closet. I hurry up and put on my new pink golf attire and grab my clubs.

"Okay, close your eyes, and no peaking." I stick my head out first to make sure his eyes are closed. Sure enough, he's going along with the program. I get into position and try not to drop the bag with the clubs.

"Okay, you can open them," I announce. He opens his eyes and he's not saying a word. Shit did I get this wrong? "I've been going to Nevada and taking lessons with Butch Harmon and I got us a tee time this afternoon at Cypress Point in Pebble Beach. Do you hate the outfit?" Jesus Christ, I wish he would say something.

"Wow, you did all of this for me? That's amazing. There's just one problem."

"You hate the outfit. Do I look like a giant Pepto-Bismol tablet?""

"I don't know if I can concentrate on golf knowing what's underneath it. Tell me the truth, is my package wrapped up in a little lacey thong with a bow on top?"

"Oh My God, are you serious?"

"Oh and while we're on full disclosure, when you blush, the girls salute me."

He's hysterical laughing and I'm a millions shades of red, I'm sure. I look down and sure enough, my frigging nipples are popping out!

"It's you! I swear it only happens with you. You will leave the girls alone on the golf course. I'll meet you in the car. Better hurry up; we are leaving in five." I toss him shorts, pick up my clubs, and head out the door.

Michael

We pop into the architect's office with me looking like a homeless guy and after a few minor tweaks, I approved all the plans. Next up—my house—to pick up my clubs and some normal clothes. Bo's shorts are too big and I feel like any minute, I'm going to lose my drawers.

"Dagen, what's our tee time? I'm so excited to play this course; we can't be late."

"One pm. My dad has a friend that's a member and he was able to get us in. I guess it's supposed to be a beautiful course."

She has no clue what she's in for. "I'm so excited; you went to such great lengths to do this for me."

"Why wouldn't I want to spend the day with you on, what is supposed to be, one of the most spectacular golf courses in the world? It's a double win for me. Just don't make fun of my golfing."

"Never." This is her first time playing a full round of golf and she picks this course, poor girl. I will have to make it up to her.

We load up the car and head out. I put on my Keith Urban playlist. "Gone Tomorrow (Here Today)" comes on and I can't help but sing along with him. "This song always reminds me of how quickly life can change. Carpe diem, baby, make the most of what we've got right here, right now."

She reaches over and turns the music down. "Is that what you really believe, live for today?"

"Yeah, tomorrow is not a given and anyone who thinks that it is, is a fool. I make some plans for my life but they are never set in stone. Maybe that's why I don't go back; it seems like a waste of time. That's the big difference between my uncles and me. They have to have a plan and everyone must follow along. Plans are good but if they stop you from having a life, then what good are they?"

"Do you think that's why Antonia and Jax are at odds?"

"Antonia and Grace have plans that go against everything their fathers want for them. There will be a lot of fighting ahead of them all."

"It seems like you're the peacekeeper in the family."

"Only with my cousins and really, only the girls. Jeff and Sam are a lot like Aunt Jackie: very easy going. Tell me what life was like growing up in California."

"Well, with my dad being in the business, I got to go to a lot of movie sets. At first it was fun, but like anything else, it got old. I love California because I'm able to be outdoors most of the year, but I have to tell you, I really enjoyed Scotland. Not just the whole castle and secret passages, there was just something so magical about it."

"Wow, you didn't even get to see it all. I will take you back again and each time, you will find something else to take your breath away. Just like every time I go someplace here, I find something that is so spectacular."

"Really?"

"I found you, didn't I? And now I have a beautiful home."

We get to the club with twenty minutes to spare. "Before we go in, I have to tell you something." I pull her towards me and kiss her. "No matter how many balls you lose, I will still think this is one of the best days of my life."

"Come on, wise ass, let's see who loses their balls."

We check in with our caddy and get started. Things are going along very nicely until we get to the fourteenth hole. Now we're on the surf side of the course and by the time we get to the eighteenth hole, she's ready to throw her clubs off the cliff. She's mad and pouting, and it's fucking beautiful.

"I have to confess; I knew what would happen when we got to the surf side. This course is legendary and the eighteenth is one of the hardest holes in the world." I put my arm around her, mainly to stop her from tossing her clubs.

"You could have warned me."

"No. If I did, then you would have been afraid, but you went into this determined to give it your all. I'm very proud of you. Did you like the game itself?"

"Actually, yes, even though it's very frustrating, it's also relaxing. I think a lot of this game is mental not just physical."

"Yes it is. Next time we go to Scotland, I will take you to Saint Andrews, the birthplace of golf. For now, let's head home and have a nice long soak in my Jacuzzi tub."

By the time we get home, she is out cold. I hate to wake her but she can't sleep in the car. I stroke her cheek, trying to gently wake her up. "Dagen, we're home."

She flutters her eyes open and all I want to do is take her in my arms and hold her forever. "Stay here for a second."

I get out, open her door and help her out. "Holy hell, Michael, every muscle in my body hurts, even ones I didn't know I had. How is that even possible?"

"Let me take care of you tonight . . . please."

"I'm too tired to argue."

We head inside and she curls up on the sofa in my bedroom. I cover her with a throw and while the tub is filling up, I let Mrs. H. know what I need. When I finally have everything ready, I help her get undressed and we both settle into the tub. Her back to my front makes it easy for me to work her back muscles. "Damn, girl, you're so tight. I might have to do this a couple of times."

"Sounds good to me."

"You need to turn around so I can do your feet and your calves, otherwise, you'll get charley horses."

She spins around and puts her head back on the bath pillow. Her calves are rock hard and I know she's going to hurt in the morning.

"If you keep moaning like that, I might lose what little control I have."

She opens one eye and laughs. "I don't think my girls or any of my other parts want to have anything to do with you right now. I don't understand . . . even my boobs hurt!"

"Well, every time you swung your club, the girls went around with you. I can massage them for you."

"Oh, I'm sure you could."

We get out and I towel her off and then give her one of the white, fluffy robes she put in here. "I had Mrs. H. set up a tray of food for us. I figure we can watch a movie and relax."

"Great, I'm hungry. What movie do you want to watch?"

"It's up to you. I haven't seen much lately."

"Do you have a favorite?"

"*The French Connection;* the original one. I would go with Grams whenever there was a showing in Edinburgh of classic movies. What about you?"

"If we are talking about classics, then I love the movie *Sabrina,* the original and the remake."

I pass her the remote, "You can look around and find something; I'm game for whatever you pick."

"Can we watch the baseball game?"

"Sure. I've never been to a game, have you?"

"Oh, Michael, that's our next adventure. We can go to San Francisco, see the city, and then go see the Giants play."

"You tell me when and I can make all the arrangements." I love her enthusiasm.

"When are your parents coming? I want to take them to the Napa Valley. Some of the best winery's in the world are there."

"I spoke to my dad the other day and he said they are coming out soon. When I find out for sure, we can go."

"Okay. I have to tell you, Mrs. H. makes the best wings ever."

"Yeah, I really lucked out with her except, I think Preston likes her more than me."

"Nah, look at him curled up on his bed. He's happy when he's with you."

I don't have to look at him to know he's sleeping, who can get past the snoring?

"Why do you have a safe room?"

"Well, that's out of left field."

"I meant to ask you a couple of weeks ago. I found it when I was working here. It totally slipped my mind."

"Honestly, I forgot all about it. Uncle Max had it installed before I moved in. We've always had them in all of our houses. Does it bother you?"

"No. I was surprised, that's all. Did you ever need to use it?"

"Me, personally?—no." She seems satisfied with my answer and goes back to eating the hot wings.

"So what kind of workout do I need to do, so when I play golf again I don't feel like I got run over by a truck?" She's licking the hot sauce off her fingers and if she doesn't stop soon, I might not be able to control myself. She has some sauce on her bottom lip and I swipe my tongue over it.

"You are so sexy, Dagen." She blushes, and we both glance down at the girls that are peeking out of her robe.

"Told ya; they have a thing for me."

"Can we please go back to my workout?"

"Let me show you. First, you have to open up your robe, just enough to let the girls do their thing." I open and push her robe off her shoulders exposing the girls. "Then, I have to work my way slowly down your chest but stop to kiss your heart, after all, that heart made me feel again. Then, I need to lavish each nipple with as much attention as you can take." I crawl between her legs and push her back as I take her nipple between my teeth and gently tug.

"Oh, Michael, it feels so good, but I don't think this is the kind of workout that will help my golf game."

"It will help with your concentration and, after all, golf is a mental game."

I continue toying with her nipple as she tries to take the other one between her fingers. I take both her hands and pull them above her head. "Keep your hands above your head until I tell you. Now, where was I? Oh, that's right; I was having some fun, kissing all of you, everywhere, anywhere my sweet, little heart desires." I push her robe totally open and her skin is so soft and golden, it prickles every time my lips touch her. "When your skin begs me to kiss it, I feel like I'm going to lose my mind." She's squirming for any kind of contact. I toss my robe aside and trail my fingers up and down her beautiful body, followed by kisses and a little nipping in all her sensitive areas. I reach over to the nightstand, grab a condom and make quick work at getting it on. I kiss her bellybutton star and whisper "My beacon, guiding my way."

"Give me your hands, now." When I take her hands, they're trembling.

I place them on the girls, my hands on top of hers. "Feel how very hard your nipples are, yet your skin is so soft." I guide her hands slowly down her ribs. "It's not a race, take your time and explore every inch that is you." She slows down and uses the tips of her fingers to feel all the contours of her beautiful body. "Now, guide me where you want me to go."

She stops.

"Michael, I umm. . ."

"I bet you've only done this in the privacy of your own room, never with a lover," I surmise. She blushes and all her skin is so warm to the touch. "Oh, Dagen, your world will be full of so many firsts with me. You have a beautiful body—be proud of it—show it to me, babe."

Her trembling fingers begin to move again, guiding me down to her little landing strip. She stops.

"Tell me what you want."

"I can't, I've never . . . Oh God." She squeezes her eyes shut.

"Come on, babe, say the words." I lean in and blow on her nub.

"Geez, Michael, I want that beautiful tongue of yours to work magic on my whooha, and I want it now!"

I'm trying very hard not to laugh, but I'm not winning. "Whoo-ha?"

"Look, I hate the words: cunt, pussy, dick deposit, and whatever the hell else it's been called."

"Well, I am more than happy to answer the call from your whooha."

I give her what she wants, what she's craving. I work my tongue in deep, flicking it from side to side. When I go up to her nub, I nip it as I work one finger deep inside her. She's lifting her hips up and now I press my pinky in her arse, and when I do, she grabs my hair and yanks it hard.

"Oh my God, more, Michael, *please.*"

I press another finger into her and when I look up, she's rolling her nipples between her fingers, pulling, tugging, and begging me for more. So I do what any fine gentleman would do, I replace my fingers with my cock and slam into her. She instantly kicks her heels into my arse.

"Do you want more?"

"Yes, oh God, yes!"

I lift her legs higher so I can go deeper. I know what she wants but I want to hear her say it. "What do you need, Dagen?"

"I need it hard and I need it now!"

I'm pounding into her and it doesn't take long for her to find her release. I'm kissing her slowly, waiting for her racing heart to slow down.

"Michael, turn around is fair play, tell me what you need."

I roll us over so now she's on top. "I need you and that wild whooha of yours to ride me hard while you play with the girls."

Her hair is everywhere and as she comes down hard, she works her nipples. Every time she comes down, I push my hips up to meet her.

"That's it, Dagen, show me what you've got." Every slam brings me closer; I feel my balls tighten and I know this is going to be of epic proportions. She takes her fingers and drags her nails over my nipples. Bam! That's my tipping point. I come and she's not far behind me. "Fucking beautiful!"

She crawls off of me and snuggles into my side while I ditch the condom.

"I'm finding a level of comfort with you that I've never had with anyone before, not even myself."

"You're a beautiful woman, not just on the outside. You deserve to be loved and treated with respect and kindness. You shouldn't have to settle. If you want something, then go for it."

"I've never had anal sex."

"Okay, that's out of left field."

"Well, when you were . . . you know." She looks up at me, her bottom lip between her teeth and her skin is flushed, and I swear I'm already getting hard again.

"Do you mean when I was servicing your whooha."

"Yeah, that, what you were doing down in the whooha zone felt very intense."

"I don't know how they do it in those books you read, but it's something you have to work up to. I want to try lots of different things with you. It's all about the journey."

She's fighting to keep her eyes open. "Right now you need to get some sleep."

"Will you sing to me?"

I pull her closer and stroke her back and as she falls asleep I begin to sing "Die A Happy Man" by Thomas Rhett. "If all I've got is your hand in my hand, baby, I could die a happy man." No truer words were ever spoken. She saved me when I never thought it was possible. When Heather dropped that bombshell in my lap, I thought I was nothing but damaged goods . . . worthless. She showed me that I'm not. I keep stroking her back and finally, I drift off to sleep.

Chapter Twenty-Two

PRESTON WAKES ME UP WITH THE SMACK OF HIS PAW ON MY face, apparently, he needs to do his business. Dagen is still sleeping, so I try not to disturb her. I grab a pair of shorts and head out back. It's a full moon and it's still very warm. While he's running around, I scroll through the emails on my phone. I have a reply from Tony.

Hey Michael,

I have a new software program that I helped a buddy of mine develop. I think it will be perfect for what you need. I started working on it when some hackers were able to crack into iPhones. When you get a chance, sync your phone with your laptop. Text me first and let me know when you get it set up. Shouldn't take more than twenty minutes to download it. The software will only let recognized numbers through. If it doesn't know the number it goes to a separate voice mail that you can check whenever you want. Right now, it's only on Jax's and Max's phones. I think eventually she will get the hint and become someone else's problem.

How is life in California? I lived in Silicon Valley for a few years. It was fun but then Max hired me away from the company I was with and well, you know the rest. I made some of the modifications to that gaming system that you recommended and it seems to be working better. When you get a chance, come out and visit, and bring your girl; I could use a break from fishing all day.

Tony

Me: Hey, thanks for getting back to me so quickly. I'll sync my phone now. I'm loving California; so much to see and do. I promise to visit soon and bring Dagen with me.

Tony: Great, I'll take care of the update now. Talk to you soon.

I'm glad I reached out to him. This should put an end to Heather once and for all. While Tony is doing his thing, I look through all my emails from work. Nothing is earthshattering, so I start researching where I want to take Dagen today. I got it—Santa Monica Pier! Oh my God, they have a trapeze school. They have so much stuff, I wish we could leave right now. As soon as the sun comes up, I'll charm her into going with me. In the meantime, since I can't sleep, I'll bug Antonia.

Me: You busy?

Antonia: No, why are you up? It's like 5 in the morning by you.

Me: Preston woke me up and I can't go back to sleep. Thought I would see what you're doing. How's everything going with school? Did you talk to Uncle Jax?

Antonia: I did and he is open to the idea of me going St. Andrews. But Grace wants to go to Glasgow. She said they have a great language program. Oh, and Jeff made the cut for the University of the Highlands and Islands for their new golf degree program.

Me: Wow, he worked so hard for that! I'll have to call him so he can tell me all about it. Dagen took me yesterday to play Cypress at Pebble Beach. She's been taking lessons and surprised me. It was amazing, and when we got to the eighteenth hole she was ready to toss her clubs off a cliff. When she wakes up, I want to take her to a trapeze school down by Santa Monica Pier.

Antonia: OMG, you have lost your mind. I better get pictures.

Me: Of course I'll send pictures, just don't tell Uncle Jax till after the fact.

Antonia: It sounds like everything is going good with Dagen.

Me: It's funny, I keep telling her she doesn't need to fit into anyone's box. She shouldn't try to be like everyone else and in reality that's exactly what I was doing. With Heather, I was going along, doing everything I thought I should when, in reality, I wasn't doing what I wanted to do. I'm not only getting a life but enjoying my life for the first time in years. Ironically, I have Heather to thank for that.

Antonia: You always see the good in everyone; you're

amazing. So, no more shit from Heather?

Me: No. I haven't heard anything more, but I did put Tony on it.

Antonia: Well if anyone can get rid of her, Tony can.

Me: Do I dare ask what's going on with you and Bo?

Antonia: Still just friends, unlike you and Dagen lol.

Me: Yeah, sure. Okay I've got to get going. Love you, ttyl.

Antonia: Don't forget my picture ☺

I think it's time to touch base with Grace. Maybe I can get the two of them on board.

Me: What are you up to?

Grace: Hey, stranger, what's up?

Me: I spoke to Antonia and she said you were thinking of Glasgow.

Grace: Yep, they have a great language program. Antonia told me that she spilled the beans to you. Thanks for not ratting us out.

Me: I'm trying to keep an open mind. Is there anyway I can talk you out of this?

Grace: Not really, look I've got my mother's love of language, and my father has taught me all kinds of self-defense since I was five years old. I'll be going into this with a leg up on the competition.

Me: Eventually, you will have to talk to him about it. Make sure you give me a heads up so I can stay on this side of the pond.

Grace: Chicken shit.

Me: Nope, just really fucking smart lol. I gotta run. Love you.

Grace: Back at ya.

Preston and I head inside, and Bo is making coffee. "Why the hell are you up at this hour?"

"I've got an early meeting at work, what about you?"

"The big guy woke me up, so I decided to catch up with Antonia." I watch his face for any kind of reaction—*nothing*. Maybe he heeded my warning.

"What are you up to today?"

"I'm going to take Dagen to trapeze school just as soon as I can talk her into it."

"Why are you trying to fit a lifetime worth of living in such a short time, are you sick?"

It never occurred to me that anyone who knows my past might think I'm sick again. "I'm not sick. I realized that I've lived the early part of my life in a bubble. When Heather came along, I fit into her nice, neat box of what she wanted. I need to find me, and Dagen is showing me a world of possibilities."

He pours me a cup of coffee and we head out back to sit down and catch up for a bit. "So, then the move here was worth it for you. What happens next?"

"If you're asking if I'm staying, the answer is yes. I like California and all it has to offer. Right now, I'm taking one day at a time."

"And my sister . . . what happens to her in all of your new found freedom?" He has every right to ask, same as I did with Antonia.

"We started out as friends, and we are building upon that. I want more with her, and we are taking it one day at a time."

"Well, I think I have the right to ask this question, so please hear me out. What happened with Heather? Why did she dump you? I mean, let's face it, you both have money, looks, everything at your fingertips. You wake up one day, she hands you an envelope and dumps you. You and your family freaked out by what was in the envelope. I think I have a right to know. I have to protect my sister."

"Yes and no. Yes you have the right to protect your sister, and I wouldn't expect anything less of you. However, my family also has a right to their privacy. I will tell you that I told Dagen, before we got together, why Heather ended it and she chose to continue our relationship. You've always trusted her judgment, trust her now."

He's quiet, drinking his coffee and staring into the morning haze. After a beat, "I trust you, Mike. I always have. If my sister is okay with everything, then you have my support. Besides, this is the happiest I've seen her in a very long time. Really . . . trapeze school?"

We're both laughing when Dagen steps outside. "Good morning, sunshine."

"You're very chipper this morning; did you even sleep?"

"I've got to get to work. Good luck today."

"Good luck with what?" She asks but he just laughs as he takes off.

"What was that all about?"

"I was wondering if we can go to Santa Monica Pier today. There are a bunch of cool things there to do."

"Why do I feel like there is more to this then you're telling me?"

Damn it, I'm so busted. "I would like to try something with you and I would really like it if you would keep an open mind."

She sits across from me and now I feel like I'm in the hot seat. "I'm listening; go ahead."

"Can we go to trapeze school?"

Her face is red and she is trying so hard to stifle her laughter. No such luck; she loses it and tears are coming down her cheeks. "Are you for real?"

"I was looking at different things for us to do today, and yeah, I'm for real."

"Is this some sort of bucket list?"

"Well, no, but like that great song from Tim McGraw says 'Live like you were dyin'.' I'm finally at a place in life where I can live life to the fullest. I'm not wasting it."

She leans in and kisses me with those beautiful soft lips. "Okay, Michael, let's make a memory today."

I kiss her over and over again. "Life's wonderful because of you."

"I already said yes. I swear you should go into politics."

We head inside and Mrs. H. is setting up breakfast, I'm too excited to eat.

"Guess where we're going! Oh, never mind; you'll never guess— trapeze school."

She drops the juice and makes the sign of the cross. "Why?"

"Because I can, and life is too short to say what if. Don't worry, it's perfectly safe."

She's cleaning up the juice and talking under her breath about keeping my feet on the ground. She reminds me so much of Mrs. Osla and my Grams all rolled into one.

"Michael, while we are at the pier, there is an antique carousel and a really cool aquarium we can go to. I'll need to stop home first to change and then stop at the office."

"Are you sure it won't be a problem?" I'm loading up my dish with pancakes, eggs, bacon, fruit and she's eating toast, what the fuck? "Why are you only eating toast?"

"How can you eat all that and then get tossed around?"

"Cast iron stomach."

"Well, not me. I'm going to jump in the shower while you finish up."

I pull her close and whisper in her ear, "I could wash your whooha."

"As much as the girls and I would love it, we'd never get out of here."

"You've got a point. You go first; I'll finish up here and then pack a bag to leave at your place." I lift a piece of bacon off my plate to pop into my mouth. She kisses me as she swipes it out of my hand and then heads off smiling. I don't know how I got so lucky, but I hope it never ends.

Dagen

His shower is a short girl's dream come true. Six bars running down the walls on each side with so many different types of jets hitting my body, while the two square rainfall heads from above drop so much water that I don't have to worry about getting all the shampoo out of my thick hair. But, the best part: the heads above are wired to a remote that lowers them for the vertically challenged. He has the entire bathroom wired for sound and right now he has Pink's "Fuckin Perfect" on repeat. "Change the voices in your head, make them like you instead." He keeps this up and I might actually believe him. This man has more products in his bathroom than I do. As much as I hate to leave this shower, if I don't, we'll never get out of here.

I find him standing out front by the Aston, messing with his phone. "Is everything okay?"

"Yeah, you want to drive?"

"Are you serious? You never let me drive."

"I didn't even realize it. You can drive for the whole day." He opens the door. I get in and he crouches down next to me. "A few things I need to show you before you take control of her." I'm trying hard not to laugh but his angst at letting me drive his baby is very funny. "First, the paddles on the wheel are your shifters. Second, I will take care of all the audio while you drive; I don't want you distracted. Remember, she's got at V-12 5.2 Twin Turbo which means, she goes very fast and finally, don't smash her." He kisses me and then closes the door.

We're now both sitting in the car and I'm too nervous to even turn it on.

"Well, are we going to sit here all day?"

"I'm sorry, you just made me very nervous."

"There's nothing to be nervous about, press the button."

I reach over and press the button. "Oh!"

"What? Are you okay?"

I have to have some fun with him and his 'girl.' "Michael, all that power just made my whooha come to life."

"Only you, sunshine."

We head out and now he's playing with the audio. "What are you trying to find?" I reach over to help him and he bats my hand away.

"Two hands on the wheel. Last night I added some more songs to your playlist."

He puts on Justin Timberlake's "Can't Stop The Feeling."

"I feel like J.T. is sitting right here singing with us."

"Do you realize you're doing 95 mph?"

"Oh shit, sorry. It's the music."

"Bo was worse, especially when Bon Jovi came on."

"I should have the approval from the county for your music studio today. If we do, then we can start right away."

"Great. I can't wait to start recording with you. Oh, and you never played your piano for me at your house. With that ceiling, the acoustics must be crazy."

"I promise tonight to play for you, but only if you sing."

"We can both sing. Have you ever been to this pier? You know some people can live their wholes lives in one place and never see everything around them."

"That's true, but I've been to the Santa Monica Pier many times. It's a fun place to hang out and when the sun sets, they have a great fireworks display."

We get to my house in record time. "I only need a few minutes to change and then we can get going." I cut the engine. He grabs his bags and we head inside. "I'll show you where you can put your stuff." *And, boy does he have stuff.*

"You realize you have more product than I do, how is that even possible?"

"Now you sound like Antonia; she's always picking on me. But, it's my mum's fault that I'm addicted to so many different products. She used to be a hairstylist and absolutely loves trying all the latest and greatest."

"Did the trapeze school give you a list of what we are we supposed to wear?"

"Yoga pants, socks, tie your hair up in a rubber band and bring flip flops and a towel. I've got a change of clothes in my bag and room for yours."

"You're the best." I stuff everything into his bag along with my bathing suit, and we head to my office. The approval for the studio is waiting for us; we double check it all and sign off on it.

Since it's during the week, parking at the pier is not that bad. "I hope the school has an opening for us."

"Oh, I already booked us in the 12:45 flying trapeze class."

"You were pretty sure I'd say yes."

"I can be very persuasive." He hits me with that million-dollar

smile and I can't help but laugh. We get checked in and we have
to sign safety waivers. I look over at our detail and none of them
seem happy. Once they belt us into a safety harness, we're ready to
go. He goes first and he's so good at it. His laughter has made this
all worthwhile. I'm taking picture after picture. I know I will never
forget this day—ever.

"Okay, Dagen, it's your turn."

My heart is pounding, but I have to do this. Not for him, but for
me. With each step up the ladder, my fear subsides and when I take
hold of the bar, I know I've got this. I push off, and the feeling of
flying through the air with such freedom is overwhelming. Through
my tears and my laughter, I'm finally letting my heart feel again.
When I'm back on solid ground, he takes me in his arms and kisses
me long and hard.

"Dagen Turner, my you've got a lock on my heart forever."

I feel my chest tighten, could he possibly feel what I'm feeling?
"I promise I'll never break it."

I wish we could stay in this moment forever, but we're being
pushed along. After we change, we continue on with our adventure.
By nightfall, I'm worn out and it's nice to lie down on the blanket he
packed and watch the fireworks.

"I had the most spectacular day, and to think, I've been here so
many times, yet today, it feels like the first time."

"I told you, you'll have a lot of firsts with me. You're falling
asleep; how about I drive us back to your place?"

"Between yesterday's golf and flying through the air today, I
can only imagine how I'm going to feel in the morning."

"We could relax in your beautiful claw foot tub, and I can give
you a massage."

"You've got a deal." I can only hope that I'll manage to stay
awake the twenty minutes it's going to take for us to get home.

Chapter Twenty-Three

Michael

DAGEN IS SO EXHAUSTED THAT SHE BARELY MANAGED TO stay awake on the ride to her house. "I'll get the bath drawn while you relax." It doesn't take much to convince her and in no time, I've got a steaming hot bath and some Advil waiting for her. We both climb in, her back to my front, which seems to be our norm lately.

"Your shoulders are so tight, how is that even possible?"

"The past few months have been crazy busy. My volleyball league will be starting soon, and I really need to get into shape."

"I know I've monopolized all of your time lately and I know I should be sorry but, truth be told, I'm not."

She turns in my arms and kisses me. "I've enjoyed every minute of it. I wouldn't change a thing, well, except maybe my horrible golf game."

"Golf is a game that gets better with time. Oh, I forgot to tell you I spoke to Antonia and she said Jeff made the cut and got into The University of Highlands and Islands golf program. It's very hard to get in; I'm so proud of him."

"Wow, that's wonderful. Does he want to golf professionally?"

"That would be his dream, but making the cut is very difficult. I think he has a good shot at it."

"I think it's wonderful that you come from such a tight knit family. I have no cousins; it's just Bo and me."

"Well, now you have all of us, good, bad, or otherwise. Come on, the water's getting cold. As much as I want to have my way with you, right now, you need to eat and get some rest. How about I make us some grilled cheese sandwiches and we can sit under the stars."

After we get dried off and dressed, I steer her towards the piano. "While I cook, you play."

"Any requests?"

"Whatever makes you happy." I head into the kitchen to make dinner. She begins to play, her fingers dancing along the keys. After a bit, she begins to sing. It's the first time I've heard her by herself, and her voice is breathtakingly beautiful. I stop everything to head out and watch her. She's singing "Bless The Broken Road." With such emotion, she's totally lost in the music. When she gets to the line "Every long lost dream lead me to where you are." I see a tear roll down her cheek. I step out of the doorway and sit next to her, then wipe away her tears. "That was so beautiful; why the tears?"

"Tears are my heart's way of saying it's overflowing with happiness."

I kiss her. I could keep kissing her all night long, but that won't get us fed.

"Will you play some more while I finish cooking?"

"Any requests, yet?"

"Nope, whatever your heart's telling you to play." I head into the kitchen and now she's playing Kenny Loggins "Forever." I finish up and I'm standing in the doorway with the food, but I don't want to stop her. She is so absorbed in the beauty of the music she creates. I wish that someday she would be at a point where she could share her talent with the world, but right now, I'm happy she's sharing it with me. When she finishes, she takes the sandwiches while I get the wine and we head out back to have dinner under the stars.

"I see you haven't killed everything I planted, yet."

"Give it time, and I'm sure I will. Although, I have to say, the thought of growing my own veggies is very exciting. How's Mick making out with his garden?"

"Remember Grams kept calling it all weeds? Well, he sent me a picture the other day, and his corn is about chest high. Now he wants to get chickens. You know we'll never hear the end of that."

"I'm really looking forward to all of them coming out for a visit."

"Hopefully soon."

"Is there a problem with them coming to visit?"

"It's hard for Aunt Raven to come back to the States. She lost so much here, but Uncle Jax said he would try to get her to come. Time will tell. Enough of that; what are our plans for the rest of the week?"

"I can look at the Giants schedule and see if they are playing at home and we can get tickets to the game."

I pull out my phone to see when their next home game is and I have an emergency text from my boss to call him. "I've got to call work. Apparently, there is some sort of emergency."

She takes the dishes inside to give me some privacy while I call Glen. "Hey, Glen, it's Michael, what's going on?"

"There has been an oil leak a hundred miles off the coast of Louisiana. It's a privately run rig and they are saying that it is contained. The company is claiming that everything is back to normal and they want to resume operation. The EPA is putting together a team to go out there and double-check everything. That area can't have another disaster like the 2010 spill. It's a deep-water rig and they need one more safety specialist. With your background, you would be a perfect fit."

"When would I have to leave?"

"You need to be at LAX for a 6 am flight. Michael, you don't have to do it; it's strictly up to you. They asked me for some recommendations and you're the only one who came to mind."

"I'll do it. Do you have any of the details about the leak?"

"Very little. Apparently, it's not from drilling; it's in the flowline that connects the different pipelines. I'll send everything I have to your email along with your flight information. And, Michael, be careful. Apparently, there's a tropical storm gaining some speed, so watch yourself out there."

"Yeah, don't worry; I'll be fine."

"You better be; I just got you broken in." He hangs up and I send a quick text to Neville, letting him know about the change of plans. Now comes the hard part: saying goodbye to Dagen. I turn around and find her curled up in the patio bed.

"Hey, I have some bad news."

"I heard; you have to leave. It's your job; you're responsible for the safety of others. I would expect nothing less from you."

I curl up next to her and kiss her sweet lips. "My flight isn't until 6 am, so from now until then, you can do what you want with me."

"Really?"

"Really." I smile. She climbs onto my lap and slowly kisses me. Working her way down my shoulder, first with a kiss and then a little nip. When I reach for the girls, she takes a hold of both my wrists.

"No touching—at least—not yet. I'm wound up so tight, I might come from you touching them." She wiggles her way down and plays with my nipples instead. She so gentle, first kissing and then she tugs a little. Working her way slowly down my abs. She pulls off my shorts and tosses them, but not before she pulls a condom out of my pocket.

"You've got that Scotland Scout thing down."

Her fingers always tremble when she touches me and it's fucking sexy as hell. She kisses my tat and whispers. "We are making it a good one." She pulls off her t-shirt and places my cock between the girls.

"Please, for the love of all that's holy, let me touch them."

"Yes."

That's it, just a simple yes, and I feel like I've won the fucking lottery. I flip her over and now my cock is cocooned tightly between her breasts as I play with her nipples.

"I don't want to come yet, but I don't know if I can hold back."

She swirls her fingertip around the head of my cock and it's like he's answering a siren's call. "Michael, wait. I want you on your back; my way tonight."

I flip on to my back, thinking it will give my cock a chance to redeem his self-control. No such luck; she's swirling her tongue around and then up and down the vein. Now she's got my balls, first one and then the other.

"Oh, God, Dagen, I don't know how much more I can take."

She takes my cock deep into her mouth and as it hits the back of her throat, she presses her finger into my arse. That's it—I'm done. Mount St. Helens just erupted.

"Holy hell, woman, that was surreal."

"I'm not done with you, yet. Remember, it's my night." She's kissing me everywhere and slowly my deflated cock is coming back to life. She opens the condom and rolls it on. The concentration on her face when she does this is a total turn on.

"My whooha needs servicing before you leave."

I can't help but laugh. "How would you like me to service your whooha?"

"First with your highly skilled tongue and then, with your cock."

"Every time we're together, you're becoming more comfortable and open with me. It's beautiful, like you." As I crawl between her legs, I push them up high so I can have full access to her. I start with a kiss and then I flick my tongue over her nub and end with a tug. When she starts pulling my hair, I know it won't be long before she loses all control. I get up on my knees and slowly enter her, then stop.

"Michael, why are you counting?"

"I need a minute or the party will be over before it even gets started." Slowly, I start moving, trying to prolong the inevitable but then she moans and takes her nipples between her fingers, rolling and pulling. She tilts her head back and lets out a deep sexy as hell moan. How much is one man supposed to take?

"Dagen, I'm—oh fuck!"

"Please, oh, Michael, yes! More, I want more."

I keep going until there's nothing left in the tank for either of us. I make quick work of the condom and then pull her into my arms. The night air is turning chilly, so I pull the throw blanket over us.

"Well, that was quite the sendoff."

"I don't want you to forget me."

"I would never forget you."

"Do you know how long you'll be gone?"

"No. I won't have any idea until I access the damage. Hopefully, not too long."

"I know you have to go, but I'll miss you."

"I promise to check in daily and you can always find your star right there." I point up, showing her right where I'll be looking every night.

It's after midnight, and we're both exhausted. I hope this inspection will last only a couple of days but I can't be sure. What I am sure about is—*her.* "Close your eyes, sunshine, you're exhausted." I put on the playlist I made for her and hit shuffle. How ironic; Aerosmith's "I Don't Want to Miss a Thing" is the first song to come on. She drifts off to sleep with me softly singing to her.

Sitting under the stars with my girl, content in my arms, is a dream come true. I never thought I would get this close to anyone ever again, let alone, this soon. She accepts me for me and not someone else's past. She stepped into my world and blew the lid off my box, the same box I'm always telling her to step out of. Richard Marx is singing, "Last Thing I Wanted" and I tighten my arms around her. The first time I heard this song, I was running with

Preston on the beach. I swear it was written about us.

When I finally look at the time I realize I'm never going to make it home to pack a bag. Maybe Bo can help me out.

Me: Hey, wake up. I need a favor.

Bo: This better be good.

Me: There's been an emergency in the Gulf. I have to head out there with a group from the EPA and check that everything is safe. I need you to go into my closet, get the bag I keep packed and bring it down to LAX.

Bo: What kind of emergency?

Me: A leak off the coast of Louisiana. The company is saying it's contained and the clean up is almost done. The EPA wants to make sure it's safe to go back online. They emailed me some schematics of the flowlines. I'm forwarding them to you. Let me know what you think.

Bo: Sure, send it now. There's a waiting area by public parking lot C. I'll meet you there.

Me: Thanks.

She's starting to stir in my arms. "Hey, beautiful, I need to get going, and I don't want you staying out here."

"I'm sorry I fell asleep on you." She stretches and winces, no doubt sore from the last two days.

"How could everything hurt so much? I mean even my hair hurts, like that's even possible."

"Book a massage and take lots of Epsom salt baths while I'm

gone. Bo is meeting me at the airport, so I could stay here longer. I'm leaving my car here. Feel free to use her, just don't wreck her."

"I can drop you off at the airport."

"My detail is dropping me off. I want you to get some rest." I squeeze her to me. She's kissing my neck and making it more difficult to leave. "Remember what I told you at the pier." I give her one last kiss goodbye before getting up and heading down the walkway. When I turn around, she's standing in the doorway, running her fingers over her lips.

At this time of the morning, traffic is light. I find Bo waiting for me at the parking lot. "Hey, thanks for doing this for me. I could have had one of the guards bring it but I wanted to talk to you about the leak."

"No problem. I looked at the schematics you sent and what I don't understand is, with all the technology they've been using, why didn't they notice this sooner?

"Yeah, that's what I was thinking. It sounds like someone dropped the ball."

"Well, just don't go pissing in someone else's pool before you have all the facts."

"I know. I've got to go. I'll text you later and let you know what I find." I slap his shoulder then head to the terminal. When I get to the gate, I find a few more people that were recruited by the EPA. The good thing is, they recruited people from all different companies to look at this before it becomes a major disaster. My detail has to do a pre-check with the gate agent and the flight crew. They can only go as far as Louisiana, after that, Neville will remain with me. I've got time to kill, so I send Antonia the photo I promised her.

Antonia: Don't you ever sleep? I think this picture might

be my favourite, so far. The look on your face is sheer joy and freedom. Did Dagen like it?

Me: I got called into work for a special project, otherwise, I would be sleeping. Dagen loved it and we plan on going back again. When you come out here, I'm taking you.

Antonia: Deal. What's the special project?

Me: No big deal; I need to make sure some lines are safe before they are operative.

Antonia: Be careful and Facetime me soon. I miss that mug of yours.

Michael: I will.

The flight is not very full and I'm able to take up a full row with Neville in the row across from me. I swear, the minute we get to ten thousand feet, he's already asleep. I'm flipping through my pictures and I find one that the instructor took of Dagen and I after the class. I decide to send it to my mum, along with a picture of me on the trapeze. It doesn't take long for my phone to chime that I have a new text. My mum is so predictable and I can't help but laugh.

Mum: So, you seem happy.

Me: I loved the trapeze and can't wait to go again.

Mum: I meant with Dagen. I know you loved the trapeze, anything to make me nuts.

Me: Yes, I'm happy. She's my more.

Mum: I knew that day you brought her home that she was different, special.

Me: I thought for sure you would lecture me about it being too soon and give it time.

Mum: I saw something different when you were with her that I never saw with Heather. It's like your heart found it's home.

Me: Have you been dipping into Uncle Jax's fortune cookies? Lol

Mum: Raven created a monster with that one. Look at the picture of the two of you together. The look on both your faces is so beautiful. Life only comes at you once, Michael, grab it by the balls and run with it. You can't always play within the lines. Why are you up at this hour?

Me: Work stuff. How's dad?

Mum: Wonderful of course. He's been very busy with this year's harvest. It looks like it will be a good year for the reds. As soon as it slows down, he promised we could come and visit you.

Me: Okay, I've got to get going. Love you.

Mum: Me too.

Might as well put my earbuds in and try to get some sleep. I put Dagen's playlist on shuffle and drift off.

The couple of hours sleep was worth it. I just wish I could have jumped in the shower before heading out. The man heading up the inspection is Ross Armstrong. He's going over all the safety precautions for the crew. When he's done, he pulls me aside.

"Glen informed me about Neville and he has clearance to go with us. The others will have to stay behind. Can I ask you something; why are you even here?"

"I was asked to do a job for which I'm more than qualified to do. I'm here just like everyone else, trying to prevent a disaster. Is there a problem?"

"No, no problem, I was just wondering what you're trying to prove and to whom you're trying to prove it to."

"Are you always this rude or just to me?"

"I have to look out for my men."

"Sounds like you're just fishing for some sort of tabloid information. Like I said, I'm just doing my job. Maybe you should do yours."

Before we head out, I pull my lead guard, Rico, aside. "Give Uncle Max the name Ross Armstrong and ask him to look into him. It's probably nothing, but tell him the hair on my neck stood up; he'll understand."

Neville and I are the last to board the transport under the watchful eye of Armstrong.

Dagen

Oh my God, when the alarm goes off, I make the mistake of stretching. My entire body cramps up and is screaming out in pain. You know when you get a charley horse, you usually leap out of bed and try to walk it off, but what the fuck do you do when your entire body cramps up? Why does my hair hurt? How is that even possible? Oh, what I wouldn't do to be in his amazing shower right now. Dreams are not going to pay the bills. I drag my sorry ass into the shower and make it as hot as I can stand it. When I reach for my shampoo, I find all kinds of different bottles. I have four things in the shower: shampoo, conditioner, shower gel, and a razor. He's got to have at least eight or nine different things. What the hell is beard conditioner? He doesn't even have a beard! I open it up and damn, it smells really good. After a while, the water starts to turn cold and I know the party's over.

I have two meetings today, one is at my office and then I have to meet with the builder at Michael's and go over the plans for the music studio. This builder is new to me but he is supposed to be the best in the business for what I need. I opt for a pink and white pencil skirt, a fitted white blouse and matching pink pumps. Pencil skirts give me an hourglass figure, and I need all the help I can get. When I head outside, the DB is sitting at the curb. Hmm what's a girl to do? Well, he said I should use it, so why the hell not? Especially now that Michael made me realize that having a guard does not mean she has to sit in the car with me. When I get in, I smell him everywhere and my heart is pounding. I've been checking my phone all morning and no message from him, yet. I snap a quick selfie behind the wheel and text it to him. When I press the ignition, my whooha tingles. Now I'm sitting here laughing and crying at the same time, how is that even possible? I have no time for this, now. I turn on the sound system and he has the playlist he made me programmed to come on.

Driving this car is a dream, even if I'm in Beverly Hills traffic. I'm waiting for the light when Coldplay starts singing "Miracles." He has such a vast love of all different kinds of music. I don't think I should attempt to parallel park; valet is the way to go today. When

I get into my office, there's a Forget Me Not plant on my desk with a note:

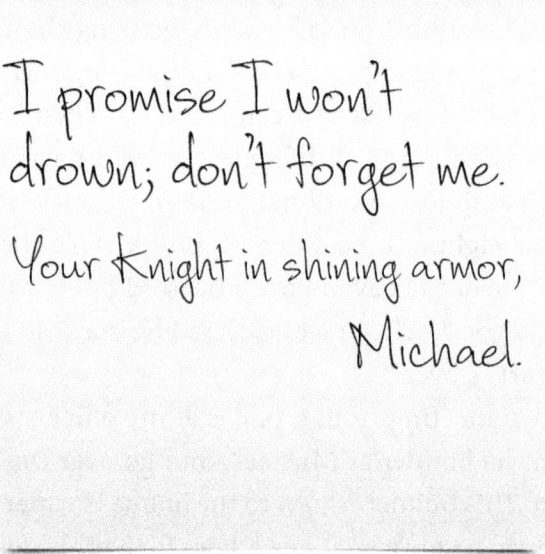

I promise I won't drown; don't forget me.
Your Knight in shining armor,
Michael.

I'm laughing and crying again, remembering that silly story he told me. I need to pull myself together; my meeting with the new client is about to start. I very rarely close my door, and when I look up, my assistant Nathan is waiting for me.

"Hey, Miss Redmond called and changed the time of the meeting. You'll be with the builder. Besides, she wants Malibu and that's my specialty, so I told her no problem as long as she didn't mind dealing with me. She was cool with it."

"I'm sorry I haven't been around much."

"It's okay. Chelsea is handling all the paperwork and bullshit stuff and I've got the clients covered. Even though she's like a drill sergeant, I'm thankful that you hired her. Besides, I haven't seen you this happy in years. So, tell me about him."

"He's very kind and damn good looking, but it's so much more than that. He's the real deal. I don't know what I ever did right to have him, not only, step into my life, but for him to notice me at all."

"Did you not look at yourself in the mirror today? You're fucking hot; open your eyes,"

"Now you sound like him. I want to try and see him as much as I can when he's in town. So, two weeks out of the month, I'll be scarce around here. I've been doing a lot of thinking and, if you're willing to carry the load, then I would like to up your percentage. The standard deal usually nets us six percent. The agency will always get one percent, but if you handle the sale, you'll get bumped from two percent to three percent. I think I should also give Chelsea a raise."

"Wow, thank you. I agree with you; Chelsea has more than earned it."

"I'm meeting the builder at Michael's house, so I will probably hang out and visit my brother, unless you need me back here for anything?"

"No, I've got it covered." He hands me the plans along with another envelope.

"I did a cost break down on the job. Just because the guy has money doesn't mean he should get hosed."

"You're the best. Let me know what happens with the Redmond deal." I snap a picture of my plant and read the note again. How could I forget someone who's turning my life upside down one memory at a time? I gather up all my stuff and head out.

No matter what time of day I get on the Pacific Coast Highway, the traffic is always horrible. At least I have this car's state-of-the-art media system to play with. I think I was able to sync my phone, but I'm really not that gifted. I'll call my mom to keep me amused. When I ask the car to call Mom, she answers like a Brit. I'm laughing, that is . . . until Bella answers the phone! Holy crap, I'm so electronically challenged.

"Michael, is everything okay? I thought you would be busy with the inspection."

"Umm, hi, Bella, it's Dagen. I have Michael's car and I was sitting in traffic, so I tried to call my mother for amusement. I'm so sorry to disturb you." I know I'm rambling and thank God she's laughing.

"Dagen, don't worry about it. How have you been?"

"I'm fine, thank you. Michael and I have been going on little adventures; it's been fun."

"I've been getting the pictures. I'm glad he's enjoying life. He sent some pictures of the house; it looks beautiful."

"Thank you, but now Michael wants a music studio. He's keeping me busy."

"He loves music. You know, Max is the one who taught him how to play the guitar."

Somehow, I still can't picture this. "Michael mentioned that. I think I would pay to see Max play the guitar." I can't help but laugh at the thought of it.

"Well, you'll be happy to know that he also sings."

"You know it's true what they say, never judge a book by its cover. When you come out, I would like to take you to the Napa Valley. There are some great vineyards and there is also the Calistoga mineral hot springs."

"It sounds wonderful. We will try and get out there soon."

"Well, I better go. I'm coming up to my exit. Thank you for keeping me amused during the ride."

"You're welcome. Be safe."

That's probably the longest one on one conversation I've ever had with her. I give up playing with everything and just put on the news. When I pull up to the guard booth at the gate, he informs me that the builder is waiting. He's early, so that's a good sign. I head inside and find him in the kitchen with Mrs. Holiday.

"Hello, Mr. Jacob, I'm Ms. Turner."

He's looking me up and down and then he glances at my guard, Ms. Salvano. Maybe I'm just being paranoid.

"Why don't you show me where the actual building site will

be." He takes my elbow and I step away from him, which causes Ms. Salvano to step forward.

"Why don't we go on the patio and I can show you exactly what I need done? Then, I can show you the site that the surveyor already staked out. The architect drew up the plans to our specifications. You just need to build it." We head outback and I spread out the plans on the table so he can see exactly what I want. He's leaning over my shoulder and I take a step sideways away from him. He's a tall man, so when he's looking over my shoulder I feel like he's looking at my boobs.

"This is a big job, and by the looks of these plans, it will take a couple of months to pull this off. Plus, the city moves really slowly with the inspectors and permits. Do you live in this big place all by yourself?"

Before I can answer, Preston comes running out the house with his teeth bared. He's inching closer to Mr. Jacob. Salvano and I are trying all the hand signs, but they aren't working. I grab his collar and try to hold him back. When a dog does this, it means he senses danger. Mr. Holiday comes running over and puts a leash on Preston.

"Mr. Jacob, thank you for meeting me, but I don't think this will work out. Please send me a bill for your time."

He leaves and finally Preston starts to calm down. What the hell am I going to do now? He was the best in the business. What the fuck am I going to tell Michael? The sleaze ball builder was more interested in my boobs and if I lived alone, than doing his job? He'll freak out.

Me: Hey, do you have a list of any other builders that I can pull from?

Nathan: What happened to the one you were meeting with?

Me: Very high on the creeper meter, plus Preston wanted to take a bite out of him.

Nathan: Maybe you should have let him. I've got a list. I will go through it and see what I can come up with. Redmond is a go; I'll be showing her places tomorrow. I'll let you know what I find.

Me: Thanks! ttyl.

I'm glad I threw a bag of clothes in the car, at least I can get comfortable while I wait for Bo to get home from work. I head into the kitchen to get something to eat and I find Mrs. Holiday set up lunch for me before she left. *A girl could get used to this.* I take everything and head in to Michael's office. By now, Nathan probably emailed me the list and I can work from there.

Chapter Twenty-Four

Michael

We get to the rig, and it's much bigger than the last one I was on. They have a lot of state-of-the-art computer stuff, but not everything is working to full capacity. Every time I question something, Anderson cuts me off. Rather than sit and listen to his bullshit, I take my coffee and wander around. Uncle Jax taught me that sometimes you get the most information by taking a back seat and just watching. When I take out my phone to make notes, I see I have two text messages.

Max: Anderson doesn't have a good reputation; there have been complaints about him. Watch your arse.

Me: Thanks.

The next one is a selfie from Dagen.

Me: Very hard to concentrate on work when my girls are smiling at me. I notice you were in my car. I have one question, did your whooha sing?

Dagen: She doesn't want to sing without you. The girls were tucked away just fine. You just have an overactive

imagination.

Me: Only with you, sunshine. How's your day going?

Dagen: Busy. I woke up feeling like I got hit by a Mack truck. Stood in the shower till the water ran cold. Used some beard conditioner on my hair, looks the best it's ever looked. Why do you have that if you don't have a beard?

Me: ROFL It's not just for a beard.

Dagen: OH!!!!

Me: I'm laughing hysterical right now and people are starting to stare.

Dagen: Well, I might as well give you something else to laugh about. I thought I synced my phone with your car. I thought I was calling my mom, that is, until your mom answered.

Me: I'm sure she found it very funny.

Dagen: She was very sweet about it. After that, I gave up and put on the news. How is it going by you?

Me: It looks like tropical storm Gaston will become a hurricane. Not sure of the severity or what direction it's going to take. Either way, there are things here that need to be addressed. Hopefully, I won't be gone too long. I've got to get back to work. I'll try and check in later. If not, sweet dreams, sunshine.

Dagen: Hugs.

Anderson called a meeting of the minds, which is what he likes to call it. Each member of the team has to present his or her findings to the board, which consist of the CEO and Anderson. Guaranteed he's not going to like what I have to say. Neville and I get there and take the last two seats in the back. It's a ten-member team and, so far, every member is saying not to reopen, but no one is giving a definitive reason why. Being picked last is not always a bad thing; in this case, it's a blessing. Over the years, I've watch Uncle Jax at work; he's a master at what he does. I'd like to think I've learned a lot from him. Be direct, get to the point quickly, make them feel like you're doing them a huge favor, and end with them feeling like they need you. Finally, it's my turn.

"Good evening. I've been following everyone's presentation and one thing is missing. You already know that reopening this drill is questionable. It could lead to another leak from the flow-line, a leak that might not be so easy to repair. What I don't see is what affect Gaston will have on the flowline if you reopen. In case anyone is not aware, Gaston has been upgraded to a category two hurricane. I'm also concerned about the level of drilling mud, the trip tank levels, and the age of the equipment. Even though the gas pressure has been capped off, if Gaston hits, the pressure builds and if the mud levels are not above acceptable levels, well, you just created the perfect storm. With outdated equipment, you've created a disaster that could have been prevented." I distribute my reports to the other members, giving everyone a few minutes to absorb my findings. Anderson's face is turning red, no doubt because, if they have to close it down, he loses a fat bonus along with his pay. "My preliminary findings suggest this rig should be shut down immediately. After the storm passes, then a qualified crew can make the necessary changes." I head back to my seat, and I feel like my back is being shot with hot spears.

The meeting quickly breaks up and as I'm heading out, the CEO pulls me aside. "Mr. Vizzano, I'm Mr. Stapleton. I'd like to hear more about your theory."

"The way Gaston is barreling in, I think it's becoming more than theory."

"How much time do you think we have?"

"It depends on the storm. If it continues on the predicted trajectory, you might have twenty-four hours, but I would start evacuating now. Things can change on a dime, and this is something you don't want to fall behind on."

"Thank you for your honesty."

He leaves, and I'm not sure what he's doing, but I know I want to get the hell out of here. "Neville, I'm thinking we need to make arrangements to leave as soon as possible."

"This storm is traveling fast, it might not be that easy. Let's go check the radar and see what's going on." We're heading upstairs when there is an announcement that the rig is being evacuated. "That was pretty quick, something must have happened." When we get to the deck, there's been a definite shift in the storm. The wind has picked up but no rain, yet. Neville grabs my arm. "We won't get any air support in this storm, but Anderson is loading up the lifeboats that are kept on the freefall ramps. We need to make sure we get on one of them."

"Don't worry, I will get on. Thankfully, each boat holds up to forty people, so at least it's not like the Titanic. You need to get on board and put on your life vest."

We are heading over when the entire rig shakes. Fuck, it's a blowout explosion.

"Michael, you have to get in that boat now!"

"There are still too many people that need to be evacuated. The sooner we get them on, the sooner we can get the hell out of here."

Some of the men are trying to contain the fire while we load the boats. Now the rain is coming in hard and fast, good for the fire

. . . bad for the rescue. This doesn't look good and for the first time, in a very long time, I feel fear, a fear I haven't felt since Uncle Jax told me I had cancer. I push Neville into the lifeboat "I don't need your death on my conscious; save your arse." It's called a freefall for a reason; it's kind of like a water ride at an amusement park. Before Neville can get out, Anderson releases the boat.

In the mist of all of this I realize this might be my last chance to tell her how I feel. I know I'm a crazy arse fool, but I can't wait. I pull out my phone and send her a text.

Me: Dagen, Things are little crazy right now. Remember what I told you, that no matter what, you've got a lock on my heart forever. I didn't get a chance to tell you, but I love you. I love everything about you. You're my best friend, my lover, my sunshine, and my end all. You've helped me get a life worth living. You complete me. You're my beacon of light in this crazy arse storm. I'm only sorry it took me so long to find you. I love you, with everything I've got.

I hit send and pull the people, fighting the fire into the last boat. I'm helping everyone get belted into the boat when there is another explosion. I hit the release lever for the boat, but I don't get a chance to belt myself in. The boat goes one way and I go another. I'm flying through the air and this time, I'm not on a trapeze with a net to catch me. This time, it's a very high drop. I hit the water and instantly feel something in my leg snap. Black smoke and debris is everywhere. The water is cold and I'm starting to get numb. I can't see the lifeboat—hell—I can't see anything. There are a series of explosions, and I'm trying to swim away from the wreckage, but it's very hard with one leg in a hurricane. Something hits me in the head very hard. Whatever it was has made my head bleed. I must have been knocked out from the blow. It's getting darker but the rain seems to be subsiding. Maybe I'm in the eye of the storm. I don't think I'm dead. If I am, then this is a major disappointment. If only I could see Dagen's star, she would guild me home. I'm floating for a while and all I can think about is the dead people in the Titanic movie. "Thanks Aunt Raven for making me watch that movie with you, now that's all I can think about." Jesus, I'm talking to myself.

I need to keep my arms moving and I need to try and keep my body temperature up. Hypothermia sets in pretty quickly. The rain is back and, this time, harder than before. The eye of the storm has passed, but I'm so tired. The rain coming down in sheets and it is hurting my eyes. I'll just close them for a bit. Oh my God, Miss Rose is here. I'm dead—that's it—there can't be any other explanation.

"Miss Rose, why are you here? If this is dead, then we need to talk about different arrangements."

"Michael, you're not dead, but you need to fight. Be the man I know you are and fight to live. You've always put everyone first, now it's your time. Don't let it slip away."

I open my eyes and she's gone.

"I'll fight Miss Rose, I'm just really tired. As soon as I rest a bit, I'll fight again . . . promise."

PATRICK

The storm is hitting a lot harder and faster than predicted. I usually leave the charters up to my crew, but with this Gaston taking a sharp turn towards land, I decided to go to the pier and help. When I get there, I notice one of my boats is still out. That's unusual. Usually, everyone follows my orders with no questions asked. I find the head captain, Roy, securing one of the boats.

"Hey, Roy, where is the other boat?"

"Pat, there was an explosion on one of the rigs. All charters are out there trying to assist the Coast Guard. It's getting really bad and most of the guys have come back. I'm just waiting on Gabe, he's the last one out there."

"I'll finish securing everything and wait here. Why don't you get going before this storm gets worse?"

He doesn't have to be told twice; he's got a family at home. I'm sure they are worrying about him. The wind and the rain is really starting to pick up. I know these men live by a code: if anyone is out to sea, and in trouble, they are the first ones out there to help. But, I don't need one of my guys getting lost out there. While I'm securing everything, I turn on the radio to listen for any updates. The storm is getting worse. I'm about to radio Gabe when I see his boat coming in. He pulls into the slip and I begin securing the boat. Gabe and his first mate struggle from the cabin, carrying a body.

"Gabe, is he dead?"

"No, but he's in bad shape. We wrapped him up in whatever blankets we could find. We need to get him to the hospital right away if he has any chance to survive."

I help them get the guy off the boat. He seems familiar, proba-bly one of the locals that were working on one of the rigs. "No way an ambulance is going to get here anytime soon. Let's get him in my truck and I'll drive him there. Does he have any identification?"

"Yeah, I found his wallet in his pocket. His name is Michael Vizzano Jr," he says. I freeze a name from the past that I never ex-pected to hear again. "Patrick, you okay?"

"Yeah, I'm fine. Just get him in my truck and I'll take him there myself." To think, after all these years, I'm going to be the one to save him. I turned her world upside down, but, maybe now, I can wipe away some of the wrongs. Maybe, just maybe, I can be redeemed in her eyes. Not that I deserve it, not for all I put her through, but maybe he's my glimmer of hope.

"Michael, don't you die on me."

I look over at him and I notice he's got a gash on the side of his head. He muttering something, it sounds like he's thanking Rose for saving him. "No, Michael, that would be me, Duke, the past coming full circle." Maybe he's delirious, I'm not sure. All those years ago, I was forced to change my name and put into witness protection. Now my past has come back to life, and he's right here in my truck. Now I have to try and keep him alive long enough to gain some sort of redemption. I crank the heat up trying to warm him up as I try to navigate our way to the hospital. Debris is everywhere and the wipers can't keep up with the rain. I make my way downtown and the National Guard is directing everyone to seek shelter. They let me through and direct me on the clearest path to the hospital.

When I pull up to the emergency room, the doors open and the nurses race out with a gurney. I give them the little bit of information that I know. While they are tending to him, I pull out my phone and try to contact Jax and Max but all I get is a message saying the call won't go through. I'm not sure if it's the storm or something more. Finally, I dial her—my sister—Raven.

Chapter Twenty-Five

Raven

THE YELLING FROM HIS OFFICE IS LOUDER THAN USUAL. OH yeah, they bicker and challenge each other like two old cronies but something about this is very different. I hear Jax let out a roar that makes my heart race and not in a good way. I'm running up the steps, taking them two at a time. The closer I get to the office, the louder it gets. When I open the door, a glass comes flying along with a slew of F-bombs.

"Jax!"

"Oh my God, Raven, I'm sorry." Our eye's lock and there is a look on his face that, in all of these years we've been together, I've never seen; it's a look of sheer panic and despair.

"I'm glad you weren't aiming for me; what the hell is going on?!"

"It's Junior; he's missing."

His words hang in the air: *Junior—missing*. I grab the chair as the room begins to spin. My mind instantly flashes back to the day on the school playground when Michael was fighting off his kidnappers. My head begins to pound and my stomach is twisted into knots. Please, dear God, not again.

"Missing?" I barely whisper out the words before my knees begin to buckle. He pulls me into his arms; his grip is tight and I can feel his heart pounding through his shirt. Max is on the phone barking out orders while Jax's grip on me tightens.

"Junior was with a team of investigators on a private oil rig one hundred miles off the coast of Louisiana. Apparently, there was a leak in a flowline and ninety thousand gallons of oil had already spilled out. The company claimed it was repaired and they were set to go back online. Junior's team was brought in to determine if it was repaired properly or if they had to do a total shut down. He found that the situation there was too dangerous and insisted that it be shut down until the proper repairs could be made. He was helping to get everyone off the rig to safety when there was a small explosion. His guard tried to get him to leave but he refused until everyone else was safe. There was a second explosion and now he's *missing*." His arms around me tighten, maybe it's to stop my shaking or maybe it's to help him keep from losing what little control he's barely hanging on to.

"The United States Coast Guard has been called in, and they are monitoring the situation. Until additional help can get there, they are dropping packages with flotation devices. Mick contacted his friend Jacob who is an Admiral out of The Eighth Coast Guard District. They are assigned to that area and they assured him that they are doing everything possible to rescue everyone. Fishing boats from the area are also helping with the rescue. The biggest problem is that Hurricane Gaston has hit the area. They are hoping they don't have to call off the search and rescue. Max just got a hold of Michael and Bella in Italy, they are already on their way to the States. Get everyone ready we are leaving right away," Jax finishes filling me in.

Dagen

I'm sitting out back, waiting for Bo when a text message comes through from Michael.

> **Me: Dagen, Things are little crazy right now. I want you to know that no matter what you've got a lock on my heart forever. I didn't get a chance to tell you but I love you. I love everything about you. You're my best friend, my lover, my sunshine, and my end all. You've helped me get a life worth living. You complete me. You're my beacon of light in this crazy arse storm. I'm only sorry it took me so long to find you. I love you, with everything I've got.**

> **Dagen: Are you okay? I would rather tell you this in person, but here goes. I love you, heart and soul. It took my mind some time to catch up to what my heart already knew. I've waited my whole life for you to find me. I don't know where this journey is taking us, all I know is, I want to spend every day of the rest of my life with you. Hugs.**

I'm reading his text over and over, what does he mean a little crazy? Why would he text me this and not at least call me to tell me. I'm staring at the phone, waiting for those three little dots that show he's answering me . . . nothing. Bo comes running through the back door nearly knocking it off the hinges. "Dagen, did you hear anything yet?"

"What are you talking about?" He can't possibly know about my text from Michael.

He sits next to me, both of his hands holding my shoulders. "There was an explosion on the rig and Gaston has hit harder than expected. Michael's missing."

"No, look he texted me; he can't be missing." I show him my phone.

"That was a couple of hours ago. Right now, he is listed as missing."

"No, no, no, no, no! Please, God, no!" I totally fall apart in my brother's arms. "I don't believe it, I won't believe it." I try to jump up, but he's still holding me.

"Where are you going?"

"I won't wait here, I just won't. I'm going to Louisiana. You can come with me or you can stay here, but, so help me God, I'm not giving up."

"No flights are going into the area; I already checked," he informs me. I grab my phone out of his hand and start looking for the number. "Dagen, I wouldn't lie to you; we can't get there."

I call Max not sure if he will even answer, for all I know, he's on his way to Louisiana. "Hello, Dagen, now is not really a good time."

"Max, don't you dare hang up on me! I need to get to Louisiana right now. All flights there are canceled. If you don't help me, Bo and I will get in that bullet of a car and drive ourselves right now, and when Michael finds out, he'll be really pissed at you."

"I'll call you back; start heading to the Burbank Airport."

"Come on, we've got to get to Burbank."

Mr. and Mrs. Holiday are in the living room, watching non-stop news footage of the explosion. I can't even go down that road. "We're on our way to Louisiana. We'll keep you posted." I then turn to my detail. "Ms. Salvano, I know I never let you drive, but I'm in no condition to. Please get us to Burbank as fast as you possibly can," I beg and she nods her head in agreement. We all race out to get into the car.

Bo and I are in the back, and she takes off. She's driving like she's in a crazy car chase. Then I remember, she told me that Max trained her. I keep whispering for Michael to hang on. My phone rings and my heart skips a beat. I want to believe it's Michael but it's not, it's Max.

"There's a military flight waiting for you. I sent the coordinates for the house we are staying at to Salvano's phone. Be safe."

"Thank you." The phone disconnects and I'm not even sure he heard me.

I don't know how Ms. Salvano doesn't get pulled over, but she speeds right it to a reserved area for military personal. There are at least a dozen military personal waiting for us, along side a huge plane, which I'm told is a Hurricane Hunter. "Ma'am, my orders are to get everyone delivered to Louisiana ASAP. It's not the most comfortable ride, but you're in good hands."

They help strap us in, and of course the aircraft fascinates Bo. All I know is, I want Michael home safe. We take off and I'm saying every prayer I know as we fly into darkness.

MAX

I was barely keeping it together when Dagen called and tore into me. Pretty obvious they are more than friends. "Why the fuck didn't he get in the boat with Neville?"

"Because Michael will always put others before himself."

I spin around at the sound of her voice. "Jackie, I thought I was alone."

"We'll find him, but staring at the phone won't make it ring." I know she's right but I still can't look away. "Dagen and Bo are downstairs. She took one look at Bella and lost it. I think it's safe to say they are more than friends."

"Yeah, I figured. Where's Jax?"

"Trying to keep everyone calm, especially An."

"I'll be down in a minute to give him a hand." She kisses me and gives me my alone time. I pull out my wallet and take out my picture of Samantha and Elliott. *I know you're both watching over me, please help me find Michael, keep him safe.* I wipe away my tears and head downstairs. I need to be the rock that everyone expects me to be. I look at Jax and shake my head no. "As soon as this storm let's up, I'll be joining the search. Jax, where is Dagen?"

"She probably went in the kitchen for some tea."

I check the kitchen and she's nowhere to be found. There are two staircases in this house, maybe she went up to her room. When I get back in the living room, Jax is on the phone and looking out back. "Max, Salvano just called; Dagen is upstairs on the outside balcony. She won't come in. I'm going to try and talk to her."

"I'll be in the office if you need me. I want to check the weather and see if I can get a call through to the Coast Guard." Right now, I need quiet.

JAX

How the hell am I supposed to help everyone keep it together when I'm barely hanging on myself? I find her on the balcony, looking up and yelling Michael's name over and over again. I hand Salvano a towel and she gives us some privacy.

"Dagen, he can't hear you. Please come back inside before you get sick."

"I can't see it, Jax."

"See what?" Maybe she's having a breakdown, maybe I need to get Raven.

"Michael had a star named after me. He said if we were apart to look for the star." She lifts her shirt and shows me her bellybutton charm. "He said this was his beacon. I can't see the star, Jax." She falls to her knees and she is inconsolable. I lift her up and carry her inside. Salvano helps me wrap her in a blanket. Dagen hands me her phone. "That's the last message I got from him. I can't lose him."

I'm looking at the message and it reads like he doesn't think he'll get out of this alive. I feel the air leave my lungs like I was sucker punched in the gut. "Raven always says we have to have faith. Maybe now we should all start tapping into that."

I don't know if I got through to her, but I won't leave her up here alone. I carry her downstairs. Antonia and Bo take over. Raven hands me a towel to dry off.

"Jax, what happened?"

"Nothing, we're just all dealing with this in different ways. I just wish this damn storm would let up. I'm going to see if Max found anything out. Try and keep everyone calm, please." I race upstairs. I can barely carry my own fear let alone everyone else's. "Hey, any news?"

"When the storm hit land, it started to die down. Mick's friend, Officer Jacob Mamire, from the Coast Guard called. He said that some of the local fishing boats picked up survivors. I'm hopeful, Jax; he's strong and healthy. What happened with Dagen?"

"Junior had a star named after her and told her when they were apart to look for it, but she can't see the star due to the storm and she's falling apart. Told her it was his beacon. She showed me the last text message he sent. It sounded like a man saying goodbye, like he wasn't going to make it."

"Jesus Christ, no wonder she lost it. He's going to be found and he'll be fine."

"Yeah, well, when we do, I'm kicking his fucking arse."

"Come on, we better get back downstairs."

Chapter Twenty-Six

WE ARE ON THE STEPS AND I STOP FOR A MINUTE TO look around. Everyone is tending to each other. Even the guards are having a hard time with this. Junior has touched so many lives, and he always acts like it's no big deal. In reality, he is the rock this family relies on. His cousins run to him for all kinds of advice. He is accepting of everyone; always willing to share. He lives life to the fullest. I keep looking at that picture from the trapeze and he's got a look of sheer joy, not a care in the world. Now, God only knows where he is. I head downstairs to check on Bella; she's very quiet. Even though Michael is with her, she is retreating within herself. A phone is ringing and my heart races. It's Raven's phone, she's staring at it and not answering it.

"Unknown number. Hello." Her face turns white like she saw a ghost. She puts the phone on speaker. "How did you get this number?"

"I tried calling Jax and Max but there is some sort of block on their phones. I know I'm never supposed to contact you, but I have Michael."

"What do you mean you have him?"

"I own a fishing charter and one of my boats pulled him out of the water. He's alive and I was able to get him to the hospital. I just texted you the information."

"What do you want for this?"

"I just wanted to do the right thing for you. I know how much he means to you. Please don't tell anyone outside of your family that it was me that found him, otherwise, I'm a dead man."

"Duke, it's Max, if this is a game or some sort of wild goose chase. I will find you and kill you."

"Duke doesn't exist anymore; it's Patrick, and yeah, I know firsthand what you would do to me."

Raven takes the phone off speaker and steps away. I want to flip out but I have to respect her decision to talk to him even if I disagree.

"Thank you, I know you put yourself in danger. Take care." She hangs up and hands Max the phone. "That's the hospital that he's at, let's go."

Dagen

The ride to the hospital seems to take forever but in reality, it's thirty minutes. I don't know who this person is that found him or why Max flat out said he'd kill him. All I know is—Michael is alive. We get to the hospital and it only takes a minute to confirm that Michael is here. Thank you, God, for answering all of our prayers.

We are not all allowed in at once. Michael Sr., Bella, and Grams go in first. While Jax and Max are meeting with the doctor, I'm watching their faces, looking for any sign. I know they didn't have to include me here, and I'm grateful that they did. I'm just happy he's alive, but when they come over, their faces tell another story. Jax pulls Raven into his arms, closes his eyes and, for the first time, I see behind the strong, powerful man that everyone idolizes. I see a man who is vulnerable, and a woman that is the glue that holds him together. Grams, comes out of Michael's room and she's pale, holding onto the back of the chair. Mick runs to her side and she begins to cry.

"Maxwell, what did the doctor say?"

"Michael has a broken leg, he has advanced hypothermia, he needed stiches, and he is still unconscious. They are slowly bringing his core temperature up, but they will know more when he wakes up. Right now we just have to wait."

"Bella wants you and Jax in the room, now," Grams informs them.

JAX

We head into Junior's room and when I see him, it takes all I have not to fall apart. I've watched him deal with being kidnapped, cancer, even rejection and none of that destroyed him, but this is bad. Max is talking to Bella and Michael but I can't focus on any of that. All I see is that little boy watching Doctor Who, telling me when he grows up, he wants to be a Time Lord. I see a little boy whose laugh could light up my darkest days, and now a man, who is lying there broken and there's nothing I can do to fix it. I've always had to make everything better for everyone, but this is out of my reach.

"Can I have a moment with him alone, please?" I speak up. Bella doesn't question me, she understands better than anyone the bond that Junior and I share.

Everyone leaves and now it's just us. The constant beep of the machines is less annoying knowing what the alternative is. "Junior, I'm taking care of Dagen for you. I know what she means to you and I promise I will make sure she's okay. Niceties aside, what the fuck where you thinking not getting in that boat? You tell me you need to experience life, and spread your wings, well let me tell you something, right here and right now—fuck that shit. I don't know how to deal with all this. All I know is when this is over, we are going to have to renegotiate." I give him a kiss on his forehead, the only place that's not bruised and head out the door.

"Dagen, they are only allowing two people at a time into the room, but Max has already made arrangements for Junior to be moved into a private room. Right now Raven and Jackie are in with him. When they come out, I will take you in to see him."

"Thank you."

Max is finishing up with the doctor, hopefully he has some good news.

"Jax, the room should be ready soon. I spoke to the doctor again and he said his core temperature is coming up nicely and when he wakes up, there are some tests they will want to run."

"Did he say if this is normal that he hasn't woken up yet?"

"Everyone's body is different; all we can do is wait."

"Jackie and Raven are coming out now, please stay with them while I bring Dagen in. I know everyone wants to see him, but I know this is what Junior would want."

Max takes Jackie and Raven in his arms, trying to stop their crying.

"Dagen, I'll take you in now. He looks worse than he really is." Before I open the door, I take her hand and give it a little squeeze. She lets go and steps inside, then takes Junior's hand.

"Jax, can you give us some privacy please?" She doesn't wait for my answer, she kisses him and as I back out of the room, I know that Junior has found his connection.

Dagen

Even though his body is broken and battered, he looks like a sleeping prince, my prince.

"Michael, you need to wake up. You need to tell me to my face what you said in that last text message." Nothing. I pull the chair close, sit down, and continue to hold his hand. I'm prepared to sit by his side forever, if that's what it takes.

"Okay, maybe you're not ready to wake up but when you do, we are going to have to discuss your career choices. You keep telling me to step outside my box, but right now, my box has exploded."

I put the earbuds from my phone on him and play the playlist he made me. Music means so much to him; maybe it will help. I hit shuffle and watch him sleep.

I must have fallen asleep myself; Bella is in the room with the nurse.

"Dagen, I'm sorry I woke you, you both looked so peaceful. They are ready to move Michael to his room."

"I didn't realize I fell asleep. I'll step outside." I move the chair back so the nurse can do her thing. I step outside and Antonia and Bo are waiting for me. "Where did everyone go?"

"They all went to his new room. Bo, can you get us some coffee, please?" Apparently, she is trying to politely get some alone time.

"Is something wrong, Antonia?"

"I never have a chance to talk to you alone. There's always someone hovering around you. I'm very protective of my cousin, we all are."

"Why don't we take a seat where we can have some privacy?" We take a seat in the corner, away from the rest of the waiting room.

"Now, what's on your mind?"

"Look, Michael is the rock of this family. I know everyone thinks my dad and Uncle Max runs the show, but the truth is, it's Michael. That being said, I see something different with you, he's different with you. All the pictures he's sent me and all the text messages, all I see is happiness. It's like the old Michael is back, the Michael before that bitch Heather came into the picture. Please don't break him, Dagen." Her eyes fill with unshed tears and it breaks my heart to think of what Heather did to him.

"I love Michael. I only want what's best for him. I would never intentionally hurt him. Here comes Bo. Let's go to Michael's room, I want to be there when he wakes up." I give her a hug and we head to Michael's room. When we get there, Jax lets us know that they took him for a test. Once again, it's a waiting game. There is a television in the lounge, and they are still running reports about the explosion on the rig. The storm has passed; now it's all about the cleanup. I don't want to watch the constant replay of what almost killed him. I put on my earbuds and let the music he made for me take over. "Last Thing I Wanted" is playing and I instantly recognize Richard Marx's voice. I remember falling asleep the last night we were together and I think this song was playing. It's like it was written just for him. I close my eyes and flash back to all of our adventures. Replaying every single one so I don't miss a thing. Every memory is a moment in time that I will have tucked in my heart for the rest of my life. The elevator doors open and they bring him back to his room. He still hasn't woken up, and now I'm starting to worry. I want to stay with him but there's so much family; I don't want to overstep my welcome.

"Antonia, I need to stretch my legs for a bit. I'll be back. If he wakes up, text me." I text my number so she has it and head to the café. Everywhere I go, the continuous news loop is on. Rather than watch it, I head towards the gift shop. It's filled with all kinds of keepsake trinkets, stuffed animals, and balloons. I wander around a little bit more and then get back into the elevator to head upstairs. The waiting area is empty so I knock and head into his room. Everyone is just sitting around waiting.

"Antonia, anything new?"

"I was just texting you; he seems to be moving around a bit. The doctor said to be patient. I don't think that word is even in our dictionary. The nurse was giving Uncle Max a hard time about all of us being in here. If he doesn't wake up soon, we'll all get thrown out."

"Maybe we should go back to two people at a time. You know . . . keep the peace and all. Bo and I will wait outside," I suggest. Bo holds the door open and everyone leaves but Michael Sr., Bella, Grams, and Jax. "Besides, the more rest he gets, the quicker he will heal." I have even less patience than they do.

We all head into the lounge area and between all of us and the guards, it's full. I'm looking through all the pictures of Michael and me on my phone, not really paying much attention to anything. The elevator doors open, Antonia leaps up and Bo is trying to hold her back.

"Oh, hell no, you fucking bitch! You're not wanted here! Take your daddy and get the fuck out before I wipe that smirk off your face permanently."

What the hell? Bo has his arm around Antonia's waist, trying to hold her back. Mick comes running over and positions himself between the girl and the rest of the family, while Max approaches her father.

"Davis, you don't belong here; take your daughter and leave—*now*." His voice is deep and demanding; only inches separate the two of them. This is the Max that everyone is afraid of.

"My daughter needs to be here, Max, I won't be intimidated by you."

"Bo, what's going on?"

"That's Heather."

I feel my face flush and not in a fun way. Since I'm about the only calm one here, I walk up to her to try and defuse the situation. "Can I help you?"

"I don't know who you are, nor do I care. I'm here to see my fiancé and they can't stop me." She waves her hand around as if everyone else is insignificant but her. Before I can even answer her, Antonia freaks out.

"Oh, hell no. He was done with you and would never take you back. You're nothing but an evil, lying bitch. Leave now before I make you." Holy shit, Antonia is like a momma bear protecting her cub and I don't think my brother can hold her back much longer.

"That's where you're wrong. I spoke to Michael the other day and he said he wanted to get back together. He said he still loved me and all was forgiven."

"That's why he had a special program to block your sorry arse from ever getting in touch with him again. Get back to reality, bitch, you blew it and it was the best thing to ever happen. He's moved on and she is wonderful."

"He'll want access to his child."

Everyone freezes at the mention of a child. My heart tightens at the thought that this evil woman could be carrying Michael's baby.

Bo steps forward, "There is no child. I know for a fact that he always used protection with you. Let's be real here; you didn't want children with him. Hell, you barely wanted him. What's your end game, Heather? What'd you find out that no one wants your sorry ass?"

She reaches back and slaps Bo across the face, hard. I'm trying to hold Antonia back from a knock down drag out fight when Jax steps out of the room.

"Enough!"

Everyone freezes.

"Davis, take your daughter and get out of here. She's caused enough trouble. If you can't control her, I will."

"Are you threatening me?"

"I never threaten anyone. I will break you, starting with your company, and I'll work my way down from there. Now leave."

Heather's father is trying to hold her back, but she steps right in front of Jax. "This isn't over, Jax. I'm not afraid of you."

He leans in closer to her, only inches from her face. "You should be." He waves to security and we all watch as they escort them out. Jax turns his focus back to us. "Junior is starting to come to; let's head inside. Max, have extra security stationed around the hospital." He's back to business as usual, like all of this is just a common occurrence.

"They have already been called. They had to wait until they were allowed to enter the area. They are on their way and have been given a picture of Heather and her father, with strict instructions not to let either of them in."

"Dagen, come with me, please." Jax puts his hand out. As I take it, he pulls me close to him and leans in near my ear, "I know when he comes to, you're the face he's going to want to see. Heather is inconsequential. Please don't let anything she said here today get to you. Desperate people do desperate things."

I look over at Bo and he's got a large, red handprint on his face. Everyone else is carrying on as if what happened was just another day at the office.

We are all sitting around Michael's room, waiting. Mrs. Osla pulls a portable DVD player out of her bag and starts playing episodes of Doctor Who. They are trying anything and everything to get him to come around but it has to be when his body is ready. I keep rubbing my star charm and, in my mind, I keep telling him to follow the beacon. I'm as bad as the rest of them. Finally, his eyes start to flutter. He opens them and quickly closes them.

"Mum, Rose was right; I'm not dead, but damn, my head hurts."

Raven is shaking and very pale. Bella is kissing him everywhere and he opens his eyes a little bit. "Really, Mum? Where's Dagen?"

I come closer so he can see me. "I'm right here. You sure took your time waking up."

"I couldn't see the star to guide me but I had a little help from an old friend. My head really hurts. Can't they give me something?"

"Now that you're awake, I'll get the doctor."

"No, stay here with me. Bo, can you?"

He puts his hand up, "Enough said, I've got this."

"Grams, please stop crying. You're making Mrs. Osla upset."

"Nonsense, Michael, I knew you were going to be just fine." She folds up the DVD player and puts it in the drawer. "When your head is better, we can watch some of the Doctor together. I was able to snag some of the original episodes. You need to get some rest. I'll be in the waiting room." She kisses his forehead and when she's walking out, I see her wipe away a tear.

There's a knock on the door and the doctor comes in with the nurse. "Mr. Vizzano, welcome back. I need everyone to step outside while I examine him."

We all reluctantly leave and once again we're stuck waiting.

Michael

He's shining this fucking light in my eyes and I have a monster fucking headache. "Can you cut the light, please?"

"I imagine you have quite the headache. You had to get forty-two stiches on the side of your head. No worries; when your hair grows back it should cover it."

"Won't be the first time I've lost my hair, just hope I'm not that scary looking."

"I don't think you'll have any problem. You have a compounded fracture of the tibia, which most people call their shinbone. Basically, when you hit the water, it caused a shock and the bone snapped. Your bones could have been weaker from your cancer, or it could've just been a very hard landing. Anyway, the tibia is your support bone, so you have a full cast. Good news is—you'll heal."

"And the bad news?"

"You won't be taking any giant leaps anytime soon. Oh, and since the storm hit, we've been overwhelmed with patients. The only color we had left for your cast was neon pink," he informs me. I pull the sheet away and begin to laugh. "Well, I'm glad you can still laugh. You're a very lucky man that the charter boat found you and brought you here."

"I don't remember any of that. Did everyone else make it?"

"There were no casualties, so for me, it was a good day."

"Can you give me something for the headache and when can I leave?"

"I can give you something for your headache but you're not leaving until I run a few more tests. Your core temperature dropped to the danger level. I want to make sure everything is running properly."

"What about my family? I know there are rules, but you might not be able to make them leave. Can you make some sort of exception for them?"

"Mr. Fleming made a rather large donation to our new heart hospital. I don't see a problem with them staying here."

"Thank you." I give him an appreciative smile. He leaves and the nurse is doing her thing. I've been poked and prodded so much in my lifetime, none of this matters. She gives me something for my head and when she opens the door to leave, Uncle Jax is standing there and steps inside.

"Hey, what did the doctor say?"

"He just went over what I'm sure you already know. A few days and I'll be good as new. I need a favor," I mention. His jaw is tight and he's got a death grip on the bed rail. "Uncle Jax, are you okay?"

"The last time someone in a hospital bed asked me for a favor, it didn't turn out very well."

"It's nothing bad. I need to talk to Aunt Raven alone."

"Okay." As protective as he is of her, he doesn't ask me why.

He leaves and it only takes a minute before she's in my room. "Hey, Jax said you need to see me alone. What's wrong?"

"I need to tell you a story. Please come sit next to me."

"Is this about my mom? You said her name when you were waking up."

"Yes, I need to tell you what happened. I was out there and the water was cold. I kept getting hit with all kinds of debris. All I could think about was that movie you made me watch with you, *Titanic*. Everyone in that movie was frozen to death in the water. I was cold and tired, my eyes hurt from the pelting rain. When I closed them, I saw Miss Rose. She told me I wasn't dead, which I thanked her for, and she told me I needed to fight. She told me I always put everyone first and now it was my time. When I woke up, I was here. I don't know what all of this means; I only know that it was very real for me. This is the second time she saved my life. I think she's my guardian angel."

She's crying and I put my arms around her and hold her as best I can. "She loved you so much, Michael. From the very first day you accepted her and made her feel loved."

"There's not a day that goes by that I don't think about her or thank her for the life I have today."

"I love you, Michael."

I pass her the tissues. "You know Uncle Jax is standing right outside that door, probably pulling all his hair out."

"I better let him in before he's bald."

Just as predicted, he's outside the door. He must have been running his hands through his hair, cause it's every which way. "Sweetheart, is everything okay?"

"Yes, Jax, everything is fine. I'll give you a minute alone."

"So, what is it that you haven't told me yet?" I ask.

"I was getting ready to tell you but then you wanted to talk to Raven. Heads up, Heather showed up with her father. Yes, she caused a scene. She even tried to say she was pregnant, but Bo knocked that down real quick. Is it a possibility that she could be?"

"Absolutely not. She's really grasping at straws; she gets the shot and I always used a condom—*always!* Was Dagen there?"

"Yeah."

"Fuck!"

"Dagen politely asked her what she wanted. Heather claimed she was your fiancée and she demanded to see you. Bo told her off and she smacked him hard across the face."

"She smacked Bo? Oh my God, and Antonia?"

"Bo held her back from beating the crap out of Heather. My daughter does have her mother's temper."

"I've got to straighten everything out with Dagen." I try to move but I can't.

"See, that's the thing; Dagen wasn't upset. I mean, she was upset that Heather made such a big scene and made everyone upset, but she never doubted you. See, I told you someday you would find that one person who will make you whole. Really, I'm a fucking genius; it just takes everyone else a little longer to catch up."

I can't help but laugh at him; he's priceless.

"She accepts me and doesn't care about DNA. She's the total package, my end all." I feel the meds kicking in and I'm finding it hard to focus. "Whatever they gave me is making me very sleepy."

"Get some rest; we will all be here when you wake."

I close my eyes and replay all the memories Dagen and I created. I wasn't looking, but she was waiting for me all along.

Chapter Twenty-Seven

I HEAR MUSIC, AND IT'S WARM. I OPEN MY EYES AND DAGEN IS asleep, curled into my side and I have one of her earbuds in. Phil Collins is singing "You'll Be In My Heart." I'm so glad I made this playlist for her. The songs really speak from my heart. She's starting to wake up. "Good morning, sunshine," I say softly. She tilts her head up and looks at me with those puffy lips. Fuck me, I need them now.

"I know I have dragon breath, but please put those beautiful lips on mine."

She stretches up and brushes them across my lips and I think my cock just jumped for joy. "Mine is not much better."

"Before everyone comes in, Uncles Jax told me about Heather showing up here. You know she's not pregnant, right? The last time I had any contact with her was the night at your house when she texted me. I let her know, in no uncertain terms, that she was never to contact me or anyone in my family ever again. I even had Tony install a special program on my phone so she couldn't bother me again."

"Michael, you don't have to explain anything. I was more upset for the rest of the family. They had to listen to her carry on with her bullshit. Remember, "You'll just keep crashing if you never take your eyes off the rearview mirror."

"Oh no, not you, too—fortune cookie?"

"No, Leo Christopher."

My leg is itchy. I move the covers to see if I can figure out some way to scratch under this damn cast. Dagen is biting her bottom lip, no doubt trying not to laugh.

"ANTONIA!"

The door flies open and she comes in laughing. "When the hell did you do this?"

I'm looking at my neon pink cast and it's covered with all sorts of drawings. There are Unicorns, rainbows, cars, explosions, and a stick figure swinging on a trapeze.

"We all signed it with something, Mrs. Osla even drew you a TARDIS."

"When did you do all this?"

"You were out for the count, and I was bored."

"You know I'll get even?"

"Yeah, I know, but it was worth it. Did my dad have the 'come to Jesus' talk with you, yet?"

"No, but I know it's coming. I can handle him."

She rolls her eyes and laughs. "Bo and I are going to get some decent food, you want anything?"

"Yeah, food, toiletries, and some clothes; I have nothing. Where is Bo?"

"He's sitting in the lounge, having a conversation with Uncle Max. I think they are starting to understand each other."

Dagen and I look at each other and laugh.

"Michael, I'm going to go with them. I need some clean clothes. While I'm gone, you can get cleaned up."

"Don't be long," I plead. She gives me a quick kiss and now I'm alone with an itchy leg.

Like clockwork, the nurse comes to check my vitals. "Are you ready to get cleaned up?"

"Exactly how is this going to work?

"Right now, we are only going to do a sponge bath. However, when you leave here, we will send you off with a plastic cover. We really want you to wait at least forty-eight hours before you shower, and let's not forget the stiches in your head."

"This doesn't sound good at all."

"You'll be back to normal in no time. The key to surviving a cast is to keep it dry and cool. I brought you some reading material to take home with you."

"When am I getting out of here?"

"Your doctor has some tests scheduled today, but I venture to say tomorrow. Now, let's get started." She pulls back the sheet and gets an up close look at my decorated cast. "Oh my, looks like your family has been having a lot of fun at your expense."

"Trust me, I'll get even with them. Is there any way I can do this myself?"

"Not yet. Don't worry, you don't have anything I haven't seen before."

This sucks, but I'm out of options. I let her do her thing and pray she's quick about it.

Dagen

The hospital is in the downtown and even though this city got hammered with the storm, there are people helping people. Stores are open for business and happy to see us. I see Bo take Antonia's hand and I realize they are a lot closer than I thought. I wonder what Michael knows about this.

We find an Under Amour store and I pick him up enough clothing for two days, along with some toiletries. Then we find a place that sells Beignets, and I think I've died and gone to heaven.

"Dagen, do you think Michael is going to go back to his job?" Antonia asks.

My stomach instantly twists into knots. "Is that what you were referring to when you asked about the 'come to Jesus' talk?"

"Yeah, my dad is going to push hard for him to leave that job. Michael will push back just as hard. They are more alike than they want to admit. It's not going to be pretty."

Bo puts his arm around both of us. "Don't worry your pretty heads off over this. Mike and I have been talking about opening our own company, maybe we just need to speed it up a bit. Right now, he needs to concentrate on getting better and that's going to start with those damn Beignets."

We get back to the hospital with way too many bags. When we get upstairs, everyone is in his room and they can't dig into the food fast enough.

"I got you some stuff. What did I miss?"

"My sponge bath, and I had to explain my decorated cast. Uncle Max, when are you springing me from this place?"

"The doctor said maybe tomorrow."

"I'm not waiting until tomorrow. I can be doing the same thing at home that I'm doing here and be a hell of a lot more comfortable."

"After my coffee, I'll see what I can do; fair?"

"Thank you."

The room is packed and I can't see how this is helping him. I slip away and into his bathroom to, at least, get somewhat cleaned up and change clothes. I'm looking at my reflection and I cringe at the saddlebags under my eyes. My hair looks like I did it with an eggbeater. I do the best I can with what I have to work with and head back out. The room is not crowded at all. I feel like I can breathe a little.

"Hey, Uncle Max is getting me sprung from this place."

"Where are you going to go?"

"Dagen, where do you think I would go? I'm going home with you. Are you worried that I would run back to Scotland with my tail between my legs? Santa Barbara is my home."

"What about work? I mean, I know it's too soon with everything that just happened but I know you; sitting idle is not an option."

"For the past year, Bo and I have been toying with opening our own business. We thought we should wait and work for someone else to get our feet wet. Maybe we need to think about it a little bit more seriously."

"I thought Jax or Max would push for you to go back to Scotland." I climb on to the bed and he takes both my hands and kisses them.

"We need to talk about the last message I sent you."

"You thought you were going to die. Things are said when we think the end is near. Don't worry about it."

His grip on my hands gets tighter. "Dagen, I have regrets—we all do. I regret that I didn't tell you sooner. I regret that I did it in a text message. What I don't regret is falling in love with you. Yeah, this is better than a text, but my sorry arse is in this stupid bed and I can't take you in my arms and make love to you all night long. I want to make the girls all perky and I want to make your whooha sing. I love you." He squeezes again then tilts his head. "Tears?"

"I told you; tears are my heart's way of saying it's overflowing with happiness. I love you, too." I smile. He pulls me close and kisses me. My whole body flushes from just one kiss.

"My girls are back and perky, so beautiful." He's running his thumbs over my nipples.

"Michael, anyone can walk in here. Besides, before you know it, we will be back home."

As if on cue, Max comes in. "Hey, Junior, I wanted to give you an update. Jax is going to get everyone back to Scotland. I'm going to go back to California with you. Once you're settled, I can leave. We have a nurse that will be traveling with us. The nurse will be in with the wheelchair in a minute."

"Thanks, Uncle Max. Can you give us a minute?" He asks and

Max quickly steps out, giving us whatever time we have until the nurse gets there. "Kiss me," he begs.

I'm trying not to laugh but I can't help it. "Don't stress about this, we will find a way to be together. Maybe I can have Bo keep him amused," I suggest. We're both laughing when Max walks in with the nurse.

"I'm not even going to ask; it's time to go," Max announces.

"You know, Max, I never had a chance to ask you, how were you able to get Bo and me on that military flight in the middle of a hurricane?"

"Friends."

Man of a few words when it comes to business. We head out to the waiting cars and make our way to the airport. Everyone is saying their goodbyes and I'm standing in the background. I don't want to interfere, but Bella pulls me aside.

"Dagen, we really didn't get much time together. I wanted to thank you for taking care of my son. He's my world and he's been through so much in such a short time. You're a very special lady. I know you love him; it shows in everything you do. If you can't get rid of Max, call me, and I'll make him come home." She gives me a hug and then boards the plane. Antonia is the last one to board and Bo is sulking as we board our own plane. Michael is exhausted and falls asleep before the wheels are even off the ground. Max is busy going over some stuff with the nurse. My brother looks lost, and my heart breaks for him. I get up and motion him to come into the back with me.

"Hey, what's wrong?"

"Nothing."

"Bo, you can talk to me. I promise I won't judge."

"I finally meet someone special and I know nothing will ever come of it."

"Why?"

"I can't believe you even have to ask that. For starters, she's young and inexperienced. Her father would kill me and if he doesn't, her uncle surely will. If it doesn't work out, I will lose my best friend. No matter which way this goes, I get fucked."

"I know she wants to come out to California. Maybe she can come and stay with Michael for a bit."

"Did you forget that's where I live?"

"Okay, maybe she can come and stay with me." What the hell am I getting myself into?

"You would do that? I know how much you and Mike want to be together."

"Yeah, but you have to help me get Max to go home."

"Why am I always stuck with Max? I really think you and Mike are getting a kick out of this." If I look at him I'll laugh, so I fiddle with my seatbelt instead.

"Let's get some rest before we land."

Michael

The drive from the airport to my house was not that long but for me, it felt like a lifetime. I don't know who was more excited to see me, Preston or Mr. and Mrs. H. Of course, she made all my favorite foods. When I finally got her to stop crying, she said if I went back to work on the rig, she would quit and take Preston with her. Nothing like a little emotional blackmail to keep me grounded. Dagen went back to her place to pack some stuff and Bo is walking around like someone stole his puppy. Trying to get around with this cast on is no easy feat; thankfully, my house is all one level. I finally make it out back without knocking anything over and find coffee and Uncle Max.

"I can see why you love this place so much, it's tranquil. Tony sent your new phone; he pulled all your pictures from the cloud."

He hands me the phone and my picture of Dagen, riding Tequila, is my screensaver. I know I must have a stupid grin right now but I don't care.

"You really love her, don't you?"

"Yeah, I do."

"How much does she know?"

"I told her why Heather left me, if that's what you mean. I didn't go into any great detail about the family's past. As far as I'm concerned, it's ancient history."

"What do you remember about the explosion?"

"Leading up to it—everything. After that, things get a little sketchy, why?"

"You were pulled from the water by a charter fishing boat. It's owned by Patrick Brown."

"Is that supposed to mean something to me?"

"Yeah, Patrick Brown used to go by the name Duke Jensen."

The name sends a chill up my spine. "How is that even possible? How did you find this out?"

"He contacted Raven and told her that one of his charters picked you up. At first, I didn't believe him, but we were desperate to find you, and I couldn't take a chance that he might actually be telling the truth."

"Why did he contact Aunt Raven and not you or Uncle Jax?"

"Remember Tony put that program on some of our phones? Well, he tried us first and when he couldn't get through, he tried Raven."

"So, she spoke to him?"

"Yeah."

"Jesus Christ, between that and what I told her about Rose, it's a wonder she didn't fall apart."

"What about Rose?"

"I know this is going to sound crazy, but after the blast I could swear Rose was there, telling me to hang on. I really believe she is my guardian angel." I pour us each some more coffee as I try to wrap my mind around the fact that Duke's guys pulled me from the freezing water.

"It's not crazy at all. When we lose someone we love, a part of them follows us forever."

The sound of the surf is a comfort, both of us dipping into a well of memories.

"Do you think you'll ask Dagen to marry you?"

"I know what I want but I don't want to push her, why?"

"You know her better than anyone, how do you think she would react to life as a Vizzano?"

"I can't imagine it would be much different than it is now. She's gotten used to security always around us."

"Junior, if you decide you're going to stay here and start a family, then some things would have to change. Security would get tighter, especially when you start a family."

"But, if I went back to Scotland, it would be different because I would be isolated at the family compound? I won't do it. I won't raise my children to live in fear. What good is it to have all the money in the world if it keeps me from having a life?"

"I've lived with the cruel hand that life sometimes deals. It took everything I had to trust myself to love again, love without fear. Sometimes it's a daily struggle, but I do it. I want you to understand everything before you make any decisions. What did Dagen say when you told her why Heather left?"

"She thought it was terrible that Heather would judge me by anything other than the man that I am today."

"If you're really serious about her, then she should know everything, including the money. There's nothing worse than going into something with only half the facts. I put a copy of the report in your safe. Take your time, think about everything and whatever you decide, I will support you."

"Is Uncle Jax okay with all of this? He wanted to keep the money quiet," I ask just as Mrs. H comes out with Preston, to leave us with a pot of fresh coffee and a plate of warm croissants.

"He's the one who suggested it. I don't know his reasons why; I only know I trust his decision. There's no rush; whatever you decide, just let me know."

"I really want to get back into my normal routine. After my doctor visit today, I'm probably going to dismiss the nurse. I have plenty of people around if I need anything."

"Is that your subtle way of telling me it's time for me to go?" He's laughing and I'm so busted.

"I planned on leaving in the morning. Have you thought about work?"

"Yeah, actually Bo and I had talked about opening our own company. We've been working on the development of a product that could change Fracking, making it safer and quicker. It will revolutionize the industry. I've been working on the business plan and when it's done, I want to run it by Uncle Jax."

"I start businesses from my heart, whereas Jax does it from his head. It sounds to me like you got the best of both of us."

"It's all about giving back, lending a hand to the person behind me. This family has set that example for me and I plan on passing it down to my children."

"So, you have decided you want children?"

"When I was floating around in the Gulf, I kept thinking of all the things I didn't get to do. The one thing I would have regretted the most was not being someone's dad."

Uncle Max doesn't always show emotion, but when he does, it comes from his heart. He puts his hand on my shoulder and gives it a squeeze. "Every day, you make me so proud."

We sit for a while enjoying the sunshine and the sounds of the surf. "So, Uncle Max, how bad is it going to be for Bo?" What kind of friend would I be if I didn't ask? It's not like everyone didn't notice the hand holding and how close they were. He doesn't even lift his Ray Bans he only gives me his usual 'I'm going to fuck with him so bad' smirk.

"Bad; let's face it, Junior, he's stepping into the swimming pool with Jax. That, right there, puts him at a major disadvantage. If that doesn't fuck him up, he's got me on the edge of the pool waiting." Now he's laughing so hard, he can barely catch his breath.

"Mind sharing what's so funny?"

"If all else fails, we can send your Grams after him." Poor Bo doesn't stand a chance. I shake my head in sympathy for him as I look down at my new phone and pull up the video surveillance of the house. I have to thank Tony for all the gadgets he put on here.

"The doctor is here," I announce. "I'll be back." I get up and by the time I make it to the front door, Mrs. H is letting him in.

"Hi, I'm Doctor Butler."

"Hey, I'm Michael; my bedroom is just down the hall." I slowly lead the way.

"The type of fracture you have will probably take a little longer to heal. You need to try and stay off of that leg as much as possible. By the way, that's a very interesting cast you have on."

"They only had pink left and my family decided to decorate it while I was sleeping. What about my stiches?"

"I will take them out next week. I will leave you instructions on wound care and showering."

"Do I still need to have the nurse?"

"Not as long as you have someone here in case you fall, then you will be fine."

He finishes up and I also let the nurse know that I will no longer need her. Finally, I'm getting my house back to normal again. Uncle Max is on the phone, so Preston and I head into my office. I want to see if I got any emails from work. The only work email I got was from human resources, reminding me that I'm not allowed to talk to the press. My spam account is filled with different emails with one thing in common: Heather. She keeps creating different accounts so I will answer her. That's never going to happen. The only way to end this is to change my email address. Sad that this is what it's come to. When I look up, Uncle Max is in the doorway. "I didn't hear you, come in."

"I just gave myself a guided tour. I haven't seen it all since Dagen finished putting it together. She really did an unbelievable job."

"I had to change my email address. Heather keeps sending emails from different addresses. I think I should put more protection on Dagen."

"Did she make any threats in the emails?"

"I didn't bother to open them."

"Then, what makes you think you need more protection?"

"A feeling in my gut that I'd rather be safe than sorry."

"Would it be okay with you if I read them?"

"Do you think it's necessary?"

"I would feel better, if I knew how crazy she is."

"I'll forward them to you now." A few clicks and it's all done.

"I'll let you know the outcome. I'm going to town for a little bit. I want to get some stuff and cook dinner for all of us tonight. After that, I'm going to take off. I don't think you need me hanging around here. Do you need me to pick up anything while I'm out?"

"No, I'm actually going to take a nap before Dagen gets here."

He leaves and I head into bed. I didn't realize how exhausted I was. My head barely hits the pillow and I'm out.

MAX

I drive myself into town. I could have had one of the guards take me but, truth be told, I love to drive and I don't always get the chance. I found the gourmet store and get everything I need for dinner tonight. When I stumble upon an old fashion ice cream parlor, I can't resist a cool treat. I take a seat and start going through the emails from Heather. With each one, she's getting more out of control. It's clear I need to put more security on Dagen, but I'm also going to put a guard on Heather. Not to protect her but to watch her every move. I have no clue what I'm going to do about Antonia and Bo. Life was a lot easier when they were all little babies and did what they were told.

Me: You busy?

Jax: No. How's Junior?

Me: Good. The doctor was here today and all is well. The nurse has been dismissed and I'll be heading home tonight. I think they've had enough of me. Junior sent me all of Heather's emails. I'm adding more protection on Dagen and I'm adding someone to watch Heather.

Jax: How bad is it?

Me: She's off the fucking rails. I'm not coming right home, making a stop to see her dad.

Jax: Come right home; I'll handle Davis. I've been buying up blocks of his company's stock. I now own forty-nine percent. He either gets his daughter under control or I break him. No one fucks with Junior—ever.

Me: Are you sure you don't want me to handle him? I could be the calming voice of reason.

Jax: Positive. Just get home safely. You calming? Since when? Forward me the emails. I'll keep you posted on

what happens.
Me: Done. Ttyl.

I phone my pilot to let him know I'm heading back to Scotland tonight and then head back to Junior's house so I can start cooking.

Dagen

When I get to Michael's house, Bo is waiting outside for me. "Hey, is everything okay?"

"Mike is sleeping and Max is cooking."

"Wow. I didn't know he cooked."

"Apparently, he's a Jack of all trades. He's leaving to go home tonight."

"I'm sure you'll be happy." He doesn't answer, which is answer enough for me.

We head inside and the place smells wonderful.

"Hi, Max, what happened when the doctor came?"

"He released the nurse and said everything was coming along nicely. I hope you're hungry; I made Chicken Francaise, roasted potatoes, and steamed asparagus. Dinner will be ready in thirty minutes."

I quickly close my tote so the smell of the In-N-Out burgers I brought doesn't escape.

"Sounds wonderful. I'm going to check on him." I quickly head down the hall to his room and when I get in, he's watching television. "Hey, how are you feeling?"

"Bored."

Oh, I can see I'm going to have my hands full with this patient. "I didn't know Max was cooking dinner." I pull out the bag with the burgers and he's got a huge smile.

"Make sure you save room for his dinner, though."

"Have I told you today how spectacular you are?"

"Yes, but feel free to keep telling me. How are you feeling?"

"Itchy and bored. Will you give me a sponge bath?"

"Why didn't the nurse give you one before you sent her away?" I can see where this is leading.

"I would much rather have you do it. The doctor said my leg might take a little bit longer to heal. I just wish the itching would go away."

"After your bath, I will wrap ice packs around your cast. The cooling will help with the itching and, if that's not enough, I picked up a couple of cans of compressing air."

"I was reading about different remedies on line; do you think those really work?"

"When I was younger, I broke my arm in the heat of the summer. I tried everything and those worked the best. The key to surviving the next eight weeks is to make sure you keep your cast dry."

"Not only are you beautiful but you're a genius. How did you break your arm?" He asks as he begins to scarf down his food. I can't believe after all this, he's still going to eat Max's dinner.

"Bo and I were playing superheroes. We climbed on top of the jungle gym and leaped off. Bo landed perfectly. I did a Humpty Dumpy swan dive. Broke my arm in two places. Go ahead, laugh, everyone else did."

"What superhero were you?"

"Really? After my sad story of great humiliation, you want to know what hero I was? Wonder Woman of course, she had the golden lasso."

"Maybe you can dress up for me."

"If you're good, I might just do that. Now, what else did you get done today?"

"Tony sent me a new phone and he was able to restore everything. I have a new number and a new email address."

I want to know if she's contacted him, but yet I don't want to know. Did he read the emails? Did he respond to any of them? "Because of Heather?"

"Yes. I found a bunch of her emails from different email addresses in my spam account. I was going to delete them, but Uncle Max wanted them. I'm putting another guard on you. Please don't fight me on it; I can't protect you right now."

"So, you think she could be a danger to me? What about everyone else?"

"Everyone is safe. It's just me; I would feel better with another guard."

I love him and if this is what I have to deal with, then I will. "Jax really tore into her and her father at the hospital. So maybe he'll get his daughter to back off."

"I'm sorry that you had to witness all this bullshit."

"I felt bad for the rest of the family. I will tell you that Jax scared the bejesus out of me."

"Yeah, most people don't want to be on the receiving end when he's like that."

"Has anyone from work contacted you, yet?"

"Only human resources, reminding me about a gag order. Oh, and I got a letter from the company that owned the rig, thanking me for my work and letting me know there were no casualties from the explosion."

"Max said dinner will be ready in thirty minutes and it's past that now. After we eat, we can do the sponge bath." His face lights up and I know exactly where this is going.

When we head into the kitchen, Max is just putting the finishing touches on the food. It looks and smells wonderful. "Max, I'm very impressed; everything smells wonderful. Where did you learn to cook?"

"My grandmother taught me. She always said 'if you can cook, you can win the hearts of all the ladies.' Not sure how true that is since Jackie only eats wild caught ocean fish and salads. None of the women in our family can cook. However, Mrs. Osla bakes some of the best Scottish desserts I've ever had."

"When she sent me the stuff for Michael's office she included a tin of some homemade shortbread cookies. They were fantastic."

"While Junior slept, I gave myself a tour of the house. You did a spectacular job. Have you found a new builder to start building the music studio?"

I should have known he would already know about the creeper. I was hoping to keep it from Michael. I should have known that was impossible.

"Dagen, what happened with the builder that we already decided on?"

"He turned out to be a creeper and Preston tried to take a bite out of him. I would have thought Max would have told you already." I'm giving Max my *I want to smack you in the face* smile but, in my mind, I'm throwing flaming arrows at him. Michael drops his fork and the clank startles me.

"Why am I just hearing about this now?"

"It happened right before your accident and I forgot about it until Max reminded me. It's not a big deal. My assistant has a few builders lined up for me to interview."

I look at Bo for help and thankfully he's paying attention for once.

"So, Mike, how about them Dodgers? Did you watch the game today? We just might make it to the playoffs this year."

"No, I didn't get a chance. If my leg heals before the season is over, Dagen is taking me to a game." And with that, we all concentrate on the food before us.

I don't know how Michael finished his dinner after he just ate a burger and fries. At least he skipped dessert.

"As much as I would love to hang out here longer, I really need to get home. Junior, I took care of everything we talked about earlier. If you need anything else, let me know. I'll check in with you soon. Dagen, why don't you walk me out?" He hugs Michael and I follow him to the car with Preston right behind me. "I wanted to apologize to you; I didn't realize that you hadn't told Junior, yet."

"It seems so absurd to me that you seem to know everything that goes on in our daily lives."

"Actually, I don't. The only reason I know what happened was Mr. Holiday asked me what he could have done with Preston to get him under control quicker. He was afraid he made a mistake. The guards know to give Junior his space unless he's doing something that could possibly put him in danger. By the way, I have assigned another guard to you and I also put a guard on Heather."

"Why are you sharing this with me? Why did you put a guard on Heather?"

"It involves you and you have a right to know. I read all the emails she sent Junior and I think she's gone off the rails. I'd rather be safe than sorry." Before I can say anything, he pulls me into a hug. "You're good for him and he's good for you. Thank you for taking care of him."

"Have a safe flight." I smile. He gets in the car and drives away. I don't think I will ever be able to figure that man out. At least I know that he's not getting up-to-date details of our personal life. "Come on, Preston, it's time to tackle that sponge bath."

MAX

Me: Hey, I'm in flight; we took off about four hours ago.

What happened with Davis?

Jax: I met with him outside of his office and showed him the emails. He agreed that she has gone off the rails and he has made arrangements for her to seek professional help. He understands that if she tries to contact or bother Junior in any way, shape or form, then all bets are off. I still want the guard kept on her 24/7.

Me: I agree. I'm glad to see that you kept it civil even without me there.

Jax: Wise arse. How's Junior doing?

Me: He will be fine. Dagen is taking good care of him.

Jax: She's a keeper. I'm happy for him. Have a safe flight; I'll see you later.

Me: Bye

Chapter Twenty-Eight

Michael

THE WEEKS HAVE FLOWN BY, PROBABLY BECAUSE I'VE BEEN very busy working on my business plan. I finally heard from my job in the form of a pink slip. My recommendations, although very effective, were too costly. They wanted quick and cheap. It was my very first and, hopefully, my last pink slip. They did send a hefty severance check, which I donated to NORACAL Boxer Rescue.

Construction on the music studio has been underway and moving at a good pace. I did pay the creeper a visit and one of my crutches just happened to slip and nail him in what little balls he was sporting.

I don't know how my uncles handled Heather's emails, but I never heard from her again. For my own peace of mind, I still haven't let up on Dagen's security.

Today is a big day for me; my cast is finally coming off. Dagen insisted on going with me but, from everything I read on the Internet, I thought Bo should, instead. Bo promised her he would take pictures.

"So, Mike, what's the real reason you wanted me to take you and not Dagen?"

"Well it is pretty disgusting getting this thing taken off."

He gives me his *are you for real* look and I can't help but laugh.

"I'm going to propose and I want you to take me to Tiffany's to get the ring."

He's very quiet and now I'm starting to worry. "Bo, what's the problem?"

"Do I have to move out?"

I can't believe this is what he's worried about. "This is not going to be like an episode of *The Big Bang Theory*. We can't live together forever. Eventually, you'll have to move out, but not till after the wedding."

"I like *The Big Bang Theory*."

"That's nice; still not going to happen. I haven't told my family, yet. I know you talk to Antonia all the time, so don't open your mouth."

He waves his hand at me and mumbles under his breath.

We get all checked in at the doctor's office and when the doctor starts to saw off the cast, Bo runs out. I'm not even looking; the sound, alone, is making my teeth hurt. When he finally pulls it off, I can honestly say it is as disgusting as I thought it would be. The nurse is kind enough to help clean it a bit and then gives me some lotion to put on. I'm glad I brought a pair of jeans with me to cover this shit up. I head out to the waiting room and find Bo playing a game with a little kid.

"What did the doctor say?"

"I can't believe you ran out. He said it will take a little bit for me to feel stable on that leg again. Take it easy and keep the crutches near."

We head to the parking lot and at least now it's easier to get in the car.

"Mike, what's that stink?" He rolls down the windows, trying to get the smell out of the car. Unfortunately, it's my leg that stinks.

"That, my friend, is my leg."

"We can't go out like this. I have an idea. We can get some Febreze and spray you down."

"You realize how nuts that sounds, right?"

He turns the music up and keeps driving until we get to Ralphs supermarket. "Come on, Mike, go inside, buy the stuff and then you go into the men's room and spray yourself."

I can't believe I'm actually considering this. "Look, you can't stay in the car with that leg; it will stink up the car and she deserves better."

Against my better judgment, I hobble inside with my detail following behind me. Who knew there were so many different scents of this stuff? Finally, I find one that is unscented and head into the men's room. It's either working or I'm getting immune to the stink. When I come out of the men's room, Rico is laughing.

"What's so amusing?"

"The things we do for love."

He's got a point. I want to be the one to pick up the ring not someone that works for me. When I get to the car Bo's on the phone.

"Hold on I'll let you talk to him yourself. Antonia." He passes it to me.

"Hey, what's up?"

"I wanted to know how it went today? Oh, and Aunt Bella sent you a care package for your leg. She said you'll get it sometime today."

"Everything went fine, except it looks and smells nasty. What are you up to?"

"The usual stuff—nothing earthshattering—that's for sure. I'll let you go. Tell Bo I'll talk to him later." She hangs up and I'm staring at the phone. I gather things between them are progressing. He takes his phone and tosses it into the cup holder. The rest of the ride, he cranks up the music and we each space out.

I've already ordered her ring from the same lady that helped me with her bellybutton charm. I knew when I saw the Grace ring that it was perfect, simple, yet elegant. She pulls it out and I show it to Bo. "What do you think?"

"It's big but simple. I mean really, what girl doesn't want her guy to give her the blue box?"

The inscription came out perfect. *"You've got a lock on my heart forever."*

"When are you going to ask her? Keeping this a secret will really test me. You know what?—don't tell me cause I suck at all this."

I thank the lady as she takes the ring back to package it up for me.

"What are your plans for the rest of the day?" I ask as soon as we get back outside and get into the car.

"Well, if you don't need me, I'm going surfing," he says as he starts up the engine and pulls out.

"You are officially off babysitting duties. Have fun."

When I get inside, I'm thrilled to find my mum's care package with a letter.

Hey Michael,
    I found all kinds of wonderful products for you to use on your leg. Make sure you use the loofah to get the dead skin off. I hope this helps, and I can't wait to see you soon.
Love you,
Mum

Leave it to my mum to send me all kinds of products. When

Dagen sees this, I'll never hear the end of it. I head inside with my new found products, run a hot bath and soak for a while. The worst of this is over, except I now have one white leg and one tan leg. I've got a lot of stuff to do before she gets here and the first thing is to arrange for her to have time off without her knowing about it. I head into my office and call her assistant Nathan.

"Hey, Nathan, I need a big favor. I want to surprise Dagen and take her away for a few days. Can you help me with this?"

"Actually, now would be a great time. We only have one house that's going to closing and it's my listing, so she doesn't have to be there. How about I tell her that it's slow for the rest of the week, so take it off because next week looks busy?"

"Great. If there's a problem, let me know. Thanks for your help."

"If you need anything else, just let me know."

Me: Facetime?

Jax: Sure

"Hey, what's going on?"

"I want to run something by you, first. I want to ask Dagen to marry me. But, I want to give her the report to read that Uncle Max left me, and I want to tell her about the money before I do so."

"There's no do-over button in life. Once it's out there, there's no going back. Are you sure this is what you want?"

"More than anything. I don't want to start off with secrets or baggage. Once she knows it all, if she wants to walk, then at least I'll never say 'what if.'"

"What do you need from me?"

"I'm going to tell her everything tonight and if she hasn't run away, I'll come back to Scotland with her tomorrow to ask her. So, if you get a text saying I need the jet, can you have it ready for me?"

"No problem, but you know the way I am; I'm going to go nuts waiting."

"How do you think I feel?"

"Did you figure out how you're going to ask her?"

"I'm taking her to the top of the hill and I'm going to ask her there. I want you to have the Aston waiting for me and put a note that you were busy and you'll see me at the house."

"Okay, got it. Now, how's your leg?"

"White, but good. I've got to run; she just pulled up. Hopefully, you'll hear from me soon."

I could watch her all day long. Everyone is always happy to see her: the guards, Mr. & Mrs. H, Preston, and, of course, me.

"Look at you; no more crutches. Was it gross?"

"Bo ran out of the doctor's office and he made me Febreze my leg before he would take me home."

She's hysterical laughing and, when I think about the fact that I went along with his hair brain scheme, I have to laugh, too.

"Well, you smell great."

"My mum sent a care package of products."

"Why am I not surprised?"

I take her hand and we head into my office. We have a seat in front of the fireplace. "There's something I need to talk to you about. Do you want a drink or something?"

"You're scaring me; are you okay?"

"Yes, best I've ever been. I want to put all my cards on the table." I hand her the envelope with the report. "That's everything about every member of my family. I want you to know it all. I don't want any secrets between us, ever." My heart begins to race, but then she hands it back to me. "Dagen, I don't understand; you need to read this. Why are you giving it back to me?"

"Everything in there is the past—their past—not ours. It has nothing to do with whatever the future holds for us. I understand what a blow it was to you to find out about your father. We've talked it through, and I love you—the man that's sitting in front of me. If you keep looking behind you, you'll miss what's in front of you."

"There's something else you need to know. I'm a very wealthy man."

"You bought a house from me for twenty-nine million dollars in cash. I think it's safe to say, I know your family has a lot of money."

"No, you don't understand. It's not just my family that's wealthy. I'm talking about me, personally."

"How? I mean you're just starting out."

I point to the envelope. "It's in those papers but the express version is that Uncle Jax had part of his company in my name. When he sold it, my portion went into a trust. It took me months to wrap my mind around it all."

"Okay, so you have your stuff and I have mine; it's not a problem for me. I can support myself. Unless, of course, you need a loan; I might be able to spot you a few."

"Very funny. Are you sure you're okay with all of this?"

"Yes. I just have one request. I want you to burn that envelope and never talk about it again."

I toss it into the fire and watch the past go up in flames. She's right; it's like a giant weight has been lifted off of my shoulders.

"I want to take you home to Scotland; can you get away a couple of days?"

"It's slow this week, so if you want, we can go. I've been wanting to talk to Antonia more about Bo and her plans, so this is good timing."

"We can leave right away."

"I have to figure out my clothes situation. I've got some stuff here and some stuff at my place. I don't' know if I'm coming or going."

"Why don't you move in here, then you'll know where all your stuff is all the time."

"Why don't you move in with me?"

"I love your place but we wouldn't be able to fit everyone. We could use your place as a getaway." I think I better pull my foot out of my mouth and shut it.

"I promise we will figure it out. For now, let's just get away for a few days. Pack for the fall and if you need anything else, we can get it."

I send a quick text to Uncle Jax that we will be at the airport in an hour.

Finally, we are in flight and I'm starving. I'm glad they have our usual In-N-Out waiting for us. I just hope I can keep this secret.

"Have you finished your business proposal?"

"Yeah, I sent it to Uncle Jax to tweak, then Bo and I can take the next step."

"I know Bo's excited about it. What do you think about him and Antonia?"

"That's a big can of worms. I'm really on the fence about the whole thing. He's my best friend, and I know him very well. She is very inexperienced and he's been around the block a few times. On top of that, she wants to pursue a career that will involve traveling. He's grounded in his community and, when we open this company, he won't be traveling. Timing is everything and I think their timing is way off."

"Do you know what she wants to do after college?"

"Yes, but please don't ask me. Antonia and Grace confided in me and I can't break that trust. All I can do it try to guide them in the right direction."

"Wow, that's a tough spot to be in. Especially considering how close you are to your uncles."

"I'm hoping once they finish their first year, they change their minds or, at least, talk to their parents about it."

"I'm going to try and talk to Antonia about Bo while we're there.

Maybe feel her out and see if it's just infatuation or what. Then, I'll talk with Bo when we get home. I mean, he's walking around like he lost his puppy. Something's got to give."

"As much as I want to say stay out of it, I think we're already sucked in. We better get some sleep or the time change will be a killer. I have to warn you, my leg is ugly."

"It's a leg, Michael, don't be ridiculous."

We head into our cabin and get ready for bed. While she's in the bathroom I put on sweats. I can't bring myself to show her my ugly leg.

"Michael, why are you in sweat pants?"

"Look, my leg is really nasty looking. I only got the cast off today."

"You tell me to accept myself and love who I am. I couldn't care less what the hell it looks like. What bothers me more is you trying to hide it from me." She's got her hands on her hips and her face is flushed. I look at the girls and they are saluting me. I push my sweats down around my ankles.

"That's it? That's what you're embarrassed about? Michael, you have a white leg with some peeling skin. Big whoop."

"That was very romantic. I think I'm going to start a book of Dagen-isms. I'll start with whooha and work my way down to big whoop."

She pushes me back hard enough and I land on the bed with my pants still around my ankles, but not for long. She whips them off and tosses them across the room, followed by her robe.

"You need to be off your feet and, now that the cast is gone, I'm having my way with you. Sit back, relax, and enjoy yourself. I know I will." She throws a bunch of condoms on the bed and then she climbs between my legs, kissing the white one as she takes a close look at it. She works her way up to my cock and then she slides her tongue around the head. I know it's been hard to function with that cast on and we found ways around it, but this is sheer heaven. Her mouth is warm and she works it all the way down my cock.

"Oh yeah, nice and slow." My hips are pushing up to meet her every move and my hands are laced in her hair. She knows I'm close and slows it down even more. She stops and gets on her knees with my legs wrapped around her. Her hands glide up to her nipples, rolling them between her fingers. When she tugs on them she drops her head back and let's out a long sensual moan that sends shock waves from my cock down to my balls.

"Oh, babe, get one of those condoms on now. . .*please,*" Dagan begs. I think I just set a world record for getting a fucking condom on.

"Tell me what you need." I pull her closer and take one of her nipples in my mouth, flicking it and tugging it to that fine line of pleasure and pain. Her entire body shakes and that's when I know she's on the edge.

"I need you now; I'm so close."

I unlock my legs and crawl out from under her. "Tonight, I want you from behind." I gather her hair into a ponytail and wrap it around my hand and sink my cock deep in her. "Oh dear God, you're so beautiful." I gather my wits and begin to move, slow at first, but then she reaches under herself and runs her nails gently over my balls. I feel like I'm on fire.

"More—*now*—I'm there!"

I give her all I've got and as my balls tighten, I feel her body flush and she comes with me not far behind her. I make quick work of the condom and lay down next to her, stroking her back.

I move her hair out of the way so I can see her beautiful face. "Hey, sunshine, are you okay?"

"Yeah, are you?"

"I've got one white leg, one tan leg. My balls feel like they got pulled through the tip of my cock, and I'm all sweaty. Yeah, I think I'm good."

She's nodding off, so I head to the shower, turn it on and step in.

I couldn't go another round if my life depended upon it, but when I turn around, she's stepping into the shower with me. "I thought we could shower together."

"Did you now? Turn around and I'll shampoo your hair." She does so and I begin working the shampoo through her hair and damn it, she's moaning. I look down at my cock; there's still life left in it. I'll be damned. She's rinsing her hair and when she turns around my girls are saluting me. "You know it's you, right? I mean, I just have to look at you and *bam*." I'm leaning against the wall, my arms crossed and my cock is hard as stone. She drops to her knees and takes my cock in her warm mouth. With my hands on her head, guiding her every move, I close my eyes and let her take all that I've got to give. I know if I died right now I'd die a happy man.

We climb into bed and, somewhere over the Atlantic, we drift off to sleep.

Chapter Twenty-Nine

Michael

WHEN WE GET OFF THE PLANE, THE ASTON IS WAITING. "I wonder where everyone is? I thought, for sure, Grams would have come to pick us up."

"Maybe they're busy. It's okay; it will give us more time alone." When she gets in, she sees the note from Uncle Jax. "See, he left you a note."

"Well, if he's busy, we can go exploring." The ring is burning a hole in my pocket. I need to take my mind off of it. I drive closer towards the garage.

"Oh look, Michael, all the cars are out. They must be cleaning them. Is that a Lamborghini golf cart?"

"Uncle Max got it for me for my birthday right before I had to leave for the States. That's how I learned to drive."

"On a golf cart?"

"Stop. Go. Right. Left. Yep, that about covers my lessons."

I pull up to the hill and help her out. "I thought we could climb to the top and watch the world go by while it's still warm out."

I help her up the incline and when we reach the top, we both look around.

"Wow, Michael, with the orange streaks, the sun looks fake. I feel like I can reach up and pluck it out of the sky."

"Dagen, I love you."

"I know; it's the one thing I'm always sure of."

"I told you, you've got a lock on my heart forever. Before you came into my world, I just existed. I was always making sure everyone else was happy and, somewhere along that road, I lost myself. Then, you stepped into my life and I realized the whole time my heart was on a journey to find you. I know I took the long way around but, somehow, you were right there, waiting for me. You made me believe that I'm worthy of being loved. You let me love you with all my heart and soul, and you gave it right back to me." I pull the ring out of my pocket and get down on one knee. "Dagen, I want to be your knight in shining armor. I want to spend the rest of my life loving you. I want to build a lifetime of memories with you. I want to overflow your heart with those memories and only see you cry happy tears. Will you marry me?"

Her hands are trembling and the tears are falling. She drops to her knees and kisses me. "Yes."

Before I slip the ring on her finger, I show her the inscription. I don't know whose hands are shaking more. I hold her in my arms for a while and as the sun starts to set, there's a chill in the air.

"It's getting cold, let's head to the house."

"Did anyone know you were going to ask me?"

"Only Uncle Jax but, by now, who knows?"

When we get to the house, it's quiet . . . almost *too* quiet. When we get to the living room, everyone is there, but no one is saying a word. I take one look at Uncle Jax and I start to laugh. He's like a little kid on Christmas morning.

"Yes." That's all I have to say; one word, and they are ready to celebrate.

"You had one job to do, just one."

"Junior, I tried. I really tried, but it was all your Aunt Raven's fault."

"Jax, you might want to remember what happened the last time you tried to blame me for something."

"Junior, help me get some more beer." He jerks his head in that direction. I head into the kitchen with Uncle Jax right behind me. "What did she say when gave her the report to read?"

"She didn't want it and asked me to burn it. She said if I kept looking behind me, I will miss what's in front of me."

"What about the money, what did she say about that?"

"I never gave her an amount; I just told her I had a lot of money. She said she has her stuff and I have mine and then she asked if I needed a loan. It was her way of telling me she couldn't care less what I have."

"Junior, she's priceless."

We head back into the living room and Mrs. Osla pulls me aside. "I'm not getting any younger so you better hurry up and do this. We need to get some babies in this family again and you're up at bat."

I almost choke on my beer. "I'll do my best."

I look around the room and there is so much love. I'm glad I burned that report. The past is just something in the rearview mirror. My future is right here with the woman who's got a lock on my heart.

Epilogue

Michael

TODAY IS IT, THE DAY I FINALLY MARRY DAGEN. I OFFERED to take her anywhere in the world and give her whatever type of wedding she could come up with. She said no to all of it. She insisted on us getting married on the Santa Barbara beach where we had our first unofficial date. Somehow, she even got a Rabbi and a Priest to go along with all of this. I offered to pay for the entire wedding but her father said no. What I did get from my beautiful fiancée, the week before our wedding, was a prenuptial agreement. At first I thought she was kidding but she had a little speech prepared, so I sat down and let her do her thing. I still laugh every time I think about her trying to explain to me that she had to protect her business. When she was done, I handed her an envelope with the deed to the building that her business is in. I purchased it and had it put in her father's name. Then, I finally told her how much I was really worth. She cried and still made me sign that damn paper. Yep, my sunshine is full of surprises.

"Mike, you ready?"

"Bo, is everyone else down there?"

"Yeah, even Preston is there with his bowtie on. We've got to leave now or you'll be late."

When we get to the beach, it's late afternoon. We all take our places. Bo, of course, is my best man. Antonia is Dagen's maid of honor. Preston is in the front row, looking very handsome in his bowtie. Dagen put Uncle Max in charge of the music. When she starts to walk towards me, Uncle Max hits play and Landon Austin is singing 'Once in a Lifetime'. She really is my once in a lifetime. She is breathtakingly beautiful and no longer standing in the shadows of her own insecurities. When she steps next to me, her father hugs her and places her hand in mine. The Priest and Rabbi give their blessings and turn it over to us.

"Dagen, because of you, I've become a better person. I've grown to be the man I was destined to be. Every day I spend with you becomes my favorite day. I promise to fill your heart with happy memories, and when we are old and grey, we can share them all over again. You've got a lock on my heart forever."

"Michael, you bring out the best of me. My heart was waiting for you to show up and when you finally did, I found a true friend, a lover, and my better half. You told me 'When you step outside the box, you never know who might want to dance with you.' Because of you, I took that step. You made me believe in myself even when I couldn't. You've given me your heart and I promise you I will never take that for granted. I love you."

We exchange our rings and now I can officially kiss my wife, but first, I lean in and whisper in her ear. "My beautiful wife, I can't wait to have my way with you."

Her skin gets that beautiful flush. We both look down at the same time and she laughs.

We kiss and everyone is clapping. Grams and Mrs. Osla are crying.

We head back to the house, and now the party can finally start. Dagen takes Mrs. Osla on a tour of the house; she especially loves the TARDIS bar. Uncle Jax found the big bowl of fortune cookies that Dagen had made just for him.

There is so much love in this room. We've all fought hard for it and we are winning . . . one day at a time. I break open one of the fortune cookies and when I read it, I know it was written just for us.

"When two hearts are destined to be together, no one and nothing will ever keep them apart."

Don't forget to add "in bed."

The End

Coming soon: *The Bench*

Mick

Everywhere I go, I hear the cries of the people. Little kids begging for help, help from me. There is no language barrier when it comes to fear and pain. No matter where I go, I can't break away from the sounds in my head of twisting metal. The smell of burning jet fuel is embedded into my brain.

Going back to Nebraska has never been an option. It hasn't been my home for years. I can never go back to Covington; too many memories. My aunt and uncle have, since, passed. Everyone else has moved on without me. Hell—life has moved on without me. New York City is my last hope. Maybe seeing where the towers once stood will help me remember why I went, why so many from my graduating class only came back somewhat alive? This isn't living life; this is nothing more than existing.

The bus ride from Bethesda is long. I fight the urge to close my eyes. I know if I do, the nightmares will come. I don't trust myself in confined spaces. I don't know if I every will again.

The Freedom tower is huge, America's way of telling the terrorist to fuck off. I walk by the 911 Memorial at least a dozen times but I can't bring myself to go in. I shake my head in disgust, give up, and try to find the Department of Veteran's Affairs. I need to let them know where I am. The line is out the door, but it's not like I have anything better to do. When I finally get to the front desk, the information clerk hands me a form to fill out and then it's wait all over again. They want a New York address. Damn it, I don't have one, and I'm not even sure I want one. The one thing I know, for sure, is that the only postal address for Hell is what's inside my head right now. When my number is finally called, I explain to the administrative assistant that I just got into town. She suggests I get a PO

Box and then come back again. It's a start; something is better than nothing. When I get to the post office, I show the clerk my driver's license with my old address in Covington, Louisiana. She issues me a box and puts in the change of address form. At least now I have something to show the Department of Veteran's Affairs.

I walk down the city streets, trying to take it all in. Maybe this wasn't such a good idea? Cars gridlocked and their horns blaring. There are so many people rushing to get nowhere fast. There's an underground subway system that I know I can't go anywhere near. There is a smell coming out of the grates along with the screeching of the train. It sounds like twisted metal, a trigger for me. This city is filled with so many homeless people, everyone with a story to be told. Some of them—veterans who could really use the services more than me. If I could get out of my own head, I wouldn't need anyone. I finally find a nice bench in the warm, afternoon sunshine. My hands are filled with at least a dozen pamphlets of services available. Unfortunately, the wait for help is more than I can handle. Most guys I know can't wait that long. If they are reaching out for help, they are at the end, hanging on to that last straw, trying to claw their way to the top of that murky water.

Day turns into night and starts all over again. It's true what they say, this city never really sleeps. There is a Starbucks across the street from my bench. I head over and order some overpriced stuff and use the restroom. I decide to leave the pamphlets in the john; maybe someone can find what they are looking for. I head out, get my overpriced food, and head back to my bench, my home for the unforeseeable future.

One day leads to another and after a while, I lose count. The manager of Starbucks lets me come in, before he closes, to wash up. There is kindness here; you only have to open your eyes to see it. I fight every night to suppress my nightmares. Some nights are worse than others. I've officially declared the bench my home. It's crazy that I'm becoming protective of it and worry when I'm gone that someone might take it from me. I've been venturing out a little bit further from my bench every day. I walk everywhere I go. Even though I have no place to be, I'm somewhere, anywhere, just not inside my own head.

Today, I found a church that has a soup kitchen. After speaking to the pastor, he allows me to volunteer. It's only one day a week, but it's something I can do—no questions or long conversations—just serve hungry people. I'm dishing out chili today and that's when I notice her. She looks familiar and I realize I've seen her before at the Starbucks across the street from my bench. It's such a big city, yet such a small world. She talks to each person she's giving food to, not making them embarrassed because of their situation.

"Hey, mister, are you going to dish that out or what?"

"Yes, I'm sorry." I go back to my job and by the time the last person is through the line, she's gone.

"Excuse me, Pastor John, who was the girl on salad today?"

"Another one of God's angels. Can you stay and help with clean up?"

I laugh "Sure, back to reality, sir. When I'm done, would you mind if I showered before I leave?"

"Of course not. Would you like me to see if I can get you a bed in one of the shelters?"

"No thank you. Save it for someone who really needs it." I know he means well, but I don't trust myself to sleep in a room with others. What if the nightmares come? What if I can't control them? What if I hurt someone? It's best I head back to my bench. It's safe and, for now, that's enough.

Other Books

The Unraveled Trilogy

The Unraveling of Raven

Darkness Into Dawn

Shattered Lies

Uniquely Mine

About the Author

Theresa Sederholt was born and raised in Brooklyn New York. She is a graduate of Campbell University in North Carolina, with a degree in Criminal Justice. Theresa now calls North Carolina home, with her husband, a professional chef, and her two dogs.

Experiencing life first hand is what she does best. Believing she can do anything has put her in many crazy situations. Whether it's babysitting a pig farm or cutting the top off of a mini truck; nothing is ever out of reach. Her list is endless, A to Z.

Theresa's beliefs are pretty simple. There isn't a luggage rack on the hearse, and give a girl Nutella and espresso and she can change the world.

Theresa enjoys connecting with her fans. She can always be reached through her website at:

www.theresasederholt.com

www.ingramcontent.com/pod-product-compliance
Lightning Source LLC
Chambersburg PA
CBHW072344020726
47506CB00004B/993